"Having been born into an Old Order Amish family, Jerry Eicher writes from a wealth of knowledge about Amish life. With that, Eicher has an uncanny ability to get into his characters' minds; the result is an authentic portrayal of Amish strengths and weakness rarely seen in print."

Leroy Miller
Writer, Co-author, *A Symphony of Frogs*;
Editor, *The Amish-Mennonites at Kempsville, 1900–1970.*

"*A Time To Live*, captured my heart and held it from start to finish. Full and sensitive characters, heart-stopping events, and a glimpse of unfamiliar cultures and beliefs rewarded me in Eicher's book."

Sidney J. Paterson
Artist & Writer's Group Coordinator

A Time to Live

Jerry Eicher

A Time to Live

Published by Horizon Books
768 Hardtimes Road
Farmville, VA 23901
www.gospelontheweb.com

Front cover photo of boy and door is used with permission from Julie Lyle of Tri Village Studio in Columbus, Ohio. The boy is David, the son of Paul and Loretta George.

Front cover photo of ox cart was taken by the author.

ISBN 978-0-9787987-0-3

FOREWORD

Eicher, Jerry S. (2006). "A Time to Live."
Reviewed by Linwood H. Cousins, Ph.D.

Linwood H. Cousins is a social worker and cultural anthropologist who holds an appointment as Associate Professor of Social Work at Longwood University In Virginia.

JERRY S. EICHER has written nothing less than a gem of a novel. It is a journey into Amish life that takes one to the most unexpected places. Whether it is Ontario, Canada, where young Jason Esh and family were part of an Old Order Amish community, or the towering mountains and rolling hills and valleys of South America and the Honduras, the reader is taken on a ride into the exhilarating drama of life among the Amish. And accompanying the reader every step of the way are characters that fit the traditional stereotypes of Amish life as well as those who push the edges of Amish culture and tradition to find deeper meaning and purpose. By the end of the novel, one has discovered not just the culture and meaning of being Amish, but how the triumphs and traumas of everyday life make the Amish more like others — outsiders — than they perhaps realize.

To accomplish all of this, Eicher centers his novel around the lives of a few key individuals whom the reader comes to see as clearly as one's own image in a mirror. Alongside Jason and his parents, Homer and Rachel Esh, is Peter Stolsfus. These individuals are with you from the beginning to the end of the novel. And it

5

is their lives that are center stage. Certainly many other individuals are involved and are crucial to "A Time to Live." But this is clearly Jason's story, based on the adventures he experienced with his grandfather, Peter, who carried the burden of missionary work, and Jason's father, Homer, who shared Peter's burden and at the same time possessed his own independent but pious and devoted approach to life as Amish and as a man.

From the fire that destroyed Peter's old house in northern Ontario Canada, to the uncompromising and off-putting Bishop Wengerd who tried to hold the line against Peter's missionary zeal, to the exciting but dangerous trek to the Honduras, to Jason's first fist fight, to a rendezvous of two young lovers in the night, to the not so crafty Honduran thieves that required constant vigilance and creativity from the Amish to protect their valuables, to a controversial new church and young Bishop, a bachelor's final foray into the adventures of life before his wedding day, to a death and, finally, a return home, this novel is an intriguing, emotional ride.

To say that one would not expect such a story based on Amish life is to not understand that the Amish are thoroughly human. The simplicity one sees in the Amish traditions that are open to public view conceals the essence of their human nature and the things the Amish have in common with the rest of us. Never denying the challenges and limitations of Amish life in the face of modern culture and society, Peter Stolsfus sees Amish culture in its "best moments as only a tool to accomplish something greater" (p. 329). That something greater is "the practical application of scriptural Christian living" (p. 328). Thus, the novel is in many ways a Christian story, a book with an appealing philosophical and Christian message about life and living. But to see only this is to miss the point entirely. More human ambitions and aspirations, as well as triumphs and downfalls, are expressed through religion than perhaps any other human institution. Why should it be any less so with the Amish? Why not an Amish life for a source inspiration and wisdom for living? Indeed, for the Amish, like for the rest of us, there is "A Time to Live" and this is a book to read about it.

INTRODUCTION

A Time to Live is a work of fiction, running from 1967 – 1977 approximately, and is based on a true story. The story opens in an Amish community in Canada. Homer Esh takes center stage in the first chapter, while the main character, young Jason, begins as a background figure. Of importance throughout the story is the inside information contained and the intimate look at Amish life. Where appropriate, the English dialect of the Amish has been used. Spanish dialogue is translated verbatim.

The first part of the book lays down a foundation for the heart of the story, the experiences of a community of Amish people as they establish a settlement in Guateteca, Honduras. Accidents, robberies, adventure, and their joy of living in this area of the world all combine to make the story.

This account of the Amish settlement in Honduras makes an interesting story for many reasons. First, it has historical significance — the Amish hadn't attempted such a missionary effort before. Second, the author clearly knows his way around the Amish world and offers a frank but sensitive assessment of the pros and cons of Amish life — and there are plenty of both. Third, the attitudes of the third-world natives clash time and time again with American attitudes and, more specifically, with Amish attitudes. This clash of cultures is told simply and matter-of-factly, with little moralizing.

CHAPTER ONE

THE YEAR WAS 1967. In the shadow of the last rays of a late fall sun, Jason Esh stood at his home waiting for his father, his hands in his pockets. He was a tall boy for his seven years, deep into the first grade at the little one-room Amish school house across the road. Born in Canada, his life revolved around his family and this young Amish community settled on the shores of one of Ontario's lakes. He knew this life, yet remained unaware of the currents stirring all around him. Still innocent of church politics and troubles at such a young age, he simply took life as it came and never thought things would change.

A visitor from the US once expressed surprise on hearing the many places these particular Amish people came from. "One would think this was a much larger community," he commented. "You have so many different names and places you come from. They are from all over."

But it was a small community with only one district. Amish from Indiana, Pennsylvania, and Illinois came here, many of whom were seeking a place to live where their young boys were not subject to the US military draft. They founded the community some years earlier.

"Something just has to be done," their bishop said, while still living in Illinois. "The draft is doing our people so much harm. It is bad enough that the government feels it must go to war, but now they want to drag us into it."

The problem was that even though the US made provisions for conscientious objectors, the resulting mandatory two years of medical service in the hospitals of major cities proved devastating for many of the larger Amish communities. Many Amish young men left the community never to return after their term of service was over. Here in Canada there was no draft and no exposure of the young men to the temptations of the big cities. Like the bishop decided, something was done. With the Amish to say is to do, and so this community of Amish was founded.

Across the open Ontario fields from the Esh home, Beth Stolsfus lifted the kettle sitting on the old stove in the kitchen and shook it. That was sometimes faster than stirring the corn, and she was in a hurry. Not that this was unusual, but tonight the supper must be ready on time. All around her on the old wood stove was supper — mashed potatoes, gravy, meatloaf, corn, and green beans. The stove had its quirks and needed to be controlled carefully with the damper on back if one wanted plenty of heat to cook with but not too much. Carefully checking the level of the ash pan, she looked at the old black oven. "Now behave yourself, you stove you."

Homer Esh, whom Jason waited for, was on his way home from a hard day's work. The clip of his horse's hooves made a mushy noise on the gravel road. The cart jerked with the rhythm of motion as his horse trotted swiftly along. Homer was a long way from town, where he worked.

"Why do I have to drive this distance every morning and evening? As much money as the business is making I could hire a driver. Maybe some day?" Homer was bothered this evening.

Underneath his two-wheeled, two-seated cart was a wooden toolbox of sorts. It contained construction tools, for Homer was a contractor specializing in homebuilding, and a quart of ice cream wrapped in three layers of paper bags. The ice cream was for dessert at the family supper that night. Homer's brother Lamar usually ate the ice cream he bought on the way home, but Homer was taking his home to share with the family. His wife Rachel waited for him, along with the six children. Jason, the oldest, especially possessed a sweet tooth. Store-bought ice cream was a rare item in the Esh home. At his house there was no refrigerator or electricity. No phone in the house, and no TV.

Homer was the oldest of twelve children, all of which still lived within a three-mile radius of each other. Their father was a minister at an Old Order Amish community within fifteen miles of Lake Winnipeg. The town of Fraserwood was their closest town, within driving distance for a horse and buggy. This was a small and young settlement as Amish churches go, containing only one district.

Homer was sixteen when his family moved to Ontario. He was now married with six children of his own.

❧

In the house behind Jason, his mom Rachel was getting supper on the table. She came from one of the better families in the community. Her father was not a minister, but by reason of his intellect and will was not unknown in Amish circles. She came from a large family also. She and Homer married young, she eighteen and he twenty. Homer noticed her soon after she started attending the youth functions at sixteen. That was the age when Amish young people normally were allowed to attend the official youth gatherings. They quickly got sweet on each other and dating led to marriage two years later. She did not seem to mind marrying him on a shoestring, as most Amish young people are not given their own wages to keep until they marry or are twenty-one. Her faith in him seemed to be rewarded now some nine years later as they owned their own home and the business was prospering.

Homer was careful to marry a girl who appeared to have no serious health problem. That was one of his private nightmares, a sickly wife at home who could not take care of the children and household duties. He knew of such cases and was determined to avoid it. Now if God sent it to him after he was married, he supposed there was little he could do about it, but why go looking for

11

trouble? He knew that one married for better or worse, for Amish did not tolerate divorce, but why start out with worse when one could start out with better? At least that is how it seemed to him.

❧

Moving along quickly, Homer was almost home. The horse seemed glad to get there as they pulled into the driveway. It was a twenty-mile round trip into town every day for work, but the church standard being what it was who would dare go against it?

There was a church rule against hiring drivers and Homer was getting tired of it. "There's no reason at all that that rule cannot be changed. Of course the farmers frown on hired drivers for day workers. They will hire a driver for themselves to go to town, but that is okay I guess. 'Once every two weeks or so is not too bad. We just cannot have it being done every day.' That is what they say. I can hear it now. Well, what if I just went and hired a driver?"

Jason standing there watching his father come was not aware of any of this. His dad was home. Nor did he understand the other problems bubbling under the surface.

His dad did in fact hire drivers at times, but now with the construction business prospering there was growing sentiment among the farmers of the congregation against these transgressions of the rules by the construction workers. There was talk that the rules would have to be strengthened again. Homer heard all about it from his brother Joseph the other Sunday night when several of the children were home visiting at their parents' place. It was a family affair with the wives and children in attendance.

Rachel made Homer attend the function even though he did not want to. She said, "You know that your parents will be disappointed if you do not come. Your family has a tradition of the children coming home for the evening, once a month or so. We have got to go."

Homer knew she was right, so they went. Jason had overheard that conversation, as Joseph told his dad that night in no uncertain terms what he thought of all this building going on in town. Jason could still remember the rant.

"The world people have always been caught up in making money and expensive homes. They have always been adding house to house and homes to homes. It is right ungodly the way the town's people build so close to each other. I have actually heard that people are putting wall-to-wall carpeting in their homes. Is this not true, Homer?"

Jason watched as his dad squirmed and said nothing, and wondered where this was going. Joseph did not let up, though. "And that is not all. I have heard that people are putting indoor wiring for TV in their homes. It is bad enough for the world people to put that horrible looking set of tails up on their roof to get television. Why, we know that the divorce rate has shot up since TV has come into the homes, and all sorts of immorality and fornication among the young people. If that is not bad enough, now they are trying to hide their sin by putting the wiring out of sight. Is this not true, Homer?"

Homer grunted something about not putting the wiring for TVs in the homes himself, and that he thought the indoor wiring was done to make things easier, not to hide anything. His response was largely lost, though, as the others were turned towards his father, who was looking at Joseph in surprise. "I had no idea things were this bad in town. It does sound all so terrible the way things are going out in the world. Maybe I can bring this up with Bishop Wengerd soon, as there may be others who are seeing this danger also now that you have seen it."

A satisfied look crept over Joseph's face, before he quickly let the corners of his mouth drop into a mournful look of deep piety. "I am glad you are seeing the danger, Father, and I am thankful you will take it up with Bishop Wengerd, as I think the ministry should get involved in this danger our people are being exposed to while working in town. I did see Bishop Wengerd last week when I stopped into his harness shop. We spoke at length on this matter, and he said some of the others have raised concerns also about the dangers of making so much money while working on these worldly homes in town."

Homer kept his mouth shut, as the others paid no attention to him anyway in the conversation that followed. The look on Joseph's face as he went out to the kitchen to ask his wife whether she was ready to go home made Homer glad he belonged to a faith that believed in non-violence. "Helps at least to cut that option out."

༄

Homer's flow of thoughts was interrupted as the horse pulled up to the barn itself. He got the horse unhitched from the cart quickly, and pushed the cart under the lean-to as Jason stood and watched. The barn was warm and musty, in that animal heat sort of way when it is cold outside, as Homer unharnessed his horse and placed him in the stall. He had been looking forward to the ice cream in his toolbox, but his thoughts left him not too sure about it anymore. "At least the children will enjoy it."

Ontario could be cold even in the fall, and Homer dreaded winter's coming. It would make the drive to and from town each day an even more unpleasant one. The smoke coming out of the chimney was inviting as he stepped outside the barn. His home was heated with a wood furnace in the basement. Behind the house was the stack of wood he split the winter before. More green wood was cut already in the woods but hopefully would not be needed until next winter.

Dusk was just falling, and he could see the glow of the gas lantern through the kitchen window. He knew that later the small kerosene lamps would be lit for other lighting in the bathroom and bedrooms, but out in the living room and kitchen it was gas. Homer heard that other Amish communities such as the ones in Indiana were getting gas piped into the ceiling and walls for lights and refrigerators, but he doubted whether such a thing would get past Bishop Wengerd or some other people.

༄

Across the fields Beth continued her preparation for the family supper. She was a girl of action, a flurry of movement even among the Amish, who were not afraid of work, whether male or female. Beth possessed a slight build and cheerful temperament, considering the intensity with which she could feel and work. Perhaps those who accomplish the most in the physical world have the most hope about other things. Right now, with supper all around her, she heard her sister Susie calling from the back room.

"Beth, would you come help me"?

"I can't right now — I am watching supper. You know how hot this stove gets."

"It will only be a minute. See if Mom can watch the stove."

Beth looked out of the kitchen door for her mother, but she was nowhere in sight. "It will only take a minute," she thought. "Okay, I'm coming."

Rachel already had the food on the table when Homer walked in followed by Jason. Handing her the ice cream she went to put it outside on the front porch for keeping until dessert time. She asked him, "How was the ride home?"

"Not too bad. The horse gets tired of the trip."

"That is to be expected. Did you take it easy enough on him?"

Homer nodded his head. "I did not push too hard."

"At least you do not drive like some of your brothers do. They act like they have no mercy on man or beast."

Homer was non-committal as the children gathered around the table. Jason sat on the side facing the window, hardly able to wait for the ice cream. The other children filled out the rest of the benches on either side. "She is telling the truth after all, so what more was there to say?"

Chapter Two

ABOUT THE SAME time that evening Peter Stolsfus walked towards his house after the evening chores. He left the barn where the milking of the cows was just completed, expecting the smell of supper to greet him at the door. Farming was hard work. Milking to him still meant doing it by hand and cooling the product in the water tank outside afterwards. Two of his daughters helped with the milking but had gone in some time ago to prepare supper.

"What a beautiful evening God has made," he thought. "No rain today, and the air still a little warm from the summer. I am so thankful for what God has given us."

His step was still sharp for his age, as the wind stirred the white hair in his long beard. The eyes that looked towards the big brick house he called home were kind and with a depth of wisdom that came from suffering. Peter had been fairly healthy all of his life. Lately, though, something was causing problems. He had been to see a doctor this past fall about his frequent pains in his upper arms and shortness of breath, but the doctor seemed to think little was wrong other than working too hard. Beyond that his physical problems were few. Peter's sufferings had been of the heart and soul, hard to lay a finger on. If you asked him, he would have told you that his spiritual journey with God was where it should be. He was Amish because he believed it. He raised his children in the faith because he was sure it was the best. His questing for spirituality at times vexed the local ministry, but he submitted to their direction because he was sure he needed their guidance and protection to watch for his soul. Yet there were times like tonight, after the day's duties were done, when for no reason in particular that hunger for something beyond he knew not what would cause him to lift his eyes higher than his farm and chores and being Amish and long for God until it hurt.

Across to Peter's right was the main road that ran past the farm. As he walked toward the house, he thought over the day. "The chores and the field harvesting have really wound down well for the night. The preparation work on next year's strawberry patch is almost done. The old stone water tank in front of the barn needs some attention, but it rarely has problems, so a problem once in a while is not so bad. The northern field behind the barn is harvested and ready for fall plowing. Maybe we can do that next week.

"At present we are not running a very large dairy herd. Although the farm could be handling a larger herd I suppose. The verdict is still out on our second year with these alternative crops. I think the strawberries should do okay." Peter paused at the front door before opening it and entering. His thoughts interrupted, he was glad to be in the house and ready to settle down for the evening.

Three of his youngest children, Beth, Matthew, and Susie, were still living at home. Fred was teaching school in Indiana at a Beachy Amish school for his second term. The others were all married and lived close by. All were still Amish and Peter had every intention that they remain so. Not that any ever went wild or questioned the Amish way, but keeping one's children was always a high concern for any Amish father.

There were some men who lost most of their children and so lost their influence and status at church. Worse was the sense of failure that came with having failed at life's most important task. Peter mused that there was no higher measure of acceptance among any Amish than that given to parents who could keep all of their children in the faith. He was not motivated much by that but by what he himself believed to be right. Still he thought of it. By that standard he should have been well liked, but the fact of the matter was that the bishop was not quite sure of him. Any Amish bishop worth his salt was always on the lookout for cracks in his members. Peter seemed to have little success in keeping the searching eye of the church off of him. He and Bishop Wengerd spoke many times, but the result rarely benefited Peter.

~

Beth walked back through the rooms to help her sister at a brisk walk. It would not take long, she was sure, but she would try to be quick. She found her sister with the ironing board up and struggling with the pleat on one of her head coverings.

The Amish head coverings for the women are complicated affairs. To make one was an art not easily learned. On the back, the main part runs in a half-moon shape that fits over the head. Around the top and sides are numerous pleats to compliment the shape of the covering. The back is straight from top to bottom when first made, but often molded to the rounded shape of the head after being worn. Some Amish communities allow the starching of their women's coverings to avoid this molding and other natural sagging qualities of the cloth, but this one did not.

The Amish believe humility is bound up in personal appearance. They believe that a sharp and professional look in one's grooming does not befit a humble man or woman. No one was sure if the men or the women were the primary promoters of this train of thought, but everyone was sure that the women needed to be watched the most lest fancy dress and fancy worldly grooming should creep into the church culture. Even though the general attitude was that women tended towards this error, the men were not left out of the equation. Men were required to do their part in taking a stand against worldly hairstyles, although it was known that the men usually supplied this with less resistance than the women. The hair on a man's head must not be altered in any manner whatsoever after it was cut with a single cut. In most cases, cutting must be in a circular fashion without any angles that might appeal to vanity. In no form must the hair be thinned out or made to look like the dreaded approach of the worldly influence called shingling. The result was not only hair cut in a circle on the head but also a resulting true circle from upturned hair on the outer tips coming from being pressed down by the ever-present hat. The resulting look had a down side in that it stirred some of the young boys from time to time to look longingly towards the world of shingling, but it also resulted in a look that satisfied even the strictest soul of the community that the fashions and vanities of the world were not being followed.

As Beth arrived, Susie was holding up the covering for demonstration purposes. "This side one right here — I can't seem to get it right."

Beth told her to hold it around the other way when she ran across it with the iron, and also to spend less time on vanity. "You know what this will look like after you have worn it even for five minutes."

"I know that, but I want it to at least look nice for a little bit."

"You ought to be ashamed of yourself, but here — let me help you. Let's see the other side."

"I really have already tried that — the ones on this side came together, but now the last six won't lay down properly. How will it look in church if I can't make them lay down flat? This is my very best Sunday covering."

∼

Across the house, Peter settled down on his rocking chair. "I guess I should not tell the bishop so much about my feelings. Seems like they just come out." The rocker settled back and Peter could see the bishop in his mind's eye.

Bishop Paul Wengerd was a tall man, his face lined with purpose and intent. He was not one to be easily pushed around or persuaded. Some bishops lead their flocks with an easy but firm hand. Bishop Wengerd favored the firmness and cut quickly through the easy part. His beard was grayed as befitting his age and reached well down his chest. Some Amish beards at that length lend a gentleness to the face by their shape. This sort of beard has a rounded look. It often reflects a heart that is merry and large. The beard of Bishop Wengerd had no rounded look. It started out the width of his chin and jaws, then narrowed on the way down, before fanning out just a little at the end. He was not a man to lighten one's eyes when he went forth on church business.

The rocking chair rocked back and forth as Peter pondered the situation. "I am a member in good standing. Why is it that I always seem to get in trouble with Bishop Wengerd?"

As Peter knew, Bishop Wengerd had no complaints of the ordinary kind to bring against him. Normal infractions for a farmer would be modern machinery, a two-bottomed plow, an updated milking parlor, or rubber tires on his tractor. Since Peter had no desire for such things or ever expressed his support for them, nothing was ever brought against him as a disciplinary offence. What he and Bishop Wengerd could not see eye to eye on were things like missions. Peter and his family had spent a winter two years ago further north helping the Indians for three months. Bishop Wengerd checked into what would be the normal violations, such as driving vehicles while away from the Amish community, failure to wear regulation hats, or any participation in other such dress code violations. As there was no local Amish bishop close to the Indian reservation to give Bishop Wengerd firsthand information, he settled for Peter's word on the matter. Peter assured him that none of the church rules had been broken. He said that they had gone up to the reservation only to attempt ministry and aid to the Indians. Bishop Wengerd did not seem totally satisfied but let the matter lie "until any evidence should come up to the contrary." Peter felt his temper beginning to rise. From past experience he knew that it was best to keep it under control. He often said things under stress that he later regretted.

The last time they were together talking after church Peter brought up the subject again. "You know, Paul, how much we enjoyed ourselves the other winter with the Indians. It was a real blessing to our whole family. Do you think the church could support more missionary efforts like that?"

The bishop then proceeded to give Peter a lecture on the dangers of mission outreach and its corrupting influence upon the morals of those who went to the mission field. Peter was forced to agree on the basis of much testimonial evidence presented by Bishop Wengerd that a sure road out of Amish life seemed to be mission work. Yet even in the face of this weight of evidence, Peter expressed his displeasure at the lack of Amish mission outreach. Unmoved, Bishop Wengerd rebuked Peter for having high ideas and disrespect for those in authority over him. The injustice of the charge finally caused Peter's temper to flare. He expressed himself further on missions in general and the lack of sympathy for it in Amish church groups. His outburst necessitated a return trip some days later to apologize. The bishop accepted the apology and to Peter's gratitude pushed the matter no further. Yet even tonight Peter could feel the eye of the bishop upon him, but inside his hunger for the work of God was still there.

Over at the Esh house the glow could be seen for miles around against the dark northern Ontario sky. Homer Esh was finishing off his plate of store-bought ice cream and had not yet seen it. The sun had set some time ago, and it was by now late evening and dark. He saw it when he stood up from the table to walk into the living room.

"Rachel, come look at this."

Something in the sound of his voice brought her running down the hall from the far bedroom where she was attending to one of the younger children. She did not waste much time looking out the kitchen window or going to the basement for her coat before going on out to the front yard. He joined her after going for his coat and boots. Several of the older children joined them on the yard looking in the direction of the glow in the night sky.

"It looks too far to the south to be Elmer's on the corner. Maybe it is no one we know," Rachel said, thinking out loud.

"Big enough to be something like a barn at least."

"I would not be so sure it is a barn, Homer; there is also something else that is big enough to cause such a fire down in that direction."

"Surely you would not suppose it is that?"

"Yes, you know what I am thinking — my father's place. Please, quick, get down there. They may need help."

❧

Not thirty minutes earlier Beth was helping her sister. She held up the white handcrafted head covering with its contrary pleats. They both heard the cry of alarm from the kitchen — "Help, fire!" It was mother's voice from the kitchen door!

Both sisters took off running through the house. Mom was at the kitchen door but could not go further because of the thick smoke.

"Quick, some water."

"The only running water we have is at the kitchen sink."

That was not reachable. What followed was a general flurry of activity that later became a blur in their memories. Such things as blankets and coats were thrown about but with little avail. The old wood-burning stove must have been angry when it exploded because the job was well done.

"Run, go tell Dad."

Dad already knew and was right beside them. His first concern was his wife and daughters' safety. He told them to keep away from the kitchen with their blankets and coats. "It looks too late for that. Go tell Matthew to run to the neighbors to call."

"That's a half mile, Dad. He can grab a horse."

"No, he's young. Matthew can get there running before he can catch the horse. Be quick about it. Tell him."

Matthew was still in the barn when Beth found him. "The house is on fire. Dad said to run to the neighbors to call on their phone." Matthew looked at the flames and smoke coming out of the kitchen window and up the side of the brick dwelling. He said nothing as he left in his best sprint down the gravel lane.

❧

"How do you think I am supposed to do that?" Homer demanded of Rachel. "How am I supposed to go and see what this fire is about? There is no use trying to harness the horse. It would take too long, and then the drive down. The horse is already worn out."

"Hitch a ride, there, out by the road." She told him. "Another car just went by. There is more traffic than usual. They must be going to see what is happening themselves. I just know it's my father's place."

The traffic of cars was indeed increasing. By the time he got to the edge of the road, one of the drivers must have seen him coming and stopped the car. It was a neighbor who rolled down the window.

"Jump in, Homer. I'm going to see what is going on. You are welcome to come along."

As Homer climbed in on the passenger's side, Jason, who had followed Homer out to the road, asked to go along.

"Up to you, Homer," the neighbor said through the half-rolled-up window.

"Let me go, please. I want to go."

"No, you just stay here."

"Please, I want to go."

"No, it could be too dangerous for you. We do not know what is going on." The car left in the direction of the glow, leaving seven-year-old Jason standing in the yard.

❧

Peter was already organizing the removal of items from the house according to importance when Beth got in from the barn. The flames were spreading quickly.

"Here girls, work on the clothes in the bedroom. Anne, just grab things and throw them out the window. Maybe the neighbors will be here soon. I will get the papers from the desk. We have to save what we can."

Some minutes later, after having run outside with an item herself, Annie found Peter in the living room trying to move a large piece of furniture.

"Don't try to move that big piece, Peter. Wait till the girls can help you or Matthew comes back. There are smaller things you can move."

"Well, let's get what we can. I'll work on some of the other things. The papers from the desk are already out in the yard. We may not have much more time. This old house is going fast."

The cars began pulling in the lane as neighbors and people going by stopped. After the driveway filled up to a safe distance from the flames, the parking was done on the road. People ran from their vehicles and offered to help. Peter told them to get what they could carry out of the house. The scene was soon one of furniture laying all over the yard with clothes draped over them.

"At least none of the other buildings should go. The barn is too far away," Peter heard one of the neighbors from down the road say. "Where in the world are those fire trucks? Did someone call for sure?"

Flames by now began to shoot out of the half side of the roof where the kitchen was. With the heat the fire spread more rapidly. Peter was the first to call off the household items rescue effort.

"Better to back off, friends. It is just worldly goods."

"We can still try for more of the beds on the end towards the road. I think one of those windows will open up wider — we might better break it out," a stranger said.

"The door towards the road could be broken off and widened. It is small, but that side jamb may give. It looks like she will go anyway," another offered.

"Any objections, Peter?"

Peter Stolsfus had no objections.

Many of the heads turned as the sirens of the fire trucks were heard in the distance. The sound wavered low at first, then grew in intensity.

"Looks like the fire trucks are here, but it's too late for this old house, I'm afraid." It was the voice of Neil Armstruck, the grain and milk farmer whose large farms were across the fields. "Everybody over here by the furniture — let's get it off the yard so the trucks can get closer."

A path was cleared at the front of the house and down the side towards the road for access to the back.

The fire chief soon sought out Peter. "Sorry about the fire, Mr. Stolsfus. We got here as fast as we could. That old timber makes her go fast. My men will do what they can, but I can promise nothing."

"I understand, Chief." Peter stood still for the first time in a while and removed his hat. Even more than usual the marks of the circle outlined his hair all the way around. Peter wiped the sweat from his brow. "We must rest in the will of God."

"No doubt," said the chief. "You will excuse me, Mr. Stolsfus. We will do our best."

Rachel gathered the smaller children around her standing out there in the yard. After they watched the sky a little longer, she took them into the house. Jason stayed out by himself, his face serious, looking at the smoke and fire billowing into the sky. How he wished right now he was over there at the fire. Things like this did not happen every day. Somehow he just knew that. "Why did Dad not let me go along? A time quite like this will never come again."

Life to Jason summed up itself in that moment, far away and unreachable. He lived down here where the days went by much the same, with one following the other. Then when the important times came, like right now, obstacles seemed to be placed in one's way. Not that many had yet come to his young life, but this big one seemed to foretell of many to come.

The children had all long gone to bed and were asleep when Homer returned. His face was serious and sober.

"Was it my father's place?" Rachel asked in a whisper so as not to awaken the children.

"Yes, that is what it was. There is not much left of it, burned quite to the ground."

"No one is hurt though?"

"Just shook up. They could not get the fire department out fast enough, with it being so far from town and the time it took to run down to the neighbors to use the phone."

"Is it really gone? I mean gone?"

"A couple brick walls left. You know that house was old, and must have been dry, too, with all that aged lumber."

With that they went to bed for what was left of the night. The children were told in the morning. Grandfather's house burned.

"Burned right slam to the ground," Rachel told them. "My beautiful old home."

CHAPTER THREE

B Y ELEVEN O'CLOCK the fire in the old house died down to a smol-
der. Little was left despite the best efforts of the firemen. The
side towards the road had charred timbers sticking skyward out
of the crumbled brick facing that had not yet fallen. Where the
kitchen had been little was standing. Even the brick fell. For a while
it looked like the two chimneys in the kitchen would stay up, but
they fell towards midnight. The shower of sparks caused the fire
chief to move the spectators even further back.

Away on the other side of the driveway some of the neighbors
still lingered with Annie and Peter. The girls were standing a little
ways off, while Matthew mingled somewhere in the tangle of furniture and strewn objects. All of the married sons who lived in the
community and son-in-law Homer Esh were there at some point.
Peter wondered how they all came so quickly. "They must have
caught rides with someone's car," because he could not see any
buggies or horses tied anywhere. All of them now left except for
Jesse.

"If you are ready now, Dad, we have a driver to take you all
over to our place for the night."

Peter turned to face Jesse. "I think we are. There is not much
sense staying any longer tonight."

"How are you feeling with your heart? Any pain?"

"Well, I am stressed of course, but seems to be nothing
unusual."

"Maybe you need to make a trip into town tomorrow after all
this to see Dr. Tenner, just to be sure."

"I'll think about it."

"First, though, let's get all of you over to our place for the night and some rest. Lois can get something ready fast, I am sure."

"We can hardly put such a burden on you and your family, Jesse. Lois will not even know we are coming, and you have a house full already."

"It will not be a burden. I suppose someone has already stopped in to tell the family at least what is going on. You will be staying only for one night; then we go from there."

They left soon after that, all piling into the van and looking back one last time at the house that was now little but a foundation.

≫

The next morning, though, the place buzzed in a flurry of activity. Neighbors were everywhere cleaning up debris, and already several of the sons were working with Peter Stolsfus on plans for a new house across the lane. The women set up a makeshift kitchen in the back towards the barn and were already carrying in food for the day. As people came and went both to help and to show their concern, the hats and bonnets outnumbered the English neighbors by far. These were people who practiced in sincerity the admonition of the Holy Scriptures to care for the household of faith. Times of suffering were times to be there for one's fellowman whether he was friend or foe.

Homer had arrived early with his crew. They were taking time off for a few days from their regular work to help out. Rachel arrived at nine o'clock with the children. Jason was the first out of the buggy. He paused at the edge of the driveway and looked towards the ashes of the old house. There it lay, the morning breezes stirring little wisps of dust into the air. He had lived in that house once — that is in one corner of it. For the first three years of his life, Homer and Rachel had rented the two bedrooms on the east side. Jason could not believe his eyes. How could so much be reduced to so little in one night? Was this not the place of such great memories for him? In his mind's eye that morning standing by the driveway, he saw himself with a stick chasing a strange dog out of the yard as a three-year-old. He saw the box under the front window where his uncles kept the groundhogs they captured in the hay field. He saw them showing him how to place fish worms on the ends of hooks. "It's all gone," he said to himself. "How can that be?"

He saw his grandfather standing off to the side. Bishop Wengerd was walking up to him. The bishop's straw hat sat firmly on his head, having seen its years of sun and weather.

"Well, Peter, you can be thankful it happened so early in the evening. If it had been late at night when you were all in bed, who knows."

"We are thankful for the protection of the Lord."

The bishop as usual was not one to beat around the bush when he knew for sure that the rabbit must be in there. "Have you been doing any thinking since last night?"

"Sure I have been thinking, but what do you have in mind?"

"Well, we of course do not know for sure — it being the Lord's will that moves in our lives. All of us are sinners and make our failings and mistakes. I for one do not point the finger at anyone, but with this fire could God be speaking to you?"

"I am sure that He could be."

"You know some of the ideas you have been having lately again. Just the other Sunday after church out at Elmer Zook's barn I heard you talking to young Amos Byler about how we ought as Christian people to be reaching out more, like mission-minded, I think you said. You know such things are strange for our people to be thinking of, and especially for you to be talking to our young ones about. I thought I pointed out the dangers to you when you came back from your time up north with the Indians. Maybe God is talking to you through this fire about the wrong ways of your thinking."

Peter paused for a moment and said nothing. His temper was crying for attention. He wanted no further outburst that would require further apologies or worse.

Bishop Wengerd took the pause as a sign of encouragement to continue. "I sure hope you give it yet deeper thought. You know how easy it is to be deceived in these last days."

Peter slowly found his voice. "If God wants to speak to me, I am always willing to listen. He is quite welcome at all times to bring His message. It would not seem quite necessary to me for God to have used this fire to get my attention."

"You know, Peter, what is it about you that just resists correction all the time? It is none of your business to be telling the Almighty how to talk to you. We know the dangers of those who claim God speaks to them personally. It is much safer to trust in the voice of the church for direction. The church is speaking, Peter."

"You surely do not mean that you are the church?"

"No, of course I do not mean that. I am just a small part of the church, really nothing at all, but the voice of the church has been heard many times on this subject of missions. Missions are a good thing, but they are a great danger to our people. There are others for whom it works to do missions. It does not work for Amish people to get involved in mission work. The church has been very clear on this for many years. Why can you not hear the voice of the church, instead of insisting on following your own direction, which could easily be leading you into error?"

Peter found his voice. "There was a time when our forefathers were great missionaries."

"That is all true, but that was a long time ago, and it is now our responsibility to carry on and keep the many great traditions which they have left us. Why can you not submit to the will of the church, Peter?"

"You are right in what you say about the fire, but not in the way you mean it. The Bible does speak of a time when Elijah stood outside the cave, and the great fire roared by on the hillside, but God was not in the fire that time nor is He in this one. God spoke to Elijah in the still small voice, and He speaks to me also in a still small voice."

"Now look, Peter, you don't have to go quoting the Bible to me like I was an Englishman. I know what is right. Pretty soon you will be quoting the chapter and verse. What is happening to you anyway? Your father was never like this."

"What my father was or was not has little to do with it. I can read the Bible for myself."

"There you go again, Peter. How can you say such things? We are not wiser than our fathers were. Why, if you were any younger, and not an old man like you are, we would have to deal with you in church."

Peter's temper wanted attention again, but Peter thought it better to leave it unattended. "What you really mean, Paul, is that since I am older I am not as tempted to break any of the church rules, so you really have a hard time finding anything against me. My ideas — you really would not want to try discipline on me for those, would you? Might cause too much discussion, now would it not? Some young men might even do some thinking?"

The bishop only shook his head. "You will maybe learn yet. Remember your heart trouble — that may be God talking to you also. A man was born from the dust, and he must go back to it. We must all be content with that."

"In the beginning," Peter said, turning his hat in his hand, "God put us on this earth to live. He did not put us here to die. Some of us have not forgotten that."

"There you go again. You know such thoughts are not meant for Amish people. You would do better teaching our young men how to obey the church and God."

"I am glad to do that, but the church must also be taught of God."

"That is not your business to decide. We must all obey the church."

Joe Yutzy, who walked up, interrupted the conversation.

Jason, still standing over by the driveway, had caught bits and pieces of the conversation. It all seemed a little strange and unimportant to him. "Why were these grown people talking about missions? Did they not see that the important thing was still the pain caused by this house, now gone and burned down?"

Joe Yutzy addressed Peter. "We need to know where you want the debris and ashes from the house hauled to. Is there a place on your farm, or will it all have be taken somewhere else?"

"There is a gully that needs filling in behind the field to the right of the barn. Should easily hold anything from the house we haul down there. Just have them take the ashes and brick no one wants down there. The wood we will dispose of some other way, and some of the bricks can be used again or someone may want them."

"We'll do that," Joe said and walked away.

Peter turned around, but the bishop had walked on also. He could see his straw hat nodding in conversation among the crowd.

"What was that all about?" Peter turned to the sound of his son Jesse.

"Just Paul and I talking."

"Anything to do with the fire?"

"Yes, that and my opinions on the mission field. The bishop thinks God might be talking to me through the fire."

Jesse said nothing at first. "Well, I don't know much about how God speaks, but I do think some of your ideas on missions are quite sound."

"I am glad someone else believes in them too."

"Take for instance what we were talking of the other Sunday night when we all were here at your place. Here we are in Ontario, Amish, knowledgeable in the soil, know how to raise good crops, good work ethic, and prosperous by and large. Have we no responsibility to others less blessed than ourselves? How much do the special lives we live add anything to the world around us? Who wants to know about the horse farming that we do, excellent though it is? Of what benefit is our self-sufficiency to a country where there is such plenty? Here in North America there is such abundance that a little waste goes unnoticed. Could not our frugality and hard work be of better use somewhere else, a blessing maybe to the culture? Could some third world countries benefit from what we know? Could we have more of an impact somewhere else?"

"Well, be careful what you say around the bishop and some of the others, even though I agree with you. Such talk is not looked on kindly. We don't want others thinking this fire was set by heaven."

Two weeks later the foundation for the house across from the lane lay in place. Rachel came to help on the day of the working frolic. The home was quickly framed and roofed. Jason was amazed at the speed of things, but found little interest in the new home. Sure, there it stood fresh and new, but it lacked the mystique and presence of the old home.

For the next month the sons and sons-in-law would finish the interior as they found time. People still stopped by to help for a day or so. Each gave, some more and others less. As was common among the Amish, there was no insurance on the house or on any of the other buildings on the farm. Donations came in both from neighbors and other Amish communities.

Bishop Wengerd made mention of the need, and as there is no offering plate ever passed in an Amish church, a person was designated to whom anyone could give money for this purpose. With the free labor and having to pay only for the cost of materials, the impact of the loss of the house was much lessened, although not without financial pain. Once in the new house, Peter lay in bed at night and looked out his window across the lane and wished at times the old house still stood there. Beth was glad to stay with her cooking around the new stove. Susie pointed out that such dedication may not always be wise; for if she had not left the kitchen at the old house that evening in answer to her call, what might have happened? She would stay with dedication, Beth said, and let Susie count the blessings of the other — although she was glad and thankful she had not been in the kitchen when the stove blew up.

As Peter sat in his rocker again one Saturday evening, the last outline of the old foundation could still be seen across the road in the gathering dusk. A brick lay here and there from what had once been a grand old house. He wondered if it really was a sign of things to come and what it all meant. His thoughts got too deep even for himself, and to shake the shadows from his mind he got his Bible and began reading. "A time to get, and a time to lose; a time to keep, a time to cast away," and then the one that meant the most to him. Only he read it in German. Not just because it was the language of his people, but because he always thought it was much grander in the old tongue. It rolled out of the mouth with such dignity and added to the splendor of the Holy Scriptures. "A time," he said to himself. "A time to live."

Jason went to sleep these nights, still thinking about the old house. He did not consider it much of a time to live in. He thought the past much better than the present. To him things would never be quite the same without the old house. "Maybe?" he thought. "If I had been there to say good-by that night, I would feel different. Now, the house has left without me. Well, good-by house, anyways. You were a good friend."

Chapter Four

Homer's brother Joseph Esh was driving happily along on the way to town. He was trouble in the making wherever he went.

Not yet far from home the road was still graveled. The horse's hoofs would soon have that clear clip-clop sound as they hit on the blacktop section of the road up ahead. He did not much care for that modern sound to assault his ears, but otherwise it was a beautiful morning to go to town and Joseph was enjoying himself with his own thoughts. He also enjoyed the buzz and the unrest in the community caused by the announcements last Sunday that communion was coming up. Everyone knew the semi-annual communion time was close, but having it officially announced heightened the tension. Boredom was always a problem for people like Joseph who did not normally feel inclined to participate in the number one solution for boredom among the Amish people — hard work. For Joseph, communion time and the upcoming weeks preceding it offered a break from the status quo, a refreshing breeze across the landscape, a time to feel important and needed in church politics. That is unless one felt insecure, which Joseph was feeling. He was sure that things were okay, but yet were they?

In the meantime, just outside of town a van was pulling into Fraserwood. Mrs. Troyer shifted her position in the second seat back by the window. She moved slightly away from her husband. He was tired also from sitting on the vinyl bench seat. The nine-passenger van was occupied, since early morning, by twelve people, one in front beside the driver, three in each bench seat, and four in the back seat that stretched all the way across. Drivers charged by the mile for any trip without any limit on the number of passengers. With this as a motivation and the fact that there were always people willing to travel, it was both necessary and easy to fill a van for most trips.

This particular vanload of travelers just home from a wedding trip to southern Illinois had about had it with traveling for the day. Mrs. Troyer's sister's boy had married on Thursday. The wedding had been a large affair even for Amish weddings. Relatives came in from miles away as was the case with these travelers from Ontario. To the Amish, weddings were major events and opportunities to break the monotony of everyday life. It was also a chance to meet relatives or friends who had gone liberal, and in some cases totally English, meaning completely forsaking the Amish way of life, who could not under normal circumstances be held too close to the heart.

It was now mid Saturday afternoon and they were approaching the town of Fraserwood. Mrs. Troyer eagerly waited to be home, as well as everyone else, their legs and bodies cramped from the long hours of close sitting. Last night the van stopped at the outskirts of the large city of Detroit for the night. It made for a long trip. "At least we can make it back for Regulation Sunday tomorrow," Mrs. Troyer was thinking.

※

Joseph slapped the reins onto the back of his horse as he passed the intersection where he could see to the south and catch a glimpse of Peter Stoltzfus's new home. Thoughts of that fire, not so long ago, crossed Joseph's mind. The bishop had made remarks about the incident to someone else. At least that was the way Joseph heard it, and Joseph was close to the Bishop Wengerd.

"I wonder why the bishop never told me anything personally? Seems like he would. He surely would not think I sympathize with Peter Stoltzfus?"

The road passed slowly under the wheels of Joseph Esh's buggy. Town was a distance away for a horse-drawn carriage that averaged less than 10 miles an hour, and Joseph used the time to think about things.

"Regulation Sunday is in two weeks, after that Communion in two more weeks. I really need to have something to say this time. Surely the bishop and ministers do not think that I am weak on the church rules. Why would they think something like that? Why is the bishop not talking much to me lately then? Is there something I could do? Maybe that is the problem. They must want me to show my support for them."

Two weeks prior to communion, the Amish would gather for a special Sunday meeting to go over their regulations and rules, hence Regulation Sunday. It was a time to have the bishop review the rules and refresh anyone's memory if there had been reports or sightings of transgressions. It was also a time to take a look at whether fresh ones were needed or further applications of existing ones. All rule changes passed by a 100 percent vote, but few dared vote against any recommendations from the bishop once he received the backing of his fellow ministers. In such cases, charges of rebellion and subversion would be brought at once against the offending voter. Any disciplinary action would again have to be passed by the proverbial unanimous vote, which was even less likely to have dissenters than the original proposal. Discipline was essential and always a priority in preserving the Amish way of life and the unity of their fellowship.

❧

Coming into Fraserwood, the van jerked slightly as the driver pulled up to a stoplight in downtown Fraserwood. Mrs. Troyer looked out her window on the left side. Her husband, Ben, had just said, half to himself, "Be home soon now. Still in time to help with the chores."

"Yes, I have been thinking the same thing. Look — there is Sam Zook's boy over there by the grain store."

"Ya, we are almost home."

"Look I said, it's not just that, look how he looks."

Ben leaned around his wife and looked out the window. The light turned green in the meantime, and the van was already in motion.

"I don't see anything, neither a Zook boy nor how he looks."

"Don't get grouchy on me, mister. I know what I saw."

"Well, what did you see?"

"That was Zook's boy and he did not have a hat on."

"Yes, you already said it was Zook's boy, but are you sure he did not have a hat on? This is Saturday afternoon in the broad daylight in downtown Fraserwood."

"It was the Zook's boy and he did not have a hat on."

"Sure, but he was inside the store, right?"

"Nope, he was walking right down the sidewalk without a hat in sight."

"He must have left it in his buggy."

"How do you know, and besides what difference does that make? He wasn't wearing it. Next thing you know they won't be wearing their suspenders in public."

"Well, I don't suppose he wears them while he sleeps, at least I don't."

"That's really funny, Ben. You ought to be ashamed of yourself. What if the children hear you talking like that about suspenders and hats? You know they are our identification as Christian people that are distinct from the world. Besides, tomorrow is Preparation Sunday. You just watch it, that Zook boy is already baptized and in the church, and he'll just try to go along with communion and not say a word even after doing a thing like that. Not a word he'll say — you just watch it."

"I know someone else who is not saying a word, too."

"I know someone who is saying something."

Mr. Troyer squirmed. His now really sweaty back slid against the van seat.

"I'm not saying anything."

"Yes, you are. This is a very important issue, and you know I can't say anything. When the preachers come around to us women, we can speak for ourselves, but we can't bring up anything about anyone else. Like someone breaking the church rules."

"I'm not saying anything."

❧

Joseph slapped the reins again and shook his head to cast aside the morbid thoughts that injected themselves into his mind. "There really can be nothing wrong. It must just look like I am being avoided." He laughed to himself, a high-pitched sort of sound that came mostly out of the upper regions of his throat. Joseph felt much better. Even his horse perked up and trotted a little faster.

"I had better propose some strengthening of the existing rules, though — farming equipment maybe. The problem with that is we already have it pretty hard. Besides, how can I go there as I have not seen anyone trying out any new farming methods or equipment lately? Some of the farmers talked of milking parlor changes, but as yet nothing serious. I guess I could give warnings on that, but a real hard case and evidence works better. Let's see, what of the carpenters in the church? Some of them are becoming quite successful. Take my brother Homer and all the money he's making. That must be putting pressure on him to bend the rules. Money just does that, like creating the desire for the use of electric saws and other modern equipment. Suppose Homer is doing something like using the realtor's generator, maybe, to run tools with? He did admit to me the other evening at Mom and Dad's that someone puts in the TV wiring for the homeowner, but that he does not do it himself. That probably won't go anywhere. What if he is using electric tools though?" Joseph was smiling to himself. "Communion time is truly a great time for the soul."

❧

In the van, Mrs. Troyer was quietly speaking to her husband's face to avoid attracting attention. "You will tell the preacher about this. It is serious that our young people are seen in town with their hats off. Who else might have seen? Ben, you know some of the other young people might have been nearby, or even with him.

What of his own brothers? What of our boys? Suppose one of them sees one of our young boys without his hat on in public? Why, Ben, this is serious."

"Serious, I know that, but I'm not saying anything."

"Yes, you are, and that settles it."

"Would you please be quiet before anyone else hears us fuss in this van?"

The van slowed down as it hit the graveled section of the road.

"Almost home," said the driver.

Chapter Five

Joseph pulled up his horse at the stop sign. He had been on the blacktop for some time now. Here was the main road, the state highway that ran north and south through the local town of Fraserwood. North from here it connected with another two-lane main highway. There was always a greater danger for any horse-drawn vehicle on these well-traveled roads. Joe slapped his horse briskly across the road, turning left towards town, and kept the buggy wheels half on the shoulder of the road. Cars slowed down some but went around much faster than on the smaller county roads.

"You know, Joe," he told himself, "Elm Street is just coming up. You ought to swing down there — it's not that far — and see for yourself what Homer is doing. He must have a dozen homes going down that street, Mom said. Let's see, around ten o'clock. Things ought to be going full swing." Joseph smiled to himself, all on the inside of course. He did not think that anyone would see him, but this was a public highway and one needed to look sober like a holy man.

Elm Street came up rather quickly. Joseph turned to the right. His horse seemed surprised at being told to turn. He had never been told to go this way before. Slapping the reins smartly Joe speeded up. To his left he passed several homes that looked finished with "Esh Construction" signs in the yard. On the right towards the middle section of the street Joe could see two horses and buggies parked in the yard. The horses were unhitched and tied to the tree with a little hay in front of them.

"Must be working there."

41

Joe listened intently as the clip-clop of his horse's hooves on the pavement sounded loudly in his ears. He put his storm front on the buggy up and leaned forward.

"That sure sounds like a motor shutting down. Wonder if the thing is sitting around back. What is that going in the window?"

Joe wasn't sure how you run these electric saws, but he had heard something about a cord between the generator and the saw.

"Sure looks like a wire going into that window. What is that wire going into the top of the storage barn? That is too small for electric. Could it be a phone wire?"

Joe passed the house with the buggies and horses in the yard. All was quiet. He could see no one.

"Awful quiet for a construction site."

He kept his horse going. At the end of Elm Street, which dead-ended, he could have turned left and gotten back on track for downtown.

"I think I'll make another swing by that place. Maybe I can see something from this side going back."

The horse turned sharply at the end of Elm Street. There was just enough room to make the turn as the front wheel on the left side rolled against the protecting roller bar on the bed of the buggy. Joe's horse was confused on the turn. It switched its tail in a show of protest.

Joe drove a little slower past the house with the horses and buggies in the front yard. There were shrubs that had not been removed during construction and he could not see anything behind the house. The front patio window from this direction allowed a clear view all the way through the house to the back French doors.

"It must be evil to even work on such a fancy house. Think of all the money Homer is making. Wonder if Homer installed those French doors for them himself? No wonder the man is tempted to use electric tools. Well, I have seen enough. I am sure that a motor shut down as soon as they heard my horse coming, and something went into the window. That phone wire has to be checked out too."

42

After he was done with his shopping, Joe thought and thought on the way home how to check this phone thing out. It finally occurred to him that if one has a phone, one's name is listed in the phone book. Why not go and check it out. So that is what he did. He stopped in at the schoolhouse. There the listing stared back at him as big as life, Homer Esh, address Elm Street.

Chapter Six

To Jason the days passed slowly after his grandfather's house burned down. For the adults they involved last-minute scurrying around in preparation for the big day. Little did anyone know how much that day would figure into their futures.

Sunday morning dawned muggy and cloudy. Church was held at Albert Mast's place. The bench wagon sat up close to the house, empty now of its load of backless benches. They were all set up in the kitchen and living room, with a few bleeding into the main large bedroom off of the living room. This was in case not everyone could be seated in the kitchen and living room. They set the benches up with a dividing space in the middle. This was the line between the women and the men who would sit facing each other when the three-hour service began. From Sunday to Sunday the routine remained unchanged — only the house changed. Each family took church for at least two weeks, four weeks when this community had had fewer families. The ideal was to have church arrive at each house once a year with those with larger houses taking their turn in the winter. In the summer those with smaller homes held church in the barn. Albert Mast was one of those with a large farmhouse. He gladly took church indoors at his place, as it saved the trouble of thoroughly cleaning the big room by the haymow, let alone having to attempt to control the fly population. Although no one said anything, each farmer knew that he got marks on farming ability by his control of the local fly population. The bishop in times past swatted at flies buzzing around his face during his sermon, but most of the younger ministers did not quite dare. No farmer wished to have the ministry remembering such things when church matters came up in which he would have to be dealt with. So that, among other reasons, contributed to a major effort at fly control when church was held in a farmer's barn. Albert thought of one of the poorer farmers in the community, Robert Wagler, who could scarcely afford the expense of the extensive fly bait or sprayer that it took to control flies even for a short period of time. He thought maybe he should contribute in some manner to the expense the next time church was at Robert's place since he had none of that expense himself. "I will have to see what I can do, although that might be hard. Robert is not one to accept help," he thought to himself as he walked towards the house at eight-thirty that morning.

As nine o'clock approached, buggies could be heard coming down the road from both directions. They pulled in the driveway, drove up to the house as close to the sidewalk as possible, dropped off the women folk and smaller children, and then drove on out to the barn to unhitch.

Homer pulled in with Rachel and the children a little late. Dropping her and the two girls and boys off at the end of the sidewalk he continued on. Impromptu parking arrangements were made into lines of buggies by an unspoken order of things as if each driver knew what the other was thinking. Jason jumped out to help his dad unhitch. It took but a moment to unhook the traces and the holdback strap on one side, and if the driver had someone with him, the other side was already done. If not, each single driver walked around the front of his horse and repeated the movements on the other side. A quiet sharp command took the horse out of the shafts and around the back of the buggy, where the bridle was exchanged for a halter and tie rope. From there it was into the barn. When the horse stalls were full, there was room at a temporary tie-up site with a small amount of hay placed on the ground for the horses. Long rows of horses ended up standing lined up side by side with not always the friendliest of feelings. It was hard, though, to hit much kicking straight back, and a horse has not much of an aim off to the side. Some of them were not above trying, which led to a ruckus once in a while. The men closest to the scene would take measures to calm things down. By the time church started all the horses usually accepted the arrangement and made peace with the fellows next to them. They had after all been here before in this same situation — different barn, yes, and a different horse close by, but still the same.

～

Bishop Paul Wengerd stood at the head of the line of men standing outside in the barn lot and on the lawn. To his left were his two home ministers and, to their left, the deacon. Conversation was low and animated at times. As each man or boy who was a church member arrived he traveled down the assembled line and exchanged greetings with each one, and then took his place in the line. The greeting was a handshake and a kiss between each man who was a member in good standing. The Bible was taken literally to command this form of greeting. Bishop Wengerd was known to remind those who had scruples otherwise what the Holy Scriptures said. Some of the younger boys from time to time were overcome by the routine. Maybe it was the cold mornings when things ran down the noses of certain ones who were less than diligent with their handkerchiefs that caused them to become artful at avoiding the center of the face.

"A kiss," said the bishop, "is a kiss. Never knew a kiss to mean anything else. When I kiss my wife, I kiss her on the mouth."

None of the older men begged to differ on the subject or buck Bishop Wengerd, and so the matter stood. Conversation didn't begin until after a person passed through the greeting line and had taken his place. Handshaking men, hats firmly in place, moved quickly down the line.

Jason watched the men shake hands and greet each other. Every once in a while someone noticed him and shook his hand too. They would smile at him or wiggle the hat he wore on his head. As his father passed Bishop Wengerd he turned to the man on his right. "Your fall plowing going okay?"

"Yes, it is. This rain we have been having has really made the weeds grow. We got the first rounds in just after the rains stopped. Heard at the store that the rain should be moving back in the next week or several days. Hopefully we will be done by then."

"Our plowing is going about the same. With this climate so uncertain later in the year, we can be thankful for any good weather we get. I think a little too much rain is always better than too little rain. Sure beats having a dry fall and the chance that next spring will lack rain after we plant."

The man at the bishop's right agreed.

Sharply at ten till nine, the long line began to move towards the house — the bishop in the lead, followed by the rest of the ministry, then the married men from the oldest to the youngest, and the same for the boys. The benches were empty on the men's side until the bishop arrived. The ministry sat off to the side on separate benches, which intersected the others in a T at the space in the middle. The men took their places from the oldest in the back to the younger generation in the front. Albert watched with concern as the benches on the men's side filled up fast. He hoped no one would have to move into the bedroom. It looked as if everyone would fit even with the visitors, as the last of the young boys filed up the side of the front benches and sat down. The youngest boys were allowed to sit by themselves across from the youngest girls, facing each other. Jason sat there and looked at the girls simply because that was what was in front of him. The benches where things were happening, though, were three or four rows back on each side. Not that you would have seen any commotion, as that was not allowed, but the opposite sides were looking at each other.

At nine o'clock the bishop said the opening benediction, a short memorized line from the traditions of the fathers. One of the song leaders responsible for this Sunday called out a number in a clear loud voice so that it might be heard by one and all. The singing began, a slow German song with tunes and rhythms of the 16th Century, while the ministry filed out to their morning consultations with each other. They would be back at around ten o'clock or a quarter till, perhaps much later on Regulation Sunday. Song number two would need no calling out, as everyone knew what it was going to be — number one in the songbook. The first line started with, "Oh, God, Father, we worship you, and praise your works." This morning the first hymn lasted twenty minutes. Several of the men who dozed off during the song included Amos Byler. He woke up when the singing stopped, collecting his wits in the silence.

"Surely it's not me this morning. I know I'm young married, but I just sang it several Sundays ago." Amos breathed a sigh of relief, "Good, it's not me."

Young Pete Mast two rows in front, on towards the side of the house by the window, got the punch in the back.

"Sing the Worship Song."

The voice was low, an intense whisper. Not many heard more than a few people away, because it was not necessary to say the words in an intelligible fashion. A quick mumble and a hiss of the lips were enough to transfer the message.

Jason noticed the activity going on behind him, but thought nothing of it. It happened most Sunday mornings. The young men and boys were introduced to lead singing by being asked to lead the "Worship Song." It was not the simplest of tunes, but simplest from the fact that it was sung every other Sunday, thus easiest to remember and learn.

Pete shook his head. It meant, "I can't." The shake was barely perceptible. A series of slight rotations of the head to the left and the right, performed at rapid speed either from nervous excitement or intense dislike of singing, so as to be hard for the eye to follow.

There was silence for several minutes. More people were waking up. By now the people behind Pete Mast knew where the punch had come from, as they could by inverse deduction figure out who the song leader was that morning. He made preparations to ask someone else. The signal went faster this time due to the lesser need to punch so many backs, as the owners of the backs were aware that further messages might be transferred due to Pete Mast not singing yet. The shake of the head led to another young boy closer to Amos Byler. This time there was immediate action.

There are no written notes in the Amish songbook. One sings from sheer memory and the imprint of repetition. Slowly and quietly the voice began, trembling slightly due to the stress of the situation and the youth of the boy. The first two notes were pitched low. From there the voice grew in volume and soared ever higher for a total of six to eight notes, depending on the experience and inclination of the singer, each note held for two to three seconds except on the fast jump towards the end. It ended with a full breath fully exhaled and an exultation of triumphant sound. After that the audience joined in. Each line was repeated in the same manner with a different set of starting notes, except for the first and third line. It was a marathon of endurance for the young and an induction into manhood. Twenty-two minutes later, the last note ended. The preachers were still not back.

In the silence that followed, Jason shifted on the hard backless bench. He wished church was over, but he knew it would be a long time yet. Over in his corner, Peter Stoltzfus looked at the clock on the wall. He could see it through the doorway into the kitchen. There was another one hanging in the living room. From where he was sitting on the opposite side of the minister's seat, Peter could not see that one. There was also one in his watch pocket, but few of the men except perhaps for the younger boys looked at their pocket watches during church services. The sound of another number being given out surprised no one as unconsciously they all were expecting it. It was song number 412, pronounced in German by the song leader, and since it was a difficult and unfamiliar tune, the song leader himself began it. Ten minutes later the line of ministers filed in from upstairs in single file and took their seats. The song was discontinued at the end of the current stanza. In the kitchen, the clock said five minutes till ten o'clock.

"Still back early for today," Peter thought. "Either they did not have much to discuss, or there was quick unity among them." As the last notes of the song died away, the first minister to speak rose to his feet, stood a little off to the side of the minister's bench, and without notes or a Bible began his sermon. An Amish sermon is completely extemporaneous. It is just done that way.

Mose Stuzman started the preaching part of the service with the opening message, his style and tone inspiring to hear. Peter could see people paying attention, as they usually did when Mose spoke. At three minutes till eleven the opening message closed, having begun at the account of the Garden of Eden and ended with Noah building his boat before God destroyed the earth with a flood. The deacon asked the congregation to stand and read the scripture reading for that Sunday. His voice carried even above the shuffle of feet as many of the young boys left for the outside. Jason went out too, although his father had told him that when he was older it would no longer be proper for him to file out during church time. For now, a little boy could not be expected to go over three hours without a bathroom break. Growing up seemed a long time in the future to Jason, as he felt like it would never quite come.

Alva Bontrager had already risen to his feet to speak when they trickled back in and found their seats. He began after the account of the flood and told the general high points of the Bible story until the birth of Christ. Alva sat down at the end of the message after asking two men for testimony. It was a quarter after twelve when the service closed.

Testimony time is a requirement in Amish tradition. At the mouth of two or three witnesses all things are established, even the preaching of the Word. No man believed himself to be a world apart. All must submit to the discernment of others. To keep the preaching of the Word pure, the role of testimonies was relied upon. Usually the ministers who did not preach that day were asked or one of the older men. Today Alva bypassed the ministry and asked two of the older men for testimony. No one took this as an insult; since the bishop would preach the afternoon session, it was assumed Alva was giving him a break.

Bert Mast said he was in full agreement with all that was said that day and all the things brought forth to the congregation's hearing. "Often we must think that the Lord's coming is near at hand. Even today the clouds may open and he appear in the sky. I am so thankful for all that we have been taught and instructed. It is good to have godly leaders to keep us from deception, as the world pulls at our young people and old people alike. We must strengthen ourselves every day, as has been said, to keep the faith and stay pure from the world. I just wish my blessing on all that has been said."

Bill Mullet was next. He cleared his throat loudly. "I am in full agreement also with all that has been said here today. We can be so thankful for these words to feed our souls as we look out upon the world and see it becoming more fallen every day. Ever greater and greater wickedness is around us that can lure us into destruction. I support fully what was said. I too think that the difference between the world and the church should not just stay the same, but as the world goes further and further into the styles and fashions of wickedness the church should look less and less like the world every day. I just wish my blessing on all who are here, and on what was said."

Bishop Wengerd rose to his feet. "The Sunday church service has come to a close. Will all those who are members please stay in. Those who are visiting and are in good standing with their home churches are welcome to stay also and observe. We have work in the Lord's vineyard to do."

The house was filled with the sound of feet moving as the children and non-members filed out. Jason got in line as soon as possible for the exit. He was very glad he did not have to stay in. Some of the adults left with their smaller children too, until they could get them settled down happily somewhere outside with the older ones or sometimes upstairs with their older sisters. Several of the mothers left to prepare the noon meal for the younger children. On Regulation Sunday there was no noon break until the afternoon session was done. This was considered too much for the smaller ones, so they were fed before the adults were done. The women would find their way back in as soon as possible.

Bishop Wengerd cleared his throat. "We know that in every vineyard there is always work to do. The vines must be kept and the weeds weeded out. So it is with us here today. It is necessary to do the work of God in his vineyard, the church. There are weeds here that must be kept out and there are vines that must be kept up. We look to the Lord to help us in these matters."

No one was sleeping now. The bishop continued on in this manner for over an hour and a half, covering in random fashion the rules of the congregation — everything from the use of phones to the width of the rims and manner of style on the men's hats.

"It has come to our attention, and some of us as ministers have noticed, that the younger boys on Sundays are turning up the rims on their hats and using smaller rims than the three inches required. There is a unity among us as ministers that this is not to be allowed and must be repented of and changed. We know that in two weeks it will be Communion Sunday, and we expect this to be taken care of in that time. Of course this will be put to a vote from the church and anyone can express himself who wishes to do so.

"One of our families who moved into the community some six months ago, it has been brought to our attention, still have their rubber rims on their buggy wheels. We are aware that this was the standard in the home church where this family came from, but that is not our standard here. We wish to be patient in this matter and give time for things to be changed, so it is our conclusion as ministers that this should be changed no later than next communion time. Again, the church is free to express itself on this matter. It is our desire to be consistent that causes us to make this standard. We have seen the dangers that come from rubber tires, especially as they relate to rubber tires on our tractors. Of course we do not have automobiles, but we believe that is what rubber leads to. If we have rubber on our tractors, then soon we will have them running around on the roads as some in other communities have been tempted to do. As far as the rubber on the buggies go, we know other Amish communities allow it, but we feel it would be best and more consistent to stay away completely from the temptation of rubber, even on our buggies.

"It has come to our attention that some have been going over to their neighbors to use the phones. This is a great danger, and also a temptation to stay around a little longer maybe at the neighbors while the television is running and watch. Already in times past reports have been given how Amish people became too close to their neighbors while asking to use the phones and also for taxi service, and have been drawn into many temptations. Taxi service must be limited to the van drivers and others who are recognized as driving for all the Amish. This is much less dangerous to our way of life than to have personal phone and personal taxi service. It has come to our attention that one of the members has installed personal phone service on his jobsite in town. This will have to be stopped at once. We have a standard here that the pay phones be used at the schoolhouses — that is what we have them there for. It has been noted by some of those who are using their neighbors' phones that Peter Stolsfus used their neighbor's phone to report their fire. We understand this concern as a ministry, and while it would have been better to go to the schoolhouse to call in the fire, in emergencies like fires we will make exceptions. So while we understand the concern of those who heard of the use of the personal phone service by Peter Stoltzfus, they should not use this as a reason to do the same thing. We also would encourage that even in the case of fires, or other emergencies, if the schoolhouse, of which we have two, is close, to use the schoolhouse.

"Then there is the grave matter that has come to our attention concerning the use of electric tools by some of the carpenters in the church. This is a grave temptation that will bring a serious problem into the church. We know how the temptations of the world pull on us. Making money can always be a problem. It is the concern of the ministry about how much work is being done in town and among the English people. This cannot help but have an influence upon the thinking and lifestyle of our people. We understand that not everyone can farm, but even though we need to go out into the world to work, we must not be like the world. The world has a lust for money, modern conveniences, and tools. These are a corruption to their souls. If we allow electric tools to be used by the carpenters, this will be a very weak link in our witness to the lost. This matter, the ministry is in unity on, has to be changed. Further steps should also perhaps be taken. The church can express itself on this matter today, but as a ministry we feel that since much of the carpenter work is being done in the town of Fraserwood, and that the town work seems to be what is having such a drawing and bad influence on the hearts of our people, it is our recommendation as ministers that carpenter work in Fraserwood be no longer allowed. We know that this may seem too hard a measure to some and a sudden shock, but the matter does seem serious to us."

Joseph Esh held his eyes straight ahead looking as unconcerned as if he were milking his cow at home in the barn. "This is going better than I even thought. Wonder what Homer will do now if this passes and he can't make his big money?"

Bishop Wengerd was continuing. "We understand further that some might think this is moving too fast, but we are concerned about the dangers this presents to our children and the influence on them. The dangers of working in town seem to be why the temptations of the world are having a heavy influence on some of our members. There are eternal values we have to think about as we consider these matters. This may just be one link in the chain as we deal with the world, but it is the weakest link that breaks the chain. If there are some who would be against this because of the effect it has on their income, we as a ministry recommend that they think of the greater cause and not of the things of the world."

The bishop then turned the time over to the two home ministers and the deacon for further expressions and clarifications. Mose Stuzman expressed his support for what had been said. "We need always to be on guard about the ways and the temptations of the world. I am in agreement with our attempts to deal with these problems that have come up. It would be easier to just be quiet and say nothing about them, but we care about the souls of our people."

Alva Bontrager raised his bowed head after Mose was done. "I too give my support to these standards of God's Word and of the Church. Of a concern to all of us at this time should be this matter of the use of electric tools on the job site. It has even been reported to us that one of the members has a listed phone number in the phone book. I would have hoped that none of our people would be tempted and drawn so into the ways of the world. It really saddens my heart that this has even happened. I am sure that all have been aware of what our standards are. This is a great disappointment to me that some of our precious people have strayed towards the world.

"Another thing that could be said about the matter is that we as a ministry have decided that even though we think that work in Fraserwood should be stopped, because of the apparent grave temptations there, we also would allow that any work that is at present started or under contract by our carpenters could be completed. This will help to lessen the hardship that this rule change will bring. Of course the church can express herself on this."

The deacon wished his support and blessings on what had been said, and encouraged any of the other brothers to express their further concerns also. When the deacon was done the bishop rose, as the rest of the ministry sat, and said that it was now time for the church to express herself and vote on these serious matters. Rising to their feet, Mose and Alva each took a side of the congregation, the one the men and the other the women. The deacon did not participate at present but waited to see if any slow points should develop, in which case he would begin at the end of the room where needed. Each minister went down the long line of benches and bent over each person. He would listen to the whispered comments and then go on to the next.

Alva was responsible for the women's side, and each said exactly the same thing with slight variations: "I desire to be a partaker with communion, and express myself in agreement with the concerns and the final conclusions that were presented. I confess to being a poor sinner. I ask for patience from each one, and extend the same patience to others." That was the extent of it for Alva until he could get over to the men, unless someone gave a confession. This was then added on at the end. For the women, comments were limited to confessions and not concerns. Alva got the usual confessions related to things the bishop mentioned. Dan's Mandy was sorry for having dressed her girls in too fancy dresses. The wife of Albert Mullet expressed her regret for some things she said about another sister. Here and there was the guilty conscience that went beyond the obvious, but those were few today. Alva was moving rapidly on down the bench line.

Mrs. Troyer took her attention off of trying to catch Ben's eye as Alva was almost in front of her. "He'd better say something. Looks like he just wants to stay quiet."

Alva moved in front of her, and she demurred to the right away from Ben's direction, sweetly turning her head with bowed and cast down eyes. "I desire to be a partaker..." and the rest of it. Mrs. Troyer had no confession to give. Alva moved on to the next person, unaware that even as he started his movement, between the cloth of his arm sleeve and his coat the piercing eyes of Mrs. Troyer caught her husband's eye. "You'd better say something."

Mose moved much more slowly down the benches of the men. The boys went by quite quickly, but the men were another matter. Some of them engaged him in quite animated whispered conversation. There was more being said than confessions. Watching from his bench, the deacon noted the delays and also the fact that Alva was still not done with the women. After glancing in the bishop's direction and receiving a nod, he got up from the bench. The deacon began at the other end near Mose. The first one he came to was Ben Troyer sitting on the backbench.

"I desire to be a partaker with communion, and express myself in agreement with the concerns and the final conclusions that were presented. I confess to being a poor sinner. I ask for patience from each one, and extend the same patience to others." Ben shifted slightly on the bench and the deacon waited. "I, ah, I have a concern to express that maybe should be said in concern to a matter of the rules of the church. I, ah, we, I mean I saw one of the boys in town when we were coming home from our trip to the wedding, you know in Illinois, well, we, ah, I mean I, we were coming through town in the van and there was one of the Zook boys walking on the sidewalk without his hat on. I, ah, think this might be a matter of concern that should be expressed. We are, ah, I mean I am, much in support and want to be supportive of the rules of the church. It is our, I mean my concern, that something should be said as correction for this, and an encouragement that it not happen again."

The deacon bent down lower and whispered back, "Are you sure you saw the Zook boy on the sidewalk without his hat?"

"Yes, we, ah, my wife did."

"I will express your concerns to the others." The deacon moved on.

Several rows up, Joseph Esh was having no such trouble talking to Mose. He was done with his opening comments. "I am glad to hear the concerns that have been brought up here today. I am just in total agreement with what the ministry has said and with the rule changes that they have decided on. It is just a terrible thing to see and to hear that among us as the church of God these things are happening. That even here we should see and hear of electric tools that are such a great evil and hindrance to the Christian life, and are making an inroad into our church. How can it be that the world has such a pull on Christian people who are so well taught in the Word of God and the New Birth? I am glad to hear the ministry take such a strong stand against this danger to our children and to the church. I am supportive of them totally and so glad to see them take this strong stand with this rule change. It is encouraging that they are acting so quickly when we are threatened by this danger. I hope to teach our children at home the Word of God and the rules of the church that we have heard so well here today. I feel we are so privileged as members of this church to have such a strong ministry to uphold the standards of the Word of God. I just desire the blessings of God on all of us." Mose was not sure, but Joseph might have whispered something more as he went on to the next person. He did not go back to find out.

When all three ministers were back, the bishop nodded at them. They were expected to say in public what each person told them, without mentioning any names. The deacon went first. "Those that I spoke to among the men expressed a desire to partake of communion and their support of what was said. Several also expressed further concerns. One brother felt more could have been said about some of the haircut styles among the boys that seem to be coming into the church. Another said he saw one of the young folks in town without his hat, and expressed his concern. All expressed their desire to partake of communion."

Alva was next, "Among the sisters whom I spoke to, they all

expressed their desire to partake of communion. Some of them gave confessions of their own, expressed their regrets and desire that the church have patience with them. Among the men and boys I spoke to, all desired to partake of communion. Many of the men expressed further concerns about the youth, our farming equipment trends, and about the use of electric tools. Some expressed a total support for the new rules on working in the town of Fraserwood. Others wished it might not have to be, but they did not obstruct the new rules." As Alva finished speaking, he glanced towards the bishop sitting on the other end of the bench.

Bishop Wengerd nodded to Mose. "I too found everyone in agreement to partake of communion from among the men that I spoke with. They were in support of the ministry and of the things brought forth. Two of the men expressed their strong reluctance to no longer allow carpenter work in Fraserwood, but they will not oppose the ministry. All expressed their need for patience from the church and hope to extend that same patience to others. There were several who confessed to having come short on keeping up the church standard. One mentioned using the tractors too much, and another said he was going to make some changes to his boys' hats. An elder brother has chosen to place himself in excommunication for two weeks until communion. He confesses indulging in the problem that he has fallen into before, and chooses this way of expressing his regret and asked the church for forgiveness."

The bishop nodded his head after a whispered consultation with Mose. "I am glad to hear what the church has said, and that all desired to partake of communion. Concerning the brother who seeks excommunication for two weeks, we as the ministry accept his choice of discipline and desire God's blessing as he seeks to improve his life. The church will accept his excommunication until communion time when he will participate. I also am pleased with the unanimous vote on all the matters that we brought up. It is so important that we have unity among ourselves and are of one mind on these matters. As far as the other concerns that were expressed, I support them all and encourage repentance from those involved. This should be done in the next two weeks before communion.

The new rules concerning working in the town of Fraserwood will be in effect immediately. We will have some patience as the carpenters comply with them. We as a ministry feel that though this will cause some hardship at first, in the long run it will be for the best of all concerned. It is important that we look not just at the short term where our eyes can see, but also out into the future for our children and for our grandchildren. We will now be dismissed and will have communion services in two weeks at Elmer Byler's place. May God grant us his blessing."

The lines of worshipers began to file out from the boys down to the older men. Out on the kitchen wall Peter Stozfus saw that the clock said a quarter till three.

At four o'clock Jason was in the buggy with his family clopping down the road on the way home. He wondered why everything was so quiet. His dad was saying nothing and mom was breathing deeply. "They must be tired from sitting in church all day."

CHAPTER SEVEN

THE NIGHT FOLLOWING Preparation Sunday was sultry without any rain. Lightning played before dawn in the bank of clouds all around the horizon. The morning dawned gray and with promises still unfulfilled. Homer Esh woke up still angry. Of course you would have a hard time telling it by looking at him. He did not believe in swearing, but he was mad.

"Can you believe they would do something like that?" His voice was low. "It was my brother who did it. I just know it was." Homer was sitting at the kitchen table for breakfast. It was Monday morning, and yesterday's church had not been a good day for him.

Dawn fast gained strength, and Homer was already in from the barn, having gotten his horse ready to leave for town. Rachel was serving eggs and pancakes with sausage. She took the extra time this morning to make the pancakes in the hopes it would help. Last night had not been a good night for her either. Coming home from church Homer said little, nor did she raise any points in the silence, but now things were spilling out.

"You cannot be sure that it was your brother. Some of the others have been upset for some time now with the carpenters. You know yourself that we have been making some good money. Look at this house. It is paid off. How many other people in the community can say that?"

"It makes no difference what any one thought, or what any one thinks. It does not matter how much money I am making. It does not matter what their arguments are. It does not matter what dan-

60

gers they see. It is just plain wrong to tell someone where he can work. Why, town is about the only place where much construction is going on right now. This county has so few places to work in already. It is not like we have very many options as Amish on what we can do for work. What are they, farming and carpenter work? Now town is closed to us. I think I am just going to join the Beachy church. They surely do not have such things as rules to forbid working in town. Then there is that little matter about Amos Zook putting himself under two weeks of excommunication for his problem again. There the bishop sits and lets Amos get by so easy with something that is really wrong, and yet he keeps us carpenters from working in town. Amos keeps falling into this problem for years and years now, but it is just ignored. How do we know how often he is doing it? He may just be confessing the times he is caught."

Rachel's face was pale as she tried to quiet him. "Be careful, Homer. The children will hear you." The plate of eggs she was carrying to the table did not shake too much for she was not shocked, just horrified that her fears were true. She spent some of last night in nightmares that Homer might be thinking of joining a more liberal church. Apparently she was right.

"But Homer, we are not going to be doing something like joining the Beachys. I don't care what you think about what happened Sunday. I feel sorry for you that you can no longer work in town. I am sure many of the others do too. None of us likes what Amos does with his girls, but I am not going to be the one from my family who leaves the Amish."

About that time Jason came down the hall looking for breakfast. What he had heard she could not tell. He looked at his dad as he took his seat at the table, but said nothing. Homer said nothing either, which was worse than saying something. They ate their breakfast in silence. Jason was sure something was wrong, but felt little interest in it at the moment.

The sun was just coming up when Homer left the house at 6:30 to drive into town. Rachel stood by the window beside the front door listening to the wheels of the buggy hit the gravel road and then fade quickly from her hearing. "He is thinking of joining the Beachys. What am I going to do? This just cannot be happening."

❧

Homer pulled into his jobsite in Fraserwood at a quarter after seven. After unhitching and setting down hay for the horse that was stored in a small storage barn for that purpose, he pushed the cart into the front yard where it would be out of the way. Neither of the other two men that worked for him had arrived yet, although they would be there by 7:30 at the latest. They were good boys, among the best even as Amish workers go, hard workers and energetic. Going around the back of the house he uncovered the generator that was also kept in the storage barn. It was not his generator but belonged to the realtor who pre-sold most of his homes for him. Of course Homer actually supplied the funds to purchase the generator. This was done by an extra increase of the fees paid to the realtor on one of the first homes sold. But since the funds were paid to the realtor and the realtor bought the generator from money out of his account and his name was on the sales receipt it was not Homer's generator.

Homer told him this when the realtor dropped off the generator. "You can come and pick it up whenever you want to."

The realtor chuckled. "You Amish have a strange way of doing things. Why didn't you just go down to the store and buy the generator yourself?"

"Well, it's like this. The church rules do not allow us to own generators, but borrowing one to use usually does not make any problems."

"Then why not just change the church rules?"

"Well, that cannot be done. It would never pass the vote. I am just satisfied if we are allowed to use a borrowed one. That, though, has never been put to a vote. It is a matter I guess everyone has decided to leave alone. In the meantime I consider it to be allowed."

The realtor just shook his head. "Whatever, Homer, just use the thing. At the speed I am selling homes in this town, you will never keep up cutting all those boards by hand."

Homer agreed. "That is why we have to have a generator."

As he pulled the tarp off of the generator that Monday morning, Homer thought of the conversation with the realtor. "How in the world am I going to explain to him now that we can no longer work in town?" Homer pulled the generator closer to the door of the storage shed so that the exhaust would vent outside. Normally after venting the generator he placed a large piece of plywood in front of the door, both to shield the generator from sight and to muffle the sound. It cut the sound about in half and still left half of the door open to help with venting on the top. On the day that his brother Joseph drove by the house he barely made it out in time to shut the generator down before Joseph had been abreast of the house. "He must have heard it that day and told the bishop. What a brother."

This morning Homer made only half-hearted attempts to situate the plywood securely across the storage shed door. "What does it matter now anyways? We can't work in town anymore. Who cares who hears the thing run?"

A few minutes later the help pulled in. After unhitching and tying their horses, they met Homer in front of the house. "I suppose neither of you were for this thing on Sunday."

Neither of them seemed surprised at Homer's abrupt start of the conversation. They both shook their heads. "Why of course not, you know better than that."

"I thought so, but just checking. Any of you have any plans? As you know this will most certainly mean closing down the business."

There were some sarcastic chuckles. "What are we supposed to do? This was all kind of sudden like. Of course we heard the rumors of how the farmers were upset with us carpenters, but that is not unusual. None of us expected this to happen. We have been thinking and talking since last night about moving back down to the states, although nothing is sure yet."

"Maybe to some of your relatives in Ohio or Pennsylvania?"

"Something like that, but not Amish anymore. Beachy maybe."

"Yea, I have been thinking the same thing."

They put on their tool belts and got to work. At eleven thirty the realtor stopped by for routine paper work signing. He was not happy when Homer told him the news. "What do you mean you are not building in town anymore? Have you decided this for some reason?"

"No, it was decided in a church vote last Sunday. The bishop has forbidden it."

"The bishop? What control does he have over where you work? This is North America, not some third world country."

"Yes, I know that," Homer said grimly, "but in our church those things can be done, and they have just been done. We can no longer work in town, and there is nothing that can be done about it."

The realtor seemed to be at a loss for further words and stood there in front of the house shaking his head. "This is too bad. I will miss the business and the sales your work has been generating. I also kind of liked you, Homer."

Homer grinned sheepishly and said nothing.

"How can this operation we have here ever be replaced? Are you sure nothing can be done about changing this decision? Maybe if I talked to the bishop or presented the situation to your church council something could be done?"

"No," Homer said, "none of that will work. The feelings are quite strong on this subject within our church, and minds will not likely be changed. Some of them think I am making too much money."

The realtor looked like he was going to say something else but changed his mind. "Let's get these papers signed then. I will think some more on this, and we will talk about it later." Homer stood there looking down the street as the realtor's car pulled on to the main road going towards Fraserwood.

At home that evening he told Rachel all about it, and that the boys who worked for him were moving back to the states. "They plan on joining the Beachys. I am planning the same thing, as soon we can find a church close around here. There is no way I am moving. The work in town is just too good. Surely there is a Beachy church around here somewhere."

Rachel burst into tears right then and there. It was impossible to hide the problem forever from the children anyway. Jason came out from the living room where he had been playing, after hearing the conversation. "Who are the Beachys?" he asked his mother.

"It's some horrible church your father wants to go to."

"Why would Dad want to go to a horrible church?"

"Because the Bishop will no longer let him work in town. They just made the rule yesterday."

"Why would the bishop do something like that? Has he got so much power that Daddy has to listen to him?"

"Yes, we have to listen to the bishop. Your daddy's brother does not like him either." Rachel wished right away she had not said that. The boy did not need to have conflicts with his uncle on top of everything, but it had been said.

Jason asked, "Why does Daddy's brother not like him?"

"Because Daddy makes too much money, I think."

"Why does Daddy have to make so much money?"

Rachel was at her limit. "Would you be quiet now? All daddies have to make money. That is how you eat."

Chapter Eight

LATE IN 1967, Homer asked for a meeting with Peter Stolsfus, largely to satisfy Rachel, but to clear his own conscience too. "You need to talk to my dad," she told him.

That meeting was on Wednesday night, as they gathered around the living room in the new house. Homer told Peter all about how he felt, and that he wanted to get out of the Amish. Jason and the other children were told to play upstairs, but Jason soon got tired of that. He came over and listened by the stairs. It sounded like a solemn meeting to him. The grownup voices rose and fell in conversation, intermingled with some weeping now and then. He wondered why everyone was so sad. Going to a new church did not seem like much of a thing to him.

The evening ended with a plea from Peter to please hold off on any plans of leaving the Amish. "I will see what I can do. It would be such a sad thing if one of our children left the Amish."

With the tug on his heartstrings, Homer agreed. He would wait and see what happened. "How are you going to change the bishop's mind, Peter? That seems impossible to me."

"I don't know what I can do, but let's wait a while and see what happens. Maybe God will open a door."

They drove home with Homer a little irritated with the decision, but Rachel was satisfied. Jason asked from the backseat, "Are we leaving the Amish?"

"No, we are not," Rachel told him. "Your grandfather is going to be working on the problem."

That was all on Wednesday night. Tonight the cloud of concern was no longer as heavy hanging around the Stolsfus residence. Beth Stolsfus felt free to walk around with something extra in her step. It was Friday evening, and the weekend was coming. Sunday, a day of socializing for the Amish, included both the young and old. After the service of each Church Sunday, versus Sunday School Sunday, a meal was served. In all Amish communities a full Sunday service with all the trimmings is held only every other Sunday. For the Sunday service in-between, communities such as Fraserwood held a slightly shorter service oriented around a Sunday School Class format. After a full Sunday service the older people got to fellowship until early afternoon — first around the bench tables set up where the services had been held, and then later in circles in the yard or inside if the weather was colder. Regardless of the Sunday, the young people got their own singing for the evening. Depending again on the arrangement, supper was served, but the singing always began at 7:30. At nine o'clock the young people, having experienced all the socializing they could handle, made a beeline for home. Depending on the weather and the size of the gathering, the horses could be a problem as the buggies lined up at the front door steps. A few would get impatient and try to break the line. It was a matter of pride to keep your horse under control, so it was usually done.

The boys hitched up the horses, and then brothers picked up their sisters and the boys who dated picked up their girls and took off on their own. Dating was done at the girl's house with the intention being to supply supervision from the parents if needed. Depending on the community, the deadline was midnight, with communities like Fraserwood strictly enforcing it. They, being still a young enough Amish community, possessed both the zeal for such moral rule enforcement and the ability to see the results because of their small size. It seemed as if the one reinforced the other. Fraserwood believed in a two-chair rule with other added details going with such an arrangement. The degree of enforcement depended not just on the conscience of the couple but also on vigilance from the older folks. There was a way of checking things out, if one really cared about it.

"Just think, Susie," Beth was saying, "Fred will be here now for this weekend. He let us know some time back that he will be off this week from his school teaching."

"Look Beth," Susie half turned towards her, "I know that you like your brother Fred, but that is not the only reason you are happy. You always get happy as weekends come around."

Beth looked like she should be ashamed of herself, but she rallied. "I guess I do, but why should I not? We work all week, hard you know, and weekends are a time to, well, to see other people and go to church."

"Yes, go to church, now is that not fun? Sing the old songs of the forefathers, wait for the preachers to come back in, listen to sermons. Yes, Beth, I can see why you are happy."

Beth was shocked out of her train of thought by this outburst. "We should be so thankful that we can go to church. Our forefathers did not have this freedom. Look at the freedom we have. Many in the persecuted church still do not have this opportunity to gather like we can. We are a blessed people."

"Yes," Susie acknowledged, "church is a privilege to go to. I would not have it any other way than being Amish, but you know what I really mean. You just want to see the boys."

"I do not. I don't care about the boys at all. Why, who is there around here that I would even care about?"

"You do have a point, but I think you still like them. Like maybe you think this motley bunch we have around here might be something else. Don't you ever imagine that they might be someone else? Like maybe Henry Zook's nose would be straight and he would not smell like the cows he milks? Just think what Mose Mast would look like if he walked straight and quit twitching nervously when he looks at you? Don't you ever think, Beth, of what a man must look like?"

Beth was staring at her sister. "You mean you think of such things too? Well, I guess I am not surprised that you would, but I do too."

Susie smiled. "I am glad you own up to it. You scare me sometimes."

≈

The hired driver pulled into the driveway at 8:30 p.m. The sun had set, its last light still lingering in the late Ontario fall sky as Beth and Susie came to watch by the kitchen window.

Peter and Anne went out to meet the car. Fred came out first and came over to shake hands with his parents standing at the end of the walk. "How do you do, Son?"

"Just fine." They exchanged warm pleasantries, as their relationship was close.

Behind Fred, the car door opened on the other side. The boy who was getting out did not fall out the best he could, but landed with his feet properly placed. His body moved in sync with his arms and legs. Each move was made in accordance with the other. When he stood his clothes were not fancy, nor did they look high-priced. They were plain, in fact — a black overcoat with black pants and a light-colored shirt without designs or marking. What was remarkable were their well-kept look and the confidence they exuded, as if they possessed a life of their own. They were a part of their owner. His face was sharply chiseled and yet looked fresh, as if the owner had seen many parts of the world and yet still believed. He smiled easily with a grace that almost lent itself to a bow as he walked towards Peter, Annie, and Fred at the end of the sidewalk. Beth and Susie looked at each other by the kitchen window. Neither of them spoke a word, but they did not need to. The air between them already spoke the words. A man.

"This is Dan, Mom — Dan Ludwig. He is staying with me now at the trailer near the schoolhouse while he studies for the Catholic priesthood. We just decided he would come along for the weekend."

"Well of course, you are most welcome." Both Peter and Anne extended their hands with smiles. Any friend of their son was welcome in their home.

"Now that we are settled in the new house there is plenty of room," Annie informed him. "Fred can have his own room this weekend, and we still have a spare one for you."

"Well, I have not been home that much, so I was not sure how the room situation was, but if there is not an extra room, I can share my room with Dan. It seemed big enough for two people last time I was home."

"This is most kind of all of you." Dan's words were crisp and precise. It was plain that he was an educated man. Then to the surprise of Peter and Annie he switched to the Amish dialect. He said the words in the same careful and exact way, with the result of it sounding strange. Each area of the Amish world has its slightly different version and accent of the dialect, but this was something different yet. Dan Ludwig spoke as if he had learned to speak on purpose, as if in trying too hard to get it right he left out the slurs and mumbles of the native speaker.

"You are welcome," Peter said, looking at his wife. Together they thought it. This was a man they were glad to have as a friend of their son.

"Fred said that you are studying for the Catholic priesthood."

"Yes, I was. I think I have decided on another course though. My background is non-Amish. I came into contact with the Amish around the area where Fred is teaching school and became interested in joining the plain people. Sounds kind of way out maybe to some, as I have come to understand that the Amish do not have many outside converts."

"That is sadly true." Peter shook his head slightly. "Not many people join, mainly, I think, because we do not try to evangelize. I am an Amish person who believes that we have much to offer the world, and that we should be more open with offering it."

Fred spoke up. "Not everyone shares that opinion. In fact, most Amish, including our bishop, thinks that we need to keep ourselves free from any influence the world might bring in by evangelization."

"I will leave those arguments to those of you who know. As for myself, I am just glad that you do accept outside converts. I find myself strongly drawn to your lifestyle and Christian witness.

There were still several years left in my training at seminary, but it just seems to me that I may be better able to live out my desire for a deeply committed Christian life in the Amish community than I could have as a Catholic priest. There is much of the Catholic life that is segregated between the religious and the secular. From what I have seen of the Amish, they try to blend the two together."

Peter smiled slightly around the corners of his mouth. "You are an insightful young man. We will see if we can talk some more about this later. In the meantime, supper is waiting, and I am sure both of you will want to clean up and get some early rest."

The girls left the window and were standing by the door waiting. They had heard the conversation out by the end of the walk. "A real live Catholic priest. Is that as bad as it sounds?"

"That's not bad at all — that sounds exciting."

"You know, Beth, I just give up. You are so hopeless. Makes one wonder about your upbringing."

"But we don't know if he is really as bad as you make it sound. Just think, a real live Catholic priest. Not everyone can be the same like some people that I know. Life like that gets kind of boring. Besides, Fred has not said anything bad, has he?"

"No, but you don't have to act so innocent about this. You really are looking forward to seeing this person."

"Yes, imagine a real live Catholic priest visiting in one's home."

"Keep your voice down. They are coming up the walk, and he is not a Catholic priest yet. Just studying for one."

❧

Fred opened the screen door first and shook hands with his sisters. He turned around. "This is Dan Ludwig, the boy who has been boarding with me at school. Dan, this is Beth and Susie."

"Hi." Dan stuck out his hand. "How happy you girls look, and such beautiful dresses you are wearing."

Both of their faces turned red. "Beautiful dresses," Susie responded, "what do you mean? These plain outfits are nothing but plain."

"They are beautiful — I really mean it. See, from where I come from, I am used to seeing so much worldly dress, even in the church people. The world thinks they dress pretty, and they uncover their bodies in such wanton fashion." This remark was delivered without any shame or embarrassment. Dan did notice the red deepening in the girls' faces. He wondered whether Amish did not talk about such things. Sensing that the men behind him were tensing up too, he kept his expression the same and continued. "It is a true beauty that I see among the Amish, coming from something inside the person, such as you girls have. It is the beauty of a meek and quiet spirit. Where I come from the beauty is on the outside, and little on the inside."

The girls nodded their heads slightly but said nothing. Dan wondered if he had gone too far with them and overstepped some hidden boundary line. Fred was moving on towards the living room, so he smiled and moved to follow.

That was when Beth spoke up. "Fred has not told us much about you, but we are glad you could come. Supper is ready. I am sure you are hungry after all the traveling."

"Yes, we are," Dan said as he followed Fred into the living room.

Susie turned to her sister. "How did you dare say that? You ought to be ashamed of yourself talking to him after he told us that about our dresses. Whoever heard of a boy talking to girls like that?"

"There was nothing wrong with what he said. I liked his sincere heart. At least he can talk, which is more than you can say about some boys I know. I like how he talks. It sounds educated. Surely there are more things that a man can do than throw a good pitch fork of manure."

Susie said nothing but followed her mother into the kitchen. They looked at each other like they were not sure if God had made certain people or not.

Dan sat down in the living room on the couch. "You have a real nice place here, Mr. Stoltzfus. I just love the way you plain people farm. So much of your work is done by hand and horses. It makes you think of how Adam and Eve must have done their work in the Garden."

Peter chuckled, "Well, we do not consider ourselves on the level of Adam and Eve, but we do enjoy the lifestyle. There is something godly in working so close to the soil. To run one's fingers through freshly plowed and disked ground does good to your soul. I imagine the modern farmers could do the same, but seems they have no time to get off the tractor. Maybe it is the power of the tractor that keeps them moving. Our horses have to rest and it gives you time to pause and see and feel the earth as God has made it."

Dan responded that he had never farmed the soil, but he liked the Amish way of doing it over modern methods. "You also keep your places up so well. How do you find time for it? Fred told me when it happened that your house burned. Yet you have quickly rebuilt. I assume that the place across the drive is where the old house stood." Dan turned around and pointed to the other side of the lane where there was still some evidence of burned bricks and disturbed ground.

"Yes, that was the place," Peter said. "Our home practically burned to the ground."

"That must have been a traumatic experience to go through. Living like the Amish do must give you an inner strength to bear such things. You and your family look quite well for having suffered the shock of such an experience."

"It was hard," Peter agreed, "but we are thankful to God that no one was hurt, and for His protection over all of us. Beth could have been closer to the stove when it blew up, as well as other things."

Dan Ludwig nodded his head in agreement. "But I still insist that it is something. Granted that I may be coming from an entirely different perspective, yet I think it reflects our larger culture. If this fire happened to my family, I am telling you, why my sister, well, you just cannot imagine. Even my father, and he has insurance that would cover most of the loss." Here Dan threw his hands in the air. "One of them at least would have to have therapy. There is just no doubt in my mind. That is just how things are out there in my world. People do not take things well. And yet I am looking at you and at your family. None of you went to see a therapist? You did not have insurance to cover the loss of the home?"

"No, and no, because none of us needed it." Peter chuckled again. "Really, what would we want to see a therapist for? They just cost money, and if we need to talk there are plenty of people around to talk to. And without television," he grinned, "there is plenty of time to talk. Plus the neighbors gave us a hand and church people gather around at such a time for support. Then there is, of course, our faith to support us in time of need."

"It still is most remarkable to find such a thing, and such a community of faith, in our modern day and age. Most of you are farmers, close to the soil. You are solid in your commitments to your families and to each other in your community of faith. You live a deep faith in God expressed not just in words but also in your lifestyle. Are you aware how unusual that is in our culture?"

Peter nodded his head. "We are aware of it. That is why so much effort is expended in keeping what we as the Amish have."

Dan continued, "As you know I was studying for the Catholic priesthood. It was for this thing that I was looking. In the Catholic faith you find this type of lifestyle only in the monasteries or in the dedicated lives of the priests and nuns. It is practically unknown in the laity at large. But here it is not just the priest who lives his unworldly life — it is the whole community of believers. You have managed to include the family, wife, husband and children, your business, your community, all incorporated into the church. This is what I want."

Peter nodded his head again. "You have touched on the best of the Amish vision, but you know surely that everything is not roses in anyone's life."

Dan laughed. "I am sure it is not, but at least it must cut down on the therapy needed to live an ordinary life. Going back to my sister. She spends who knows how much on her psychologist. Where I come from, no one has time anymore it seems — time for each other, time for themselves even, and so little time for God. They are always running everywhere. Everyone is gone most every night. Their cars are always on the road. Most people I know have left off using public transportation — trains, buses, and such things. I hardly feel safe driving on the highway anymore with the number of cars on it. Here, why look, no cars in the driveway, no tractors in the field. I have hardly heard a car go by on the road even. This is such a peaceful setting. Heaven feels close to me."

"Yes, sometimes," Peter Stolzfus said quietly. "And sometimes it seems far away."

Dan seemed not to notice as he continued. "This is so wonderful, and I would like so much to be a part of it. I would like to be as secure and unpretentious as you people are. I would like to live my religion all the time, not just in church. Here I could marry, have a family, and still have the holy life that I was seeking in the priesthood.

Annie interrupted them as she entered the room. "Supper is ready. Would the two of you come to the table? And Fred — where is Fred?" She went to the bottom of the stairs and called up. A faint voice answered from the bedroom, followed quickly by footsteps and Fred's appearance.

Peter led them into the dining room where the girls were already seated surrounded by steaming bowls of food — mashed potatoes, gravy, green beans and a meat casserole. After they were seated, Peter led in grace. His voice rose and fell as he said the German words with feeling and emotion.

After an appropriate silence Annie encouraged them, "Everyone help themselves. There is pie out in the kitchen."

Chapter Nine

Dan Ludwig wanted to be awakened in time for chores.

"That will be at 5:30 a.m., Dan. Think you can handle that?" Fred asked. "This is not like getting up for prayers."

"Just be sure and wake me."

It was dark the next morning as they entered the barn, Fred swinging the gas lantern he had lit in the house. "We will light some more once we are in the barn. The girls will be out too. They help with the milking."

Dan breathed in the morning air. The sun sent up its first slight coloration in the sky behind them. "This is better than morning prayers, Fred, the air is so sweet. It is easier to smell it here than from the inside of the chapel."

Fred did not respond right away, but then mumbled something about never having been to morning prayers.

"You know what I think? I think there is a part missing from my life. I never even knew what would satisfy it. Yet here I get a glimpse of it again. Somehow your lifestyle has found a connection between the natural and the spiritual. This morning draws me to God, more than saying prayers ever did. It is as if you not only put God first, but you are finding him in the first things, the natural world around you. Who would have thought that doing chores would open one's heart to the Almighty? Did you actually say you milk by hand?"

At first Fred only nodded his head to the question, but he remembered it was dark and said "yes" after receiving no response. "The whole family helps at one time or the other, everyone except mother."

The barn door creaked as they entered. Fred hung his lantern on a nail hammered into a beam. He went to open the door to the outer yard and the cows began filing in. They found their way to their own stanchions, banging loudly against the holding bars, waiting for their feed. Dan Ludwig was watching Fred scooping it out when the barn door opened behind them. Beth entered and with a muffled good morning took a three-legged stool from against the wall and grabbed one of the stainless steel pails from the milk house. Fred soon joined her with his own musical swish, swish of milk squirting against stainless steel, followed by the deeper sound of milk into milk through a layer of foam.

"Your milking sounds great, Beth. I wish I could learn."

"How do you know what milking should sound like? Have you ever heard it before?"

"No, but something tells me that it is making the sound of a capable and well-done job."

Beth pretended not to hear as she moved on to the next cow. After finishing her fourth one she headed for the door. "Breakfast will be on the table in fifteen minutes — eggs, bacon, the works this morning."

An hour later Fred and Dan left on the way to town for Saturday business. They made a strange sight on the open buggy — an Amish young man sitting on the right side driving, and on the left a young man who looked sort of Amish. The hat looked right with its three-inch rim pressed straight out all the way around. It was hard to tell about the pants since the young man was sitting, but they looked homemade. The sports coat created a problem. No one in town ever saw an Amish boy wearing one before.

Dan Ludwig was chuckling. "We do look strange. As soon as possible I would like to get Amish clothing. It would feel good this morning to have on what you are wearing. People look at you differently than they do me. They look at you with a certain expectation on their faces. It is as if they have already drawn conclusions in their own minds that could not be easily changed."

"You may be dreaming, but what conclusions would that be?"

"They seem to have already decided that you are a good person who would do no wrong."

Fred did not think that anyone looked at him like that. Dan told him that it was not him personally that he was referring to, but the looks seemed to be caused more by the clothing than anything else.

"See, this is what I want, Fred. It is what you Amish have. Now when people look at me they look as if they have a blank mind concerning my character. They look as if they do not know me, but it is more than that. One likes an opinion to be drawn, a conclusion, and an absolute to be placed about oneself simply by one's presence. This is what you Amish have. People are convinced that you are good, and you would have to prove them wrong. For me as I am now, they look as if they do not know, and I would have to prove that I am good. It would be much better, I think, to have it the way you have it."

Fred looked rather unconvinced. "We have always been taught the value of our clothing, but not for those reasons. We are not trying to make ourselves special. Rather it is things like unity that we are after. By having uniformity in our clothing it draws us together into a unity with one another. What better way to be one with each other on the inside, or spiritually as some would say, than by being one with each other on the outside? Such oneness lends itself to maintaining our unity first with each other, and then with God. A simple dress code brings more agreement and equality amongst us than a thousand sermons against the self-life. In being called away from our own desires on how to dress, we lay the foundation for the larger decisions when self must be ignored to be our brother's keeper. You are making it sound as if our clothing should be worn for personal selfish reasons."

Dan was nonplussed. "Not at all. I am just seeing another angle of this that may not be apparent to someone like yourself, who is living on the inside. I am still looking at it from the outside. What I see today driving in town with you is what I want to have. There is a longing that I feel to be surrounded by people who are at peace and in unity with each other. It would be wonderful to share a common identity, a common hope, and a common face that is presented to the outside world. One would not feel so alone then, but rather surrounded by a sense of belonging. When you are by yourself the task of establishing your own place and purpose in the world seems so hopelessly difficult. That is why there are so many lonely people in this modern world of ours."

Fred nodded his head slightly. "There is a lot of truth to what you are saying, but we are lonely at times too, even when we are among people who are like us."

"Well, that is probably true, but look at some more of the benefits. Take this sport coat I wore today. When I bought this coat, it was, now that I stop to think about it, purchased with very impure motives. I bought it first of all just for myself, because I liked it and wanted it. How much better would it be if I bought a coat thinking about others and not about myself. In this way I would be practicing a constant turning away from my own selfish motives. All my actions could then become motivated away from selfishness and self-satisfaction to a concern for the well-being and consideration of others. I would be laying a foundation for Christ-like behavior in my life."

Fred could not resist a grin even in the face of Dan's expressions of devotion. "You are forgetting that this coat I am wearing cannot be bought in any store. It takes a sewing machine pedaled by someone's own feet to make it. There is a lot of work involved."

"I would be willing to do that, and that is how it should be. The people who follow after God should be so separated from the world that they cannot even buy the world's clothes. It should be that clothing designed for the lust of the individual and the satisfaction of self cannot be purchased by people who desire to be holy. The cost in human effort is well worth the result. You have clothing that reflects your spiritual values and furthers your walk with God and each other. The world does not make clothes like that. Of course they have to be made. I have never thought of it like that before."

"Well, that does put sewing by hand in a different light," Fred observed wryly. "I am sure the girls and Mom will be inspired to hear that their sewing machines have been the source of your lofty thoughts."

"You can be amused about all this if you want, Fred, but I think you should give a little respect and reverence to what your upbringing has given you. That must be a problem for those who have been brought up around these things. I am sure, though, that the older ones like your father — and yourself even when you get older — will appreciate the value of what I am talking about."

"You are right," Fred nodded. "Our people some five hundred years ago were moved by high motives and intentions. We have tried in our day and age to follow that. Things just get a little dim after a while. Maybe that is hard to explain to someone who has not grown up around these things. It is hardest to see what is closest to our noses."

Dan thought for a long time in silence as he watched the landscape go by. "I suppose it is, but I feel as if I should have grown up here. It feels like home. By the way, Fred, you have two nice sisters."

Fred said without turning around, "Which one would that be?"

"Well, the oldest one."

"You wouldn't, would you?"

"Oh yes, I would."

⊗

That Sunday morning Jason got his first look at Dan Ludwig. He liked what he saw. Rachel had told him that a visitor would be in church, a good friend of the family. Jason was always on the look out for new friends and found an interest in people. This was an interesting person. "He walks so dignified," Jason thought. "No up and down in his step like the Amish boys."

On the way home from church Jason asked Rachel, "Why does Dan like Fred so much?"

"Well, they are good friends," she told him. "They got to know each other where Fred teaches school."

Jason thought for a while. "I think he likes him a lot."

Later in the day, Dan sat with Fred on the bench with the first row of boys. It was Sunday evening at precisely 7:28 p.m. in Albert Yantsey's basement. The clock hung on the furnace wall to their left. As one of the oldest boys, Fred felt a responsibility to sit there, and his visitor was to be taken along. Behind them sat four more rows of teenage boys followed by three rows for the married men. Tonight most of the benches were full. Directly opposite Fred and Dan, separated by a mere six feet, were an equal number of empty benches behind which were a corresponding set filled by older and married women. There was total silence. Hardly a muscle moved on the front benches. Behind them, on what sounded like the third row, Fred heard a foot or two being moved across the concrete floor. Songbooks were being held and opened soundlessly.

Then down the basement stairs they came. It was 7:29. Alma Chupp was in the lead. She was 29 years old and never known to have dated. Following her was Martha Byler, a sunny girl just turned twenty. Her boyfriend was sitting to Fred's right. They were now dating for two years. He was smiling, and Martha was too, but Fred did not think it was at each other. They both seemed to be enjoying life. The third girl was Esther Schrock, followed by Fred's sister Beth, and so on. They all filed in and sat down till all three rows were filled. These were the girls. Not that anyone in the room felt the need for questions.

Fred moved in his spot on the bench, ever so slightly. Even after going through this since he was sixteen years old, it still caused emotion in him. It was like putting magnets close together with the polar ends turned against each other. The effect cut through the humdrum and haze of Amish living. It made life seem immediate and clear. It was like turning the pages of a blurred book and finding the letters clear and readable. It was like having asked many questions and finding they all had one answer. Fred shook his head and tried to think of something else. He glanced over at Dan. To his surprise Dan looked like a boy who was enjoying himself and quite at home.

"No nervousness around our girls at all." Fred was not sure he liked this. "Looks too much like a duck coming into his own pond. He must be used to being around girls."

The German song number was given out and started from the girl's side of the group. It was 7:30. The Amish hymn singing began. German singing would continue for 30 minutes with fast tunes sung on the same songs as the slow tunes had been sung on Sunday morning. Dan Ludwig thought those had sounded like the Catholic Gregorian chant, but Fred told him he thought there was no connection between the two. After that a ten-minute devotional was followed by English singing till 9:00.

Albert gave the devotional that evening. As the hosting family, the father of the house took his turn in presenting scripture and commentary to the youth. Amish public scriptural presentation was strictly controlled by the ministry. Within the ministry team, commentary was carefully guarded. Only on special occasions like this, and in some Sunday School and Parochial school functions, were the lay people allowed to expound scripture publicly.

As Albert cleared his throat and gave out the scripture text, the young people gave him their attention. There was no rustling of the pages of Bibles opening to the text. Amish people do not carry the Bible into services, except perhaps for Sunday School Sunday. Even the ministry does not carry Bibles into the church service. Only after all are seated on Sunday morning is the Bible given to the presiding bishop for use in the service. It is considered a great mark of pride to carry scriptures around in one's hand. Such an individual would be regarded with suspicion as believing he possessed superior learning and abilities. To carry the scriptures would be interpreted as believing one contained the powers of private interpretation. Walking into a church service with the Bible in hand would be stating for all to see that one needed not his brother and his brother's guiding hand in life but only one's own grasp on scripture.

The text was the third chapter of John, the story of Nicodemus and his night visit to Christ. Albert read haltingly through the High German. As he prepared to make his follow-up remarks, he searched for German words. Not being a minister, he was not used to speaking fully with German words. It is only when an Amish person tries to talk completely German in his dialect of Pennsylvania Dutch that he sees how many English words have crept in. Albert was embarrassed as he searched for German words for what he normally would have said quite fluently in the English-afflicted version of Pennsylvania Dutch. The English words were like bright red salmon going through the water. He was looking for the gray, for the acceptable, and then here came another one. Fred felt for him as the stream of his speech continued haltingly. Dan Ludwig asked Fred about it later and found the explanation surprising.

"You people have to be careful about this. What is wrong with you that you cannot speak German? It is good that there is still at least the consciousness of the dangers to your language. I was glad to see that the man was trying to leave out the English words. Where I learned the Pennsylvania Dutch they were careful to teach me Pennsylvania Dutch, not English-modified Pennsylvania Dutch."

Fred agreed but mentioned how easy it was to pick up English words. "There is no written language for the Pennsylvania Dutch dialect. What we know is learned only by ear, by what is verbally passed down. So the temptation always is to use the English word when one does not remember what the German word is. Some of the words the old people do not even know any more. In that case we have to reach back to the High German for guidance, or use that word itself. There is also the conflict between the High German language and the Pennsylvania Dutch dialect. Put in the different variations of Pennsylvania Dutch spoken by the different areas of Amish Communities, and things can get difficult."

Dan Ludwig said he was glad to see that the people were trying. As for himself, he was going to stick to German words from the beginning.

The last song was given out at 8:57. It was "Blessed Be the Tie." Conversations began within a few minutes of the last sounds of singing. A few of the boys and girls talked across the front benches, but mostly the buzz of conversation was within the male and female zone.

Outside the first buggy could be heard rolling past the basement window on the graveled driveway. Fred nudged Dan and said he was ready to go. Together they went out to harness the horse to the buggy. Dan was not much help, but he wanted to know what was going on. "When is the courting done?"

"It is done mostly about right now. As soon as we have this horse hitched up we will pull up to the line over there." Fred pointed his chin towards the sidewalk coming out of the basement door. There a buggy waited at the end and two in line behind it. "My two sisters will come out as that girl is coming out right there. In my case it is my sisters. If I am dating it is my date. I would then drive her home and stay for the time allowed. The parents may set that time, but in our situation the church has the rule of midnight. At midnight I would go home."

"Is that all? What happens on your dates? Does your buggy serve as your car? They seem a little tighter than a car. Not much need to sit any closer together, is there? Does a buggy lend itself better to kissing than a car?"

Fred was not amused, but since it was dark Dan Ludwig could not see his face. "No, we do not do that stuff around here."

"You don't? They do at the Amish community where I learned my Dutch. At least some of the boys I talked to spoke of kissing, and something about a broomstick under the rocking chair, but I never learned how it was all done. I just figured Amish were male and female like everyone else."

Fred was glad his red face did not show in the darkness. "We have rules against those kinds of practices. I have dated but never kissed a girl in my life. Hopefully it will stay that way until I marry. We believe that strong marriages start with strong disciplines, and those include keeping your hands off of each other until marriage."

They got in the buggy and pulled up to the end of the sidewalk. Beth and Susie came out of the basement door almost immediately. They climbed in the back seat of the double-seated buggy, as Fred had borrowed his parent's buggy for the night. The conversation on the way home was chatty between the girls and Fred as they caught up on community and family news that meeting people brought to mind. Dan Ludwig did not have much to say as the buggy rolled along in the darkness. He was thinking of dating, and of Beth, and of how much he knew that he was finally home.

A week later Homer and Rachel were at Peter and Annie's place for Sunday evening. No one felt like attending the evening sing with the young people, so they gathered at the new house. Homer raised the point, foremost in his mind, with Peter, "Have you thought anymore about what to do about the church situation?"

"Yes, I have, but nothing has come up yet. I am praying that God will open some door that we can all walk through. It looks impossible from man's eyes, but with God nothing is impossible."

Homer responded, "I admire your faith. As you keep praying, hopefully God will do something soon. I am having a hard time waiting, that is all."

"It is hard, I know," Peter said. "But waiting is better than doing something we will all regret later."

Rachel cleared her throat, anxious to change the conversation. "Did Dan Ludwig actually ask Beth for a date before he left?" Her eyes shone with intense interest.

Annie smiled, "Not really a date. He asked her whether she would write him."

"He did. Really, that is wonderful. What did Beth say?"

"Yes of course. She fell pretty hard for the guy."

"Isn't that exciting."

"Now you're sounding like the girls do."

Jason was playing on the floor in the living room. No one paid any attention to him, or asked him to leave during the conversation. He was not sure what dating and letter writing was, but if it concerned his favorite aunt he was interested.

"What is writing letters all about?" he piped up.

"Now Jason," Rachel told him, "you should not be listening to adult conversation. "Your aunt is dating Dan Ludwig."

Jason shook his head. He was not sure what dating was either.

CHAPTER TEN

No one is sure how the church trouble in their lives would have turned out if a visiting minister none of them ever saw before had not shown up. Peter and Annie were on their way to church that morning. The carriage bounced on the left side as the wheels hit the rut in the gravel road. They were not yet aware of how little things turn the course of one's life into strange directions.

"Oops," Peter commented on the bump.

"Ya, Peter, you could drive a little more careful."

"We are not going that fast, Anne. It was the rut."

"Whatever it was, it's not good to get shook up in one's Sunday clothes. If there had been water in that rut, you could have splashed us on this side with mud, or it could have hit the girls in the back. Do remember to be more careful on these gravel roads, especially when it has rained."

"I'll try. Maybe the highway department will get around to fixing the ruts. It is only lately that it has been this bad."

At the intersection Peter pulled the horse to a halt at the stop sign. Two buggies coming from the west passed while he waited, with their occupants in Sunday attire.

"I heard there is a load up from Southern Illinois, a minister along. I have never heard of him — Robert Troyer." Peter pulled away from the stop sign, slapping the reins to get his horse moving at a faster rate so he could catch up with the two buggies in front of him.

"It will be good to hear different preaching. Not that our home ministers are all that bad, but something else for a change. You know how it is, Peter."

"Should be a good Sunday."

Ten minutes later they pulled into the farmstead where church was being held. Peter dropped Annie and the girls off at the end of the sidewalk. Buggies were already lined up to the left of the barnyard, with some in various stages of unhitching and others already parked. Peter did a half circle with the buggy and got in place. He could not fit into the parking structure, so he pulled farther up and pushed the buggy back by hand. As he hopped out, one of his older boys, Jesse, came over to help unhitch.

"Nice morning, Dad, don't you think? Hardly a cloud in the sky for this time of the year."

"Yes it is, Jesse. Thanks for the help. I am not as limber anymore as I used to be. The horse threatens to go sometimes before I am done unhitching both sides."

"Now don't try to sound old, Dad. You are still quite spry. Seems like only yesterday when I left home and got married. Now we have eight children ourselves, but you and Mom are still young, at least you seem so to me."

"Well, I guess the Lord will see how many miles we all have left in us. I do get tired easy at times. You know, Jesse, I have been thinking this week again about the needs we have on these church matters. Homer is getting mighty impatient just waiting. This thing of not being able to work in town is really hard on him.

"I guess I wonder if maybe my burden for the mission field could be a part of the answer. I still get this longing to reach out to others less fortunate than us. We have so much as Amish people that would be useful in the third world countries. Here in Canada, who needs our farming and old-fashioned values? It seems like the world is just rushing by and inventing new things every day. What uses have they for us? We clutter up their blacktop highways, when graveled roads would suit us better. We have to drive miles into town when the little country store would suit our purposes. I do not feel like we are of much use to this modern culture. In the third world countries I hear they still use ox carts and horses, if they have them. They plant corn by hand, on the mountainside. Even in my old age I long to be of use to others, to expand that usefulness to where it is really needed. Maybe if we moved to a third world mission field, Homer would come along. That would really solve a lot of things. Plus to see new cultures, their faces, and their countries. Would that not be better than growing old on my rocker?"

Jesse looked around to see if anyone else was in hearing distance. "As I have told you before, Dad, I get excited myself about such a thing. I don't know about Homer. We shouldn't decide the matter just because of him. It seems more important than that. But you know what Bishop Wengerd thinks. Maybe he could be made to understand how you think and feel if you explained it all to him."

"I have tried, Jesse. It's no use. He is dead set against any such talk. Says we ought to be upbuilding and thankful church members right where we are. Says Amish people do not do such things. That it never works. That you only end up losing the good things you already have."

"I guess there isn't much of a record of Amish missionary work. Why is that? It does make one wonder."

"Yes, why is it like that, Jesse? Why can't we do mission work? If what we have is so good, is it made worse for sharing? There is a use for our ways somewhere, Jesse. There must be."

"You should hear Dan Ludwig talking. Fred wrote that he is still all wound up from his trip up to your place the other weekend. He and Beth are writing, Mom said. He even plans on moving up here when Fred comes back from his term of teaching."

"I guess you have a point, Jesse. Sometimes people can see things from the outside better than we can from the inside, but I still think we could share more than we do. Dan Ludwig is an interesting boy. Beth is all excited about him. Seemed to be sincere enough, but he has not been the one living this life for some fifty-six years. I guess that is just my perspective from the inside. Then of course there is Homer to think about."

Jesse glanced around nervously. "We'd better get in line, Dad. People are looking this way, probably wondering why it is taking us so long to unhitch a horse. They might think we are both real old, or something else."

At nine o'clock sharp the line of men moved towards the house. Peter and Jesse got back from putting the horse in the barn in time to get in their place in line but didn't have much time for handshaking. Jesse greeted several men around him, and Peter did the same. Jesse hoped those he did not have time for would take no offense. He thought to himself that he would find those he missed after church and greet them then. Jesse waved to one of his younger sons to join him in the line.

The line continued to move on towards the house, entering by the kitchen door. Jesse took his hat off and placed it with the pile on the table. He reached for his son's hat to place it on the table.

"How am I going to find it again, Dad? That's my new hat."

"Its got your name written in it, doesn't it?"

The little boy smiled in relief. "That's right, it does — Mamma wrote it in last night."

Jesse smiled at his son and pushed him gently forward to fill in the gap in the line.

"Come on, move."

≈

The preaching started at a quarter after ten. Home minister Alva Bontrager preached the opening message. At eleven the visiting minister got to his feet.

Peter Stolzfus remembered little of the actual sermon. What he remembered was the zeal, the earnestness, the look on Bishop Wengerd's face, and the way he shifted on the bench. This man was a preacher — young, articulate, and interesting. Peter listened in rapt attention. The words went by him in single file — missions, responsibility, obedience, God, short, responding, and alive.

The hour message passed quickly, at least for Peter. At the long lunch table, served with a special blend of peanut butter, bread, meats, pickles, and other minor foods, he was seated across and down several seats from the ministers, but he could hear.

"You are from Southern Illinois, is that right?"

"Yes, that is correct."

"Are there Gingerichs living there? Seems like I heard that

name mentioned once, by someone I met, who said they were from Southern Illinois."

"There are some around, I think, but not close to our district."

Peter's peanut butter sandwich tasted good, so he concentrated on it and his thoughts and stopped straining to listen. One of the servers came back with coffee.

"Want some coffee?" It was one of his older granddaughters helping out with the serving.

"Sure." He held out his cup, being careful not to upset his cheese perched on top of his peanut butter sandwich in the other hand. As his granddaughter moved on down the line, he absentmindedly stabbed at the pickles. They were sweet pickles, his favorite.

It was a half an hour later when their table was done eating and cleared out that Peter got a chance to speak with the young minister, Troyer, in semi-private.

Peter introduced himself and got right to the point. "I liked your message today."

"Well, it was not really anything much."

Peter continued, "We are kind of in a church crisis around here right now. Because of that and because I have thought much of missions and how an Amish outreach or missions group ought to be started, maybe in a third world country, I would really like to start an Amish mission outreach. Have you ever thought of something like that?"

Minister Troyer did not act surprised. In fact, he smiled slightly. "Yes, I have in fact, and so has another minister in the district next to us. We know each other well and have spoken often about it. There really ought to be Amish missions work done somewhere."

Peter was silent for a while. "This is so good to hear you say this. I have been feeling much of late, as I am getting older, that I would like to be involved in missions work, without all the modern emphasis as you see in others, you know."

"That has also been in our hearts. An Amish community of faith and witness in some foreign country is what we have been thinking. A country south of Mexico, perhaps — there are several small ones there, I believe."

Peter was silent again. "We must talk some more about this, as I am more than willing to support such a venture."

"We are leaving this evening for home, but I tell you what — let us think some more about this, let me take your address and I will give you mine, and we will stay in touch."

"That sounds right to me. Let us stay in touch."

The conversation took five minutes, and they exchanged addresses.

❧

Peter and his wife pulled out of the driveway at 2:30. The scattered groups of men visiting in the front yard were almost gone. As they turned left, several buggies were in front of them, and to their right Peter could see one in the distance.

"I saw you were talking to the visiting minister."

"You did. I only spoke to him for a little bit."

"I know you." Anne did not say anything more; she did not have to.

Peter took that as her assent if not approval and began. "Robert Troyer says they have been thinking themselves about starting an Amish mission work in Central America, and that there is another minister that lives in the district next to his that is interested also. This may be our answer that we need for our church problems around here. Have you ever heard of anything like it?"

"Well, I have heard it from you."

"Yes, yes, of course, but Amish ministers who want to do missions work. I have just not heard of that before. Sure, there must be some, but I have not found them yet, and you know neither have I been looking for them. I never thought such a thing would be possible. That is just like God, though, to do what we think is impossible. Do you think we are too old for such a thing?"

"Speak for yourself, Mr. Stolzfus. I am still young."

"Of course you are, Anne, and so am I. Young enough to move to Central America. My, what that would be like!"

"I hope you know what you are doing, Peter, but I suppose you do. You usually do."

91

"After talking to Robert, I invited Jesse's, Albert's, and Steve's over for supper tonight. We need to talk about this. If they support the idea, I will tell Homer and Rachel about it."

"You do not really expect them to go too, do you?"

"The boys have expressed interest in the past. You have heard us talking about it, haven't you? As far as Homer and Rachel, I think they might go along. It certainly would be better than joining the Beachys."

"Of course, you have talked before. This sounds like more than that to me. But I suppose you know what you are doing."

"Would you quit saying that. I do not know if I know what I am doing. It is just that something seems like it needs to be done, and well, why not us?"

"Yes, but Central America? Are they still frying people in pots and putting their skulls on poles in front of their homes?"

"No, Anne, I am sure they are not."

"I guess we might find out then. Would you drive faster, Peter? I have a big supper to get ready for this evening."

Peter slapped the reins and the horse increased his speed.

Chapter Eleven

That evening after supper, and now the beginning of 1968, the men folk found a map of America and got it out on the kitchen table. They turned it in the right direction, with North facing north. Before them was Canada, then the United States, and hanging off of Texas on the lower left-hand side of the map, Mexico. Central America started wide and got narrower as it went down. The strip of land swung down and then to the right: Guatemala, San Salvador, Belize sitting on top of a little swirl, Honduras, Nicaragua, Costa Rica, and then the thin long little line of Panama ending where the land mass bulged out into South America. The map stopped there.

They scaled the map after someone brought out a ruler. It was a long ways down from Ontario, Canada.

"Where are you going, Father? Costa Rica?"

"We will have to see. Nothing has been decided yet. I will do some studying in the encyclopedia on the lay of the land, geography, populations, and poverty levels. We will want to go somewhere where there is a need. I am sure Robert will have ideas also."

"Are you actually going?"

"We don't know yet, but this does sound like the most promising thing I have heard of yet. As you all know I am not a minister and so could not conduct Sunday services. That has always been a barrier for me when I thought of starting a new missions outreach anywhere. Who would lead in the meetings and minister to the congregation?"

"Maybe Steve and his family will go along. He is a deacon," Jesse said, nodding to his younger brother across the table from him.

"Yes, it would be good if Steve came and the rest of you as well, but we would need more than a deacon to have services. What we need is Amish ministers and a bishop who are interested in missions. Robert said he has another minister who would be interested in going along. That leaves the bishop, of course. With ministers and a deacon, that is assuming Steve goes, we could have services, but not ordinations or marriages."

"You would not actually need a bishop living there as long as he would travel down for official duties," Jesse brought up.

Peter nodded his head in silent thought. "All this is happening so fast, and we need to take it slow. I am sure God will help us, if it is his will. He will supply all our needs. As for now He has already given us so much — an Amish minister who is actually interested in missions. That is such a wonderful thing indeed. I say we should not pass up this opportunity that may be given to us of God. I believe we should be of good courage and think seriously about walking through this door. Such a thing may not come along again for us Amish people very soon. I believe, as all of you know so well, that we as plain people owe something to the world. Things like our farming skills, our ability to work with the land, our simple lifestyle. Would it not be much more in order for us to be in a country that wants and can use our skills, instead of here in a modern society that has so advanced past our way of life? Would it not feel wonderful to be really wanted in a society? Think about how much easier it would be to keep our children if we did not have to work only with the negative and keep them from something that looks good, but could offer ourselves as a benefit and a blessing to those around us. Wouldn't that appeal much more to our families and those who are coming after us? Look how hard it is to keep our young people now. I say let us try this idea of mission work, and we may well be blessed of God."

Everyone was looking at each other and at the map. Someone said, "We will stay Amish though, won't we?"

"That would defeat the whole purpose if we didn't," Peter said, and several of the others were nodding in approval. "For that very reason, I am taking such care that we do things right from the beginning. We must have ministers involved in our efforts so that it is a solid commitment to the direction we wish to go. Then when others join, perhaps, it will be clear that we are an Amish missions outreach church. It is not my intention to leave the Amish fellowship, or to have anything other than an Amish mission. If I wanted anything else than that, I could have done something like this a long time ago, as the more liberal churches have many mission outreaches I could have involved myself in. They would even have let me start something on my own without ministerial help."

"We were sure you felt that way, Dad, but it is good to hear you say it anyway," Albert said. "It would be sad if we left the Amish faith just to do missions work. That kind of defeats the purpose, doesn't it?"

"You are right, and that is what I do not wish to do."

"What are you going to do about Amish fellowship, Dad? You know that Bishop Wengerd here will not support you in missions. Do you think there are other Old Order Amish groups who will be interested in risking fellowship with a missions church, let alone the problem of finding a bishop?"

"Those are questions we will have to answer in time. I wish the answers were easy. I wish Bishop Wengerd would support it himself, but I doubt it. As you know, missions are considered a dangerous thing with the Amish churches. We all grew up in the faith, and I believe you are all already aware of the reasons. Missions-minded people usually become more liberal after they are on the foreign field, or even here around home for that matter. I have tried hard not to be that way or to give offence to the great traditions of the Amish church."

Steve spoke up with some doubt in his voice. "Is this not all true, though, about the dangers of missions? How are we to know that it will not go that way with us? I do not want to go liberal, or see my children grow up like that. Once we are on the field, how do we know what the temptations and pressures will be that we face? I just wish there were others who had tried this before us and found it to work."

Peter nodded his head. "That would be a good thing. I wish too that there were others before us, but just because no one has done it before does not mean it cannot be done. I plan on being very careful with laying the groundwork. That is why we must have ordained Amish ministers to lead us, and once we get there and the community is begun we must be careful about the dangers. I will also look into whether the New Order Amish would support a foreign missions group. Seems like I have heard there is a bishop in Indiana who is more open to spiritual ideas, and who might be willing to fellowship with us and give us guidance. Maybe that is where the bishop could come from. This would be an important part also of laying the foundation, and I would not want to proceed without the blessing and guidance of an Amish bishop. He would of course not have to live with us as Jesse said, but would have to be willing to visit as the overseer."

The talk continued on. Jesse asked after a while, "Are you just doing this, Dad, because of Homer, so he does not leave the Amish?"

Peter pondered the question. "That is a part of it, but only a small part. The big part is my burden for missions."

Jesse nodded. "That is true. I have known your burden for missions for many years now."

Steve and Albert with their families left a little after nine and Jesse around nine-thirty, just as the young people drove in from the singing. After the usual greetings and partings of family, Peter stood listening to the buggy wheels at the front porch door, while behind him he could hear the voices settling down upstairs for the night. He looked up to the stars that stretched out across the sky and prayed to God that it would work. He prayed from the depths of his heart.

A few days later Peter stopped by Homer's in the evening and told Homer and Rachel about what was going on. Homer was interested. He said it sounded like a better idea than joining the Beachys. The more he thought about joining the Beachys the worse the idea looked, but he really had to do something.

Jason heard them talking, but it did not sound interesting. He was not sure what moving meant. Far away to him were grandfather's house and the town of Fraserwood. That did not seem too serious.

Peter started writing letters to Robert Troyer, keeping him updated on information from his end. Two months went by without much response. Then the letter came. Robert said that Vern Miller and himself were ready to make an exploratory trip to Honduras, Central America in search of the possibility of founding an Amish mission outreach. Could Peter be ready to go shortly? Peter was, and wrote back in the affirmative. More letters were exchanged and the plans solidified. The date to go was set.

Chapter Twelve

THE PLANE BANKED slightly to the right. Wispy clouds passed by on the wingtips. Through the window on the right a coastline could be seen coming up. Peter Stoltzfus sat in seat 21A by the window with Robert Troyer in the seat 21B beside him. Across the aisle was Vern Miller.

Peter leaned over and asked Vern, "Is that British Honduras coming up, do you think?"

"I might figure it out if this plane held still for a little bit."

"It is not that bad, really, now is it? The old buggy has worse bounces than this."

"At least they are sharp bounces, and not this queasy swaying up and down. These bounces feel like they have rubber in them."

"By the way, Peter, whose idea really was this? I have never been this far from home. If things go wrong we are holding you personally responsible."

"Remember, you were just as eager to come as I was. Look at that coastline. Isn't that something?" The window showed a smooth line of land and water meeting. There were no jagged edges to the lines such as are caused by mountains or bluffs. The coastline flowed in and out in sync with itself. "Looks like a gentle land, as if it kept pleasant things on its mind."

Vern was not so sure. "Looks strange to me. Like it's not exactly normal. From up here it is hard to tell, but those trees look droopy."

"What do you expect — highways, overpasses, miles of concrete, thousands of cars? That is what we are trying to get away from."

"Not really that as much as, well, it's everything, the land, the vegetation, it's not natural. It feels different already. I can tell from up here. It looks like it never got cold."

Peter ventured gingerly, "I don't think it does."

"I wonder what my wife back home would think of this. Do you think she will actually want to move here? Some of my children are too young to care. The oldest ones are still young enough that things like this are an adventure to them."

"We do not even know whether we like it, but I think God will help us with the families if it comes to that. They would probably reflect our own views and feelings by the time it is over with. I know that Annie has always been willing to go with me on our other mission outreaches. Let's all remember what this is. It is not just adventure and seeing new lands. We want the hand of God to guide and give his blessing to what we want to do."

Robert shifted in his seat as the plane did another bounce on the turbulent air. "That is why I wish our wives could have come with us. It would have been nice if they could have come all the way down here or at least to Miami to see us off on the plane, but Canada for you Pete, and Illinois for us, is a long way from Miami, as well as from Honduras."

"If we move," Vern said, "they can all see this then. I think we are doing the right thing for now. It would have been way too hard to bring more people along for this first trip. I feel enough stress with the decisions we have to make. Seeing strange country like this is tiring also. Then there was the Greyhound Bus Robert and I took to Miami. That was tiring enough, without taking the bus all the way from Canada like you did, Peter. Why didn't you fly all the way, Peter? There must be air service closer to you than Miami. We thought of doing that. Now I wish we had. That return Greyhound Bus trip from Miami is not something I am looking forward to. At least Robert and I could travel together for company on the bus. You were alone, Peter."

"I brought along some books to read. And it was not really too bad. Greyhound traveling has always been enjoyable to me. I think the Lord wants us to stay as simple and peaceful as possible, even in our traveling. Going by bus seems more in line with our life-style than this plane does."

Vern must have missed the spiritual nudge in the conversation for he continued. "I would not use the word 'enjoyable' and 'Grey-hound' in the same sentence — my knees cramped in the small seat space, traveling all night, with all that starting and stopping at every little town. When Greyhound says it goes everywhere, I was thinking of something more majestic, maybe mountains or things like that, rather than stopping every other mile along the way. Seems like everywhere to them is every little town and hamlet there is. That whine of the engine in the middle of the night is still in my dreams."

Robert chuckled, "I guess we could have bought plane tickets from closer to home instead of driving all the way to Miami to fly, but I thought you agreed it was cheaper."

"I did, but in the future I will fly whenever possible."

Peter cleared his throat. "We can be thankful we are flying at all, even if it is only from Miami down. We could well be on a boat crossing over the Gulf of Mexico, or driving down all the way overland through Mexico and Guatemala by bus. This trip of ours is already pushing the limits at home in our church of what are acceptable things. I not only enjoy traveling by bus, but I think it is wise that we all be discreet about things. Flying is still allowed among our group of Amish at present, partly because it is such a new thing that little discussion has been done about it. It just looks better, as well as fitting my personal beliefs, if we take our travel-ing by bus whenever possible. There was already some mention by two of the brothers in my home church about how lawful flying by plane is for Amish people. It does not help that flying and missions are now being joined in the same sentence. We are going to have to be careful about things like this."

"Are they really serious, Peter, about outlawing flying for the Amish people?"

"Yes, but the rule would only apply to our home church, although there are other communities I am sure who would have similar feelings. At home this past communion the ministry prohibited any more new construction work in our local town. I did not fully understand all the reasons for that, but I support our Amish faith. If they felt that such a move was important to make, I would not be surprised if they felt the need to restrict people from flying in the future like we are doing. I hope that does not happen. Hopefully we will not be a threat to the ministry with our mission outreach in Honduras. That is if it is God's will that we move there. It would make things much harder for us to even think of starting an Amish community in a third world country if all the travel was done by land. I do so hope that God will see fit to help us in this matter. We want this to be an Amish project, and we want it to stay Amish."

Robert nodded his head in agreement. "Let us hope this all turns out well. Vern and I also want to be careful in what we do, and not to be an offence to anyone. We feel too that it should be possible to start an Amish church in a foreign country. There are many who say it cannot be done, but they have never tried it. We wish to do our part to make this venture a success."

Peter was silent as the intercom crackled on. "Ladies and Gentlemen, we are now preparing for landing in Belize City. Please fasten your seatbelts."

"Here we go, our first landing on foreign soil."

The plane touched down gently on the concrete runway. Outside, low trees and bushes could be seen. The trees were of medium height, some looking like palm trees. Their observation from above was being confirmed through the small plane windows.

"Looks like stunted versions of something, certainly not the US variety."

"Probably the heat. I read it gets pretty hot here in British Honduras."

Robert chuckled, "You might be short and stunted too in so much heat."

"Let's get out of here. I sure hope the land looks better where we are going, instead of this swamp-like look."

Peter said that he thought it would. "From my memory, I believe Honduras has a higher elevation and is mountainous, having mostly indigenous pine trees."

Some of the passengers disembarked and a few came on. In fifteen minutes the plane lifted off to land in the capital of El Salvador thirty minutes later. Military vehicles lined the landing strip and were parked in front of the terminal.

"Well, well, what have we got here, some kind of war?" asked Peter.

"Maybe some local thing, indigenous too," Vern ventured. "Some need perhaps to parade their military hardware for the benefit of tourists."

"Looks serious to me. I am going to ask."

Peter turned to an American-looking man sitting in the row in front of them. "Do you know, Sir, anything on why the military vehicles are here?"

"Yes, in fact I do. A local row, I believe between Salvador and their neighbor Honduras. Border dispute, I was told."

"That's interesting, because Honduras is where we are going. Is this anything serious?"

"Yes, serious enough in their world, but from our point of view mostly blow and puff. They really have not enough military hardware to do much damage. That is, of course, from the English point of view, and I would believe American too. A few pot shots and it is all over. Nothing like a declaration of independence or such sort of thing."

"Well, yes." Peter cleared his throat. "I see your point. We are visiting Honduras, I and these two others." Robert and Vern nodded their heads, leaning forward to hear better now that their presence was acknowledged. "Are you familiar with Honduras?"

"Most certainly, I live there. Have lived there for some fifteen years. I moved from outside Dallas, Texas, and liked it so much I married a local girl and have a farm some four hours north of the capital."

"That is interesting." Peter was leaning out of his seat. "Could you tell us about the country and how the climate and farming is in your area?"

"We live in a valley of sorts, at least it levels out for some distance east and west of us. El Salvador and Honduras are countries of moderate mountain ranges with multiple foothills scattered around at random. The same scheme of things carries for both of them. So it is difficult to find much flat land for long. Our valley has a large range of mountains to the north with its accompanying foothills. These are fairly close to us. To the south is a larger range, but they are farther away, barely visible at times. Weather is beautiful all year around, anything from a rare low 40 degrees Fahrenheit to the more normal 80s and lower 90s. The elevation is between 2000 – 3000 feet, so there is no humidity like the coast has. There is none of the intense heat that goes with the costal regions of this area.

"Farming is sporadic at best, not because of unavailable land, but because the natives do not know how to farm. I don't believe I have seen as much as a tractor since I left Texas. Work is done with oxen, primarily; the plows are a disgrace to any proper concept of plowing. They are wooden instruments that barely scratch the surface of the soil. Perhaps that is why little plowing is done. The most common method of planting corn, which is the main crop they know of — that and beans — is to take a sharpened stick, punch a hole in the ground, drop in the seed, and push it all shut with the foot. One is amazed that they get a harvest at all. Fertilizer is unknown to them, or maybe too expensive, unless they have some native fertilizer they are using that I am not aware of. As far as land to farm, streams are fairly abundant as they are the main source of the people's water, both for drinking and other uses. Although I have never paid much attention to it elsewhere, on my land the stream bottomlands are of a nice black soil and lend themselves handily to farming. It's just that proper farming is not done much.

"Honduras has a rainy and dry season, weather wise. In the rainy season it rains often in the afternoon, sometimes daily. In the dry season there is no rain for up to four months or longer. The natives take no preparations for this annual occurrence. They could lay up crops and prepare one would think. Any good farmer where I come from would make plans in expectation of the usual fluctuations of corn and bean prices. But it is a poor country."

"Yes, it sounds like it."

The plane began to taxi again away from the terminal. The gun barrel of a tank went by the window. The fasten-your-seat-belts light on the small screen above the entrance door flashed on as the plane made a circle in preparation for takeoff. Out of his window Vern could see the steps being rolled away that were used at the front and back doorways of the plane. The plane paused a moment and then turned on full power down the runway.

Peter turned towards the American as everyone got settled in his seat again. "We are planning to talk with the Mennonite Central Committee offices in Honduras, once we get there. A Mennonite friend in Canada gave me information and contact referrals. Our hopes are to find a location for founding an Amish Community in Honduras."

The stranger registered no surprise. "I am glad to hear that. These countries could use the industry and work ethic of the Mennonite people. I have heard only good things about your faith. Certainly you should be welcome anywhere in Honduras or El Salvador. If you don't mind, I would like to extend a personal invitation to all of you to visit where I live. I would be glad to see you move to the valley where I am. There are several farms in the area for sale. I would be glad to show you around the area. The name is Gilbert Benton. I live north of the capital near Guateteca. Just ask for my name, and the area people will tell you where I live."

The three men looked at each other. Robert spoke for all of them. "I would be interested in visiting that area."

Mr. Benton continued, "Our mountains are beautiful, with the main peak coming in a little to the east of my house. From the peak the range tapers down on each side. To the south is the other range. It is much more rugged and harsh-looking. At least that is how it appears from the distance, as it is maybe thirty miles away. I have never been there myself, but they tell me no one has ever climbed to the top and returned to give a report. I suspect that is more out of a lack of interest than of any danger. Hondurans take no interest in mountain climbing for the sake of climbing. It takes Americans for that.

"The valley has several streams flowing through it. One goes close by my place. The river bottoms have fertile black soil, but for some reason no one farms those places. I have not yet been able to figure out why a mountainside is preferred to plant corn on over a river bottom. Past my place runs the main road. It is gravel and pothole-filled, of course, but this is not Texas. Takes about four hours to reach the little town of Guateteca from the capital where we will land. My place is fifteen minutes less. From my calculations, that would be going fifteen miles an hour, as Guateteca is sixty miles from the capital. Someday someone ought to count the curves on the road. In Honduras you do not carve out the mountain for the road, you fit the road on the mountain. That would be a series of loops to climb up and then another series to get back down the other side. But it is beautiful, gentlemen. My wife and I are very happy."

Five minutes later they were preparing for landing again. Mr. Benton turned towards them again. "This airport in Tegucigalpa is one of the most difficult anywhere for the larger planes. Not only is the runway quite short, there is no buffer zone on either end. There are mountains all the way around the capital with the city built right up to each side of the airport. If you had looked beneath the plane just before it hit the runway, you would have seen that they shut off the traffic on the road that goes past the front of the airstrip every time a plane lands. Of course that is only two or three times a day."

"So this is called a third-world country for a reason."

"I am afraid so, gentlemen. Now do not forget about my offer to visit. I will be more than glad to show you around Guateteca and my farm."

"Thank you, Sir," Peter said. "We will keep that in mind, but first we will meet with the MCC fellow who is scheduled to meet us at the airport."

"Be careful, now. This is another world, but you must see the country and a little civilization at my place also, if at all possible. Until then, welcome to Honduras."

"Let's see now, he said his name was Mark Weaver, and that he would know us before we would know him. Well, we will have to assume that is correct. Although I guess we do kind of stand out."

"Better that, Peter, than blend in with the world."

"I know, Vern, but I was thinking more of the world we are walking in right now. Look at this, fellows." Peter was pointing towards the whitewashed airport terminal as they got down to the bottom of the steps from the plane. His hand then moved to either side as the building continued its attempts at decency but degenerated into a woven wire fence. Small trees were intertwined in the wire and growing at will. In the distance the streets of the city could be seen — bicycles, ancient cars, and men on foot. On one street a small stream trickled alongside, with what looked like children playing in it.

"Am I seeing — what I am seeing?"

"What is that, Peter?"

"Over there, with those children."

"Looks like — no, it can't be."

"Maybe it can, or maybe it can't, but back home we would call that a pig."

"You know, Peter, you are right. Our lifestyle might just stand out around here."

They entered the airport terminal through the gate they were directed to. The line was still long even though they were in the middle of the people from their plane.

"Passe aqui', senor."

"Do you have any idea what that meant?"

"Sounded like 'pass the key' to me, but I don't have one."

The man motioned them on towards another desk where two officials sat grimly. They meekly filed in that direction.

"We must have the key," Vern chuckled.

Ten minutes later they were at the desk.

"Your passports, please."

They handed them over.

"Are you all American citizens?"

"Yes," they all three nodded.

"What is your business in this country?"

"We are on a trip to see what the country is like."

"Oh, yes, tourist, isn't that right?"

"Well, yes, but more than that. If we like it we might move here with our families."

The official looked at them over his glasses. He muttered, scratched on his paper, and then stamped all three passports with a sharp quick movement.

"I have given you visas for three months. That should be enough time for you to see the country. You may go through that gate to have your bags checked, gentlemen."

While their bags were being looked through quite thoroughly, a young American-looking man entered the back of the room. He waved to them and motioned for one of them to come over. Robert looked around questioningly, but no one seemed to care, so he walked around the checkout table.

"I am Mark Weaver." He stuck out his hand.

Robert shook it. "I am Robert Troyer. Good to see you."

"Good to see you, too. What I motioned you over for was to tell you to watch your bags while they are checking them out. Things have a way of ending up under the table."

A look of "are you serious?" passed over Robert's face, but he said, "I will tell the others."

He went back and whispered to the others, and they all moved up closer to their bags. After they were through the line they checked for missing items.

"You learn quickly," Mark laughed.

As they left the terminal through the back door a crowd of young boys accosted them.

"Una limpera, una limpera."

"What is going on here?" Peter turned in Mark's direction.

"Beggars, homeless, some fakes, most of them in some kind of need. They want money." He reached into his pocket, pulled out some red-looking money, and handed one of the bills to several of the boys. "Let us through now. Hang on to your bags, gentlemen. Let no one carry them but yourselves." He started through the group of boys, and the way parted for him. The three men from the north followed him. A short walk brought them to the van.

"You will be spending the night at our complex here in town, and then we'll see where you wish to go from there."

The three men were busy looking out the windows of the van. Colorful one- and two-story adobe houses lined the streets. In the distance they could see the outlines of the center of the city, but no high-rise buildings were in sight. They could see the steep rise of foothills on what looked like most sides of the city. On some of the slopes were built tin-roofed shacks and various other assortments of buildings made out of wood and mud stacked like dominoes, one behind the other. On what looked like the better part of town, the rising foothills held red clay-tiled homes and brightly colored homes ringed by small fences, many having extensive trees and plants.

"How long have you been here, Mark?"

"I have been here for a year now into my two-year assignment."

"Do you like the country?"

"The country, yes, I like it a lot. The climate is beautiful. The people are friendly in their own way. What gets to you, at least in town, is the poverty, the hopelessness of the people. They are good at basically two things, stealing and lying. One lies awake at night wondering what could ever be done to turn it around. Our mission puts in quite a large budget that goes to the needs of the people. We staff members are volunteers. But the dent is hardly noticeable. As to long-term affects, who knows?"

"You do not sound very hopeful about things."

"Perhaps not when I am looking at the large picture. The small picture as we go about our own work is enjoyable and rewarding. It does not take much to make a difference in these people's lives. A little medicine will go a long way. A little money can help much more than it does in the States. We have had several adoption successes in the past months, in which we helped couples in North America adopt children from here. Our food outreach program this past dry season was able to help several villages in the mountains west of here that were in need. During the dry season prices for the basic foods they eat can go very high, and some are not able to purchase food at those prices, or it is just hard to get to back in the mountains."

"That sounds encouraging, but as you said the need does seem to be great."

"Yes, it is, but now here we are," Mark said as he brought the van to a stop in front of a well-kept complex of buildings. "You can spend the night here, get cleaned up, have some good meals, and then tomorrow we will see where we go from here."

"We appreciate this all very much," Peter said. "We will try to take care of ourselves as much as we can, lest we be too much of a burden."

"That will not be necessary. You are welcome here."

"I hope Honduras feels the same way," Vern chuckled. Robert and Peter did not look amused.

CHAPTER THIRTEEN

THE MORNING DAWNED with a promise of a clear and bright day. Over the capital of Honduras hung the slight mist of smoke from the cooking fires in the homes on the hillsides surrounding the city. Breakfast was being served at the MCC complex, made with a lot less smoke than breakfast on the hillsides. The three men from the states had been up before dawn, and Mark came around to announce breakfast. They were now eating breakfast with the rest of the staff.

"How did you sleep, Vern?"

"It would have been better if that pig had quit rooting around in the alley outside the window."

"Is that what it was? I did think the sound was familiar."

"I thought of getting up and yelling out the window, but thought maybe not, this being a strange country and all."

"Yea, someone might have come after you instead of the pig."

"Entirely possible, but I did not find it funny at all. Another thing, did I hear horses going past on the street not so long ago? About dawn, I think it was."

"Right again, it was horses. I saw them myself when I went to the door. Several of them were going past with packs on their backs. Rough burlap bags looking like some kind of backpacks, full of I don't know what. They seemed to be packed quite full."

"Downright western-like, huh?"

"No," Peter mused, "something was missing. They did not have the prairie windswept look. No marks of either grass-brushed legs or prairie mud, for that matter. The look was entirely different, totally lacking in the rough and tumble type." Peter leaned back in his chair. "It is hard to put my finger on it, but they looked like this country does. As if they were sick, tired, and had too much time on their hands."

Mark walked over from across the room. "Well men, are we ready to sit down and go over your plans for the time you are here? Let's go over to the office where we have a table and can be more comfortable."

When they were all seated, Mark brought out a map of Honduras. He spread it out in front of them. "This is Honduras, a country wide at the top and narrowing down like an upside down triangle. On the east side is the Gulf of Mexico, or more properly the Gulf of Honduras, and on the west side the Pacific with the Gulf of Fonceca. As you can see by the sharp differentiation of coloring, it is a quite mountainous country. We are here, almost at the center, a little to the left and lower. There is one good paved road going from where we are here in the capital to the north coastal town of San Pedro Sula; also some paved roads going to the border with San Salvador and to the coast on the south. Beyond that it is mostly gravel and bumps. There is little in the way of a highway department."

"Where are the Mennonites based? Any related mission outreaches?"

"There is us, off course. We are based only in the capital and go out in the country as needed. To the north, there is a small children's home near San Pedro Sula. On the islands just off the north coast there are some individual Americans living, although I think they have no connections to Mennonites. That is about it. Of course, we may not know of everyone down here, although it is not that big a country."

"What is this curvy road going out here?"

"That is a gravel road going out to the county of Olentego in the east of the country. The road stretches from the capital all the way out to where it ends here in this town, also called Olentego. Beyond that there are still roads, no doubt, but not officially, shall we say."

"Would a town of Guateteca be on that road?"

"Let's see, I believe it is, right here, about half way out to Olentego. I was through there once. The town sits in a nice valley. How did you know about the town?"

"On the plane coming over we met a Mr. Benton who lives near Guateteca, and he invited us to visit if we came through the area. Said he really liked the area and it would be a good place to settle in."

"That's interesting. Was he American?"

"Yes. Said he was from Texas."

"I have never heard of this guy, but that does not mean anything. I have only been here for a year. I don't know, though, of any other missions out that direction, so that may be a good place to go. There is also this place between the road to Olentego and the coast, in the town of Maiyapa. The elevation is quite high there from the mountains. That is a rare thing for Honduras — I have heard they even get frost at times, which is most unusual for this country. As a general rule for this country even the mountains do not produce frost."

"Well, what do you say?" Peter turned to the others.

"I say we stay away from the frost thing. We are coming from the cold north, so why mess around with cold? Now if it were an issue of it being really hot everywhere else, like I understand it is along the coast, that might be another matter. But I understand from Mr. Benton that his area rarely gets higher temperatures than the lower 90s, with hardly any humidity like the coast has."

"Sounds like good reasoning to me," Vern said. "Like Robert just said, why not just make the change all the way and stay away from the frost thing? Sounds good to me."

Peter turned back to Mark. "You heard what they said. I go along with that."

"In that case we will stay around the capital for the rest of the day. That allows me time to get things together for the trip, and tomorrow we will go see Mr. Benton's valley. We can use the missions four-door 4x4 pickup. I think we can all fit in, and tomorrow we'll see what we can see. In the meantime I have some business downtown, so why don't you all come along."

They left thirty minutes later with Mark in the van.

"This here is the business district, what there is of it, scattered about in the downtown area." They all followed the direction of Mark's pointing some ten minutes after they left the missions compound. "There are few factories, but small machine and repair shops here and there. There are wholesalers, although not a lot, of the advanced metal, steel, and general American technologies. We have several banks, one of which we will be stopping at soon. Most of the business is done on a much lower level, shall we say. For starters you have the street merchants who sell their individual, usually handmade crafts, then the larger individual stores who do much the same on a larger scale. Then most of the commerce is really done in the downtown market area. We will be going past that soon — before you can see it you probably will smell it. A right lively bustling place, where you will want to hang on to your wallets and anything else you are carrying both inside and out of your pockets."

"They run some pretty good scams, too," Mark chuckled. "A month or so ago, one of our guys ran, literally, into someone on the street. When he bumped into the man a glass bottle crashed and broke on the pavement. There it lay on the ground, glass thrown around, and liquid running down the street. The man was near tears, wiping his eyes and groaning in agony of soul. Said it was the medicine for his young daughter, purchased that morning at a high price, his last limpera, in fact. Without it she was sure to die. Our guy was skeptical of the whole story, and refused to pay. Instead he marched on down the street leaving the man standing there with his glass and medicine lying at his feet. At the corner, our guy went around it first before pausing to look back. He stuck his head back around to see what would happen. For a few minutes the man stood there looking forlorn, then he shook his head, pulled another bottle out of his coat pocket and went on down the street."

"Is it really that serious?"

"I am afraid so. This is the third world. Most friendly people, but do not let that fool you. Smile and keep a sharp eye out."

"What is this place like, then?"

"You will see in a minute. We are about three blocks away. Roll down that window and take a deep breath."

"Say, what is that? Smells like, I don't know, a quite strange smell. A little like, well, the barnyard back home, but no it is not that sharp. The smell is muted in some way, sweeter, more of the smell of food mixed in with something. But that would be strange."

Mark looked quite amused.

Peter turned to Vern. "Don't you think you should be more careful with your descriptions of the smells of our host country? After all, we are visitors here."

"I meant no harm, you know that, nor was I trying to be insulting. If any one should be insulted it should be us with what we are smelling."

"You do have a point."

Mark laughed out loud. "You do get used to it. It really is a friendly smell."

"A matter of opinion," Vern ventured.

"We can't drive through it — you have to walk — and I don't have time to stop. But there it is," Mark said as he made a right turn. The street thronged with people and stalls. Before them lay three to four blocks of streets going off each way, all without passage for vehicles. The sidewalks and most of the street were filled with stalls, the rest of the area with pedestrians walking past the stalls of all sizes and shapes. Behind actual storefronts there were stores in their normal places where stores should be, but almost blocked off from sight by the sidewalk stalls.

"That is the market. They have most anything you could wish, that is anything to do with the basics in Honduran life: machetes, saddles, trinkets, pots and pans, paintings, clothing, and, of course, food. No refrigeration, so everything is out in the open, which I think is where most of the smell is coming from. Lettuce, tomatoes, fresh eggs of who knows what age, carrots, all your regular garden products, meats (some of it live and some of it slaughtered on the spot — again the smell, I think), all sold, sliced, and fresh on the spot."

"You didn't get breakfast from here, did you? Those eggs were a little questionable, now that I think of it."

"No, no, never fear, we can do better than that. Although it costs more, we have our own private supplier. We do not buy any food products from the open market."

"Well, my breakfast resteth safely then," Vern quipped.

"Would you two be quiet about breakfast and think of something else."

"I was not the one who brought up the subject."

"Another thing," Mark said, "if you move down here, lesson number one on fresh produce is no buying unless you know who grew it and what he used to water it with."

"Why, does produce grow with something other than water?"

"Would you quit it, I said."

"In fact it does," Mark interjected, "but the most common concern is the quality of the water itself. Wells are almost unknown, and the water comes from the creeks, which are used for everything else that water is used for, like laundry and bathing. So the local water supply comes with many unknown added quantities which tend to leave their residue on the produce that is watered with it."

"You don't have to use such big words. I understand you. Don't drink the water or eat what has been watered — it might have bugs on them."

"Ah, a correction please. It *has* bugs on them. Don't take any chances."

"Whatever you say, I am not drinking or eating, thank you very much."

"Just with great care, that is all," Mark said.

"I hear you."

"We will be stopping up here at the bank next," Mark said as the van rounded the corner.

"Where is the bank? Up there? It looks fairly modern, not all that different from at home. Why the guards out front, though?"

"That is their way of doing things. Saves time on the police work if the policeman is right there, although I believe those are private guards. The banks and other high profile cash businesses hire them."

"Things are that bad, then. I mean the stealing and all."

"You don't think these businesses spend money just for the fun of it, do you?"

Chapter Fourteen

They got up early the next morning and planned their strategy around the breakfast table.

"Here is that road again," Mark said. "It is not as straight as it looks on paper. This road climbs the little mountains by going up the side horizontal with the peak, making a sharp turn and climbing up some more going the opposite direction. It takes quite some time to do that, and the whole road is gravel. No blacktop."

"How far is it to Guateteca?" Vern asked.

"In distance it is around 60 miles, in time it is four hours at least, unless you want to risk damage to body and limb plus whatever is done to your vehicle. The local buses travel around 10 to 20 miles an hour. Of course everything is kilometers down here, but it takes some time to convert all that over, so we are still on miles. If we get moving we should get there in time for lunch."

Robert turned to Peter. "Are you sure about this? Sounds kind of hard to get to."

"That should be just what we want. A place where there is need, and not so accessible by just anyone. I think I like it."

"Let's go then, boys. I will get the truck out."

Two hours later found them in the middle of pine hills and curves.

"These curves," Vern said from the back seat, "how many of them are there? Maybe Mr. Benton was right and someone will count them some day, if we actually move here."

"What I like," Robert said, "is going around them. There is a certain mystery involved, since you cannot see around the curve."

"We have not met anything unusual yet. Everyone else seems to be staying over on their own side. Are there ever any problems, Mark?"

"Not more than usual, I guess, with these roads the way they are. As you can see there are no guardrails, so you have the occasional vehicle that goes over the edge on one of these curves. Sometimes it does not take the curve because of too much speed. See down there — looks like an old rusted-out vehicle to me."

The others looked over the edge, as Mark took the truck around the curve. Below them, down the rail-less sharp drop-off, lay a valley from which other hills rose up again. Pine trees grew everywhere right up to the edge of the road. Far below they caught a glimpse of metal, rusted out from much time and exposure.

"It reminds me," Peter said, "of the story we often use at home in church matters to illustrate from a natural story how things are spiritually also."

There was a pause as the others waited. "I think I know what you are referring to, but tell it," Vern ventured.

"Once there was this gentleman who needed to hire a coachman to drive him around in his carriage. When he advertised for the job three applicants showed up. After interviewing all three and looking at their references, there seemed to be little difference between the three, and the gentleman was at a loss on what to do. He then decided to have each of the applicants take him in the coach with all six horses for a drive. There was a certain wicked hill near his home with a very sharp curve in it that the gentleman decided would be a crucial part of the test for each of the three drivers.

"Nothing was said about this curve, though, as he told the three applicants about the proposed test. The first driver got in the seat and followed the directions he was given for the drive. As he approached the hill, the driver discerned that the hill was involved with the test, so he was ready for something, and when the curve came up he thought this must be part of it. The driver took the carriage out close to the edge of the cliff, expertly handling the horses so that everything stayed tightly under control, and the carriage wheels passed about two feet from the edge. They continued on up to the top of the hill and circled around back to the easy slope down the hill.

"When they arrived, the gentleman stuck his head out the window of the carriage. 'Good driving there, driver. Next.'

"The next applicant changed places with the first driver, and they left at a fast clip. As they approached the hill again, the second driver reached the same thoughts that the first one did. He thought this hill must have something to do with the test, and when the curve came up, he was sure this was it. His hands took a firm grip on the reins, and his lips got firm with determination to make a good impression. As they approached the curve the driver saw from his high seat on the carriage that there were wheel tracks going out to within two feet of the cliff.

"'That must be where the first test drive went. I must do better than that,' he thought. He got a better grip on the reins, pulled the horses in a little and took the carriage out to within two wheels widths of the edge. The gravel rattled down the edge of the cliff as the carriage continued on, with the gentleman still inside. They got to the top of the cliff and circled around the slope back to the house.

"When they arrived the gentleman stuck his head out the window of the carriage. 'Good driving there, driver. Next.'

"The next applicant changed seats with the second driver with his hopes not too high. How was he going to do better than what these two guys were doing? They must be doing quite well to be getting compliments from the gentleman like that. Again the carriage approached the hill and got to the curve. The third driver took the situation in from his seat on his first glance. He could see from the tracks the situation was hopeless. There were the two sets of marks, one two feet from the edge and the other right up to the edge.

"'This is hopeless,' he said to himself. 'We might as well get this over with.' So taking the reins firmly in his hands he slapped them briskly and drove the carriage right close, not to the cliff edge, but right close to the inside of the road where it was cut out of the hill.

It seemed, to him, like the closest way to the top of the hill, now that the test was over anyway. They got to the top of the hill, took the slope down, and arrived in front of the house.

"When they arrived the gentleman stuck his head out the window of the carriage. 'You are hired, driver.'

"The other two applicants looked at each other with puzzled looks. The one said to the other, 'I wonder what he did — he must have really got close?'"

"That's the story all right," Vern said. "A few little changes from the way it's told to us, but the meaning is the same. It sure has a powerful spiritual lesson."

Mark appeared to be squirming in the front seat. The other three looked at each other. They did not say anything, but they knew what it was. "He's feeling how liberal he is," they thought to themselves.

Peter pulled his watch out of his watch pocket and looked at it. "It is almost eleven. Do you think we have taken a wrong road or something? With all these gravel roads, one looks the same as the other."

"I don't think so," Mark answered. "This still looks like the main road; if we came off of it you would be surprised how quickly it would change. But just to be sure here is a man coming up. I will ask him."

The truck pulled up to a stop beside an older man riding on a donkey with what looked like his grandson walking along beside it. Twitching its ears, the donkey showed no other signs of interest in this truck that stopped beside it, raising a cloud of dust. Mark leaned out of his window. "Can you tell us how far it is to Guateteca?"

The old man on the donkey nodded his head vigorously, "Si, senor. It is twenty minutes."

"Gracias." Mark pulled his head back in and started off with the truck.

Robert turned to Peter. "Have you noticed how many little streams we have been crossing lately?"

"Yes, I have. For a while it had been just little hills and little curves and little pine trees, but the ground has leveled out now. As you know, this is good for farming if it keeps up."

"I thought your farmer eye would have noticed." Robert continued, "If we want to have an agricultural-based community, the one thing we will have to have is some flat land and, of course, water."

"It is looking good. What do you think, Mark?" Peter asked.

"Still does not look like, say, Lancaster, Pennsylvania land, but yes, I think you could grow something in this valley." Mark responded, "The streams certainly help. I for myself have no desire to settle down in this country, though. It will be my three years of service and then back to the good old United States with my memories to think about."

"Come on, you do like this country a little bit? Just look at the mountains, now that we are out of all those foothills. To our left there, look at that range, and the taller to our right, farther in the distance," Peter noted. "The one on the left looks like you could reach it rather quickly."

"Looks nice, I guess. It is certainly better here than in the city. I guess I have been staying in town too much, but that is where our work is, although I have always been a country boy, raised on the farm, you know," Mark explained. "It was a nice place in Pennsylvania, just north of Lancaster a bit. The farm has been in the family for I don't know how many years — my grandfather would know. He and grandma still live in the dowdy house, quite up in years. We didn't use horses like you folks do, but even with tractors it was still farming, I guess — at least the crops grew."

"That is the general idea of farming, to grow crops, but they do taste better with horse farming," Peter said quickly.

"Strange indeed, I never noticed the difference; did you get better prices for your milk too?" Mark grinned.

"We should have, as hard as we worked for it. Do you still have to throw the silage down by hand?" Peter continued the conversation.

"Yes, we did when I was still at home, but Dad put in mechanical equipment now. They have to work almost as hard to unclog the thing sometimes as they would have throwing it down by hand in the first place. The bugs get worked out eventually, I imagine."

The truck bounced on another bump in the road that Mark did not think was worth swerving for, just before they crossed a little concrete bridge. "Oops, that was harder than I thought."

Peter leaned out of the window as they went over. "Nice little creek. Large enough for the government to put some effort into building the bridge. I like the amount of water it is carrying."

"It's large, isn't it? Must be fed by several other creeks to become that large. There does seem to be water in this valley, and speaking of the valley, look how much more open the land is becoming. Not exactly flat, but the foothills are giving way."

"Let's go on into town and see where this Mr. Benton lives," Mark broke in. "They should be able to tell us where he lives."

"I have a better idea," Robert said. "Let's stop at this little, shall we say store, from the looks of things, and ask them."

"Sounds good to me," Mark said as he pulled the truck over. "And this happens to be a restaurant, the Honduras version of one. They sell odds and ends, groceries, soft drinks, beans, rice, and food. Shall we have lunch, gentlemen?"

Peter looked at the others. "Why not? Let us sample the local cuisine."

"Cuisine," Mark chuckled. "The food is what it is everywhere in Honduras. Your basic tortilla, with beans, cooked and at times mashed and fried with fat for a tasty version — that is an extra, though — and rice cooked plain or mixed with vegetables, tomatoes, squash or pepper. The vegetables are safe if they are fried, but never eat them raw, as I said before. Then there is meat, beef one hopes, but there is always chicken and the occasional brown lizard. If we stopped at the market in town you could see them live, with their legs and tails tied together. I tasted some of the meat once. It was fine, I guess — kind of tough. Might be hard to distinguish it from the cattle meat, looking at some of the cows that run around here."

"Please, please," Vern said. "I am sure the food is fine. The people do look healthy, and we will survive. Let's go inside."

"Would be more encouraging if that had not been a dog who just came out the front door."

"At least that way we know he is not in the food pot."

"Come, come, gentlemen," Mark interrupted. "I know this is not Pennsylvania or Canada, but since you are planning to move here, you should taste the food."

They entered the door of the restaurant; over their heads was a large bulbous Pepsi sign. The floor was tiled in a native style of red and green colors. The edges of each tile did not have the crisp clean look of North American tile, nor were they holding up too well under usage, but someone clearly did make tile around here. Two tables were set with four wooden chairs each in what was obviously the public dining room. All four of the men crossed the floor and sat down. Through an open counter area they could see the shelves lined with goods for sale. Apparently the owner was waiting on a customer who was buying a bag of corn and a soft drink that came from the refrigerator standing just on the other side of the wall.

She came over as soon as the transaction was done. "How are you?"

"Oh," Mark said surprised, "you speak English."

"Just a little."

"Where did you learn to speak it?" Mark asked.

"From a Mr. Benton," she said.

"Ah, the very man we are looking for. Does he live close by?" Mark asked.

"Yes, just around the corner."

"Well, after the meal we can get directions then," Mark concluded.

"What do you want to eat?" she asked, standing there.

Mark turned back to her. "Just bring the food you have on hand. The usual, in other words," he said with a wave of his hand.

"I hope you know what you are saying," Robert said hopefully.

"I do, just trust me. If the food is not okay I can tell by looking at it."

"And how would that be?" Vern wanted to know.

"I know what normal food looks like, from the times that I have seen it here, so I should be able to tell if it looks unusual. Don't you think so?"

"Really comforting, really comforting," Vern responded.

"Just what I was thinking," Peter joined in.

The woman returned with two platters of food balanced on her hands and was soon back with two more.

"We can be glad there are four of us. If there had been three, she might have brought the other platter balanced on her head," Mark ventured.

"You are not really serious," Robert asked.

"No, not really, but these natives, that is the women, are excellent at carrying things on their heads — water jugs, produce to the market, even firewood for the daily cooking."

"Why not just stick with the facts from now on, and a little less humor. We are trying to eat."

"It just comes naturally."

"What is that, your humor or this food?"

"The humor, of course. Don't spoil a joke by asking questions. This food was prepared by human hands. Here are the tortillas, a thin-baked round bread made from ground corn meal. They are really good. Then I see we have beans — no fried ones, just baked — a little rice, and some meat. Try chewing it to see how tough it is. That should tell us something about the source. Over here on the side of the plate is some lettuce and tomato, as I am sure you can see, but do not eat them — surface water, gentlemen, surface water."

"It does come naturally."

"What comes naturally?"

"You said not to ask questions after a joke."

"That I did."

CHAPTER FIFTEEN

They finished their meal inside of fifteen minutes and to a man declared it good and tasty, although Vern thought he would like it even better after he got used to it. After getting directions and paying for the meal, they left.

"The directions I have say to go back across the bridge we just came from and it is the first house on the left. It should be easy enough to find."

They got back to the bridge quickly and crossed it slowly as Mark got ready to turn into the driveway.

"That is a really nice-sized creek," Peter said again.

The others were looking up the driveway as Mark pulled in. It was a short driveway, lined with trees on both sides, and the yard contained an occasional palm tree here and there. Low bushes were planted around the front and sides of the house as far as they could see. The house itself was a one-story building with red-tiled roof and yellow concrete adobe walls.

"No signs of any mud hut. This looks American with local materials to me."

Mark parked the vehicle and they all got out. Peter walked up to the front door and knocked. A native woman answered and looked at them without a word.

Peter cleared his throat. "Is Mr. Benton in?"

A quick smile flickered on the edge of the woman's face. "Yes, I will call him."

She shut the door gently and the footsteps faded away inside. The front door soon opened again followed by Gilbert Benton himself. "Hello, hello, if it is not my fellow plane travelers themselves. So you decided to try and find this place and you have found it. That is great. Please come on inside."

Peter expressed his thanks but mentioned that they would like to see some of the farms in the area that were for sale. "We should be looking around as soon as possible, as we need to return to town tomorrow morning."

Mr. Benton was quick to agree. "Most certainly. I am glad that you came. Let us go look around. First, though, let me get your names straight. I remember three people from the plane — Peter, Robert, and Vern. Who else have we?"

"This is Mark from MCC in the capital," Peter made the introduction. "He has been kind enough to drive us out here to see the lay of the land."

"Sure thing, I have heard good things of MCC. This country can use all the work of the kind that they do. The needs of Honduras are indeed great."

"Thanks," Mark said, while the other three looked at each other.

"That brings us to why we are here," Peter said. "As you know we would like to start an Amish community in Honduras with the hopes that it will serve, among other things, as a model for local farmers who do not have access to modern equipment. Our hopes are that this will be a form of mission outreach that is not commonly used by others, but one we believe can be very effective. Since we would be doing all of our farm work either with horses or by hand, it should be more accessible to the locals who cannot afford modern equipment. Plus we believe we can be a demonstration of what hard work and good industry can do for any land, even one as poor as this." Vern and Robert nodded their heads.

"Your idea sounds good," Mr. Benton agreed. "I have been thinking about what you said on the plane traveling down here. I like it. It is just possible that improvement could come to this country other than by a large investment of money. Most of the locals think improvement can only come with big money. I do not know where the idea comes from, but the prevailing view is that you have to steal money or be born with it to have any. Hard work is not considered to be any way out of poverty, or rewarding in any other positive way. As soon as one of them gets any money he quits working, with the foreseeable result, of course. It seems like we can see that, but they cannot, and they ascribe their return to poverty as the luck of fate, or to an abusive unseen rich force out to get them.

"But enough on that. I have been making inquiries about land just in case you people showed up, and I have some good news. There is a place about two miles on towards town from here that the owner would sell. I think it would make a fine place, some 200 acres, rolling, and not developed, but it has some fine creek-bottom land from what I could see driving in the other day to talk to the owner. In fact, this very creek that you cross out here at the end of my lane is the one that borders on the west side of the property. The owner is at home most of the time and said we would be welcome to visit."

"That sounds interesting," Peter said, and the others concurred. "I think we would be interested in seeing this place."

"In that case, let's go. This is my dog, Billy. He is going with us." Mr. Benton opened the back seat of his jeep and the dog jumped in. "And now one of you is welcome to ride with me in the front. The rest can follow. I think we will go into town first to show you around, and then out to the farm."

Peter volunteered to go with the jeep and got in. At the end of the driveway they waited for the others to catch up before turning right towards town.

"I believe you already know that the town is called Guateteca. It is an old Indian name from way back, although no one is sure what it means. The town is known in these parts for its practice of witchcraft. Not that such things bother me much, but it might interest you in the light of mission work." Peter nodded his head.

"This country, like most of Central and South America, was occupied by Indians before the Spaniards came. Now you have little pure blood Indian left, except for way back in the mountains where I am told there are still a few. That would be way back in, where there are hardly any roads at all. They say even the Catholic priests have not gotten a foothold in those mountains yet.

"But back to what I was saying. What you have now in the general population are mixed bloods from the intermarriage of Indians and Spaniards. The other legacy that the Spaniards have left is their religion. Most everyone is a Catholic, at least in name. It seems that the centerpiece of every little village that amounts to anything is a Catholic church, with the best architecture in town. Some of them are quite imposing.

"The other interesting piece of Indian history is on the money of the country." Gilbert dug around in his pocket and came out with a red piece of money. "Printed on their one dollar is the Indian named Lempira, who led the war for independence. But they have little in their history of law and order. The foundational issues that are so taken for granted up north are in short supply down here. What they have are copied poorly, and applied even more so. Torture is still common with prisoners whether they are guilty or not, and since everyone is guilty of something I imagine there is always something to confess. I am told that prisoners are given no food by the government, but have it supplied by their families. Pity the poor soul who has no family."

"A quite dismal picture," Peter ventured.

"That it is in a manner of speaking, but in other ways it is a great country. Take the weather as an example. With our altitude of between two and three thousand feet above sea level, the climate is moderate all year around, anywhere from the high nineties to maybe the low forties. No frost that I know of, although Honduras does have frost at the higher elevations. Just beautiful weather. We all just love it."

"That part of it does sound good. What have we got coming up here?"

"This is the town of Guateteca around this curve." To their right the road swung into a gradual long arch with a downhill run into town. "We just passed the farm I want to show you back there a ways. I was going to show you the entrance but I got too busy talking."

Gilbert slowed the jeep and gestured to his left. "This is the entrance to a farm close to the one that is for sale, a quite gigantic spread of over a thousand acres. I don't think it's for sale, but that would be too much for what you want anyway. And here is the town," Gilbert said as they came over the top of the hill.

Before them spread the town of Guateteca. The street ran down the hill past a gas station on the left. The road led in a straight line bottoming out a quarter of a mile in front of them. It then rose again as it entered the town. Mud adobe huts spread out before their eyes. Coming towards them was an oxen cart with two oxen yoked together. The man walking in front of the oxen led them with a long stick laid on the yoke. In the back his son was riding with the dog. Billy barked a greeting from the back window of the jeep as they went by. Little boys with rubber band slingshots walked the dirt streets along with the sparse pedestrian traffic.

"So this is the town."

"That it is, indeed. This is as good as it gets town-wise around here. I will take you to the town square and then we will go back to the farm."

"How do people live like this?" Peter asked as they passed a hut with pigs penned against the side of the house.

"They are poor people with poor ways, and no one has taught them any better."

Three minutes later they were downtown driving around the square. Storefronts lined the street on the north side. The police station was on the west side across from the vegetation- and tree-filled town center. Over on the east of the square stood the Catholic church, its doors standing open in the middle of the afternoon sunshine. Inside its cavernous space showed the faint flickering of candlelight. Incense smells hung faint in the air. The exterior was made of exquisite carvings and ornaments. The Catholic Church made a statement of its presence in town.

Gilbert took the road back out of town and up the hill. To their right the mountain range with its center peak rose high in the afternoon sun. The air was clear and the blue of the mountain glistened. Peter caught himself looking in that direction for a long time. Something about the sight of it held his attention until they rattled on down the road as it turned to the left. He could see it again just as the road made a sharp right-hand turn and then lost the sight behind a little mountain as they crossed another bridge. A sharp, well kept place was on their right now, as Gilbert explained that these people lived here only part of the year. The local help took care of it the rest of the time.

"A few workers can be found who are trustworthy. The rest are not." Gilbert glanced at Peter for emphasis. "Give a man a place to stay, maybe a small home right on your property. Let him keep his family with him, and pay him a decent regular weekly wage, nothing more, and his self-interest will kick in. He might just not steal from you and keep his relatives from doing the same. Always the relatives, you always have to deal with the relatives."

They passed a small lane going off to the right. "That is the road up to the mountains, and also used as the entrance to Lagrange, I believe. Lagrange is the ranch right next to the one I will be showing you. About the same size or so as 'El Sanson,' but not quite as nice. Also, I do not know whether it is for sale."

Gilbert turned on the blinker of the jeep and slowed down for the driveway. A small stone marker rose about five feet high on the left hand side and said "El Sanson." "This is it."

Peter was hit again by the view of the mountain as they turned right into the driveway. The lane went straight in and then up a small knoll. From there they drove up and down gentle rolls of the land, but always up higher towards the mountain. Ten minutes later found them on what was clearly the home stretch to a residence. An orchard stood on both sides of the lane. Peter thought they looked like orange trees and maybe the smaller tangerine. The orchard stayed with the lane right up to the edge of a clearing that contained a simple two-story boxed home. The edge of the clearing was lined with palm trees on the east side and a gigantic spreading tree on the south side. The simplicity of the house defined its surroundings as well as any American or Canadian house standard. The orchard and the shade from the surrounding trees almost shadowed the entire clearing and made one expect a more substantial investment in the house. Even the most unimaginative designer of the proverbial North American cracker box could have done better than this.

Yet Peter hardly noticed the house. He was thinking of other things. Only a week ago he left Canada. It all seemed so far away now, like another world of which he claimed only a distant memory. Time seemed to stand still for him as he stared at the clearing. Could this be home for him? Could this be the place where God would have him come, with only a dream and a passion for what needed to be done? Could this place on the earth be where he was to live and maybe even die for a cause that he had longed for, for so many years? He brushed the thought away. Why was he thinking of dying? He was not even 60 years old. If this was where God was leading him, then there would be many years left in which to see the vision take root and grow strong. God would have an Amish church here, among these palms and spreading trees. Surely this could be the place; his heart was telling him so. He knew it ever since the mountain fully caught his attention driving out of town. Had not King David written so many long years ago, "I will lift up mine eyes unto the hills, from whence cometh my help"? He felt as if he knew what that meant now; for he too looked, and in looking found strength in a strange land.

Gilbert got out first, followed by the others from both vehicles. The door of the lower level of the house opened before Gilbert got there. A local man came out with that slow smooth motion of the unhurried tropical native. He graciously nodded towards them. "Good afternoon, Senores, can I do something for you?"

"Yes," Gilbert answered in Spanish. "We are looking for Senor Lopes. Is he at home?"

"Most certainly, Senores, he is even at this time in the mango orchard." The man pointed to the north and a little path that led between the trees. "I will take you to him."

"Do you feel it too?" Peter asked Robert as they walked between the mango trees.

"Feel what?" Robert wondered.

"The feeling of home," Peter stated.

"Not really," Robert answered. "It all still seems kind of strange to me. It is nice, though. Quite a well-kept ranch and orchard. I can see how I would like it after I got used to it. This land does appeal to me; my feelings have just not caught up yet."

"Mine have," Peter said. "This is the place. It is here where we will come and live."

"Should you not at least wait until you hear the price and other such information?"

"The price will be right — I know that it will be. This is where I am bringing my family too."

"Well if you do, then Vern and I will certainly consider coming too. It will just take a little more time. But it makes it all easier if one of us is so sure that this is all right. There are just so many things that could go wrong."

The voices ahead of them chattered first in Spanish and then switched to English as the introductions were made.

"This is Mr. Lopes. The owner of the ranch."

They all shook hands and exchanged small talk, then got right down to business.

"Mr. Benton tells me that you wish to buy a place in Honduras. Well, mine just happens to be for sale. My wife and I have wanted for some time to return to Arkansas where we are from. We are getting up in years, and our children never took to Honduras. If we move back to Arkansas we can be closer to them. You know, this is still a third-world country. Beautiful, but still third-world. We came here thirty years ago and have taken this ranch from bare ground to what you see now. Have greatly enjoyed it, but it is time to move on. But even if we sell, Honduras will always be with me. Seems like the place grows on you. I am not sure why, but it just does. Maybe it is the culture, the language, maybe the countryside, I don't know, but I do know I will always love this place."

Peter cleared his throat. "I believe I want to buy your place, but we have not discussed price. What are you asking for your ranch in US dollars — or Canadian, because that is where I am from — but US will keep it simpler?"

Mr. Lopes named his price. It sounded reasonable to Peter in

Canadian terms, but this was the third world and so he turned to Gilbert. "What do you think, Mr. Benton — is that a good price for around here?"

Gilbert nodded his head. "I believe so. Mr. Lopes is being very reasonable, and from what I can see the ranch is in good shape. This orchard of mangos and oranges is well kept and the trees are mature. I do believe, Peter, you would be getting a good deal. If you want to, I can have much of the legal work done for you tomorrow, and you can return to Canada for your family while I take care of the rest of the business. The ranch will be waiting for you when you return."

"It is a deal, then." Peter extended his hand to Mr. Lopes. "Let us get down to the details."

"First I will show you around the ranch, and then tomorrow I will meet you and Mr. Benton in town, at what suffices as a courthouse, and we can sign some papers. This is all kind of sudden for me, but we did want to sell. The Mrs. will be glad to hear that we can go back to the children."

Mr. Lopes then gave Peter and the others the tour. The orchard extended back over a half mile to the creek on the north side. There was a dam to the east, just close to the middle point of the property on the north line. Irrigation ditches came down from the dam along the west side of the orchard and turned to the east and then south again parallel to the house. Mr. Lopes explained the need for irrigation during the six months dry season.

"It rains around here for six months right regular, and then things dry up. If you do not have some way of irrigating you cannot grow things during the dry season. That makes it hard on the orchard trees. Thankfully with the dam we can access water for the trees year around."

The stream from the dam ran west and then south for the property line on that side. On the east side was the Taft road, which led back to the mountains and also gave access to the Lagrange ranch and the Taft ranch. The main road they came in on was the boundary on the south. Peter was well satisfied with his purchase and said so. Mr. Lopes seemed pleased himself that his ranch was being left in good hands. They parted late that evening with plans to meet in town in the morning. Gilbert offered them a place to stay for the night.

In the morning Peter signed papers and left a deposit check, with arrangements for the rest. Mark drove them back to town, and the party of three Amish men flew out of airport the next day. Peter arrived in Canada later in the week and the others in Southern Illinois. By the next Sunday the Amish communities near and far were buzzing with the news that an Amish community was to be started in Central America, and that Amish ministers were involved. Everyone expressed an opinion, but all agreed on one thing — that such a thing had never been tried and that such a thing would never work. All, that is, except a few hardy souls here and there who dared not say much, but at night they prayed to God that it would work. They were not sure why they were praying, but they just prayed anyway and said nothing to anyone else about it.

Sunday night they met for the big meeting at Peter's place. The married boys were all there, Steve and his wife Kathy, Jesse and Lois, and the youngest married brother Albert and Barbara. Homer and Rachel were invited too, along with the one unmarried brother, Abe, who lived in the community. Beth, Susie, and Matthew were there of course. They lived at home. Fred was still at his school teaching job. They had written him about Peter's trip, and he wrote back in no uncertain terms to let them know that Honduras might be for them, but not for him.

Peter told them all in great detail of what Honduras was like. He described the valley surrounded by the mountains. He told of the local food and of the people who were so poor. He told them of the pigs in the street and of the cattle in the road. They listened in rapt attention. Jason listened too, standing beside Rachel's chair. It all sounded exciting and grand, although he still could not imagine where this all could be. The world sounded more and more like a big place to him. Whatever, he really did not care, and went back to playing with the cousins.

Homer, to the surprise of no one, was the first to commit himself to going. Rachel had no problem with it either. If her dad went, any place was better than the Beachys. Beth raised the point that she was writing to Dan Ludwig and wanted nothing to jeopardize that relationship. She doubted if Dan would want any part with missions. "You know, Dad," she said, "that he will not want anything to do with an Amish missions outreach. He is himself becoming Amish. That is what he is interested in."

"Yes, I know Beth. He will not want to come down to Honduras, but you can still write him from there. If he asks you to marry him" — Beth turned red — "Then you can move back here. That is fine with me."

The three married boys said they needed some time to think about it, but they were interested. Abe said he was going. "Sounds like an adventure to me. Wouldn't miss it."

So it was planned. The months went by quickly. Peter soon placed his farm on the real estate market and sold it. He held an auction for his tools and animals he was not taking along, and made plans to move. The others followed suit, although at a slightly slower timetable.

They all gathered at the bus station to see Peter, Annie, Matthew, Beth, and Susie off on the Grey Hound. The parting was not too sorrowful for they fully expected to see each other when the others followed in a few months. Homer said Rachel and he would be there quickly. Jason asked on the way home, "Am I going to see Aunt Beth again soon?"

"Yes," Rachel told him, "very soon."

Chapter Sixteen

It was now the latter part of 1968. Peter Stolsfus sat in his living room on the upper floor of his Honduras residence. He thought of all that had happened so quickly in the last few weeks: the move, the decisions, and the purchase of this place. Before that, the research trip to Honduras and the months of planning that followed. A dream of his lifetime was before him, and somehow it still felt like a dream.

Here he was on foreign soil. Surely here in the third world God would give him the desires of his heart — desires to see hope come to many who knew nothing of the things he did. Perhaps here at last he could give of his heart to others without hindrance from church authorities, men with other interests in the forefront of their hearts and minds.

Yet Peter astounded himself at what else was on his mind. Here he was, barely settled and already feeling something he hardly ever felt before. A concern for church drift into liberalism kept pressing into his thoughts in ways it never did before. "Why am I concerned about church drift? Suppose it is all true, this thing they said always happens to missionaries?" He found himself wondering why here, stripped of the ever-present watchful eye of Amish bishops, these feelings of concern were rising in him. He already knew his own feelings on how strongly he felt that he must never leave the Amish church. What bothered him was that this new concern for the church was so strong and in the forefront of his mind. Previously his first and foremost concern had always been missions. He pondered the change that had come over him.

Outside the darkness fell rapidly even though it was only a little after six p.m. He thought this sudden early darkness would take some getting used to. Here is came quickly, unlike Canadian winter darkness when night came slowly and felt expected. There the twilight lingered awhile even in wintertime. Here it felt as if the light would go on for a while too, and then it was suddenly over. Summer evenings in the north hung around even longer, and this was summer, was it not? But it was not the north, he reminded himself. This was the third world. Not that his mind needed any more things to remind him of that. It was his body that needed it, he concluded. Mere mortal flesh could hardly keep up with selling one's home place in the last month, setting up auction and moving 3500 miles.

The chair he was sitting did not fit well. It looked comfortable when he purchased it at the market in town, but it no longer worked. He thought it must be the body again, refusing to follow the mind. He shifted around in the chair and found a better spot. "Get used to it — this is home and you will be happy." The sleepiness of earlier fast overtook him, and it was not even suppertime yet. "I wonder why I am so tired lately. It must be the moving and everything, or this higher altitude here in the valley." He thought of the mountain and found comfort in the thought that he would be able to rest well in this place.

Earlier in the day the local police stopped by and made themselves understood that danger lurked in the air. They wanted a lights-out condition for a while until the war with El Salvador was settled. Peter listened to them but felt no real need for concern. He was aware of the ongoing dispute from what he heard on his first trip to Honduras. It all sounded childish to him and not all that serious. The border, from what he could tell, was quite a distance away, and after all this was the third world. What were they going to do? Throw bananas at each other? He did, of course, not offer this opinion or another one he thought of, which was to ask how long it would take the army to drive here in its oxcarts.

Peter kept these thoughts to himself under his friendly smile and listened to what the police said. The border situation has really flared up again at this time, they said, and fighting has begun. This was a real serious situation, they said, and people could get killed. They had just received word from the capital that El Salvador sent planes marauding into Honduras the last few nights. That was why the lights out was being requested. They were afraid that a large rich plantation like this one could be used by planes as guiding points to the town or other points of military interest.

Peter smiled some more and assured them that this was not a rich plantation, but yes they would be careful with the lights. "That is good, that is good," the police nodded happily at his agreement. "Rich places can give off much light. You will be careful. We do not like to have bombs in the town. All our lights in town are no more. All gone. Click, out."

"Yes, yes," Peter said, "we will be careful." He sat here now thinking about the conversation and smiled to himself. "I suppose if I sent Matthew out to look, the place would be lighted up like it always is." The more he thought about it the more sure he became, until soon he was so sure that he must send someone to see for sure if it was true.

Peter called to Matthew who had just came in from outside. "Matthew, I am curious if what those police said about lights-out is true. Saddle up the horse up and ride to the top of the knoll and see if you can see the town lights from there. My guess is the whole place is lit up."

Matthew chuckled a little and left. Ten minutes later the sound of a slow trot went up between the orchard trees. The light of the flashlight bounced up and down and then quickly faded through the trees. Fifteen minutes later the sound came back again. Peter got up and waited by the upper story front door. "What did you see?"

There was silence for a while as Matthew came up the stairs. "You know, it is strange — there was nothing. It was all dark. I even went out a little farther, and there was nothing. Not even a flicker of firelight. Last night I saw what looked like hut lights on the mountain side, but there is nothing now."

Peter grunted, "Well, I'm surprised. I wonder how they did that."

They said nothing more on the subject during supper, and afterwards sat around reading a while before retiring for the night. The girls, Beth and Susie, along with Matthew were with him. Others of the extended family would be along soon. But for now it was just them. There was no gas for the gas lanterns, so the only thing for light was the kerosene lamps. "You have to get into town and look for some gas, Matthew. This dim light is hurting my eyes," Annie mentioned, looking up from her copy of *Family Living*.

Peter felt sleepiness coming on soon after that. Getting up he went to the door, holding it open a minute before stepping outside. "It is so peaceful around here," he thought. Turning to go inside he paused for a moment before he shut the door and turned the heavy lock attached to the inside. "I wonder why this thing is here. Hardly seems necessary. Such a heavy door and such a large contraption this lock is." In spite of his puzzlement, since the lock was there, he locked it. The thing made a deep solid sound as the bar slide into place. For some reason it bothered him, but he could not quite tell why.

Sleep came easily enough, but something awoke him with a start. Not a ray of light shone anywhere. Peter went to the window and looked up towards the sky. Surely the stars would be out, but it was hard to see through the tree branches. What awakened him? Then he heard it, a low moan of a motor far in the distance. The sound did not come from the ground but the sky. It could not be a motor vehicle. He was sure of it. The sound was too high above the ground to be traveling any road that he knew of. Waiting a little longer the sound only became louder. Now he was sure. They were planes. He found his way back to the bed, stubbing his toe smartly on the leg of something. It would be long after before he felt anything, and the morning would show the black and blue mark. He shook Annie. "Wake up, there are planes in the sky."

"What do you want?" was the only response from the sleeping wife.

"Wake up, there are planes in the sky."

"No, Peter, you are dreaming. This is Honduras, and there are no planes down here."

"Yes there are. I hear them. Come to the window."

Annie got up slowly and came over to the window. Her feet made shallow scuff sounds as she crossed the wood floor on her way over. "Shh, listen."

They listened. Through the window came the unmistakable sounds made by the engines of small planes. The hum filled the air. Peter whispered, "There is more than one." He felt the movement of Annie's head in an up-and-down motion brushing his shoulder. How long they stood there they never knew, but it could not have been long. The planes headed on towards the east and their sound grew less and less. The listeners were still holding still, waiting for the sound to die out, when it came — a solid concussion, followed by two more. It was a low-throated sort of sound, with all the sharpness gone out of it — a muffled boom sounding from far away as if great power was behind it. Peter knew that only the distance kept the full effect from them.

"That was a bomb," he whispered. Again she nodded her head without making a sound. It felt like a year while they stood there. At least it was a year's worth of thoughts. Slowly they walked back to bed. What else was there to do? Yet it was almost dawn before Peter even dozed off a little. He woke up thirty minutes later and got out of bed. Rarely in his life did the sun look so good. The night's fears seemed so foolish now that the sun was shining. Outside a flock of parrots landed on the fruit trees up close to the house. They were making a terrible racket. He reminded himself that he would do something about those parrots. They could hardly raise fruit around here with that many parrots eating freely from the orchard. Already thoughts of bombs did not stay in his head.

The rest of the family was getting up, as he could tell from the background noise. The clatter of dishes was muffled in the kitchen when he came in where he could see Annie telling the girls about the planes. At least he did not dream the whole thing. Matthew was sleepily rubbing his eyes as he came in from outside somewhere. "Did I hear something last night?"

"Yes, your mother and I were up. There were planes in the sky, and they dropped bombs somewhere."

Matthew chuckled, "You are just making this up."

"No, I am not. You can go ask your mother — she heard it too. After breakfast why don't you ride into town and find out what they hit with those bombs. It sounded like three or more to me."

Matthew still looked skeptical after breakfast, but he left for town on horseback. He came back an hour later with the report that there indeed were bombs dropped last night. They hit the sawdust pile of the large sawmill east of town. The town was full of anxious people with many versions of the story, but this one Matthew verified by several sources and this seemed the correct one. "I don't believe we have much to worry about. If they can't do better than that we should be safe out here."

It turned out he was right. No more planes were heard that night, and a week later the police visited again to report that the border dispute was settled. To Peter the events were all kind of running together those first weeks. His confidence that this war was nothing serious seemed well justified. He wrote the news home to the others who were coming and assured them there was no need for alarm. Apparently they agreed with him because no one saw any reason to back out of their plans for moving to Honduras.

When the letter arrived from Honduras at the Esh house, Jason overheard Rachel telling Homer about the bombing. His interest was peaked. "I want to go there. I like the boom, boom," he said.

CHAPTER 17

IN THE FIRST months following his own move, it seemed to Peter Stolsfus as if they poured in, all through the late end of the year and into 1969. It left little time to think of Canada or of the coming years. The immediate was too pressing before him. First came his daughter Rachel and son-in-law Homer, followed by Jesse, Lois, and their family. Soon after that his son Steve and Kathy arrived with their family.

Peter took Jason aside the second night the family arrived and started teaching him to count in Spanish. Jason was more than willing. Spanish fascinated him. So did the rest of the country. The first night driving in the long driveway, with the trees drooping down over the lane, feelings stirred him deep inside. It was a new life, a new start, and a great place for young boys to grow up in. Jason could just tell.

Then before they could barely catch their breath, a family that none of them heard of before arrived from Ohio — the David Bunker family. David and his wife Mary brought four children with them. They all spoke a strange version of Pennsylvania Dutch. It sounded even stranger than what the Stolsfus family heard being spoken by the ministers, Robert and Vern, from Southern Illinois. But Peter welcomed them into the fold, and David found no problem fitting in. He was a tall fellow with a dry sense of humor. One thought of great wisdom when meeting him, as if he knew much and was telling little. His wife could bake the most wonderful shoofly pies, although Peter never took a liking to them himself.

"It must be the molasses, too much I guess. I don't think shoofly

142

pie and Honduras make a likely fit," he thought to himself, after hearing someone talk again about Dave Mary's pies. "Just slows a fellow down."

The only buildings on El Sanson built by the original owner were the few surrounding the main house. This made housing a major concern those first months. Yet somehow, in the way those things happen, they made it. Peter took to giving room in his basement for new families until they could build homes of their own. In Honduras, with weather of only warm and a little less warm, appropriate homes could be built quickly. The Amish settlers decided to build them almost entirely out of wood.

But a problem arose which nobody saw as a problem at the time, a kind of unseen problem that only became evident years later. The local homes in Honduras were made primarily of mud or stone, except for the occasional shack built for temporary purposes, but no one gave any advice to these white people from the cold north. Not that they would have much advice to give, or rather that they knew of to give. Long forgotten in the midst of their poverty was the real reason that permanent homes were built out of mud or other solid substances. The termites. None of those born in Honduras knew what termites did, for how could they know, having never seen what termites do to homes made out of wood? Nor did the people from the north know that termites flew in those warm climates instead of crawling through the ground like any self-respecting termite who valued fair play did up where they came from. So the locals thought they built their homes out of mud because they were poor. The white people thought so too, and besides they were in a hurry to put homes up. After that, when the first people completed their homes, the Amish reflex habits kicked in. Everyone just followed the pattern. Some of the Amish were quite capable of thinking out of the box if they had just thought of thinking it, but they did not. So the thought was left unthought-of and the houses were all built of wood. The termites started eating right away, digging up from the ground and flying up to anything they could not reach by crawling. It was just that no one noticed.

For land they took Peter Stolfus up on his offer to divide his acreage. This worked for the first few families. David Bunker took land to the east of the main house. Jesse and his brother Steve took sections out along the main road. Homer Esh took a small portion north of Jesse that contained no low fertile land along the river, since Homer expressed no farming plans. Then right in the middle Peter reserved the smallest plot for charity purposes. He was not sure at the time what, but it would later become the Children's Home. On the highest point east of the Children's Home the church house would be built on the little knoll. Later when more land was needed the La Grange ranch next door would be purchased. Together these two ranches would form the boundary of the Amish Community.

The church house was a surprise. No one seemed quite sure why it happened. None of them could bring up in their memories any recollections of Amish church houses, at least not in recent times. But for small reasons that somehow meshed together to become one big one, they needed it. That was how the church house would come to be built on the hill. Years afterward some would wonder what possessed them, but at the time there was no disagreement on the subject. Maybe it was the excitement of the move and the new land that got into all of them? Maybe it was the distance between them and their roots in the States? Maybe it was that mysterious something that grips missionaries every-where — the hope, the faith in what God would do, the hunger to reach the less fortunate? Whatever it was, the news made many an Amish man in the US shake his head.

In Ontario, Canada, old Bishop Paul Wengerd did more than just shake his head; he made a point of saying that this was a sign of serious trouble. "Amish people are not good missionaries," he said. "God has not called us to such work. That is for the English to do. Already trouble is starting with this building of a church house. Our people are called to meet in their homes. That is the only place fitting for a humble people to meet their God. Church houses make for pride and all sorts of evil things. Before long the world will be coming in that church house door." He said this with great confidence while his hand passed repeatedly down the full length of his narrow white beard. He said it again standing in line Sunday morning waiting for church to start. Albert Stolsfus just completed his auction the prior week in preparation for moving to Honduras, but he was still there to hear what was being said. On the way home in the buggy he told his wife, Barbara, what Bishop Wengerd was saying. She already knew, having heard it from the bishop's wife. Barbara did not seem too worried, and Albert calmed down himself just hearing her talk about it.

"It is just a church house. How can that be such a serious thing? Anyway your dad must know what he is doing. You know that he has no plans to leave the Amish. That is one thing they were so sure of. This will always be an Amish outreach. You know that was your dad's dream and vision."

Albert was satisfied with that and continued with the plans for moving. In Honduras, the building continued at breakneck speed. Everyone pitched in and helped each other. The projects were a marvel to the locals. They looked at the Amish as modern and highly advanced. This was a new experience for the Amish, to be considered the most modern in the culture, for before in the US and Canada they were looked upon as backwards and out of touch with the times. Here in the third world even their out-of-touch ways were considered ahead of their time. It made Peter's head spin.

Again without debate or controversy, the Amish found themselves using electric tools to build their homes. There were no public or private power lines, but generators could be purchased in the capital. Homer was the first one to purchase his generator. With the generators went the tools of the trade. Electric skill saws that would have been forbidden at home were used freely and without shame. Homer Esh bit his tongue when he first unloaded his generator at the site of his house construction.

"I'd better not say anything. Maybe if I don't bring the subject up they won't either?" In case someone did bring up the subject, Homer was ready with his arguments. "It is simply impossible to buy gas powered skill saws in the third world. They do not make them down here. Look how easy and more useful electric tools are. We have to build these houses quickly."

But no one brought up the subject. Maybe the touchiness of the issue was why no one brought it up. Besides, it was true you could not buy the gas-powered skill saws here, and Homer being the only full-time construction guy from the north on purpose left his at home. He smiled to himself and drank in the sweet sound of three electric saws running off the generator in the back, all this while building his own house and home. To Homer, life seemed good indeed.

Homer's home was a simple affair. It contained running water but no indoor plumbing. Not because Homer had any beliefs against it, but because they were not sure how sewer systems could be installed. The locals had no knowledge of the process, nor could the materials used up north be purchased in Honduras. Jason's memories consisted not of cold nights in the outhouse, since there were no cold nights, but of outhouses in general. None of them were pleasant ones. Only later would the Amish design their own septic systems.

Homer set the house on cement blocks for a foundation. It featured a finished floor of tongue and groove pine boards, paneled interior walls, and an outside metal roof. All the supplies could be found locally at the sawmill or by hiring a truck to haul them from the capital. The building went quickly. When he was done with his home and moved in, Homer started on a building to house his business. It stood to the north of his house, towards the hill where the church house would be built. There was a little corner up front for his office, with the local version of windows — horizontal panes of glass that folded on each other through a hand crank, forming a solid piece of weatherproof glass when cranked down. He used the concrete mixer they purchased in shares, he and several of the others. It was a process of days to haul gravel from the creek, then mixing and pouring the concrete floor. Using a regular wagon frame they made an excellent gravel-hauling unit. Pulled by horses, and loaded by hand, it contained a floor bed of individual boards that were not fastened down. When you arrived on the jobsite from the creek bed, it was a simple matter for two people, one on each end, to pull the boards out sideways. This dropped the gravel on the ground without any more shoveling required. Jason found this a fascinating process. In a world that knew little but manual labor, even he could feel the wonder that man must have felt when he first turned the wheel.

Jesse built a one-story bungalow to the south and out close by the road. He and his boys started working on their barn almost immediately afterwards. Plans were made to purchase cows and begin a dairy. The barn stood downhill from the house, which was perched on a small knoll. You could see the house clearly from Homer's place, although if you walked a little way in either direction it would drop out of sight because of the trees or the surrounding knolls. Jason got so that he could make the trip between their places in short order, going at a brisk run up and down the knolls. There was a joy of living that came on him in this place. Nothing he felt while living up north was quite like it.

Steve and his family built to the west of that, on another knoll closer to the river that ran on the western boundary of the property. His home was completed with a finished basement adding needed square footage. Without modern machinery, the walkout basement was dug out with horses pulling an earth-moving contraption. The Stolsfus brothers put their heads together and came up with the design.

Matthew said, "If we were to take a piece of metal bent into a u-shape shovel, only a huge one, on the forward end teeth could be welded, then we could attach two handles to the back. Each side could have traces attached that run out to the horse harnessed on the front."

The others agreed and they succeeded in arriving with the contraption at the proper depth without hitting hard rocky soil.

"With this thing, why, we could have continued going even if we hit rock," Matthew proclaimed, buoyed by his feelings of success.

Jason watched and wanted to help, but at eight years of age how much can a fellow do? His uncles were mountains of motion and enthusiasm to him. All of them were big broad-shouldered men who worked with the vigor of those facing a new world of danger and challenge.

Matthew's theory that even with rocks the contraption was still faster than digging with pick and shovel could not at the time be put to the test. Three years later Homer would dig a basement for a more permanent residence. They hit rock quickly and Matthew's theory was disproved. Homer's basement was finished by pick and shovel. Two men, brothers Fostor and Peto, enticed by the offer of permanent employment in Homer's service, toiled away for four months on the hole. Jason spent a lot of time with them, honing his Spanish skills and learning the local lore. He was not much help with the pick and shovel. He tried it with his boy muscles more than once. The ground was shale, having to be picked loose and hauled out by wheelbarrow. When completed, the shovels of the men were worn into half-moon shapes going inward, not outward. It cost Homer twenty dollars a week, in US currency, for their employment.

For now, when they were done with Steve's place the side of the walkout basement faced west towards the barn on the next knoll, which they built soon after the house. A small shed sat to the north of the house, serving as their all-around equipment storage building. An orchard with sprouts from the trees at the main house was started on the other side of the driveway going past the shed. Below the barn, land was cleared of brush in preparation for planting. They were not sure what yet, but the soil was black and good.

Everyone pitched in on the main two-story house for the Children's Home with plans in the future for three smaller ones. To the north, David Bunker built his home and laid out the foundation for a feed mill building right up close to the northern property line. Only enough room was left for a future driveway linking that end of the land with the main house at Peter and Annie's to the west. To the south it would link on to the Taft road coming in from the main road and provide access to the ranch at Lagrange.

It was during Homer's basement digging time that Jason got into his first fistfight with one of the local boys. Honduras locals are deep into the macho side of male life. Young boys are seeped in the culture of exerting your brawn and sexuality. Failing to sleep with a girl as one matures is considered a deep disgrace. Their constant questions and probing soon revealed Jason's status and celibacy. Failing to draw him into their lifestyle, they laughed at this perceived lack of manhood and taunted him to prove it by fist fighting. Jason was not interested for any particular reason other than maybe the chance of getting hurt in the process. He felt no inhibitions from his religious training for some reason, as he did on sexual matters. Finally he decided, why not.

"Let's do it," he told them.

It happened over by his grandfather's place, and the three local boys proposed going out to the mango orchard. That was fine with him. Out they went to the orchard, and he faced off with one of the boys. Jason possessed not the slightest clue of how to fight. He took two hits on the chin and neck before totally by accident catching the local boy on the chin with an underhand stroke. The power of the blow carried the boy off his feet and sprawled him unconscious on the ground. Jason stood there in surprise until the boy regained consciousness two minutes later, scrambled to his feet and fled the scene. All this was taken as great bravado and coolness by the observers. The boys spread the word of this new macho fighter, who coolly and without emotion knocked boys out cold. The news went far and wide. Jason, though, wanted neither the attention nor the notoriety. He did that evening proudly show the two workers digging his father's basement his bruised fist. They did not approve of any of it. A month later, after constant taunts and requests for a rematch, Jason did so with another boy, getting himself beat up. From then on, with the aura gone, no one asked for any more fights.

It was during the basement digging time that Homer purchased the first horse for Jason. A man came walking in on foot one afternoon leading a horse. It was brown, not too skinny, and looked like it could still run. Jason had never ridden a horse in his life, but he wanted badly to start. Homer was agreeable, and for fifty-five US dollars the horse changed owners.

"I want dollars," the man said, "not limperas. It must be dollars. US dollars."

So Jason fell in love with horses — horses one could ride, not put in traces. The mountains now became reachable, as well as the town of Guateteca whenever he wished to do so. No modern boy ever experienced more pleasure or freedom with his automobile than what Jason did with his horse. His horse became Jason's ever-present friend, an extension of his own existence he would hardly know how to live without.

Chapter Eighteen –

It was one of those afternoons they were all getting to enjoy so much — eighty degrees, a slight breeze blowing, and no sight of rain from the puffy clouds overhead. The year of 1969 was well on its way. Everyone gathered to unload and unpack the huge crate that finally came. Several of the Lagrange families had by this time arrived and settled in on the adjoining ranch. They were there to help and enjoy the fellowship. The crate in question was packed with disassembled farm machinery and implements, as well as some household items of the Stolsfus' families. Several of them went together in stocking the crate. First it was sent overland from Canada, and then across the Gulf of Mexico by ship, getting bogged down by months of paperwork at the Honduras border and what seemed like bribes to the Stolsfus brothers — money they paid to the officials for supposed legal fees and paperwork. Matthew declared he saw one official put the money in his pocket. Now it sat on the back of a hired truck in the backyard of the newly built Children's Home. The truck it sat on was one of the old ones locals used to haul logs around with, flatbed affairs with small limbs sticking up the side to hold the logs in. Only this one sported stout sideboards where the limbs usually were, some five feet high, giving it a box-like appearance. At present the backside was down with the crate visible on the floorboards.

Hanging over the truck was the stout limb of an oak tree around a foot and a half in diameter. It stuck out in a nearly horizontal angle over the floor bed of the truck some ten feet above the ground. From there the limb angled back to the main body of the oak. Between the truck and the tree was some space to walk through, but not too much. Albert wanted the truck moved closer to the tree, but the driver refused on the grounds that he needed to be able to open his door and climb out if necessary. Albert pointed out to him that he could climb out the passenger's side, but the driver insisted. He had to have room to open his door and climb out. The resulting discussion in their yet halting Spanish with the driver did not get anywhere. Jesse asked for someone who could speak better Spanish, but the Lagrange people were in even worse shape with the language lessons, having only just arrived. The Stolsfus brothers then abandoned the Spanish and discussed the issue in their own tongue. Everyone in the near vicinity got to put in an opinion, unless he was a child, in which case he knew enough to keep his mouth shut. If the child was too small to know how to keep his mouth shut, he was also too small to care where the truck was parked, in which case it amounted to the same thing and proved to be no trouble to anyone. Jason was just old enough to know enough to stay out of the conversation.

The adults discussed angle, limb strength, tonnage, and probable weight bearing points. Someone raised the point about whether North American and Central American trees would have different structural integrity. Jesse thought they would not, as the only difference would likely be the cold, and cold would not cause a tree to be stronger. Albert did not quite agree, but concurred after the others thought the theory sounded correct to them. They decided to leave the truck where it was.

Wrapped around the limb above the truck bed was a block and tackle, its lead chain hanging down to the crate below. Block and tackles are among the handiest and most effective devices available to lift heavy objects by hand-power. A rotating circle chain through one side of the block and tackle operates the internals. Running the circle chain around in one direction moves the main chain either up or down, and the reverse direction of the circle chain changes the direction of the main chain. With this simple device, very heavy objects can be lifted without any mechanics but the pull of the arm. Albert stood ready with his hand on the circle chain, having climbed on to the back of the truck after the truck-moving discussion was over. He placed the hook of the main chain into the center of the two tow straps that were wrapped around the crate. The bottom of each tow strap was held in place by the supporting boards under the crate that kept the main body of the crate slightly off the ground. These boards were fastened securely and having survived the trip down, with its no doubt rough usage by forklifts, were not likely to give way. If they did give way the tow straps would come together at the center, giving the whole lifting project a sudden jerk down and a possible tipping of the crate to one side or the other off of the tow straps. Albert gave all this a final look and decided the boards would hold, as they showed no damage or excessive wear.

"Everybody move back and we will see how this works. The two straps look okay. The big danger is if the limb breaks. I should be okay though if the limb breaks. The box will protect me. If it goes I will drop beside the crate on the floor board."

The heads around the truck nodded, and Albert began to turn the chain. Things creaked and groaned as the weight of the crate pulled on the limb. On the outer edge the leaves shook slightly and the smaller branches trembled. Albert continued to rotate the circle chain. Slowly the crate lifted off the truck floor bed. When it was six inches off the bed he stopped. The branch groaned deep down at the base where it attached to the oak.

Albert waited and nothing happened. A smile crossed his face. "Looks like we made it."

Again the heads around the truck nodded. "I need some help up here."

Jesse jumped on to the floor bed from the back, and Steve climbed up the sideboard. He put his foot in the space between the floorboard and sideboard, and pushing up he swung over the top, his feet straddling the upper edge. That was when it happened. The branch broke with a sharp crack. It could be heard clear across the field to the lane out in front of the Children's Home where some of the people were standing.

"Jump," Albert yelled all in one breath as he and Jesse hit the floorboards hard. Jason heard the crack from the front yard of the Children's home. Looking towards the truck he saw Steve trying to leave his perch on the sideboard, but his body at the chest line was still on top when the branch hit. It was all in slow motion as the branch came down, squashing Steve's chest between itself and the top of the sideboard. The bounce lifted the limb back up in the air, and Steve's body fell out on to the ground as the branch crashed down again on the sideboards without rising this time. There was dead silence as time stood still.

From the Children's Home a few curious faces looked out the window and then the door. Around the truck the men approached cautiously. Steve's body lay crumpled and on its side, his face hidden from view by his hat that fell over it. No one said anything as they stood there. Albert and Jesse crawled out of the truck and looked around. Jesse was the first of them to get close enough to touch Steve. Not only was Jesse the oldest of the family, but he was also known to have some medical knowledge of a self-taught nature. The Amish are always open, when such help is available, to people from within their own groups who learn something of the higher disciplines. As Jesse took Steve's hand they waited because they knew he would know the answer to their question. "His heart is still beating. Come help me carry him where he can be comfortable." The men around him responded, and with many hands under him they started walking, carrying Steve towards the front of the Children's Home.

From the Children's Home the doors burst open as the women came out. "Who is it?" "It is Elmer Hurst." Elmer's wife Betty burst into a run, her face white. When she got to the men carrying Steve, Jesse shook his head. "No, it is not him. Go tell Kathy it is Steve." Betty turned around to go, too dazed to respond. Already someone had told Kathy and she was running from where she was watching in the front yard.

She took Steve's head in her hands, all business like. "You must take him to the front yard, beside the road. We will keep him there while we get transportation to the hospital. Someone get a sheet quick."

Jesse nodded his head in agreement, silently staying by his side as they carried Steve to the front yard. The blanket sheet was already spread by the time they got there. Steve groaned as they let him down gently on the sheet-covered grass of the front lawn.

A frantic search ensued for options. The first suggestion to get acted on was to send someone into Guateteca to see if the doctor was in. Several of them knew the schedule of the doctor who came out from the capital Tuesdays and Fridays to run his clinic in town. That information was uncertain, though, because sometimes the doctor came a day early or a day late. Sometimes he stayed over an extra day. It was worth the try, so a rider was dispatched to go look. One of the older boys placed in charge of the doctor search asked to use Jason's horse. Instead of agreeing to the loan Jason said he would go too. The two young boys ended up going together. They rode their horses at breakneck speed into town using the main road instead of chancing a short-cut that Jason knew of, but to no avail. The doctor was not in his clinic, nor could the nurse be found who lived in Guateteca.

Back in front of the Children's Home the family was gathered around the sheet spread out on the grass. Steve's breathing was getting shallow and his lungs were rattling. Jesse and Matthew were standing with Beth and Susie beside them. Steve's immediate family was on their knees around him in a circle. It was the four boys, Kathy, and their one daughter.

Steve motioned with his hand raised weakly from the ground. "I am going soon. You have to be brave now, boys. Take care of mother, all of you. It is hard for me to breathe. It hurts somewhere in here." He motioned with his hand again, crossing his chest at the middle section.

The boys wept, as one by one they told their father how much they loved him. They told him how much they wanted him to live and how much they cared about him. The voices went around the circle, hushed and low. Their sound rose and fell mingled in with the sound of their weeping. Kathy held them all together in their sorrow, her arms spread out on each side. The little girl did not know what to do, as tucked under her mother's arm she joined them all with her tears. She could not understand why her father was lying on the grass and why he did not get up.

Kathy was holding Steve's hand. "I love you, dear. You have always been so good to me. I wish I had been a better wife to you. I am so sorry."

Someone started singing softly "Gott ist de liebe." It is a German song roughly translated "God is love," only that does not properly translate it. In the English, love can be understood as a verb, but in the German, love is distinctly made to be a noun. So it says that God is *the* Love — that love is as God is, and that really they are not different at all. It says that when one has found love, one has found God, because God has never ceased being love.

They sang it that afternoon, gathered around the sheet spread out on the grass — fifty souls far from home, in a strange land, and now facing a familiar foe of mankind, death. They sang it as only those to whom things are real can sing. The German words came easily off their tongues, for they had all sung it so many times before, but never quite like this. Before them was the body of a man in whom life was now a frail thing. They heard the words of the song that day and understood its meaning. Somehow they knew that even though none of them knew how to ask God, or what to ask him for, their hearts were asking it in tears. They wept together, young and old, so that the words of the song were muffled and they hardly could tell where they were in the stanza had they not known the words so well by heart.

Heads started turning when they heard the sound of a vehicle coming in the driveway up past Homer Esh's place. None of them drove vehicles and few came on to the ranch, so it was unusual when a vehicle went past. When this one got closer they saw that it was the driver of the truck that held the crate. He was in the passenger seat of a pickup truck. This was another of the options that were acted on. The driver was sent to look for transportation after the two boys left for town on horseback looking for the doctor. They backed the truck up close to the sheet and made motions to load it.

Without being asked, the women brought out blankets from the

Children's Home and spread them in the bottom of the truck bed. Five thick made for a scant bed, but it was all that was on hand. With Jesse and Albert leading, the men picked up Steve and laid him in the back of the pickup truck. Kathy got in front with the girl, and all four boys sat in the back on the sideboards. Jesse got down on the floor. He asked for a thermos of water to take along and some sheets to protect Steve from the dust, he said. Some of them knew what else sheets were used for, but they only thought it and said nothing. It was a four-hour trip under normal speeds to the hospital at the capital. This would be no normal speed.

"I will go along," Jesse told his wife, having motioned her to come over. "Maybe I can help with keeping him comfortable, and anything else I can do. The boys can do the chores. They should be okay. Just make sure they shut everything down for the night. The heifers need to be kept out of the barn when they milk. I think the boys know all this. They have done it with me many times now. I will let you know what happens, but it may be tomorrow night before I can come back."

It took them five hours to reach the hospital in the capital, and Steve was still alive. In fact, he seemed stronger than when they started. Jesse pondered on this and wondered if God was helping them. He left Steve with Kathy in the care of the hospital, returning the next morning with the children on the early bus for the colony. The following morning as many of the family as could went in to spend the day with Kathy and Steve. That evening things turned for the worse again. They gathered around Steve and wished the children were there, but there was no way to reach them at the colony. Again they were moved by something unexpected. Somehow in the north things did not go quite this way, but here heaven drew close as they sang around Steve's bedside. They sang the old song written and arranged by Aldine S. Kieffer in 1904.

There's a city of light 'mid the stars, we are told,
Where they know not a sorrow or care;
And the gates are of pearl and the streets are of gold,
And the building exceedingly fair.

Chorus — Let us pray for each other, not faint by the way,
In this sad world of sorrow and care.
For that home is so bright, and is almost in sight,
And I trust in my heart you'll go there.

As the evening continued, Steve rallied. He was home and starting to move around his place three weeks later. The first task he took on was directing the boys to clear off the river bottoms to the west. The knoll from the barn ran down towards the river, bucking up slightly again before dropping down to the bottoms. Spread out north and south was a strip of land a thousand feet wide of rich, black soil. It was overgrown with brush and small trees, and looked like it never was farmed before. Clearing it proved to be little problem as the overgrowth came out easily.

Peter came over to watch the work in progress the week after Steve came home from the hospital. He also came to talk. Standing out by the barn with Steve they looked out over the river bottoms.

"I am glad to see you back and on your feet. We thought we had lost you a couple times."

"So did I. It seemed as if I was going lying out in front of the Children's Home with the pain and all. I was at peace, though, and put myself in God's hands."

"We are all glad you are still with us." Peter paused before continuing. "What do you think of the present church situation?"

"First of all I am glad to see that you are concerned about it. At home you were never involved in leadership like I was, and you did not seem to pay attention to church discipline much."

"Yes, things have changed since I moved. Not that I am involved in church leadership. There is of course you, and then Robert and Vern. Yet I feel concerned and responsible for things. Without my input I doubt any of us would be here. That puts an awful weight on one's shoulder."

Steve continued, "Secondly, I am glad to see that you are concerned because I am too. There is trouble afoot. I am not sure what exactly it is yet, but something is not right. Vern and Robert of course come from a different place then we do, but still they are

Amish, ordained Amish and all. There is nothing that I know of being said about them by their bishops at home. Yet I feel as if they do not value it all as much as we do. We have to stay within the Amish faith, or it will all be in vain down here. Look at how much you have sacrificed and the rest of us. We have left our homes up north and risked a lot of other things for this. If we fail to hold the line on the church discipline, we will fail."

"I feel that now better than what I used to, but what are you referring to?"

Steve thought for a little bit. "As yet it is just the little things. The church house bothers me now a little, but we found such unity building it. I felt myself at the time that it was the right thing to do. What is there about this place that is causing these changes even in me? I know that up north I would never have given my word to a church house. Just stop and think, Dad — a church house. Yet down here we have done it, and the scary thing is it seemed right."

Peter nodded soberly, "I know."

"Then there is the electricity issue. I know that there are no power lines down here, and likely will not be for the foreseeable future. That will keep things to just generators. Yet some of our people seem to have so little sense or caution about this. Take Homer, for example. He is the worst, although the Lagrange people are just as much into them. There is, what shall I say, a happiness about them when they use these things. These are dangerous issues. It could mean the downfall of the whole endeavor if things get out of hand. Yet even Vern and Robert are not all that interested. They do not seem to sense much danger. That really concerns me. It would be one thing if they did see the danger. At least then I would feel like they might stop at the next sign of danger. Now, I do not know. What will it take for them to see a danger?"

Peter nodded again. "I have been thinking about all this even before talking with you. I wonder if God was telling us something with that limb that fell on you. That limb looked so strong and stable. We all looked at it and we were sure it would hold up the crate, but it broke. Could that mean something for us? Obviously you did not die from your injuries when by all counts you should have. Even the doctor thought so that night in the hospital. That must mean God did not mean for you to die. Was it instead a message He was sending to us? 'Be careful in what you are trusting. It might look good to your eyes, but the limb can break.'"

Steve said nothing as he stood there looking out at his fields down by the river bottom. Then he turned away with a sad look in his eyes. "I love this place already. I love it very much. I love this country, and I want this church to work. For all those reasons and more we must listen to what God is saying. I will speak to the ministry about this. We must look carefully at what we are trusting in. It would be such a terrible thing if this limb broke."

Peter agreed. "One thing that comforts me though is that Bishop Bontrager has agreed to have oversight of the church here in Honduras. He also wants to stay Amish, and from what I can see has no liberal tendencies."

Steve nodded is head. "Yes, it is good to have a solid Amish bishop in charge of the church."

CHAPTER NINETEEN

BY THE END of 1969 problems were already brewing. Homer Esh could feel it coming in his bones. It was Sunday morning around a quarter till nine. Jason and two other of Homer's boys were sitting beside him. Church was just about to begin. "He is going to do it again. I know he is. Why does no one else seem to be concerned about this?"

They were all in the church house, fifteen of the Amish families, other than those sick with the flu or some legitimate reason. The church house still smelled of new wood, its straight back handmade benches lined up with each other on each side, with an aisle in the middle. Homer was sitting halfway up on the left hand side, the men's side, considering his options. He just knew it would happen again. It happened so often and this was one of those mornings when it was most inopportune for it to happen.

"He is going to sing that confounded English song again. I just know he is. Here on Sunday morning of all places. I know the Bishop will think it is terrible."

Bishop Willy Bontrager was there that morning. He flew into the capital on Friday from northern Indiana. Robert and Peter went in on the bus to pick him up. This was the second time he was visiting and he had just agreed the night before to formally supplying bishop oversight to the young Amish community. Homer got word of it that morning on his way up the hill when he and Rachel caught up with Jesse and his family. Jesse dropped back a little bit to pass the news on to them. Both of their sets of children ran ahead up the hill while the parents slowed their walk to give themselves time to go over the point of interest. The children waited, though, for everyone to catch up as they all properly filed in on their sides of the church house.

"How can this be happening? Why have we not dealt with this man sooner? The bishop is never going to give us oversight for very long if he hears us singing an English song on Sunday morning." Homer really was quite beside himself on what to do. He was a great admirer of the bishop.

Vern and Robert knew of Bishop Bontrager while they still lived in the States, having first made contact when the bishop visited their home church area in southern Illinois. Bishop Bontrager was noteworthy even in northern Indiana with its vast network of Amish churches from north of Fort Wayne to within two hours of Chicago. He was known for his fervor and willingness to stand out for authentic biblical beliefs. Bishop Bontrager was from the South Bend area, the east district of the four districts the old Bishop Helmuth formerly was in charge of. He was in the forefront of pursuing many needed reforms within the Amish community of faith. He stressed the need and importance of each individual believer acquiring a personal faith and assurance of salvation in Christ. For this emphasis on personal faith versus reliance upon church tradition and affiliation, he acquired the negative attention of many Amish bishops. It also attracted the attention of ministers Robert and Vern, and when they brought his name up to Peter he seemed like a natural to ask for help.

From the first trip down, Homer Esh knew that he liked Bishop Bontrager. "This is really a nice change from what we are used to. No mention of electric tools or of working in town. Of course, around here we do not work in town, but he saw my shop and never said a word."

Partly because of that visit Homer was sure Bishop Bontrager would be a good bishop for them. On this morning he wanted quite badly for nothing to happen that would change that. "If things would just go the way they were supposed to go. I know the bishop would help us out for a long time to come. How we need that."

Not that Homer was just out for the impression's sake, although that was part of it, but he wanted Bishop Bontrager to be comfortable. "Back home, I am sure things go the way they are supposed to."

The way they were supposed to go was to sing the proper songs on Sunday morning, especially on a main Sunday morning with a visiting bishop there to conduct the service. The proper song was "The Praise Song."

Now Homer was waiting. He felt constrained to wait before starting the second song, because how can the second song be sung before it is the second song? He also was waiting in the hope that Dennis Faber would go ahead and sing his song. "Maybe Dennis will start his song first. Just go ahead and sing it. Please, sing the thing." Homer's thoughts were so loud inside his head he glanced around to make sure he was not saying them out loud.

Dennis Faber was the man who all the fuss was about. Dennis was the new supervisor at the Children's Home. He and his wife, Hetty, were from Pennsylvania, but were not well versed in Amish ways for some reason — or, as Homer already thought darkly, "Maybe they did not want to know." They looked Amish from what Homer could tell. Their dress certainly was acceptable for an Amish person, but neither of them could speak German. Anyway, Dennis started singing English songs for Sunday morning church. The sheer horror of it gripped Homer. Why no one took Dennis aside privately and spoke to him about it, Homer did not know. He certainly did not have the inclination to do so himself, with his feelings the way they were. Maybe someone had spoken to Dennis, Homer thought the other day, and he was not listening. That thought just made matters all the worse as far as Homer was concerned.

As Homer was waiting to sing the proper German song someone started the old German hymn "Loben see Gott." Fifteen minutes later the last sounds of the song were dying down around him. This was where Dennis always did his thing. Not only had he started singing English on Sunday morning, he added insult to injury by starting to sing what Homer was sure was an intended replacement song for "The Praise Song." At least it was always the same song, at the same time, for the assumed same reason. Neither did Dennis sing his song as the first song of the service, as he well could have. He sang his song as the second song. Homer felt his breath coming in shorter spurts. Now the time had come to sing the second song.

Homer was ready. He went through this last Sunday and won. Under ordinary circumstances no one would lead out "The Praise Song" two Sundays in a row, but these were not ordinary circumstances. Homer was ready to go ahead and do it. It would no doubt cause some questions to be raised about himself, but he was willing to pay the cost. He was ready and prepared. The last notes were gone now, and he should be starting the song. Dennis was sitting two rows in front of Homer with his songbook open.

"Okay, Homer, now is the time. Do it."

Homer was ready, but his training and scruples got the best of him. It was not right to jump in so quickly after the first song was done. The singing of "The Praise Song" required a proper pause for gravity and reflection before beginning. There was no way Homer could bring himself to jump in so quickly, as if "The Praise Song" were just some common English song sung in common English words that everyone spoke. The German tongue deserved respect and proper gravity, especially when attached to sacred singing.

"Come on, come on, start it."

Homer wanted to and tried to overcome his feelings, but could not do it. While he was struggling Dennis apparently overcame whatever feelings he felt or didn't feel and did it. He gave out the English number and started singing, "Brethren we have met to worship, and adore the Lord our God." It was number thirty-three in the black hymnal, written by George Atkins and composed by William Moore in the 19th century.

The sound of the song caused icy feelings to linger around the back of Homer's spine. The feelings spread slowly upward until his entire back tingled from side to side. In-between there were extra sharp nerve endings firing at intervals in vertical dashes to his brain.

"How could this be happening? This was Sunday morning. The Bishop was here — how could someone even think of causing such a transgression at this of all times?"

Homer looked around in slight glances out of the corner of his eyes, lest he draw attention to himself. No one else seemed to be all that disturbed. Jesse and Albert were singing right along, as if it were nothing out of the ordinary. Homer wondered what got into all of them. Was it the weather of this country or the far distance from home that was causing this amnesia?

Homer lived through the Sunday and never really got his answer to his questions that day. He brought up the subject at the next members meeting. The meeting was on a Friday evening and held at the church house as most of their other meetings and public gatherings now were. It started at six-thirty, just after darkness set in. This allowed the farmers to finish their chores in daylight but left little time to finish supper with any leisure. In the north this situation would not have been tolerated, as there they would have started most evening meetings no earlier than seven o'clock. Down here in the third world they were doing things differently. No one was objecting for some reason. Maybe it was how the darkness felt that did it. The way it closed in made one feel as if one should be home and preparing for bed, instead of roaming around at night. Whatever it was, it just seemed like the right thing to do.

All the members were there that evening except for some of the younger ones. They found it hard stirring up much interest in such a meeting in this land that was still an adventure to them. To the hiss of gas lanterns, the informal meeting was called to order with prayer and a short song. From there, formalities were set aside, and place was given for any subject anyone cared to bring up. What followed were free ranging discussions joined in by both the men and women. This was also a break from Amish tradition in which only the men spoke in all public meetings. No one said that they were now allowed to speak; the women just spoke up with questions and joined into the ebb and flow of the conversations.

In a slight lull, Homer brought up his question. Why were the German songs no longer being sung faithfully in church services?

No one seemed offended or upset with the question, just disinterested. Several raised the point that German was just not as needed down here in the third world as it was in the north. Not that they could really explain that logic, it was just the way it was. One of them tried to explain it by saying that it was not the national language, but neither was it in the north he added at the end.

No one could really come to any final conclusion, but from the ensuing conversation Homer came away with some general impressions. German had been to them in the north the dividing line, the separation between the outside and the inside, between the good and the bad. Yet here it did not have the same feel about it, as if the world they so much feared was no longer calling at the door. In the north they were the backwards ones, the ones behind, and the culture was so far ahead of them. Here they were the modern ones, and the culture around them was like seeing people stuck in time. Now their language barrier seemed unnecessary, even a waste of time, a hindrance to where they were going. Not that any of them thought it out in these terms, or even knew entirely what they were feeling. They simply brought up the point that with the large number of both visitors and natives who were attending church, some of the former who could speak only English, and the latter who could speak only Spanish, German seemed to be improper.

Homer responded that he thought it was a great shame and tragedy that the mother tongue was being given second place. "If we continue this, soon we will quit singing German completely. In my opinion, that will be the wrong thing to do. I know that the English is easier to sing, but these are sacred songs that came down to us from our forefathers. Many of them were written in jail cells before the writers were martyred."

The only one to make much effort to speak in support of Homer was Steve. He said that he too thought about what was happening with the German singing and was concerned about it. Steve even mentioned the past Sunday when Bishop Bontrager had been there, and how he thought it was inappropriate that an English song was substituted for "The Praise Song." This warmed Homer's soul, and he decided to leave the subject alone while he was at least a little ahead. At least the deacon supported him.

From there the conversation shifted to their need of income-producing enterprises. Many of them were not yet building their own businesses. That seemed to be what one did to produce income in the third world. There were no employment positions available with local businesses that would supply anywhere near the level of income they would need to exist. Up to this time they had been living on what monies they brought from the north. Plus they had been kept busy building their own homes and helping out the neighbors. Now with the building of their homes caught up, their monetary situation was foremost on their minds.

Suggestions were made on produce-raising, poultry farming, a weekly vendor's route into the capital, and many other worthy thoughts on finance. It was going on towards nine o'clock when they heard the sound of a generator starting up in the distance. The sound was loud enough to attract their attention and interest. After some discussion and noticing that Homer was missing, along with his wife, they decided that it was his generator.

"He must be home getting some extra work in yet before he retires," Peter chuckled about his son-in-law. "So like Homer."

The irony of it did not miss them. The meeting broke up to the sounds of their laughter. They left amused with the thought that working might solve their money problems faster than talking about it.

Chapter Twenty

IN THE MONTHS that followed the two side-by-side ranches hummed with industry and activity. All of the new year, 1970, was full and front end-loaded. The locals never saw anything like it. "Even when the rich rancher owned this place, nothing like this happened," Martes Martinez, Peter Stolfus's new hand, was heard remarking one Monday morning. He attended for the first time the church on the hill the day before, after being invited by Peter himself. It had been the day of the monthly fellowship meal held after the service. Everyone brought along a dish or two and spread it all out on the top of the hillside afterwards. Martes left with his belly full of American food that he would never have dreamed existed before, let alone eating it.

It must have produced no ill effects on him because he was beaming now on Monday morning. "My, my, that was really something. The food, huh, it was out of this world. The ladies, I have never seen anything like them. Our women, they are nothing. All they know how to do is make little tortillas and beans — that is nothing. Around and around they go with a little corn, and then they spread some rice on it and think they have made food. These women, they have some weight to them, good legs and arms. Some of them, you can tell, you can just tell by looking at them. They have eaten well in their life. They make food, huh, good food. Food that makes a man's stomach see a different day of the week every time he brings food to his mouth. You can close your eyes and see another kind of food somewhere. Everywhere you look, all over the hill, there was food and more kinds of food. I have never seen anything like it."

Peter laughed when he heard Martes tell the story of his day at church. "You did hear what the preacher said? You know, the sermon — you did hear the sermon, Martes?"

"Oh, yes, the sermon, it was good. Good sermon the preacher gave. It made my soul better, but the food, huh, the food — it was something."

"Yes, the food. Well let's see if we can get some work done now. With all that good food you should be able to work harder than ever?"

Martes was not sure about that, but he agreed that it was true. "We will work now."

Peter headed out to his store by the main road. Where the driveway hit the road to the capital, there was land frontage from the ranch a quarter of a mile to the east. Jesse bought this end of the ranch but was willing to let Peter use a small portion of it for his store. All it took was a small section right off the main drag, about 150 feet long by 100 feet wide, halfway in-between the driveway and the end of the Sanson ranch. With a fence around the back, attached to the main fence Jesse and the boys put up on their lower pasture, it did not take up much of Jesse's land at all. The driveway came in off the main road, followed the road along the front of the store, and then went back out in a sort of u-shape without much of a u — just an on- and off-ramp with a place to park.

Stirred up by the constant traffic on the main road, dust sifted through the open shutters and on to the groceries and soft drinks Peter stocked his store with. There were no glass windows anywhere, just stout panels of wood that lifted up from hinges attached to the inside. When shut, they made the place look like a solid clapboard building. When the store was open Peter lifted the shutters to the outside, attaching them to the ceiling of the front porch, until he wanted to close for the day. Business proved to be good. Motorists stopped in for quick refreshments, since he soon became known for the variety and quality of snacks served.

The place quickly became the bus stop for the colony and did brisk business for some 100 Amish people who owned no motor vehicles of their own. The early bus to the capital ran at three a.m., bringing you into town in time to catch the first stores that opened. A later one ran at four-thirty and then the last batch at six o'clock. The three o'clock bus was the one most traveled. Business was serious business for most of them, and arriving in town at ten o'clock was not a good start to the day. Better to lose the sleep up front like a man and get a running start at things. Besides, the first bus left the capital for the run back at twelve, the late bus at two, putting one back at the ranch just by dark.

Most of them did the capital trip in one day. Catch the early bus at three, dash around town with the excellent street bus service, do your business, and catch the noon bus back home. It made for a full and fulfilling day. Fulfilling not in the pleasure sense, but fulfilling in the sense that one tackled the horrible things in life and lived to tell about it. The buses were small things, little midgets of cramped room and tight seats. There was a larger bus, but it ran all the way from Dolente and did not pass Peter's store until the six o'clock run. Dust went without saying, as well as the four-hour bounce and jostle of the road. Windows were kept open for air and for whatever else wanted to come in. Maybe it was the smell that stayed with one the most. It was of an unknown quality, produced by mixing dust, sweat, smoke — both from cigarettes and exhaust — packed lunches of corn and beans, greased hair, and unwashed bodies. The occasional animal in transit, packed either above the bus tied on with string or in the baggage compartment, added that little extra whiff of odor to the whole mix. One arrived back home in the evening sick of life in general and of travel in particular. It was a life for the hardy and stout of heart. It produced some of the best — and the not-so-good — memories one can have. It was life lived on the edge.

At his store, Peter established a clientele for the staples of life — corn and beans. He built the two-story building by the road as his effort at producing an income for the family, and this line of his business proved his best income producer. Proper storage facilities for corn and beans were almost non-existent in Honduras. The resulting infestation of insects was a real problem. At harvest time, Peter purchased corn from the locals and later from the

Amish themselves. Storing it in a controlled environment, he could provide a stable supply of corn and beans for sale later. It did not hurt that these prices were usually up with the market at the time. He sold them for less than the going price and this, along with his soon-established reputation for bug-free merchandise, proved to make the store profitable. There was, of course, the income from the orchard surrounding his place, but it did not keep him busy full-time. He figured that even with the dairy herd he was in the process of acquiring, he would still have time to run the store. If bad came to worse he figured he could hire one of his relatives to help out.

Jason going on nine years of age was old enough to help out here and there. Peter sent him on errands between the house and the store on several occasions. The errands involved transporting money, and several limperas found themselves in Jason's pocket. His conscience never bothered him or stirred itself. Beth began running a produce route for her father twice a week into Guateteca. She would hitch up Peter's horse to the wagon, load produce from the store, and drive up and down the streets of Guateteca. Jason took to going along with her to help, and again money found its way into his pocket — twenty-cent pieces and fifty-cent pieces in Honduras coins. Beth either never missed it or never said anything about it. Jason highly enjoyed these times with his aunt, for reasons having nothing to do with money. They did not last long though. A letter arrived from Dan Ludwig proposing marriage. She accepted willingly. The catch was the letter stated in no uncertain terms that Dan Ludwig was not coming down to Honduras.

"I will not be coming down to the wilderness. If you find this proposal acceptable please consider in your acceptance that we will be married in Canada."

To Beth that was no problem, and if Peter thought it strange he said nothing about it. Jason cared only that Beth was leaving. He would miss her when she left. None of the family in Honduras made the trip home for the occasion. It was simply too far in their minds. Besides, Fred could handle the affairs on that end of it.

Steve and his boys soon got finished with clearing the river bottom. It stretched north and south for almost half a mile. The soil looked dark and full of nutrients. There were no signs of flooding from the river, which was a plus, they thought. From the signs of it the land had not been in cultivation for many years.

Farther to the north a somewhat smaller strip of river bottom lay with the same characteristics. The first year no attempts were made to tackle this piece. Later it would come under the care and cultivation of Peter's son-in-law, Josiah. Peter himself started the clearing after the first year of success with Steve's piece of land. Jesse, whose property was on the east side of the ranch, owned no river bottom to work with. His efforts to cultivate the lower field by the road where Peter's store sat proved limited in its success. Corn grew there all right, but for produce crops it had its difficulties.

Produce, they quickly learned, provided the best monetary yields. With this in mind, Jesse crossed the creek just below Steve's river bottom where the good land ended in search of the same type of soil. Across the creek he found it. It belonged to the ranch adjoining El Sanson on the west. His efforts to purchase the property came to nothing, as the owner wished to sell the whole ranch or nothing. La Prez was almost twice the size of El Sanson with a hefty sale price attached to it. The owner must have caught on that rich Northerners were buying ranches in the area. Jesse was able, though, to negotiate an agreeable rental price for a small section of the strip of river bottom on the west side of the river. Together these pieces of land along the river would prove to be the most productive land the Amish would have on either of the ranches. Lagrange held its own river on the east side, but the banks were much steeper. The river lay deep in the ravine it cut for itself. Apparently there never were enough dirt deposits made on the surrounding land to provide the same quality of growing soil as was found on the west river off of El Sanson.

Produce raising went into high gear. For six months of the year the skies supplied sufficient water for the crops. The next six months they were unreliable. For up to four months at a time not a drop of rain fell from the sky. Everything dried up. The grass got brown. The forest got dry, and only in the mountains was any moisture found, and even that was hardly worth mentioning. Forest fires started and burned without any hindrance from man or nature. Toward the end of dry season they got worse, as the locals believed in burning the grass off in preparation of the rainy season returning. Clouds of smoke filled the air by day, and by night rings of fire could be seen in the foothills surrounding the Amish ranches. The problem, other than the occasional smoke, was when the locals misjudged the coming rains. This produced big problems when the grass was burned and no rains came. Their local cows already were skin and bones and this just made things worse. They roamed at will except for those of the occasional stockowner who bothered outfitting his animal with a fence-proof contraption of crossed sticks tied to its neck.

To solve the water problem of the dry season, Jesse, Steve, and Peter put their heads together and came up with a solution. They dug an irrigation ditch that flowed all along the west side of the ranch. Actually it was an extension of an existing idea already placed in practice by the former ranch owner. He or someone damned the river on the north end of the property. It was a homemade concrete thing that did what it was supposed to do, dam up the water. From there the irrigation ditch started and ran completely around the orchard down to the home place. This was where the former owner stopped his irrigation project, letting the water reenter the river just below the house. Peter was sure, after looking at the lay of the land, that the ditch could be extended, maybe even to reach Steve's field on the south end of the property. They put their heads together and decided it could be done. With local help they extended the irrigation ditch along the property, keeping to the high knolls in order not to lose more fall then necessary. In four weeks they reached the high bluff that overlooked Steve's river bottom. From there it was a simple matter to reach the crops. A side extension was put on the next year to reach the first section of the river bottom that had been bypassed in reaching Steve's section.

The ditch was around two feet wide and maybe a foot and a

half deep at its deepest point. The water flowed at a brisk pace and transported a large amount of water if one kept the ditch clear of growth. This needed to be done on a yearly basis, although they did not always get to it. With the irrigation ditch in place the entire strip of river bottom was able to raise two crops of produce a year — one in the rainy season when they diverted the water from the irrigation ditch, and one in the dry season when every drop of water was cherished and shared. A system was worked out in which one parcel of land was watered one night and another the next night.

The waterworks that really interested Jason was the pond they built close to the Children's Home. That was his idea of water. Many were the hours he would spend fishing and swimming with the other children in its waters. He never swam alone, though, for the waters looked unfriendly when one was alone.

Over in the center of the plantation, Homer Esh got his machine shop up and running. The new driveway for the ranch, branching off from the original one soon after it came in from the main road, ran right beside his house and the shop. North of his shop there was a side entrance coming in from the Taft road, joining on to the new driveway that continued on north past the church house on the hill, the Children's Home, and on to David Bunker's place. A few vehicles would use the Taft entrance, but most found the new driveway off of the main road the best way into the ranch. The result was that most of the traffic on the ranch came past Homer's place. As his machine shop increased in popularity the traffic could be quite busy on a weekday morning.

Homer owned every tool needed to repair and maintain the heavy log trucks and the equipment at the local sawmills. If he did not have the tool, he made plans to purchase the item. In the center of his shop sat the lathe. It was a huge affair with its spinning head and fifteen-foot length. Homer trained himself how to run the lathe, turning out any piece of metal configuration the sawmill might break or a trucker wear out.

Welding machines were of course a standard feature. Homer kept a unit in front by the twelve-foot metal garage door having the capacity to wheel outside for spot work on trucks. One learned to be careful about getting hung up on the welder when the ground cable was attached to the metal frame of the truck, and the job required that one climb on to the truck body to work. With the ground cable fastened the electric current could use the body as easily as the truck frame to complete its circuit while the person was welding. Elmer Hurst, who was soon helping Homer full-time at the shop, came up with his own form of protection. He grounded the truck body firmly to the ground with a metal plate or some such piece of iron of sufficient strength and thickness. When the welder was running, Elmer never carried both of the cables at the same time, for the same reason. Not that Homer owned welders with defective cables, but the chance was just too great of getting caught on the negative and positive currents. The ground end was completely bare where it snapped on to the object being welded, and the end, which held the welding rod, was bare in spots too. Even wearing leather gloves was no guarantee of safety. No one knew or was interested in finding out what the high voltages would do to a person, but Jason did get hung up on the welder between 120-130 volts. He was carrying both cables across the floor at the same time. The result was complete immobilization, with the arms arched as round arches on each side of the body while clutching the negative and positive cables.

Jason said the voltage produced a tingling, steady, pulsating current running from side to side and up and down each arm. Thankfully the resulting paralysis did not affect his vocal cords. He hollered to have the welder shut off. It took a while for Homer to figure out why he would want such a thing done, as Jason looked perfectly capable of walking over and shutting the welder off himself. After it was all over with, Elmer Hurst thought the episode highly amusing, but apparently not enough for him to try it himself. From then on he was just extra careful to carry each cable by itself when he was working outside on the trucks, or carry them a foot back from the end of the cable. He also checked twice to make sure the trucks were grounded when he was up on them.

Homer's tools included a band saw, iron bender, twelve-inch

grinder, drill press, metal pressing bench, keyway cutter, and an assortment of hand tools scattered around the shop. A large metal table provided a working area to the rear and the right of the shop. The locals never saw so many small and large tools in one place. They concluded with their sense of logic and justice that such riches were not meant by God to benefit only one man. Since they apparently were cut out of the loop, they took it upon themselves to cut themselves into the loop. This was done without the slightest sense of guilt or remorse, although they did it when no one was looking so maybe their consciences did bother them. One simply, according to their logic, did not leave good fruit to rot on the tree, but picked it for one's own use. This was as natural to them as breathing. That's what things were made for, wasn't it? Made to be taken. Anyone was considered rich if he owned more than he needed to survive for two days. Excluding only their own families as exceptions to that, you took from those who possessed more than you did. They considered it their divine right of birth to take from those who had.

Homer soon found this out when his tools disappeared at a rapid pace. He made a serious attempt to keep his eyes on his tools, but how can one work and watch his tools at the same time? The tools just kept disappearing. It helped when he put up signs at various places, "Eyes are Watching You," with the words below a pair of eyes that looked at you from wherever you could see the sign. He had the biggest one placed on the open top of his big red toolbox on wheels. Not that it stopped it completely, but it slowed things down. Homer took to being suspicious of any of the locals in the shop. He would ask them to leave and wait outside. When he got tired of making words about the issue he turned to other things at hand — things like his rotating metal hand grinder came in handy. While grinding metal the tool made a nice stream of sparks that extended out across the shop for some distance. Normally you would keep this stream focused downward towards the ground, so as to not injure anyone. The stream produced a slight burning sting when it hit you at a distance, and the pain increased the closer you were to the tool. This stream of sparks could be made to innocently extend towards a person who was wandering around his red toolbox or other such object of interest. When the stream hit the offender, he would glare towards Homer's direction while he was leaving. All that was to be seen, though, was Homer looking down and hard at work grinding down his piece of metal, having already located the direction and desired line of trajectory for the stream of sparks before he turned the grinder in that direction.

In the end, though, Homer learned to get along with things the way they were. Losing hand tools was just a part of doing business in the third world, he concluded, and calculated it into the fare he charged. The truckers always wanted to borrow tools. Even checking carefully when they brought them back did not always cover it. Some truckers slipped back their own cracked and broken tools in place of the tools they borrowed, or they offered the help sardines and other food tidbits in the hopes that friendliness would blind his eyes.

The work came in faster than Homer knew what to do with at times. One guy showed up on Sunday afternoon and wanted his work started right away, under the plea of great necessity. Homer refused. He told him the Sabbath was not to be violated, and that he would not start till the next morning. Besides, the sound of Homer's generator starting up could be heard halfway across the ranch, and there would be no way to cover up his transgression even if he were weak on the issue. The shop could simply not be operated without the generator. There were no public power lines, and Homer installed a massive diesel engine to run the generator that produced the current he needed. The poor fellow made one last plea with a theological argument. He mentioned to Homer that the Jewish Sabbath was from sundown to sundown, and that his work could really be started legally then at six o'clock that evening. Homer said no, he would not do it, but he would come out after twelve o'clock and do the work. They settled on that, and the fellow camped out in the shop yard. At quarter after twelve Homer rolled out of bed, got his generator fired up, and got the work done in two hours. None of the neighbors ever mentioned anything to

Homer about the noise. Maybe they were in their deep sleep, or maybe they thought if anyone was stupid enough to work at that hour of the night they would leave him alone.

In the background of it all, a plan by people not stupid at all was in the works. Under the darkness of night and in the daylight at times, whispered plans and schemes were being made. The peaceful Amish community was being watched and designs laid against its very existence. Honduras does not possess thieves for nothing. They were moving about under the most innocent of disguises.

Chapter Twenty-one

THE YEAR CLOSED and the new one, 1971, began. With it came the evil eyes longing for the growing prosperity they saw. To the east of El Sanson lay the Lagrange ranch, purchased to provide room for the growing Amish community. Between the two ranches ran the Taft road. If one followed the Taft road north of both ranches, a driveway went off to the right into Lagrange. The first property on the right belonged to Elmer and Betty Hurst. The next piece still on the right after crossing the little bridge belonged to Manny and Linda Hershberger. On your left straight across from Manny were Vern and Kathryn Miller. East of Vern the lane turned to the left and continued on. Going straight brought you first to Robert and Elisabeth Troyer and then to the right again, Albert and Barbara Stolsfus. Back to where the lane turned left brought you to Lee and Mary Stuzman. The final place would belong to Jacob and Salina Mast, but they had not built yet. They would do so a year later making them the farthest east; but for now, Lee and Robert were it. Beyond them was the river with its steep bank, lying between the Lagrange ranch and the adjoining ranch.

That Sunday morning dawned bright and clear. By eight-thirty the slight fog along the riverbank lifted and the sun was left by itself in the sky with only a few fast-moving clouds as company. The Amish were on their way to church. In pairs, by singles, and in large family groups they walked to church. Even from the outskirts of Lagrange they rarely used carriages. On this Sunday morning it was no different as they left for the church house. Dressed out in their white shirts and dark pants, the men cut a straight figure beside the women in their long, two-piece, one-color dresses and white headdresses. It is strange that none of them thought much of it or that it ever became an issue, but the men rarely wore hats to church, nor did they take to wearing their straight-cut coats. Maybe it was the weather and the warm temperature, but up north no self-respecting Amish person would ever go outdoors, much less to church, without his hat. The straight-cut coats were more understandable yet would still have raised eyebrows if a man came to church without at least his vest on over his shirt.

Before leaving for church, Stuzman made sure that everything was shut up. He checked the barn door and his tool shed. Both of these and the house held locks installed when they were built, but Stuzman saw little reason to use them. They usually locked things up for the night but never did so on Sunday morning. What Stuzman was looking for were open doors in case it rained. Not that it looked like rain, but a shower could quickly come up in the afternoon. He, as well as the others, learned this from past experience.

What none of the Amish saw that morning, because they were not intended to be seen, were about a dozen eyes peering over the river bank. The number would change from time to time, as some of them got tired of watching the Amish families leaving for church and would climb back down the bank. There the bodies attached to the eyes would take a stretch from the prone position they had been lying in on top of the riverbank. Conversation issued only in low monotone. All of them were in the river basin since well before sun-up. They crept in from the south in the dark, staying on the borderline between the two ranches so as to meet no one from either of the ranches.

At a quarter after nine, the watchers on top of the riverbank gave the all-clear signal. This produced some consternation among the group, as several of them raised the issue of stragglers. What if someone was late going to church? Some of them thought they ought to wait a little longer, and the others were nervous enough to agree. So they waited, and at 9:30 the group, gunny bags in hand, broke over the riverbank. Keeping to what natural screening from human eyes they could find, they scurried towards the homes of Stuzman and Troyer. Rather than split up into two groups, they stayed together. Stuzman's house was the first target. Like the flying locusts that come in for landing and eat what lies in sight, they picked up anything that looked usable — first from the barn, then from the shop, and then from the house. They could not believe their good fortune, that the doors were all unlocked. Not that locks would have helped, because they brought crowbars along. At Troyer's place his shop was locked. They busted the window out and kicked the door out from the inside.

Leaving one person outside for watchman, they moved quickly through each building. The gunny bags became heavy with shop tools, house wares, saucers, kitchen knives, and any money they could find. The search for money turned every dresser into a mess of strewn clothes. Every closet was emptied, with the clothes and shoes thrown outside on the floor. Kitchen cabinets were apparently a mystery to them. The hollow places behind the drawers and shelves looked suspect. What corners of the kitchen cabinets they could not access by pulling the drawers out were accessed by busting in the paneling on the opposite side. Some money was found in a jar on top of the refrigerator. That caused an intense search of the pantry for more jars. When no more jars were found that contained cash, there must have been temper tantrums with empty jars smashed on the floor. The jars of food, though, that could not be pushed aside for the search were carefully set on the floor.

An hour later the group disappeared over the riverbank with their gunny bags full. At the bottom of the bank, by the flowing water, they paused to adjust their bags. From the bags containing too much weight to comfortably carry they moved the heavier items to the lighter bags. When everything was comfortably adjusted they headed back south, staying within the riverbanks. A problem soon became obvious to them now that the gunny bags were full. None of them thought of it before, but they made quite a sight hauling these bags. Now there was no question about it. If anyone saw them, he would instantly know they were up to no good. No one in the third world walked around on Sunday morning carrying gunny bags. During the week it might have passed muster, but not on Sunday morning.

Honduras was a deeply religious country with a stringent moral code. Large shops were closed on Sunday, and this amount of shopping was simply not possible. Moving was also out of the question. Families simply would not think of moving on a Sunday. Nor for that matter would they move in this manner. There was no way that any explanation could be arrived at by anyone seeing them other than the correct one — that they were up to no good. It took them a whole half hour to discuss the problem and come up with an answer. They would all go as far as they could before the riverbank hit the main road. There was a thick bamboo patch that one of them knew of. That was where they would hide for the rest of the day with the loot. It was decided that not everyone would have to stay at the bamboo patch waiting for darkness. Only a few would have to stay while the others could go on home and return after darkness to help carry the gunny bags away. This plan could get no traction, though. None of them trusted the others to stay. Even after the suggestion that four of them stay, leaving one for each of the interests represented in the group, it was a no-go. Everyone was sure that when he came back the others would have left for parts unknown. No agreement could be reached, so they all stayed in the bamboo patch all day until darkness fell. Everyone got good and hungry, but at least there was water close by to drink. They checked the gunny bags for food, but they knew before they started looking that there was no food in them. Other things seemed more important a few hours before.

At twelve-thirty the first of the Amish came back up the road, walking home from church. Stuzman's young people were the first to arrive at home. The swinging front door caused some curiosity, but they just thought their dad forgot to shut the door properly. When they walked in, though, all belief that things were normal was removed from their minds. The littered indoor landscape lay before them. Their first response was to run back out and down the road to find their parents. The story was not fully believed until their parents got to see it for themselves. Robert arrived with no young people to get home first, and he got to see things for himself before anyone told him. Fifteen minutes later when Lee came over he was sitting on his front porch in stunned silence with his wife and three small children around him.

Lee sat down with him on the front porch. "We have the same thing at home. Who do you think did it?"

"I have no idea, but what a mess it is. What do you think we should do? I just never thought anything like this would happen down here. It was so peaceful, and the people so friendly. Even the new help we hired a few weeks ago made us feel so welcome here."

Lee nodded. "Do you think we should go to the police?"

"We almost have to, don't you think? What will happen if we don't? Something so awful as this cannot just be left to itself."

Word spread quickly throughout the Amish community, all without the help of telephone or modern communication systems. Lee and Robert thought of calling an emergency members meeting at the church house but decided against it. They met instead at Vern's place that evening after their places were restored to some semblance of order. It was a gathering of long faces and sober talk.

"Who would have thought something like this would happen? We were just starting to feel at home here."

"Will any of us be safe anymore? Will we be safe with anything?"

"What will life be like if we have to lock up everything we own?"

"Not only lock things up," Robert brought up. "We are looking at bars on all our windows and maybe even the doors. Look at how they broke my window and kicked the door in."

The talk went on till after nine o'clock, when a consensus was reached that the police should be contacted in the morning. Vern was not so sure about that but gave in after the others were unanimous in their thinking. He brought up that the Amish possessed a history of not using the police with their strong beliefs of peace and non-resistance. His arguments made little effect on his audience. Outside it was dark now, and the memories of how their houses looked that afternoon was still fresh in their minds. Besides they were far from home and all alone in this strange world. The afternoon's events made that world seem even stranger than it ever did before. Maybe if they had called the members meeting things would have turned out differently, but they did not call one. Without that meeting, the others in the community did not interfere on the basis of the unspoken code of conduct they all practiced. One did not jump in to others' affairs uninvited, unless the ministry invited the move. In this case, two of the ministers were the ones involved, and they did not call the members meeting. Whatever the reason, plans were made to contact the state police department in the morning about the break-ins.

CHAPTER TWENTY-TWO

MONDAY MORNING DAWNED bright and clear. Lee's workers showed up at seven o'clock as usual. Honduras time starts early, and work at seven. After exchanging good-mornings with them, Lee filled them in on their instructions for the day, as well as the happenings on Sunday. There were general expressions of consternation from all three of the workers.

"This is terrible. We cannot believe this would happen to you. You are a good man. You have always been good to us. Do you want us to watch your house for you on Sundays? We can do that too."

They all nodded in unison. "For you, we watch house on Sunday. We watch first two Sundays for free. No one else watch better than us."

Lee thanked them but said no. They would look after things. "There will be no more easy pickings around this place. Now we will place protection on the windows and doors and lock things up well."

The workers received this information with enthusiasm. "This is a good plan. We will help you do this. Put locks on doors. Better protection on windows. No more will anyone break into your house."

Again Lee thanked them for their concern and willingness to help, but told them that things would be taken care of. He repeated his instructions for the day to them. "I must go now to the police station to report this matter to the authorities."

"That is a good plan," they said as they headed off to start their work.

Robert met Lee at the junction of their lanes. Together they walked out to the Taft road, and from there down to the main road. Before they reached the main road a pickup truck coming down the Taft road and going into town offered them a ride. They hoped to hitch a ride at the main road, or at Peter's store, but this was even sooner than expected. The ride was accepted gladly.

When the driver yelled back, wanting to know where they were going, he was curious when they said the police station in their halting Spanish. "You have trouble, you want police. Police here no good, they bad police. They want money for help. No good police. You no go to police. I will help you."

Robert shook his head firmly. "No, we will go to the proper authorities."

"Huh," the driver yelled back, jerking his head sideways with an abrupt and upwards movement. "I have told. The police are no good. I can do much better, for much less money."

Robert and Lee ignored him as they bounced along. Twenty minutes later they topped the hill looking down into Guateteca. Dust stirred up even this early in the morning as they sped down the slope into town. A pig barely made it across the road in time to miss the truck. What slowed the driver down was a couple of dogs who took their merry time in getting out of the way. The horn did little good as the truck came almost to a halt to avoid missing the dogs. No one in the cab said a word about all of this that Robert or Lee could hear.

"Do you see anything strange about this?" Robert asked Lee.

"You mean about what just happened?"

"Yes."

"It is strange, isn't it? Somebody's values are messed up. They nearly hit that pig, which has value, market wise and money wise. Some of these people could make a good income raising pigs for market. Yet that is what they paid no regard to. Then the dogs they went to all kinds of grief for. What value do dogs have down here? Nothing. They serve no useful purpose whatsoever. No economical work. No watchdogs that I can see. None of them are taken care of. They are all as skinny, as starved, and as worm-eaten as I have seen. Yet that is what they slow down for. Something is really wrong here."

Robert nodded his head as the truck bounced into a space in front of the police station. "I wonder if you could change things?"

The driver got out of the vehicle and let them know that this was the police station. Lee told him thanks as they got off the truck.

"Are you sure I cannot help you?" The driver was trying one more time. "I can look into your trouble much cheaper than the police. Better too. If your daughter has run away with some man, I can have that taken care of. Find the man and bring the girl back. If you have lost something, I can find it. If something was stolen, I know all about who is being paid by whom. Your things will be returned for a small fee. Much cheaper than the police."

The two Americans looked puzzled and shook their heads. "No, we do not work like that. We will talk to the police. That is what the police are for, to keep the law and order. They are already paid by the government, and police do not need to be paid any bribe to do their work."

The driver laughed as he got back into his truck. "You will see for yourself." With that he drove off.

"Do you think he knows what he is talking about?"

"I doubt it. Probably was just trying to get some money out of ignorant and helpless Americans."

With that they walked towards the police station. The station was just off the public square in a plain-looking building with a white stucco front. Across the front in black letters were written the words "Municipal State Police of Honduras." Inside the building the front office consisted of a room with a low countertop for the transaction of business and a room immediately to the left looking like a horse stable with iron bars across its full-height door. A lone officer in military uniform greeted the two Americans. He shook hand with them both. "Is there a problem that you have?"

"Yes, we do. Our homes were broken into yesterday, and we would like to report it."

The officer nodded. "I will tell my boss. Where are you from?"

"We live at the Lagrange ranch."

Five minutes later the officer came out from the back with another officer in tow. Both of them shook hands with Lee and Robert. "Our boss is not in right now, but we will go out with you and look at the situation."

Lee and Robert agreed with the arrangement and they set out for Lagrange riding in the back of the police pickup truck. When they arrived the two officers took the full tour of the damages at both places, and then consulted each other. "We would like to speak with the workers that you have."

"With our workers? We only hired them on a couple of weeks ago."

"We would still like to speak with them."

Lee looked at Robert. "I wonder what this is all about? What should we do?"

"Go call them up, I guess."

While Lee kept the officers occupied, Robert left to get the workers up from the backfield. He found them hard at work cutting the brush that was being cleared for future grasslands.

"There are two officers at our place who want to see all of you."

"See us? Why do they want to see us?"

"They did not say, but they want to see all of you."

They shrugged their shoulders and followed Robert up to the house after gathering up their tools and bringing them along.

At the house the officers were waiting. They asked to speak with the workers alone. Robert and Lee didn't care, so they went on in the house while the officers spoke with the workers. Animated conversation issued with much waving of arms and gesturing. The men watched with interest from the house window as things heated up outside. Without warning one of the workers took off at a fast sprint across the field towards the river. This sent the officers into high action. They assaulted the remaining men with their rifle butts, swinging wildly from side to side. Robert and Lee came out of the house running. From what they could tell from the shouted Spanish, the officers wanted the workers to stay on the ground.

They stayed there, except for the one who was fast disappearing from sight still running towards the riverbank.

"What is the problem here?"

"These men are the ones who robbed you on Sunday."

"Robbed us on Sunday? That is not possible. They work for us. We trust them to take care of the place. It could not be them."

"Ah, you are ignorant Gringos. You trust people. Here in Honduras you do not trust anybody. These men and their families are the ones who robbed your homes on Sunday."

Lee and Robert stood there with looks of incredulity on their faces. "How do you know that these are the ones who robbed us?"

"We will show you. Come with us to their houses and we will show you. We know who did this."

With that the officers began loading the workers in the backs of the police vehicles, snapping handcuffs on each one as they forced them at gunpoint to board the trucks. After everyone was loaded they told Lee and Robert again, "Come with us, we will show."

Lee went into the house to let the others know what the plans were and where they were going. "We are going with the police to the homes of the workers. The police claim they are the ones who robbed us and want to search there, I guess. Robert and I are going along."

His wife Mary nodded in agreement. "If the police think so, then you should go, but this is all kind of strange. Why would our workers rob us? We trusted them."

"That's what I told the officers and they seem to think it a strange concept, trusting people. Anyway, we still have not seen whether this is really true or not. Let's see what we find at the workers' homes."

This time Lee and Robert rode in the front of the police vehicles, one in each truck. Robert knew where the workers lived and gave directions as they went. He got the impression that the officers already knew the way, as they barely paid attention to what he said. Together the two police vehicles wound their way out the Taft Road, turning right past Peter's store. A little past the Sanson entrance they turned left into a semi-road/trail back into the foothills. The officers put their vehicles into low gear as they pulled up and down the shallow inclines of the road.

Arriving at the workers' homes, a small complex of houses hidden behind one of the knolls a mile or so off the main road, they jumped out and motioned for Lee and Robert to join them. Leaving the other men sitting in the back of the police vehicles with their handcuffs on, they prepared to enter the houses. No one in the back of the trucks made any motions to flee. Maybe they thought there was little hope in running away with one's hands cuffed behind one's back. Yet their attitude was more of anger than hopelessness. They were looking darkly at each other as the police officers approached the houses with Lee and Robert following.

As the party of men got to the doorway of the first house, two women were blocking their way. "Please Senor Officer, why are you coming to our house? Why are our husbands handcuffed in the backs of your vehicles?"

"We will search your houses, Senora, for stolen goods. These two Gringos, their homes were broken into yesterday, and we have reason to believe that the items in question are here."

"This is simply not true. Our husbands would never steal anything."

"Please Senoras, step aside — we will search the house."

The one woman broke out into a loud wail of anguish. "Why are you doing this to us? You know the agreement that we have with you. Please, please do not do this. There will be much money in this for you all. My husband can do even better than he promised."

The two officers ignored her entirely. "Step aside, woman. We will search the house. We do not know what you are talking about. Your husbands have stolen many things, and we have come to find them."

With that they drew their weapons and forced the women out of the doorway. They motioned for Lee and Robert to follow as they headed across the dirt floor to the one room in the house that apparently served as the bedroom. The hard-packed dirt left no imprint of their shoes as they walked past the earthen cooking stove with its lid of a fifty-gallon drum for a top. Tortillas were still warming on the lid from the morning preparation of food. Out of the only window in the back a chicken flew off into the yard from where it was sitting on the sill. Pushing aside the cloth curtain that served as the door, the officers entered the room. Stacked from the floor to the ceiling, on all three sides, was American merchandize of all manner and sort: tools, hoes, rakes, kitchen utensils, and gunny bags of things still unpacked. The officers turned to Lee and Robert. "Is this yours?"

They could only look at each other as they nodded "yes."

CHAPTER TWENTY-THREE

LEE AND ROBERT were standing in Lee's living room at eleven o'clock, surrounded by their wives and children. Outside the sun was shining in all its third-world glory — that warmth so peculiar to the mountain elevations in the equatorial regions of the world. Close, but still not one's enemy, as it became in the summertime up north; friendly, but with that proper respect that should be shown to the poor sons of Adam. The weather cradled one as if to make up for all the wrongs in the world. It was hard to be afraid on such a day. Those gathered in the living room were not feeling fear so much as astonishment at the news the men brought.

"You mean to tell us that it was our workers who robbed our homes on Sunday?"

"Yes, I am afraid that is who it was. We saw the stolen goods ourselves. The police took everything they could find in the three houses at the complex where our workers live along with the workers themselves. All of it barely fit into their two trucks, but they somehow got it in. I am not sure that everything was there that we lost, but the police have what was not sold or sent off somewhere else. Robert and I helped look for things and rode back with the police after they loaded things up. We were dropped off at the end of Taft road and walked in."

"But how could they have robbed us? They were such nice people. Look at how hard they worked around the place. There was nothing they would not do for us."

"That may all be true. I feel the same way, but Lee and I were at their places ourselves with the officers. Our stuff was there. We saw it. They are the ones who robbed us."

"Why did the police not bring our things back right now?"

"They said it all needed to be catalogued and recorded at the police station."

"Well, this is another country, I guess. They don't do that in the States, do they?"

"No. It did seem a little strange, but what could we do? Another thing that was strange was what one of the women said just before the officers entered the house. My Spanish is not too good, but it sure sounded to me like she was trying to strike a bargain with the officer."

Lee chimed in, "I thought so too. Something about her husband offering them a better deal if they did not search the house."

"Wonder what kind of deal that would be?"

"This whole thing is just fishy all the way through. How did the officers know this morning to go after our workers? They seemed just a little too certain it was the workers to be acting on a mere suspicion. It looked like they knew for sure. Then there was the attitude of the workers, too. Did you notice Lee? They all looked more angry than scared."

Lee thought for a minute and then agreed. "Now that I think of it, that is right."

"Do you think the police are planning on keeping our things?"

"I sure hope not. The officer said they would be by in a few hours. We will have to wait and see if they come."

From there the two families went on about their business for the day. Some of Lee's girls ran over to Vern's place to get their cousins up-to-date on the news. The adults found plenty of other things to keep busy with.

At three o'clock the police vehicles came up the lane from the Taft road. Dust rolled up the driveway after them as the two trucks made a fast and grand entrance into Lee's place. Climbing out the passenger's side of the lead truck, the sergeant introduced himself to those at Lee's house and presented the goods with a flourish of his hand.

"You will forgive me that I could not be here this morning when you came to the office, but I was otherwise occupied. Did not my officers do a good job? Your things have been found and those responsible have been arrested."

Everyone, including the other police officers who were along, proceeded to help unload the items into the house and storage shed where they belonged. The sergeant just stood there and kept smiling as the others unloaded. Robert's things were set aside on the ground until the bottom of the truck beds could be seen. Then they loaded Robert's items back up and sent them over to his house with Lee's two oldest boys. The sergeant stayed behind to speak with Lee.

"You have a reward posted for the return of your goods. Is this not true?"

"Ah, no, not really. We never got to talk about it, but we are glad that the things are back."

"My officers told me you and the other man spoke this morning when you came to report this crime of a large money reward for the return of your stolen items. I believe this is true. You and the other man told them so. This has been a great favor that the things have been found so soon, and there were many things stolen. You will find everything there that was taken except for some minor items, maybe. We got the full confession out of these thieves. They are really small-time people. They do not know how to steal things well. That is why we catch them so easy. With a little persuasion they have told us everything and where they have hidden everything. My officers went back to the thieves' homes to search again, and also in the hills by their house. We believe everything has been found by now. If not, then when more things are found these will also be returned when we find them."

Lee was finding it hard to know what to say. "This thing of the money. We certainly are grateful to you and to your officers for finding our things. I suppose we can give a reward for their return. We have just not spoken of it yet, but I will speak to Robert and the others about it."

The sergeant smiled and smartly nodded his head. "I will be

expecting your decision then in several days, yes. In the meantime the thieves remain in the prison for a long time. Your large reward will ensure that they stay there for a very long time — maybe a year, maybe two years. Our prisons are very good — hard ground to sleep on. We keep our prisoners from wanting to come back too soon. We do not feed them, so you do not have to worry about having that being an extra expense to you. Unless the family feeds them, they not eat. They all get very thin in prison. A year, huh, a year is a long time to be in prison here. But your reward for the stolen goods will help that these men not steal again. Yes, I am looking forward to when you come in a few days to my office. We will speak then of how long the sentence will be for these thieves. When you have brought the reward."

Lee cleared his throat. "Excuse me, Sir, but what if we do not bring a reward in for you? We have not really spoken of it yet, and maybe it would not be a good idea."

"No reward." The sergeant's face flushed. "No reward. No, Don Stuzman, there will be a reward. Yes, there will be one. If there is no reward, as you and the other man promised, then, well, we usually shoot the prisoners. That is what we do. Yes, we take them back to the hills and shoot them. That is what we do with thieves here, but you are rich gringos. You would not want that to happen. You have much money, do you not? You can give a good reward. That way the thieves do not get shot, and they do not seek revenge on you."

"What do you mean, seek revenge on us? We have not done anything to them."

"Oh yes, if we shoot them, their relatives will blame you because they will know that you did not pay the reward. Us? They do not blame us for shooting them. They will know that it was your fault."

Lee was at a loss for words again. "I will tell the others what you have said, and we will let you know what we decide."

"Yes, that is good. You will decide."

With that the sergeant left off the conversation and started walking towards Robert's place. Before he got very far the two police vehicles took off from Robert's driveway, made the u-turn, and headed out towards Taft road. At the intersection of Robert and Lee's driveway they picked up the sergeant, discharged the two gringo boys from the back of the lead pickup, and took off. In five minutes they disappeared from sight, leaving a cloud of dust hanging in the air all along the dirt driveway from the intersection to the little footbridge where the trees hid them.

Lee met his boys coming up the driveway, told them what to do as far as immediate chores, and then continued walking towards Robert's place. Robert met him at the door of the house.

"Is this not great, Lee? We can be so thankful to God for how he has brought everything back to us. Elisabeth has yet to find anything missing, but I am sure some things must be. It would be unreal if everything were fully recovered. I am so thankful to God for what he has done. We could have suffered the loss, I guess, if it was his will, but this is so good of God."

"Uh, Robert," Lee interrupted, "I think we need to talk."

"What do you mean, talk? Is something wrong, Lee?"

"Yes, there is something wrong. The sergeant said that we told the officers this morning that a reward had been offered. A large reward for the return of these stolen items."

"But we did no such thing."

"I know, but that is what he said, and the sergeant would not take no for an answer. The sergeant told me that the reward would be used to determine the thieves' — or rather our workers' — time in jail."

"But will there be a trial, a sentence, and all that?"

"It sounded like there won't. Only the reward and then the prison sentence of maybe a year or two. Also something was said about their upkeep in jail not costing us anything. Apparently the relatives must feed them or they starve."

"No, this is unbelievable. What is going on? You know what? We will just not pay the reward, or whatever it is called."

"In that case the sergeant said the thieves, that is our workers, would be shot."

"They would be shot? That is ridiculous. They cannot just shoot them."

"Apparently they can. Remember this is the third world, and we do not really know that much about how things are done down here. The sergeant also said that if the workers were shot the relatives would be looking to take revenge on us because they would know that we did not pay the reward money."

"I cannot believe this. This is incredible. Shooting people, what are they talking about? You cannot just shoot people for stealing things. This is ridiculous."

"Yes, you already said that. Now don't we need to talk about this with the others?"

"Talk? I think it will take a little more than talking to get us out of this mess. How in the world can simple things become so complicated? Someone has stolen from us. We now know who it was, and the things are back. Yet we are here talking about the thieves being shot or of reward money that will place them in prison without food for a long time. What is wrong with this world down here?"

"We need to talk to Vern about this."

"Okay. I guess we do."

They met that evening after six o'clock at Vern's place. Outside, the night settled in. A full moon was rising over the horizon just above the riverbank where the thieves came up on Sunday morning. It shed its beams over a world hushed and waiting. The round size of the moon that night was immense even for this country. In Vern's yard the younger children were already playing by its light, confident that as soon as the moon rose higher they would be able to see even better for their game. Tonight it was "wolf." One person was it and closed his eyes at the chosen tree and counted to one hundred, enough time for everyone else to hide. From there all was fair game as the wolf went looking for his prey. Any child sighted by the wolf and his name correctly called out got only one chance to beat the wolf back to the tree. If he got there first, he was safe. If the wolf got there first, then the child also became a wolf and joined the wolf pack in the search of the others. It was extremely difficult to outrun the wolf, who usually kept himself well placed to make a fast dash to the tree. The number of caught children soon swelled the wolf pack and brought each round of the game to a conclusion.

Inside, the adults were gathered in the living room discussing the issue at hand. What was to be done about paying the reward for the return of their goods? Everyone joined in.

"This is simply wrong, making us pay for something the police should be doing anyway."

"These police are corrupt, that is all there is to it."

"They must have planned this all from the start."

"It is all about money, that's what it is."

"Makes me think now that they knew who did this before we ever reported it."

"What was the wife talking about at the door of the house — this thing about making a better deal? Does that mean they made a deal with the police?"

"It sure looks like it. Then the police must have double-crossed them when we walked in this morning. What do you think it was, Lee — our clothes or something?"

"Neither of us was wearing anything expensive, and we certainly weren't driving anything expensive."

"Must just have been this rich gringo mentality they have down here. Everyone who is white is considered rich."

"Must have been when the two of us walked in that they thought about the money. Why didn't we think of that, Robert? Just one of us should have gone."

"It may not have made any difference at all, for all we know. Something did cause them to change their plans and go for bigger money."

"Think there is any chance of making these accusations stick to the police if we tell someone, like maybe their higher authorities?"

"Hardly a chance in the world, I would think. With this kind of corruption going on it may go who knows how high."

"What do we do then? Keep our mouths shut and just take it? This is awful."

"I'm afraid something in that order is all we can do. If we accuse the police of this it could just make things worse and still not solve our current problem."

"Okay, so tell us what our current problem is again."

"The police want money, and how can we ethically pay what amounts to a bribe?"

Vern cleared his throat. "If you had just listened to me from the start and not gone to the police, we would not be in this predicament now. Our people have always felt a deep distrust of the police. This just goes to show why this has always been so. Up in the north the police have become so nice that we have easily gone to them for help. But even then we have questioned the wisdom of it. Our roots go deep into the conviction that God's people should never depend on the secular force for their physical protection, but instead trust in God. Look at the story of the Jews when the time came for them to return from exile. They had miles of territory to cross with their possessions and much silver and gold that the king gave them for rebuilding when they arrived back at their beloved country. This territory was full of robbers, thieves, and killers. Yet Ezra and his men were afraid to ask the king for soldiers to protect them, because they had just told the king how great their God was. Instead they fasted and prayed for certain days and then made the journey without any soldiers from the king going with them. All of them got safely to Jerusalem without any loss of life or property. It seems to me that this is part of the guiding vision of our forefathers and why they were against trusting in the armed forces for their protection."

"Well, I guess that is something we should have thought of sooner, but it just seemed so natural to go to the police with the problem. Any suggestions now?"

Vern paused again like he was thinking. "I think I have a suggestion. I think there is something we could do that would clear up this whole matter."

"And that would be?"

"We can go to the police and tell them we are sorry that we started this whole thing and offer to pay bail for the arrested thieves. That would free the workers without any prison sentence like paying the reward would. It would also give the police some money, which seems to be what they are after. What do you think? Sounds like a good idea, right?"

Lee and Robert looked at each other and thought awhile. "Maybe that is what we should do."

They talked far into the night about many things but came up with no better plan. In the morning Robert and Lee found themselves at the police station again.

A very happy sergeant greeted them. "Yes, you have come to pay the reward. You are glad that my men have returned your things to you. This is good. Now both of us are very happy — you because all of your things are back, me because you will pay a good reward. How much will the reward be? Before you say, look over here at these men and think of how long you would have them stay behind bars. These are wicked men in this prison who have stolen many things from you. Now we have them here safe and sound where they cannot make trouble anymore. Think of how good this will be, and of how long they should stay here. Much time, I think it should be. Their relatives have already brought them food once, so you need not worry about a thing. They will eat well, no doubt. Ha, it will be a long time that they stay here. Is this not true? You will pay a big reward, I think. Yes, you will."

The sergeant rubbed his hands together in anticipation while he looked at them, waiting for an answer. Robert was sore afraid to break the news, but he would have to start somewhere, so he started in slowly.

"There is some mistake, I am afraid. We have not come to pay a reward."

"Not come to pay a reward? How can this be? These men will die. Yes, they will die today, and their relatives will be looking for you. They will hear the news and know who is to be blamed for their deaths. In the nighttime, swish, they will cut your throats, all of you. You must pay a reward. It is the thing that must be done."

"No, we will pay no reward." Robert was getting braver. "What we will do is pay the bail for these men, so that they can come out of jail."

"Pay their bail? Why, this is madness. You not pay their bail. No pay bail — these men belong in prison for a long time."

Robert was firm. "You see, Sergeant, we are sorry about having come to you in the first place. Our faith teaches us to place our trust in God for protection and not in the use of arms. We should never have come to your officers, and we are sorry. To right this wrong we would like to pay the bail for these men so that they can come out of prison and return to their families. We are willing now to place our trust in God for his protection over all of our things that we possess."

The sergeant was utterly flabbergasted. "You will not pay a reward, but you will pay a bail? You want these men to go free?"

"Yes, that is right."

"How much bail will you offer? There are six men in there that stole from you. It will take a big bail to get them out of prison."

Lee named a price in US dollars. It seemed like a small sum to him, but he thought they needed to start somewhere.

"You will pay that amount for these men's bail?"

Lee thought a moment about raising the number, but thought against it. He decided to go one more round on the amount before he raised the sum.

"Yes, that is what we will pay."

"You will pay that much. Then the offer is acceptable with me. I will tell the prisoners."

Fifteen minutes later the money exchanged hands and the workers were let out of the cell. Without a word they left, looking backwards several times before they turned into the street and disappeared out of sight.

"Well, we have done it, and now we will see what happens."

"You don't have any doubts, do you?"

"I think that sergeant held no intention of shooting anyone. He just wanted the money. Did you see how quickly he accepted the offer? I was ready to give twice that amount."

"Yes, I saw that. We will just have to see. I sure hope it all turns out all right."

CHAPTER TWENTY-FOUR

FOR THE REST of 1971, the news spread like wildfire hither and yonder, into every nook and cranny of the world, it seemed. Gringos paid the bail for those who robbed them to get out of jail. Homer Esh could hardly contain himself. He said he never heard of something like this. Who ever thought of this being done? He told Elmer out by the shop while the generator was running.

"We might as well put out a welcome sign to one and all. 'Come rob us. You are welcome. Take what you want. We will do you no harm. Help yourself to whatever we have.'"

A week later Lee and Robert were both hit again with a break-in. This time it was not on Sunday but during the night. The thieves simply took out the slatted glass casement windows everyone uses in Honduras. If you pry hard enough, each pane can be worked loose from its metal frame and dropped out. Once one piece is out, the others quickly follow. This time no one went to the police.

Vern was hit the week after that, and then Albert, who lived the farthest south. All the break-ins came through the windows. Two weeks later Lee came out in the morning to find the windows out again and the tools gone. Still no one went to the police. They did show up, though, at Homer Esh's shop and talked about bar designs for windows. Homer went over to look but was still thinking about things when the shed behind Peter's place was broken into. From then on it was full steam ahead with the bar design. In two days they arrived at a final conclusion for the plans. For two weeks Homer and Elmer worked on little else than making bars for everyone's windows. All their other work was forced to take second place in their effort to slow down the pace of the break-ins. Homer got Jason to cut some of the metal in the afternoons after school and on Saturdays. It was a repetitive job easily grasped by a youngster.

The bar design was a simple affair made to fit the rectangular shape of the window with a steel frame of ¼-inch by one-inch metal turned on edge. This rectangular outline was then filled up with the same size metal, creating crossbars running horizontal and vertical through the frame. What was left were small spaces through which no one could crawl and barely reach very far inside. Some of the people chose the squares to be evenly stacked on top of each other, but most of them chose a random design. Homer even tried a version in which the spaces were larger with a tapered piece of metal sticking up in the middle to prevent someone from using it as access. The result was too much of a prison look, and that design did not catch on. After completing the frame in whichever design was chosen, four side legs were attached on each corner with flares going off to the outside through which carriage bolts could be run. These bolts were run completely through the exterior wall into the inside where the nut was fastened. Since the houses were not built according to the finished specs of the north anyway, the result both inside and out fit the overall décor just fine.

In the middle of building their bar orders, Homer and Elmer were pausing one evening around 4:30 to assess where they were with the time schedule they set for themselves. Everything looked okay to them, and Elmer had just left for home when the manager from the sawmill north of Guateteca pulled in. He brought along the main shaft from his saw on the back of his truck. The length and thickness was what caught one's attention first. It was all that one man could do to move it off and carry it around.

The local sawmills operated their saw blades by attaching them to end of this shaft. For the whole length of the shaft keyway was cut in. This keyway was used to attach two holding clamps, one on each end, and the pulley that ran the thing. The one end of the shaft was threaded. This was where the saw blade was attached. It was this end that was broken off. The manager did not even bother to bring along the broken piece. It was obvious what the problem was.

This was an occurrence that the sawmill operators were all too familiar with. The saw blades were immense affairs attached to the threaded end of the shaft. From time to time the pressure and force of sawing the huge logs would break the blade off of the threaded end of the shaft. When this happened, the entire shaft needed to be taken to a shop to have new threads cut into the end. The shaft was purchased at an extra length than what was needed, so that this repair could be done several times without having to purchase a new full-length section of shaft. The sawmill manager spent all day taking the shaft out, and now he said he needed it repaired by morning. Cost was no consideration, he said. The job just had to be done so the saw could be placed in operation by the next day.

Homer knew when necessity trumped everything else, and he showed the manager where to place the shaft. The manager said he would wait while Homer ate supper. At six o'clock Homer fired the generator back up and got to work. He worked all night and by five o'clock the next morning the manager left with his repaired shaft. Honduras had never seen anything like this. That a man would work all night for any price was unheard of. That the job would be done properly in that period of time was an even greater story. The manager told the story around and it spread the length and breadth of the area. Homer's reputation as the maestro of steel and of the lathe was cemented.

It would take more than reputation, though, to stop the thieves. With bars on the windows they just kicked in the doors. When those were replaced with solid wood frame doors, they bored around the locks in circular patterns until the piece fell out and they could open the door or reach inside if a bar was placed across the door. The Amish learned how to place solid steel plates around the lock. This plate needed to be wide enough so that no hand could reach a bar placed on the inside or large enough so that drilling around it would take all night — not that anyone can remember it ever being tried when the plate was of a fairly large size. Here the proverb was proved true, that we are best at what we care about. The locals manifested energy and ingenuity when practicing thievery, but apparently drilling around a large steel plate in small hole increments was too much for even that spurt of enthusiasm.

Before the steel plates were placed on the doors, some of boys took to sleeping out in the barns and businesses where the worst break-ins were happening. The soft sound of a wood bit going around and around in the door above your sleeping bag is guaranteed to cause some tense moments. After waking up and nudging each other, the boys conferred in whispers as to the proper course of action. All the brave and bold courses of action planned the day before, when the sun was shining and no pieces of wood shaving were falling on their heads, fled far away. They settled for simple yells. In the morning they imagined these to be blood curdling in strength and power, but in reality they were not. It was enough, though, for the drill smith to cease his work for the night. After the running footsteps faded away, the boys checked their watches with flashlights covered in cupped hands and managed to get some sleep for the rest of the night. The next day their fathers belatedly got the steel plates installed. Jason heard all about the story from Matthew.

Elmer kept telling Homer about the racket out by his barn. Not that it happened every night, but often enough to keep Elmer from getting sleep when he wished to. No one was succeeding in breaking in that Elmer could tell. He worked, of course, at Homer's machine shop and so obtained first access to bars and steel. His barn was well protected with them. The racket was getting to be a nuisance, though. Elmer's dog would raise a fuss, and then sounds would follow that could be anything in the dark. Elmer put up with the mystery for a while but finally got tired of it. The next night when the dog got going again he snuck out the back door with the revolver no one but his wife knew he possessed. Hoping with great hope that the neighbors would not hear him, he fired the thing twice into the air. There was a pause in which everything was still, and then a satisfying thrashing occurred in the bushes behind the barn, receding in the direction of the Taft Road. Elmer smiled deeply to himself and told the story next morning to Homer with far too much satisfaction even for his own comfort. After enjoying themselves fully with thoughts of the frightened fellows running through the bushes and tearing themselves up good in their haste, they mentioned the matter no further and kept the story to themselves. There were no more noises from then on out by Elmer's barn.

Jason heard this story too, firsthand, but told no one. There was no one really to tell it too, besides, who would have believed a little boy anyway. People talked right in front of him like he did not matter. Why would it matter what he said?

Homer himself stayed ahead of the curve. Because of his generator he could obtain ready access to electric power that the others could not. Homer wanted to put up lights for security and visibility around his place. The problem was that the generator must run in order to have electricity. It took a lot of fuel to run the big diesel engine, so it could not be run all the time, and for that matter the thing made a tremendous racket. The roar of the diesel could be heard almost to Peter's place and past Elmer's on the Lagrange side. Homer was determined, though, that the correct route to go was security lighting. Did not the scriptures say that evil deeds were done in the darkness? What better way was there of thwarting them than to throw light on the subject? With this in mind, Homer went to thinking. There needed to be a way to start the generator up on demand, day or night. This could be done easily from the shop, but that was not the answer. Who wanted to run out to the shop while evil men were practicing their arts in order to throw light on them? One might be accosted in the process of throwing the light. His solution was to run wires underground from the shop to the house, placing the wiring and switches right beside his headboard. One switch was needed to start the diesel and one switch to stop it. To top things off, he mounted a siren above the rafters in the engine room of the shop. This required the placement of a third switch.

When this all was ready he placed security lights all along his driveway and in front of the shop, wiring them into the power source from the generator. To keep the lights from coming on in the daytime when the generator was running, he placed a switch breaker in the line. This breaker needed turning on each evening when he closed up the shop for the night. The bother of remembering to throw the breaker was well rewarded, though, when the dog barked in the middle of the night. Homer reached over his headboard and pressed the button. You could not hear the starter working or grinding from the house. Homer knew the timing needed to start the diesel from starting it during the week. If you held the button for too short a time, nothing happened. If you held it too long, the starter could be burned. But held for just the right amount of time the diesel roared to life. The result was that, at will, Homer could flood his place with light. One night soon after installing the lights they revealed three men approaching the shop from the back, facing not towards the church house but towards the west river. He lay on the siren and the wail was heard way over at Peter's and half of Lagrange. With his lights, the roar of his diesel, and the wail of his siren, Homer kept his shop from being broken into. The effect was also such that it threw a cordon of safety for a quarter of a mile to the north and on each side of him. For some reason it never reached to the south. Homer believed in praying for protection from God, but he also believed that one should turn on the lights when it lay in one's power to do so.

❦

Sometime later Jason heard his father and mother talking about it after supper. There was trouble with the Bishop. Bishop Bontrager no longer wanted to continue his trips down to Honduras.

"He will do some more," Homer said, "but he wants to cut back, probably entirely. I'm sure it has something to do with all this English singing he has to put up with."

"How do you know that Homer? It could just be the travel, or maybe he does not like to be away from his family. What is being done about it?"

"There is talk of ordaining our own bishop."

"Our own bishop, that would be wonderful."

"Maybe, and maybe not. All depends on who gets it. If it's someone liberal, who knows."

"Well, I am sure God will give us a good bishop," Rachel concluded.

Jason, listening to the conversation, was not too interested. He was more concerned with getting a good night's sleep.

CHAPTER TWENTY-FIVE

IT WAS IN February of 1972, at two o'clock on a Friday afternoon, that Taca Airlines flight 537 circled the capital of Honduras for landing. Only the crackerjack pilots with experience under their belts were used by the airlines to fly into Tegucigalpa. It was an airfield located in the heart of a city surrounded completely by range after range of Honduras mountains.

"It is one of the world's shortest runways for this size plane," the bishop heard a flight stewardess say to an inquiring passenger. "Our pilot is the best though. He is used to flying under all kinds of conditions."

"What if the weather is bad?"

"If the weather is bad enough to affect the landing, we would not have left for the flight."

The plane came in from the north going south-southwest. It cleared the last ring of foothills by a mere three hundred feet and immediately began the descent into the airfield. Banking sharply to the east it hugged the ground, houses and knolls rushing by right outside the plane windows. Bishop Willy Bontrager was hanging on to his seat in 23A. He did not care to look out the window, nor did he care for much else about this trip. Glancing out of the small window he caught sight of the city police standing by their posts as they blocked the street in front of the airstrip. That was all the time there was to remember why the road needed blocking, as the wheels of the plane hit the runway with a sharp bump.

"Just in case we come in too low."

Immediately the pilot reversed the engines with full force and hit the brakes hard. This was necessary in order to get stopped on the short runway. All passengers were forced forward in their seats by the accelerated braking. It felt to the bishop like a fitting metaphor for the nature of this country and the church work that drew him here.

He got his bag down from the overhead compartment and headed down the plane steps. Jesse Stolsfus met him on the other side of customs. "Glad to see you again. Was the landing okay?"

"Good as can be expected. I have not learned to enjoy it yet."

They got out to the settlement by the usual time. It was already well dark. He was staying at Jesse's place this time. It is customary in cases like this to give the bishop a rotating place to stay. Never was he put up in a hotel or other such English place. Always in the home of someone, and to avoid the appearance of partiality a different home each time he visited. This, of course, only added to the bishop's discomfort. If he had known where he was going to stay, a sense of familiarity would have aided his relaxation efforts. In this case he was always a little tense till he became familiar with his surroundings and with his host. This was usually about the time he left in the good cases and never in the bad cases. Not that any overt conflict would ever erupt, but the feelings were there depending on personalities and church politics.

With a new community such as was being formed at Guateca, it was important to have all the appearances and evidences of impartiality in full view. A new community has yet to form its parties and sides. The bishop, therefore, was ill advised to choose any particular faction, both because it was the right thing to do and because he did not know how the factions would develop.

"It is strange," thought the bishop, "how freshness and newness brings out the best in men and women, be it a baby's smile or a new beginning in the church world. We must all have been made to face the sunrise and to begin each day on our knees. Would that things could stay like this rather than rising into the chasms and fissures of the settled communities."

"Saturday and Sunday are going to be full days," the bishop mentioned after supper. "Would it be okay if I retired early?"

Jesse gladly agreed and directed the accommodations to be made ready. He then saw to it that things were kept quiet around the house. This may have seemed like a difficult thing to do with eight children under the age of twelve, but at the Stolsfus' house it was not. A simple talk to the children by their mother was all it took. The Stolsfus family began its child training early, and at times like this, the results were there for all to see. Jesse did not believe there was such a thing as an un-trainable child. He gave his children an unbreakable sense of belonging and an unbendable requirement for obedience. The one, he said, did not work without the other.

"With the two together," Jesse was wont to say, "you have a home where righteousness can dwell."

The bishop for one was thankful. He noted the quietness and was comforted from his weariness and the weight of his official duties. Early Saturday morning he was up, eating breakfast with the family, and left with Jesse to begin his Saturday duties. Those duties would include a visit with both ministers, Robert and Vern individually, and then with deacon Steve Stolsfus. From there he would have supper at Peter's place, followed by more church discussions, no doubt. At issue was the ordination of a local bishop for the congregation at Guateca. To accomplish this there was the first step of an ordination of another minister. In Amish church circles, a bishop could be ordained only from the minister pool, and the minister pool needed sufficient size. Two was not enough, and deacons did not normally qualify. Technically they might in some cases, although the matter was a little fussy in the verbally handed-down rules. In any case, it was unlikely that anyone would vote for the deacons when the time came to cast the ballots.

Bishop Bontrager thought it better to ordain another minister first before proceeding to the bishop ordination, and Vern, Robert, and Steve concurred. As a courtesy to Steve, the bishop mentioned that he would permit congregational votes for him when the time came to cast ballots. Steve was grateful for this even though they all knew it would be a long shot. He took it as a high compliment from the bishop, as indeed it was.

211

Also on the plate was a detailed discussion about the status of the congregation at Guateteca. Jesse was under a great desire to discuss the status with the bishop and thought seriously of broaching the subject as he escorted the bishop over to Vern's place, but he decided to stick with protocol. Little good could come from going outside the accepted channels, and besides the bishop might resent it. This could do little but harm the cause as Jesse saw it. Besides, there would be plenty of time later in its proper place to discuss all of this — maybe at supper this evening, as Jesse knew that his father also invited them over for the evening, as the host family. Jesse saw the bishop to Vern's place and then left him. He would be able to find his way around the community on his own. This was his third trip down.

Vern welcomed the bishop, and they left immediately for Robert's place. Even while walking, the bishop was ready to get right down to business. "So, where are we at, Vern?"

"Things are going well, I think."

"What about all this thieving? Are the people becoming discouraged?"

"I believe not. It has slowed down quite a bit, now that we have taken measures."

"That would be what kind of measures? Surely no one is shooting, are they?"

"No, of course not. You don't really think that any of us would use weapons, do you? Why that is completely out of the question. We have not even gone to the police since that first time."

"Well, just checking. There are just a lot of strange things going on."

"Strange? Like what?"

"Things like living behind bars on the windows, and all the doors look like steel plates to me. Even Jesse placed bars on his windows. It did give me a safer feeling, though, and that is what really bothers me, I guess. What was I doing in a country where I needed bars on the windows to feel safe? There is just something about this place down here. I notice it every time I come down. It is like I am in another world where different rules apply."

Vern did not know what to say. "Well, we live here, of course."

The bishop nodded and continued. "That is what I mean, too. You live here and I don't expect you to notice it as much, of course. Have you any idea how much you have changed since you moved down here? I doubt that you do, because of course you live here. I, on the other hand, really notice it. I notice it every time I come here. Coming straight from the States, I guess the contrast is more evident. You do things so differently. Little things. At first it bothers me, and then in a day or so it kind of goes away. Like right now, I was wearing my hat yesterday when I flew in, but this morning when Jesse brought me over, he was not wearing his, so I left it at his place. Here we are now without our hats, just walking down the road. Yesterday I never would have thought of being without it, but now this morning it feels like the right thing to do. What is really happening? If I tried to explain this to the home church, you can imagine how it would go. It worries me, it really does, and that is not the only thing like that."

Vern was thinking and finally said, "Do you really think it is wrong to go without hats?"

The bishop just sadly shook his head. "See, there you go. Asking questions. Is there something wrong with it, you ask? Don't you see what you are doing? This is exactly what I mean. It goes to the point of what I am saying. How can you even ask such a question? Is there something wrong with it? You even have me thinking about it. Is there something wrong with it? Can't you see what is happening? We are thinking and questioning about things that would be unthinkable at home. It really worries me what is happening down here. This just has got to stop. The problem is, I am not sure what it is, or what must be stopped. It is the air and atmosphere of the place. It changes you, just being here. Here it seems like the world is closer to you, more in your face, more like it possesses some other purpose than what I understand."

"Would it be like living in a fish bowl up north, or that they look at us like we are a specimen lying on the table?"

"Yes, that might be a good way of saying it — not that I have ever been a fish, but yes, that could be part of it. We, meaning we the Amish, of course, live the plain life in the north sort of as a great experiment. At least that is how the world looks at us. We try to live our life as a work of perfection within the culture. It is removed, like somewhere else, from where everyone else is. The problem is that we have to be left alone — no, more than that. We need help from the culture for that to happen. In the north the culture helps us. It is in agreement with our experiment. It goes along with our need for isolation. It even protects and encourages us. There it lends a hand. Here there is no helping hand. The bubble of protection is gone. It is as if things can no longer be practiced in a vacuum. They must now be practiced as if we were in the real world.

"Here, I feel, just as you do, drawn to questions. There the need for questions does not exist. Reality is so much more fixed, secure, and unquestionable. Maybe it is not just that the need for questions does not exist, but that we cannot find that need even if we looked for it. To find the need, one would have to break out of the protected abstract into the real world, and that we would never do because we believe that world to be the enemy. So questions are only possible when we contact the world, and they are the sign of ultimate betrayal to ourselves and to our way of life. That is exactly what it is, Vern. That is the problem here. There is no separation between you and the world. You are experiencing the world directly without any buffer between you and it. There has not yet been time to build your own reality.

"Do you not see, Vern? Our forefathers experienced a buffer put in place for them by the persecution they were under. It was a persecution long enough and severe enough for them to have both the motivation and the time to build their own reality. The world helped them, Vern. It helped them. Sure, it is no longer helping us in the north with persecution, but it is helping us just the same. It is helping us with approval. Down here in the third world, you have neither of those things. There is neither persecution nor approval of our separate status. Here, I think the world actually wants to be like us.

"If you are to survive, I think, you will need one or the other.

You must somehow find it, Vern — you must or you may not survive. Yet I wonder whether it can be done?"

It was all getting a little deep for Vern. He just nodded his head and was glad that they had arrived at Robert's place. He really understood little of what the bishop was saying. Earlier he thought he was following the conversation, but now it lost him. At Robert's place he knew that things would be brought up about ordinations and church rules. Those things he could understand and discuss at length. As to these things the bishop spoke of, he did not really know. It was high time, he thought, to steer things in another direction.

"We do like it down here. Everyone as far as I know is really into keeping this congregation going. Even with the thieving going on, the people still want to stay and see an Amish church community be established here in Honduras. I think you will find in talking with some of the people today that the vote to proceed with the ordination will be almost unanimous."

The bishop nodded his head. That was about what he expected. With the enthusiasm level that he sensed every time he was here, it came as no surprise. What could he do even as a bishop with a unanimous vote from the congregation? That was unstoppable in the Amish world. "Let's go talk to Robert, then. We still have a long way to go with our planning."

Two hours later it was decided and Bishop Bontrager returned to Jesse's place for the night. The ordination for a minister would be tomorrow. As was customary the new minister would then be allowed to preach for a year or so, at which time Bishop Bontrager would return and a bishop could be ordained from the three ministers and their one deacon. That would then be it. He was getting tired of the whole thing with the trips down and the pressures of the new congregation. Bishop Bontrager was promising them only one more trip. Robert and Vern quickly concurred with the plans and they all hoped nothing would come up to interfere.

Chapter Twenty-Six

The Sunday morning after their planning went as well as could be expected. It was now a year and two weeks later in 1973, and Bishop Bontrager was back. Standing there in the church house the bishop was reaching the halfway point of his sermon. He was approaching the time of the judges in his story of the Old Testament. The church house was well filled by the membership as well as many visitors from the local population. Today was the big day, and even the natives could understand the excitement. A bishop was to be ordained.

"A bishop," they said to each other when the plans for this Sunday were announced several weeks before. Jason, who hung around a lot with the locals and his father's worker, heard all about it.

They well knew what it meant — honor, respect, and above all power. Power to sway people and their actions. Power to officiate at the public services and to command the timing and events that guided the lives of the church people. The locals knew what it meant mainly from their Catholic backgrounds and experience — the incense, the highest place of seating, and the reverence when the man of God was present. Of course here there was no incense, but they thought the rest might be.

Now Bishop Bontrager was standing at the pulpit in this church house of Amish people. He was still not used to the idea even after having been here a few times. The feelings would have been much better if he were standing in the archway of someone's home, turning first to the men seated in the living room and then to the women in the dining room, or even if it had been a barn. Here he felt so out of place, like he did not belong in this sterile environment. At home in a barn service there would have been the soft smell of hay coming out of the haymow, the sound of the cows shuffling in the barnyard, and a chicken or two making noises not so far in the background. Here there was none of it. Sure the people were dressed up in the normal way, just like home, but it was still different. Anyway, he shoved the thoughts from his mind and got them back on his sermon. Not that he was thinking too much on this particular sermon.

It was the sermon all Amish ministers and bishops preached at communion time. He himself preached it so many times before, it kind of came by itself. You began at Genesis, with the first minister, who told the story in his own words, up to the time of Noah. The second minister took the story up to the time of Christ, or twelve o'clock. After a break for lunch, the service continued with the bishop taking the story through the New Testament from the birth to the death of Christ. All of this without once opening the Bible or consulting a single note. Life in the Amish world is spent without computers, video games, or major musical instruments, but it is not spent without its drama. The good Amish ministers pour much energy and effort into the memorization of scripture and the structure of their sermons. Sermon time is the high point — the opera of Amish living. It is the glue that holds much together. Without the oratory of their preachers, it would be fair to say that Amish life would not long exist. Hardly would one think that any of them had read Dale Carnegie on the art of public speaking, but it is truly a unique experience to hear a good Amish preacher stand and with one hand do battle with the world and with the other call down heaven to the earth. It has been said that the German language was made for war and for poetry. The good Amish preacher is trained in the arts of both.

As the Bishop preached he remembered back to over a year ago when the ordination for a minister was held. At that time, like they were doing today, custom had been followed and communion and ordination coupled together. It consisted of the usual

Old Testament stories in the morning, the New Testament stories in the afternoon, the serving of communion, the ordination from the lot of candidates, and then the feet washing for the close of the service. It had been a full schedule then and it would be a full schedule today. He still remembered how united and excited these people had been and were. That Sunday he had preached only in the afternoon. A bishop was always required to preach the afternoon New Testament sermon and so would not normally preach until that time. Today Bishop Bontrager decided to do the last morning sermon plus the afternoon sermon himself. It would expedite things and give him more control over the timing of the services. Besides it was not a big thing to him; he knew the sermons nearly by heart.

So with 11:30 approaching he sped up his sermon towards its conclusion, hitting only the high points. As he spoke he remembered back to a year ago when he had completed his afternoon sermon and then served communion. Afterwards he had called attention, as he would today, to what they were about to do. Sitting down, he had waited while Vern, Robert, and Steve passed out the ballot slips. Women and men voted, and it took three votes to get into the lot. If you were a member, you were given the paper and wrote a name of your choice on the paper, folded it, and gave it back to whichever minister was gathering up ballots in your vicinity. He recalled how Vern and Steve took the ballots out to the adjoining room to count them, while Robert waited with the bishop. Ten minutes later they were back with three songbooks. They had held a whispered conference with him, but the congregation already knew part of what they were saying. Three men had made the lot. He remembered how he got to his feet and walked over to the pulpit.

He recalled clearing his throat as he said, "We have three brethren who are in the lot: Albert Stolsfus, Elmer Hurst, and Manny Hershberger. Let us have prayer."

Placing the three songbooks on the front bench of the church house, he then led the congregation in prayer. He used the prayer book, praying a prayer of adoration and praise to God for his

218

mercy and longsuffering kindness with mankind; a prayer for aid for them, mortal men, who knew not how to find their own way in the darkness, that is this world; a prayer for direction and help to discern the will of the Almighty, that on this great occasion when men were groping for the light, He the light of the world would deem it His will to shine upon them. He brought the prayer to a close, and when he got to the end of it closed the book. Stillness and a hush came over the congregation. Even the children were quiet.

"Would the three brethren come forward and choose your books," he had said. Until he announced it before the prayer, no one, other than those counting the ballots and the bishop, knew who the three men were. Albert was Peter's son; Elmer worked for Homer Esh and was from Southern Illinois; Manny was Elmer's brother-in-law, having moved a month or so before Elmer did and living to the east of Elmer on the Lagrange ranch. They came up in the order in which their names had been called. Albert first walked up the aisle, picking whichever songbook he wanted from the three and sitting down on the front bench. The songbooks were not stacked on top of each other but rather were standing side-by-side, balanced upright with a book-holding object. If you took out any of the songbooks, the rest stayed standing. Albert took the middle songbook. The right and left ones stayed up, tottering a little but standing upright without touching each other. Elmer came next, taking the left songbook. He sat down on the bench with sweat messing up his grip on the songbook. It simply would not do to wipe his hand on his pant leg, so he tried to hold the book still and keep it from sliding out onto the floor. Manny came next and took what was left over.

Bishop Bontrager recalled how when all three men settled in, he had walked over and reached for Albert's book. He flipped through it once, twice, and then gave it back. The lot paper was not there. Next he took Elmer's book. The sweat on the book from Elmer's hand nearly caused him to lose his grip, but he noticed it soon enough to quickly bring his other hand underneath and keep the book from falling to the floor. No one noticed as the ministers on the front were keeping their heads bowed and the people on the benches behind them could not see on that level anyway. He then brought the book up and flipped through it slowly. There was no paper. He gave it back to Elmer. Moving on to Manny, no one was making any quick conclusion. They were waiting for the paper to be actually found. Until that happened you could not be sure the paper was not somehow missed in the first two books checked. Taking Manny's book he had simply opened it, and there it was, the paper.

Manny knew it, too. In fact he knew it all day but figured it was just a feeling. Through his surge of emotions he heard the bishop ask him to kneel and then read what was on the paper.

"Do you," the bishop remembered how each time you had to insert the correct name, "Manny Hershberger, accept the holy call of God and of the church to this office of a minister? Do you commit to teaching the Word of God, to be responsible for correction, for doctrine, and for rebuke as is needed in the work of the Lord?" Manny said he would.

With that Vern and Robert had come over, and with them standing there the bishop read another prayer and then concluded the ordination service. During the prayer he had kept his hands on the prayer book he was holding. It was only when a bishop was being ordained that he would set the prayer book aside and lay his hand upon the minister's head.

As these thoughts of a year ago went through his mind, Bishop Bontrager thought he had better get his mind back on the present circumstances. He sermon was going along by heart, but if one thought of too many things even while doing things by heart who knew what could happen. Glancing at the clock he saw that it was time he closed for the noon meal. Wrapping up the story he quoted the last few verses of Malachi and brought the congregation to prayer.

At one o'clock the service continued after each family gathered around a picnic lunch on the church house hill. Bishop Bontrager got through his New Testament sermon by three o'clock and started serving the bread and wine. Amish people will not drink wine during their everyday lives, but at communion time it is the real thing. They believe the scriptures mean what they say, and though they may not understand why, they obey. The bottle had been brought in wrapped in plain non-see-through cloth to hide the evil they believed was hiding within. First the bread was passed around and then the wine poured into a single cup for all to drink from. Today the ministers were wiping the top of the cup with a white cloth between every person, but it was not always done so. Homer did not care much either way, but it was nice to see an effort being made.

After the bread and wine were passed, blessed, and partaken of, the voting procedure of a year ago was repeated. Manny, functioning in his pastoral duties, helped gather up the ballots. No one thought it a conflict of interest that the ministers and Steve were gathering up ballots on which the people might be voting for them. This time the bishop, though, went off to the side room by himself to count the ballots. Vern, Robert, Steve, and Manny sat on the front bench waiting. It would take three votes for one of the ministers or Steve, whom the bishop mentioned was also included in the voting, to get into the lot. From there the same rules from a year ago would apply, as books would have to be drawn between those in the lot.

Bishop Bontrager came out when he was done counting, carrying three books. He set them on the front bench like before with the book holders on each side. Standing behind the pulpit, he cleared his throat. "The church has chosen to vote for all three ministers — Vern, Robert, and Manny — for the bishop candidacy." Steve's expression did not change even the slightest. "Would the three of you come forward and draw the lot?"

Well, they already were forward — that is, on the front bench — so they just stood, starting with Vern first, took their choice, and sat down on the next bench facing forwards away from the congregation. The bishop repeated the procedure from a year ago, starting with Vern, then Robert, then Manny. The paper was in Manny's book.

Bishop Bontrager was a little surprised himself but showed

nothing by his actions or facial expression. Who was to argue with God, especially he? First he asked Manny whether he would accept the call. Upon receiving an affirmative answer, the bishop, after motioning with his hand for Manny to kneel, laid his hand on his head and read from the paper. "It is here this day declared by the will of God, and of this church, that you should be bishop. Now it is you who is responsible to give direction, to lead, to comfort, and to build the church according to the most holy faith. You are now charged before God Almighty and these witnesses to keep the church pure as long as you shall live or until the last day shall come when Jesus shall return for His bride. I charge you with this Holy Office in the name of the Father, in the name of the Son, and in the name of the Holy Spirit."

No one heard him, but Bishop Bontrager sighed deeply inside. The thing was done, and tomorrow he would leave for home. For now he brought the service to a close, and as they sang songs they washed each other's feet — the men up front and the women in the side room on the right. It took a while, but there were many stanzas in the old German song, and it was a simple matter to just keep going. Homer wondered how this would be done if the songs were in English. He reckoned it would take four or five songs to last long enough. Maybe Bishop Manny would insist that the German continue to be sung, but he doubted it. "This English stuff was coming for sure."

In the morning, Steve and his wife talked the matter over between themselves. They decided the future held little but trouble for the Amish church here in Honduras, and made plans quietly to move back up north. Homer agreed to buy their place, as it would be an excellent addition to his own land, adding on some river bottom that he did not have. A month later Steve and his family were gone. "It was as if," one of the locals mentioned to Peter, "they never were even there."

Jason took to roaming freely throughout the now expanded property of his father. Homer took to farming, although he had never done much since his youth. It fell to Jason to help out with that also. He never learned to like farming. Horses had to be harnessed, plowing for days on end to work up the ground. It seemed like drudgery itself. Whenever Jason could get free of school and his farming duties he traveled the mountains and surrounding community with his horse. Homer lost most of his guns to thievery, and a pellet gun was all Jason could find that the thieves did not want to steal. With it limited damage could be done to birds and waterfowl in the orchards and at the pond. Dennis Faber, director of the Children's Home, accosted him more than once about the situation. Jason would not listen, though — he said his father was part owner of the pond, and it was his own business what birds he shot.

Jason was also well acquainted with a certain bachelor who lived on the end of the lane, an eccentric sort of fellow who was always kind to him. In a land where every man kept a woman, Jason wondered why Cedric Gaiuano never did.

CHAPTER TWENTY-SEVEN

SOON AFTER THE ordination, it had been one of those evenings, a Saturday to be exact. The moon rose early, casting long shadows across Homer's backyard. But now it was higher in the sky beaming bright enough to read by. Rachel and Homer had been to bed for more than half an hour. Eight o'clock was bedtime for them, and tonight had been no different. After a leisurely supper, served at six-thirty, the family had sat around reading and relaxing until retiring. Now Homer was in no mood to be awakened.

"Did you hear that?" Rachel was shaking him by the shoulder.

"Hear what? Would you please just be quiet?"

"I heard something. It was coming from over by Jesse's place, I think."

"You didn't hear anything. You are always hearing things. This is the third world. Start the generator if you have to, but things make noise down here. Just go to sleep, please?"

Rachel thought about it for a while — "There is no use starting the generator. No light reaches that far south of us where the noise came from" — and then lay back on the bed. Their bedroom window faced to the east. If it had not been for the trees and slight rolls in the land you could have looked out to your right with a clear shot to Jesse's place. From there the sound came again, a high-octave drawn-out scream that warbled at its end as if expressing a real passion of rage or something. Homer heard it faintly this time, and if not he would have felt the violent shaking of the bed as Rachel propelled herself out of it. She was standing by the window when the next two came in rapid succession.

224

"It's human," she said to herself. "A woman's scream would have fear in it, and an animal would be different from that. Besides, if it were an animal, Jesse or his boys would shoot the thing." She waited awhile by the window for the sounds of a shot or human voices in pursuit. All she could pick up were the faint irregular sounds of what sounded like metal clashing against metal. "Wonder what that is?"

"We should do something, Homer."

"What is there to do? It sounded like an animal to me. Just come to bed, will you?"

Rachel got in bed and tried to sleep, but she was sure the noises were still going on. At least there was no more screaming — or was there? She could not tell if she had been dreaming or whether it was real when she woke two hours later.

Over at Jesse's place they stayed up a little later, mostly because it was a Saturday evening. With a farm such as theirs, extra chores needed doing in preparation for Sunday. There were a multitude of little things to do that would make for less work the next day, so the boys were working that evening in the barn by lantern light. They had just completed the work for the evening and were sitting around the supper table when the first loud knock came at the door. Afterwards they could not remember why they did not open it immediately, or why the boys locked all the doors coming in. Both the front door and the door coming in the side by the washroom were locked for the night, though usually that was the last task before settling in for the night. Jesse went to the door but did not open it. "Who is it?"

"Open up," the voice said. "I am come for love. I want love, much love. Love, love is what I want. Love for my heart that aches and aches inside of me. Much pain, I want love." The voice was high and garbled and wild sounding. A loud whack came on the outside of the door, not lending any inducement to Jesse to open up.

"What was that?" one of the boys asked.

"Sounded like a machete, whacked on the door."

Jesse went over to the window on his right and looked out.

Standing there in the moonlight, his face visibly puffy, was Cedric Gaiuano. He waved his machete towards the window Jesse was looking out from.

"What's wrong with you, Cedric?"

"Nothing is wrong with me. I am come for love, for love. I would have love."

Jesse was not sure what to say. "Why don't you just go home, Cedric? It is about our bedtime, and we are settling down for the night."

Cedric shook his head. "I want love, oh love." Here he warbled some notes of a song Jesse never heard before. It was doubtful, Jesse thought, that anyone ever heard them before. "I am come for your daughter, your sweet, sweet, so lovely daughter. Ah, how beautiful she is, how adorable. She is a most desirable one, and she will love me I know, yes she will."

Jesse was highly indignant. "She will do nothing of the sort. You are drunk, Cedric. Now go home."

"I am not drunk. I am in love. Ah, love, love, she will love me, you know. Let me in to get her and take her home right now."

"You will not."

"Yes, I know what the problem is. You want me to marry her. I will marry her. I will marry her right now."

"You will not marry her."

"Why not? I am in love with her, and you now have a new bishop. He can marry us right now. Can he not? He can marry us right here." Cedric went into a slobbering laugh at the thought of it.

"My daughter is not marrying you. She is just thirteen years old, and we do not marry at that age."

"Then it is I? Is it not I? You will not let her marry because it is me?"

"It makes no difference whether it is you or anyone else. We will not talk about marrying here."

"It is just me, that is what it is. You gringos think you are something. High, big, great people who will not let your daughters marry us. That is what it is. You will not let her marry Cedric. What is wrong with you?"

"We like you just fine, Cedric. Now go home and get some sleep."

"Why do you not like me? I work for you. You work the land with me. Am I not good enough for your daughter?"

"You are drunk, Cedric. Now go home."

"I will not go home, and I am not drunk. If you do not give her to me, then I will take your daughter myself." With that he reared back off the door, threw his head back in a wild scream and charged. The machete went all the way through the hollow door, but the deadbolt and bar on the inside held. Cedric pulled down on the machete but got nowhere with the cut. The bars Homer spent so much time making were doing their job.

With that Cedric proceeded to circle the house, letting out his yells and attacking the windows with his machete. It was all to no avail, other than to break a few panes of the glass. The bars held up nicely even though they were not exactly designed for whacking with a large knife. After the first several windowpanes were broken, Jesse sent the boys around the house ahead of Cedric to crank them open. This minimized the damage largely to punctured screens. While Cedric was behind the house, Jesse thought of sending one of the boys out the front door for help. Cedric must have gotten the same thought, or else he ran out of hope of entry from the back. Before Jesse found time to formulate a plan, Cedric was back at the front door. He looked prepared to stay there for the rest of the night.

It was now going on ten o'clock, and on the front porch step, Cedric Gauiano, the apparently confirmed bachelor, sat singing love songs he was making up as he went along. What was the family to do? Jesse decided to proceed with their regular family devotions. It might calm everyone's nerves inside the house and maybe outside too. Calling on the Almighty was not a bad idea, he thought, especially since human help seemed out of reach.

"Something simply will have to be done about communications with the neighbors."

That would have to be done tomorrow at the earliest though, and not tonight. "Come Monday morning, if we survive this, I will have the boys build an escape hatch on the back wall of the house. That way we can send for help at least."

His boys were fast runners, and he was sure they could outrun anyone, even in the dark. The boys knew the lay of the land like the back of their hand, but nothing could be done now.

Gathering the family around the living room, he called to his wife Lois to join them. She was in the back bedroom with the crying Rosemary. They came out together, but Rosemary could not stop crying. Jesse motioned for them to sit as far from the front door as possible. His wife stayed by the girl's side with her arm around her. Jesse took up his place closest to the front door and began reading.

～

"I will sing of the mercies of the LORD for ever: with my mouth will I make known thy faithfulness to all generations. For I have said, Mercy shall be built up forever: thy faithfulness shalt thou establish in the very heavens. For who in the heaven can be compared unto the LORD? Who among the sons of the mighty can be likened unto the LORD? God is greatly to be feared in the assembly of the saints, and to be had in reverence of all them that are about him. O LORD God of hosts, who is a strong LORD like unto thee? Or to thy faithfulness round about thee? Thou rulest the raging of the sea: when the waves thereof arise, thou stillest them. Thou hast broken Rahab in pieces, as one that is slain; thou hast scattered thine enemies with thy strong arm. The heavens are thine, the earth also is thine: as for the world and the fulness thereof, thou hast founded them. For the LORD is our defence; and the Holy One of Israel is our king." Portions of Psalms 89.

After the reading of the scriptures, Jesse led out in the first song and the others pitched in. For twenty minutes they sang German songs they all knew by heart. Maybe they should be singing English so Cedric could understand, Jesse thought, but then decided against it. Cedric did not understand either German or English, and they did not know Spanish well enough to sing it and be understood. Prayer followed the singing, and by that time Rosemary was no longer crying. A peace settled on the house. Even the noises from the front porch were quiet.

"Has he left?"

Jesse went to the window and looked out. "No, he is still there. Sitting on the front step. He looks sleepy, though."

That was when Lois suggested that they give him some blankets. "He might go to sleep, and then we can sleep."

"How are we going to give him blankets? We surely cannot open the door."

"Right over there, the glass is broken anyway. Pull the screen apart and bunch the blanket up. You can just get it through the bars."

With the blankets ready, Jesse called out. "Cedric, come over here."

"Yes. Have you changed your mind about your daughter? It is still not too late to marry us."

"You are not marrying my daughter — just get that straight. Here are some blankets. If you are staying the night, you can sleep on these."

"Thank you, ah, much thank you. I will wait out here then until your daughter can marry me." His snoring soon began ascending into the night air. Overhead the moon shone in all her glory. It was not so late yet that the crickets and the little frogs were settled down for the night. Jesse listened until he was sure all was staying quiet, then he told everyone to get ready for bed. "We might as well get what sleep we can. God will continue to watch over us."

∼

Rachel woke at the first light of day. Just around 5:30 you could begin to see a little. She walked out to the back of the house at 6:00 to see if Jesse's were doing their chores. Normally the boys were in the barn before 6 o'clock. There was nothing going on that she could see. If she could just be certain, it would help, but the dreams and the screams all ran together this morning. She felt kind of foolish now that the sun was shining, but why weren't they doing chores? Probably Homer was right, and it was just some animal making that noise. She would wait, she decided, and went back inside to fix breakfast for the family. It was Sunday morning and there was the usual rush to get ready for church at nine o'clock. At six fifteen she checked again, and then fifteen minutes later. Still nothing. Homer told her to calm down. Jesse's, he said, were well able to take care of themselves. They were a quite competent family and probably just decided to sleep in this morning for once. No one, he said, should always have to be on time for everything.

When the clock ticked past 6:30 and was climbing towards 6:45 Rachel could stand it no longer. She marched out on to the driveway and down the road towards the main highway. A short distance, then the trail to Jesse's went off to the left. Left she went, down the ravine and up the little knoll. At the top there was a clear view of Jesse's place. There was nothing to see. Of course that was the problem. Why was there nothing to see? Down the knoll she went and through the little gate guard by the fence, up the slight slope to the house. There was not a soul stirring.

She called out, "Jesse. Jesse." Not a sound.

Her courage never failed her, nor did she feel any fear. Up she marched to the front porch, under the roof, stepping aside for the edge of a blanket, and lifted her hand out to knock on the door. That was when it stirred — what looked, now that she noticed it, like a pile of blankets Jesse might have left lying outside by the front steps. First there was just a little movement, and she thought for sure she was mistaken. Her hand stopped in mid-air as she looked at the pile of blankets. The stirring continued until a hand broke out. The hand proceeded to yank on the covers, and her horrified, overwhelmed brain knew what was coming. Out came the unshaven, grizzled face of a man.

She screamed — piercing shrieks of sheer terror. She turned and ran. She never looked back or knew how she got through the gate guard at those speeds. All the training from her childhood running games and the muscles developed from farm work were called upon that Sunday morning. Homer finally believed her when she pulled up to the front door, and he headed out at a run for Jesse's. By the time he got to the top of the knoll and could get a clear view there was no sign of Cedric. What he saw instead were Jesse's boys rushing out to the barn with their buckets to do the milking. Already the cows were starting to complain. Their mooing would only increase unless something was done soon. Jesse told Homer the short version of the story and said they would be late for church.

As they climbed the church house hill at a quarter till nine, it was not appropriate for Homer or Rachel to mention anything at great length before the church service started. No one ever, before the morning service, stood outside the church house and held a conversation long enough for such a story. They simply told Peter and Annie that Jesse's ran into some trouble and would be late. This was satisfactory information and understandable, as there were a multitude of things on a farm that could go wrong. Jesse and his family slipped into the pews at ten o'clock and gave no indication by their expressions or actions of anything being amiss. Peter wanted to know, though, right after the service, and Jesse told him the story outside the church house. He did not feel like telling the situation in front of too many people. Emphatically, Peter insisted that on this matter the police would have to be told.

"But Dad, you know how we feel about the police."

"Yes, but this is not just the thieving of material possessions, Son. This is your daughter. You will have to let them know. Maybe they can help. Up north this would be a federal matter for the FBI or something. It is really more serious than you may think. The least you must do is send someone to tell them what happened last night."

So it was that after lunch Jesse sent his two oldest boys into Guateteca to report the matter at the police station. The sergeant in charge got a big chuckle out of the story. "So one of our locals wants a white girl. Well, well, at least he has good taste." Hee, hee, hee, and they all enjoyed a good round of laughs.

Jesse's boys felt their faces turning red, but the oldest one felt more than that. He felt anger over this attitude towards his sister. In his anger he forgot most of the Spanish he learned, and his words came out half English and half Spanish. He told them they ought to be ashamed of themselves. Did they have no respect for their women or for their sisters? He told them of what the night was like and what this man said he was planning on doing. He told them they were officers responsible for the protection of the innocent, and that if they were real men they would do their jobs. Whatever the language was in, the officers got the message.

"Yes, Son, just calm down. We will take care of this man. Tell your father the next time there is any trouble to let us know, and we will come. But you must let us know while the man is doing something. Okay, now run along, and let us know."

When the two boys got back, Jesse did not say much about their story but thought about it for a while. "We will have to see what happens."

They did not have to wait too long. At four-thirty they spotted Cedric walking the ridge to the southwest of them pacing back and forth, swinging his machete, as if something was agitating him. When he showed no signs of either approaching the house or leaving the ridge, Jesse sent the boys back into town. A half hour later they were back, with the police arriving before they did. There was no sign of Cedric, though. He was gone from the ridge.

They were all standing outside the house talking with the police when someone shouted, "There he goes."

Sure enough, there he went. Cedric was making his escape at a fast run after apparently hiding behind some trees on the ridge. The police needed no instructions as they gunned up their pickup and raced out the lane around to the left and over the hill. They overtook him down by the main road in a cloud of dust. Cedric was unceremoniously thrown to the ground, dragged into the back of the police vehicle, and off they went. What they did with him no one ever knew exactly, but he was seen alive and back home several weeks later. Jesse exchanged no money with the police (nor would have even if asked), and Cedric minded his own business from then on. That is with matters of love, at least. The Amish would always know him from then on as a local menace. Some of his actions justified that opinion, and some were no doubt imagined, as such things are.

On Monday morning Jesse told his boys to start on their escape hatch in the back of the house. It was quite a clever affair and needed to be shown to you before you noticed it. In their years of living in the third world they never encountered such a situation again, so the hatch was never used for an emergency situation. The whole family did get over the affair of that night rather quickly, bonded together by their love for each other and for God. In the good and the bad, they remembered mostly the good.

❧

Jason got to speak with Cedric several months later. He was a little scared, but Cedric made no threats towards him. In fact, Cedric was laughing.

"Your mother. She is something. My how she can run." Cedric doubled over in his mirth. "I would have done her no harm. But she ran away, my how she ran. Whish, like the wind."

Jason only nodded his head and made no response.

"That new bishop you have. Is he doing well?" Cedric asked.

Jason nodded again. "I like him."

Chapter Twenty-Eight

Throughout the rest of the year, Bishop Manny took to his duties like a natural. As a young man in his early thirties, he never obtained schooling in the ways of preachers, yet he took his place as quickly as his ordination happened. Being of average height and broad-shouldered, whether anyone noticed it before or not, Manny now turned out to have a soft heart for people. On a person-to-person basis, one felt instantly comfortable with him, as if one just came home and there was nothing to fear. People open their hearts to such a leader, and Manny was one of them. The road to his house was soon well traveled. People dropped by on Sunday afternoons after church or in the evenings just after dusk. Elmer Hurst soon reached his limit of tolerance with people constantly going past his place, but what could he do?

The trail to Manny's place cut across from the Taft road over a long truss bridge put up between Manny and Elmer's places, and that was where the people could, by rights, travel. Elmer was married to Manny's sister, and they purchased adjoining lots from the Lagrange ranch. Between their places a steep ravine cut deep enough and long enough to make climbing up and down it quite impossible. To get around it on each side required far too much walking. Hence the genius of what minds put together can do. The truss bridge came into existence. The two families were related, after all, but now Elmer wished the ravine had been left the way it was.

The locals took to coming too. Manny already was putting a lot of effort into learning his Spanish, and now that he was ordained the process was accelerated. Although he never got the accent quite right, as would the children of the Amish, he soon could converse at length about scripture and spiritual matters with those of the Spanish tongue. A subject much in demand was the matter of non-resistance. A cousin of Manny's worker visited him on a Friday night, after things settled down for the day but dusk had not quite fallen. Manny knew the fellow would want to be in town by the time darkness was well settled. The locals were not much into being abroad after dark.

"So why is it that you Amish, like, let people steal from you?"

"We do not let people steal from us. That is in God's hands. See over here. I lock my barn where the tools are, and at night we lock the house. I have bars on all the windows, as you can see. It is not right for us to ask people to steal, which we would be doing by leaving everything open, or to help them steal. Where we can, we should help them not to steal, but to kill is not in our hands. Killing belongs only to God."

"But a little bullet here and there does much to discourage stealing. I know, because I have lived here much time, and that is the way things are. We grew up like this — our father, our mother, they all steal when they can. From family no steal. My father said family does not steal from each other. Only the uneducated mountain people, who know nothing, steal from their family. But from others, if there is opportunity and you do not get hurt, then why not take it? That is what my father said."

"That is, of course, all wrong, even if your father said it. We should not steal from each other, no matter if they are family or not."

"Well of course you say so — you are rich and need nothing. We are poor and have to live by stealing."

"There have been times in my life when I have been poor — not that I am that rich now — and I have found nothing is to be gained by stealing. Stealing teaches us all the wrong lessons about life. It teaches us to leave God out of our everyday needs. God wants us to earn our money and possessions by working. When men or women look to working as their hope for improving their life, it

235

takes faith in God to do that. Maybe it may not seem to you like it does, but it does. Working teaches us about faith and about God. If you look to stealing as your hope for improvement, that takes no faith at all, just a chance to steal, and you are never sure if that will come or not. If it does come, you are still not sure whether you can pull it off or not. Work, on the other hand, takes first of all faith in yourself. When men or women expect to improve their life by working, they look around for something to do at which they excel. They find something they believe they can do. Come rain or shine, come cold or hot, they know that they can get the work done. Such a person does not work just for the money, but because he likes to do what God has given him the strength to do."

"Well, I work for the money. What else is there to work for? I work from seven till four o'clock chopping weeds, fixing fence, and whatever I am told to do, but it's for the money. Of course it's for the money."

"Have you ever thought of doing the work you do just to do a good job? Have you ever seen your work as being the answer to a better life for you and your family?"

"Most certainly not. Work, here — you do not know, because you do not live here — is not the answer to anything. We work because we get hungry, but as soon as we are no longer hungry then we do not work. Work is not good for anyone. It helps nothing. How is it that you gringos do not know this? We all know that to really get ahead, a man must steal it from someone. No one gets ahead by working. Ha, that is really funny."

"Is that why you people never save up any money? You do not even cut enough firewood for more than one day."

"Well, my wife cuts the firewood. Why should I cut it if I am not hungry right then? Besides we might die tomorrow, and then whose would the pile of firewood be? Stacked there behind the house, it would do me no good once I am gone."

"But God does not want us to live like that. He wants us to live with faith in our lives. Faith that we can work with our hands or with our minds, and things will get better because of it. Faith that even if we should die tomorrow, the effect of our work can touch others. With that kind of faith, it then leads us to also believe that God will work for us. That as we are working for the good of others, so He is also working for our good."

"Bah, who believes that kind of stuff? God, He is up in heaven where everything is well and fine. What does He care? Maybe the Virgin thinks of us. I pray to her, Blessed Holy Mother, and I think sometimes she hears, but how do I know?"

"See, that is just what I mean. You do not believe in anything for sure. This is one of the reasons we do not believe in shooting people who steal. Why should we shoot someone instead of trying to help him? Once he is dead, how can we be of help?"

"You are trying to help us? Then why not give us some of your things, some money maybe, or some tools? That would really help."

"The truth is that it would not. Money and possessions are not what you need. What you need is to have God change your heart and mind, so that you think right. We also believe that such a thing is possible for anyone if he is willing to have it happen."

"For me, I would just take the money. The money would make me as happy as I want to be. Would you let me take your money right now?"

"I would tell you that it is wrong, and that it will bring you no happiness in the long run."

"What if I told you that I would shoot you for your money? Would you just stand there and let me do it?"

"If you would shoot me, I would not stop you, because I believe that Jesus was the Son of God, and that He came down to this earth and died for me. As a follower of His, I would rather follow His example and lay down my life for someone rather than killing him. I believe that following the example of Jesus would result in much more good for you than shooting you would. Because we believe that we are here on this earth not just for our own good, but for the good of others."

"Well, you are a strange people. I have never heard of such things before. I think you all better go back to the United States or Canada where you came from. Such strange people will not make it down here."

"I believe that we will make it, and that God will work many great things yet in this country."

"I have never heard of such things like this. This is 'loco.' A man with a gun who will let others shoot him. If I owned a gun I would never let anyone shoot me. May the 'Holy Virgin' be blessed." With that the cousin crossed himself, bid goodnight, and headed for town while there was still daylight to see by.

To the south of Manny's place a little knoll tucked itself in the lower corner of the Lagrange ranch. Nothing real big like the mountains that stood in the background, but tall enough so it took a few minutes to climb to the top. The main driveway off the Taft road went right by its base to the south. You could drive right by the knoll many times and in the hilly country of Honduras never really be aware of its presence. There, on the knoll, Manny went early on most Sunday mornings to pray. Not too many people on the ranch were aware of this activity, and if someone saw him, he would have appeared to be on an early Sunday morning walk. Such a thing was acceptable, but the praying would not have been. The image of an Amish bishop out on a hillside praying on a Sunday morning would not have sat well with many in the congregation. Not that they were against prayer or would have objections if he did it at home, but doing it up on the hillside smacked of liberalism up one side and down the other. That would have indicated, to some, that the Amish settlement was going in only one direction, the wrong one — which already some of the church members were feeling. Amish people are trained, in church matters, to always be on the lookout for trouble. Here they saw a big problem. Manny was perceived not just as nice, but also as lacking in the area of discipline. His soft heart got in the way of his ability to enforce the church rules.

In the meantime on Sundays, the church house filled up, not just with the Amish but also with visiting locals. Before long, conversions began occurring — not that many at first, but enough to bring the first problem to a head.

"It is simply unrealistic," some said, "that we expect these converts to learn English rapidly, let alone German. The sermons will have to be preached more often in Spanish so that the converts as well as the other locals can also be fed spiritually. How can they be expected to mature without good solid spiritual food spoken in their own tongue?"

So the argument went, and Manny openly cast his sympathies with it. In rebuttal the other side made the point that the locals were being converted without a lot of Spanish preaching, hence they would get along quite well as things were. "They came to us while we sang German songs and preached German messages. Why is that still not good enough?"

That sounded a little caustic to Manny, and so he began to promote Spanish preaching wherever he could without causing too much of a problem. "We will preach the opening message and other comments in German, but the main message will be done either with an interpreter or in Spanish," Manny said. "That is how it will be." He also said, "That is how it will stay."

This worked fine for a few months, but that is not how it stayed. None of the preachers knew Spanish well enough to preach it completely without interpretation. So both sides got to hear their language on the basis of necessity if nothing else.

A certain lady was heard to say, "It sounds much more sanctified when the words of scripture are at least read in our mother tongue before they are repeated in some unknown gibberish that this Spanish sounds like."

Of course problems arose, as they always seem to do. Manny and Robert soon knew the Spanish language well enough to preach it without an interpreter. Robert approached Manny after one Sunday morning service. "I can speak the language well enough now to preach without an interpreter. That way I can get much more said then if two of us have to say the same thing. Is it okay with you if I preach Spanish without an interpreter?"

Manny was not sure. "I don't think we should do that. It will cause trouble."

"What trouble can it cause?" Robert asked, but Manny would not agree with it.

"We cannot preach Spanish by itself. I tell you what we can do. If you want to preach Spanish then do so, and we will have it interpreted into German." After thinking about it Robert agreed, and that is what they did. There was interpretation of the sermons going from the German to the Spanish, or from the Spanish to the German. So the peace was kept and with that the hopes of many that things would remain as they ought to be.

From there the conflict that was quieted seemed only to escalate into other areas. Some of the Amish families came from Southern Illinois, where the church rules allowed bicycles. Southern Illinois was an old Amish settlement, and those who came from there raised the point in a members meeting. "The bicycles have never done anyone any harm where we came from. Everyone still stayed Amish. Why can't we have them here?"

To which it was replied, "Maybe the bicycles did more harm than you knew of? Maybe the bicycles and other lax rules contributed to some of the problems you experienced. Things like the rowdiness practiced by your youth. Are your youth not infamous for their wild parties on Saturday night? Did they not in one instance trash the trailer of some hapless young couple and have the police force called in on them? Could the bicycles have contributed in some way to luring the young people out to the world and its atmosphere?"

Having these questions raised and directly addressed to the Southern Illinois people in a pubic meeting caused great consternation. Feelings were hurt and the possibility of any connection between bicycles and worldliness was considered as inflammatory and impolite. So bicycles became the dividing line between those who feared an influence of the world upon their young people and those who looked on all such thinking as bull-headedness and obtuseness.

Bishop Manny ignored the issue for the longest time in the hopes that it would go away, but when it did not he brought the matter to a vote. That is, he planned on bringing it to vote. Those on the conservative side told him that the matter was considered too unacceptable to even vote on.

Jesse laid it out clearly to the bishop on a Saturday night. "It is simply not possible for us to even entertain the thought of bicycles being ridden around the community by Amish people, especially the young ones. Regardless of how the vote turns out, the very fact that it was voted on will open doors we would better leave shut."

On Friday nights and Sunday afternoons the grass caught little chance of growing on the trail past Elmer's place. Elmer entertained thoughts when the dog barked at eleven o'clock at night and woke him up. It did not help that he knew it was someone going home from Bishop Manny's place, after having spent the evening talking about church trouble. "Why do people not just go home and sleep, instead of wasting their time on such stupid things? God gave us the night to sleep in, did He not?"

Bishop Manny worked hard and talked long until everyone's nerves settled down a little. That was when the next big issue hit. Certain of the mothers began to let their daughters run around during the day, in public, dressed without the double top garment called the "hals-duch." This double piece of dress is an Amish staple. Roughly translated it means "throat or neck garment." Worn as an extra outside piece over the dress, it is a sort of flap with a hole in the middle, slipped over the neck and pinned at the waist, front and back, under the dress belt. It provided a covering over the front and the back for things the dress might fail to hide.

After seeing one of the girls in town without her "hals-duch" on, Rachel Esh spoke up on the matter. She could plainly see what was going on with this problem. "It is like this," she said. "With the outside piece of dress on, it is obviously of no use trying to make your dress too tight or form fitting, as the effort and hard work would be quickly undone when the "hals-duch" is put on. Without it, though, the dress can be worked on. The possibilities," she said, "were endless. You can pull the dress a little here and make it tighter there. That might then make something else look larger and more prominent than it was before. A little touch," she said, "could go a long ways. With the 'hals-duch' on, you just can not do that."

Certain wiser heads among the women were well aware of

this and agreed with Rachel. In the meantime the grass did not just turn brown on the trail past Elmer's on weekends — it gave up growing altogether.

The mothers involved made the strong rebuttal that no mischief was abroad. "It is all just an innocent affair of simply trying to dress cooler in the tropics. None of the locals wear an extra piece over the dress and they are in fact quite modest. Please quit thinking about all these rules and think outside of the box," they said. "There is nothing wrong with this, and everyone is still planning on dressing appropriately."

Manny could not keep track of all the arguments, and besides the situation interfered with his ministry to the people. So he did nothing, except try to keep everyone happy.

He did take a stand on the suspenders, though. That one he stood firm on. The converts must wear suspenders like everyone else. He would not budge on it, even when pushed on the subject by one of the above-mentioned mothers. This stand produced the effect of preventing the spread of the conflict into another area, because it never became public knowledge that suspenders were being debated. Manny started getting more sleep again on weekends. That improved both his temperament around his family and his preaching on Sundays. The church house was always full on the Lord's Day. Somehow, even in the midst of the dissension, he succeeded in establishing an influence and presence in the community. The conversions increased both among the locals and among the Amish themselves.

"God put me here," he said, "to lead this church."

Jason's heart melted under the preaching of Bishop Manny. Not any particular sermon was the cause but the atmosphere he kept the church in. Holy things were on the wind. At home, Jason broke in repentance for his sins. Amish church is not a place where one does those things. Altar calls were for the liberal churches. Rachel found him one evening in tears, and they had a long talk about things. She got Bishop Manny to stop by and talk with Jason about his conversion and about baptism. Manny told him that God would understand how young he was, that baptism was only for older people. Manny said around fifteen years of age was a safe age. It was then that one could be sure that the conversion was a stable conversion and not just emotions.

That was fine with Jason as long as God was fine with it. His conscience was what concerned him at present. It seemed to be making up for lost time. He told his mother about what he had done in stealing money from his grandfather and aunt. She helped him return the small sums without making a fuss. Dennis Faber, though, was another matter. He had to go that one alone. On a Saturday afternoon he arrived at the Children's Home to apologize for his former disrespectful attitude. It turned out to be a nice talk, as Dennis inquired all about his conversion testimony. Years later, Dennis told Jason it had been one of the clearest conversions he ever got to observe. Maybe that was because Dennis was so personally and intimately involved in the former and latter state of things, but it made Jason feel good. God must have been working in his life even when he was so young.

Chapter Twenty-Nine

B Y NOW, DURING the year of 1973, the Amish learned that potatoes were the cash crop to tap into. The locals grew the corn and beans, so that base was pretty much covered. Not that those were unprofitable things to grow, but they did not hold a candle to potatoes. Sure, the seeds needed to be special-ordered from out of the country at considerable expense, but the chance was worth taking. A man could double and perhaps with the right kind of timing even make four times the normal returns in raising produce. It all depended on where the market was at the time of harvest. With several tries they of course figured it out and got the thing down pat. Irrigation gave them control over the planting time and then the harvesting time. Soon, round, fat, healthy potatoes rolled out of the ground at just the appropriate time, were hauled up north to the main seaport of Honduras, and sold for big profits. One-hundred-fifty-pound bags of potatoes became the staple for young men to carry around on their backs as the trucks were loaded after harvest.

All the activity drew the attention of the thieves. They at first could not figure out the value of these round objects. The locals hardly knew what to do with potatoes, as they did not fry too well on the top of a fifty-gallon barrel lid. Their homemade ovens were made of clay and topped off with whatever metal was available. Baking or boiling them was unheard of — besides, why did one need potatoes when corn and beans were available?

The thieves, whoever they were, and not lacking in brains when it came to thieving, did put two and two together. There was really money to be made in potatoes, and where there is money why not steal it? A discouraging sight it was indeed for the hapless owner to come out to the potato field and find rows of potatoes just ready for harvest all dug up and carried away in the night. It was enough to make a grown man do things he should not.

Homer took to hiring a guard for the last two weeks before the potato harvest. He filled the whole river bottom with potatoes out behind the place he purchased from Steve. The field was large enough to justify the money invested in guarding services. Plus one might just be lucky enough to have hired the brother or cousin of the thief as a guard, in which case the field was safe without a lot of guarding. Homer became suspicious of this when his guard insisted that he be paid a higher fee for his services than the one agreed upon. Usually the local workers were not like that at all. After considering the matter, Homer snuck down to the field one night to see for himself what was going on and found the guard fast asleep, wrapped up in his blankets by the tree line. He let him sleep and paid him the extra money the next day, considering it a good investment. Let him pass on a little extra to his brother, or cousin, or whoever it was, and leave the potatoes alone. When the harvest rolled around, the potatoes were all there in Homer's field.

Matthew Stolsfus and Enos, a cousin who had moved down in the last year or so, took charge of the lot of ground just north of Homer's potato patch. It was a smaller piece of land, and they were not as inclined to hire guards. Plus, since neither of them lacked anything in brains or brawn, they decided to take care of things themselves. Being of the adventurous type, they let their imagination do the planning for them. Why not sneak down to the potato field and catch the thief in the act?

Two weeks before harvest they put their plan into action. While the guard slumbered soundly over at Homer's place, they got up at ten o'clock, then at one, and then again at three, crept up to the potato field and swept their flashlights up and down the field. Nothing turned up, but the next morning half of a row was dug up with a shovel.

The next night they alternated the hours, and again nobody

was there, but a fresh row of potatoes was gone again. All neatly done, you could see, so as not to hurt the potatoes and damage them for the market. They said things about this person who lived off of other's labors. After another night of checking and turning up nothing, it was plain that a new plan was needed. They developed a simple plan and wondered why they had not thought of it before. Why not just simply sleep out in the field in sleeping bags, wait for the digging to begin, and — snap — spring the trap?

"We will take our sleeping bags to the far end of the field, right under those trees. From there we can see everything going on."

"How are we going to know when the thief gets here?"

"If we are awake, we will know it. If we are asleep, both of us are light sleepers. One of us will wake up."

So the plan was made and executed. The first night it started raining around nine and chased them inside off of the field. Apparently the thief did not like getting wet either, because there were no potatoes dug up the next morning. At eight o'clock the next night they settled in again and were soon asleep.

Matthew awakened Enos sometime later. He could not tell what time it was and did not want to turn on his flashlight to find out. A soft film of mist hung over the potato patch just below the tree line. Its outline followed the river and hung even lower at the riverbank. Enos awakened without a sound, instantly alert. They held their breathing to shallow breaths and listened. Clearly it was there, the soft sound of a shovel going in and out of the ground. Earth thudded very gently to a landing between the rows of potatoes. What sounded like a bag was being pulled at intervals. Its rustle as it brushed the potato plants was unmistakable — a sound like leather squeaking on a saddle could be heard in even spaces of sound.

"It's his shoes squeaking."

"He's here."

"Get ready. Let's go."

Together they came out of the sleeping bags and over the top of the potato plants, flashlights blazing. These were battery lanterns whose sharp beam carried a thousand feet. They swept the field of potatoes from the left to the right and then back again. On the third pass in the middle they caught the man in their cross beams. Both beams fixed and stopped. Neither Matthew nor Enos could think of what to say. Apparently neither could the thief. Leaving his bag lying on the ground, he slowly walked towards the riverbank and disappeared over the edge.

"Well, that is that."

"Think we scared him off?"

"Hope so. It sure scared me."

"Let's go over and see what he was doing. Maybe he left something we can identify him with."

With that they walked towards the bag lying on the ground. It was about two hundred feet into the potato patch. Just getting there chilled them in the night air. They were nearly there when out of the mist a little lower down on the riverbank, where the thief entered before, the figure of a man formed. He kind of popped up fast, as if he meant business. As soon as he cleared the fog his flashlight came on and began sweeping the field back and forth. It was nothing in strength like the flashlights Matthew and Enos used — just a household kind of beam you can use to walk by and throw a beam thirty yards or so.

"Shall we make a run for it?"

"Let's turn our flashlights on him."

"Something tells me we'd better not."

"What shall we do then?"

By that time it was too late to run. The beam of even his flashlight could have followed them, and the man was coming fast.

"Hit the ground. You in this row and I will go there."

Matthew went to the left, and Enos went two potato rows over on the right. Potatoes are grown on a slightly built-up area, leaving a sort of trough in the middle. The plants are twelve to sixteen inches with the raised ground providing even more height. It was this hiding place between the rows that Matthew and Enos found themselves in. They managed to slip into rows three or so apart without being seen. The man kept coming. The sharp slap of his pants hitting on the potato plants could be heard, left right, left right, as he came. Matthew knew that he was close enough and that something must be done.

"What do you want?" he said sharply, keeping his head down both to remain hidden and to defuse the sound from its source.

The steps stopped. There was nothing, just silence, then a sort of soft click and the slightest little sound of movement on leather. Six shots followed in quick succession. Soft pops of dirt sounded around them. Sounds of footsteps running away followed.

Matthew waited for the pain, but there was none. Surely it would hurt if he were hit. What if Enos was hit? There was only silence.

Enos dared not move. Thanking God he survived, he wondered if Matthew still lived. He could hear nothing. How could he, as the oldest, ever face the responsibility of what happened if it turned out Matthew was shot? Waves of nausea went through him. Slowly he picked up his left leg and stuck it into the next row of potatoes. Nothing. Into the next one, and still nothing. Just as he was ready to pull it back, a shoe hit his knee. It scared him so badly he forgot to be glad Matthew was alive.

"Are you hit?"

"No. Everything works."

"Let's get out of here."

Together they left in the opposite direction the thief took, leaving the gunny bag where it was. They used no lights until they got back to the house, running by heart over the landscape and through the fences. In the morning they told their story and went to look for the gunnysack the thief left in the field. It was gone.

"Must have contained something real important in there."

"Important enough to kill over, I guess."

"From now on we leave these fellows alone or find some other way to deal with them."

That is what they did. For that season anyway, it made no difference, as there was no more potato thieving and the harvest went off without a hitch. Matthew and Enos kept the story hush as much as they could to keep the embarrassment for having gotten caught in such a situation at a minimum. Homer and Rachel were close family and got to hear the story. Such stories, especially when true, do not do much to calm the nerves when you are out after dark. Jason developed paranoia about nightfall.

So it happened that on a Friday night Homer and his family were over at David Bunker's for supper and an evening of socializing. Eight o'clock found them on their way home in the open wagon, with old faithful Molly in the traces up front. It was pitch dark as they pulled up to the cattle guard that separated their property from the adjoining property to the north. From the cattle guard all the buildings of the place could be seen, as the line was only a few hundred feet from the house. Cattle guards make a terrible racket when you drive over them, compounded by the horse's hoofs and the wheels of a wagon. As they approached the property line, they thought for sure there were lights in front of the house.

"You did not leave anything on in the house, did you?" Rachel asked.

"No, I checked before we left," Homer replied. "What could the light be?"

"I don't know, but stop before you drive across the cattle guard."

Homer pulled on Molly's reins and waited. Now the light was moving and what looked like people were walking around in the yard.

"Are those people?" Rachel asked again.

They waited and watched. The light moved some more and now they were sure. It was people.

"Those are people, Homer."

"Yes, I see it. Shall we go up and talk with them?"

"No, let's get out of here."

That was all Homer needed to hear. He wheeled old Molly around on the dirt road, and away they went. Homer got the old horse up to a gallop in the traces. The faster they went the more noise they made and the more scared they got. Flying past the Children's Home buildings, the Esh family hung on for dear life and never slowed down till they pulled up in front of David Bunker's place where they had just come from. David met them on the front porch.

"Is there a problem?"

"There were people in front of our house with lights," Homer said.

"Do you think they were thieves?"

"We don't know, but neither do we want to find out."

David could see they were all badly spooked. "You are welcome to stay here for the night."

That is what they did. Where they all slept David never quite knew, but he stuck them in the basement and all over the place. In the morning when the sun was shining, Homer went to look the place over. Nothing seemed to be amiss. Coming back to David's place he took everyone home.

Later in the day they found out it was Abe Stolsfus, Rachel's brother, who was there the night before. He was on the way home, with some of his help, from the produce route in the capital. They just wanted to see if Rachel could use some produce that was left over. That was a story that was not told around much either. If David Bunker thought it amiss, he never mentioned it to anyone. After dark, there was enough real fear to go around that I guess he was glad when one fear proved to be unfounded.

Jason did not want to leave anymore after dark, but there were still functions that needed attending. Those rides home became symphonies of terror to his young ears. Not that anything happened, but the flashlights were kept handy. Speed of foot and flight were always on one's mind.

Here Homer fudged the rules a little and consulted with his worker. He lived on the next little rise to the north of Homer's house on Homer's land. It was an employment arrangement. He mentioned to Homer earlier that he was purchasing a gun for himself. Now Homer approached him about whether they might call on him if ever there was real trouble.

"I know I can't make you do it," Homer told him, "but it would be nice to call on someone close by if a dangerous situation should develop."

"Sure," the worker said. "Call on me anytime — night, day, it is all fine. Just call loudly and I help."

Homer told the family about it and told them to use the help if ever it was needed. "Needed" happened sooner than they thought it would. Rachel woke Jason up one night, when Homer was gone, having to stay in town overnight on business.

"Jason, the thieves are out tonight. I can hear them over at Jesse's place. They are coming here next. You have to call for help to the worker."

Trembling with fright they crept together out to the window facing towards the worker's house. Jason yelled as loud as he could.

"We need help. The thieves are out."

Receiving no response he repeated the call.

Two shots sounded, followed by two more. All was silent while they waited. When nothing more happened, they went back to bed, being careful to make no noise. The next morning Jesse came up to the house all alarmed. He said they heard shots the night before. Was anything wrong? Rachel told him no, they were scared and called to the worker for help.

"What was the noise anyway?" Rachel asked him.

"Some of the cows were out and the boys and I had to get them in. Well, I am glad there was no real trouble."

Soon though, there would be real trouble, a trouble of a different kind than thieves and robbers. This one was trouble not of the body, but of the soul.

Chapter Thirty

A SURPRISING SHOCK CAME in 1973. One no one was looking for. It was one of those dark deep Honduras nights when the late moon has not yet risen. Around ten o'clock a girl stirred in her bed from a pretended sleep and quietly got up, sliding her feet on the ground. Slipping her dress on over her head, she softly opened the door of the bedroom and made it out the front door without waking anyone. Her sister, who used the same bedroom with her, was not sleeping either and heard her go. The sister was briefed the day before with a bare minimum of the plans when they had been doing chores around the house. It sounded innocent enough to the sister. She figured it was just a midnight stroll with someone they both knew and so promised not to tell anyone.

The Amish girl's bare feet brushed the gravel in the lane. It was hard to see anything in this darkness. She slowed down lest the noises of disturbed stones give her away. In five minutes she reached the fence that was the arranged meeting place. By now, her night-adjusted eyes picked out the form of the man waiting for her. Running to him, she embraced him and kissed him. It was not her first time.

He quickly drew away from her and motioned that they must be going. Together they ran carefully towards the trees that outlined the lane. Once safely inside their shelter, they slowed down. Now they felt safe from the searching beams of any flashlights if someone discovered their flight. There were no signs behind them that gave evidence of such a thing. All was quiet. He led her deeper in the trees and then paused. Opening the bag he was carrying, he whispered to her that she must change her clothing.

"Put this dress on."

"Why do I have to do that?"

"Because you cannot be seen in your Amish dress. It will attract too much attention."

He lifted up what he held in his hand for her to see. In the darkness, she could not see what it looked like, but the logic made sense. Even though one could hardly see, habit went deep. She turned around and walked behind a tree before removing her dress to change. He followed and she did not resist. The rest took only ten minutes, and this time it was her first time.

She still could not see the unfamiliar dress but somehow got it on in the dark. It felt all strange with its zippers and buttons, somehow like her heart was feeling right then. Even when it was obvious the thing was put together it still felt as if it was apart.

Joining hands they made their way out to the main south road. It was hard to reach it the way they were going, but neither of them felt safe using the lanes or the Taft road. Reaching the main road he flagged down a passing car, and together they climbed in the back. All she could tell from the direction they were heading was that it was towards the capital. Before this she thought she did not care where he took her, but now riding in this car with its headlights cutting a swath in the darkness, she was not so sure.

Morning broke like it usually does in Honduras, early, bright, and with vigor. The sister awoke with a start and to her horror saw that the bed was empty. She jumped out half-dressed and headed for the kitchen. Her mom was preparing breakfast.

"She's gone. Mom, she's gone."

"Who is gone?"

"She is gone. She did not come home. She said she would be back."

"Calm down, and tell me what is going on."

"She told me yesterday that she would be going out to see Bento for just a little bit last night and then she was coming right back in."

"You mean the Bento that works for us?"

"Yes, he has been working for us about two months."

"Why did she want to see Bento? She can see him every day."

"I don't know. Maybe she wanted to see what it was like to kiss him in the dark."

"What are you talking about? You mean she has kissed him before?"

"Yes, many times."

"Many times?"

"Yes, I saw her do it myself out in the barn, or some other place like that when no one was looking."

"Why haven't you told us this before?"

"She said not to tell anyone. That it is a perfectly normal thing for girls to do, and that I would want to kiss some boy myself some day. Will I, Mother?"

The mother failed to respond, taking rapid steps towards the front door instead. Tearing it open, she screamed her husband's name like an animal does that has lost its cub and knows it can do nothing about it. He came running — not that he failed to come before when she called, but today he knew it was different.

"What's wrong?"

"She is gone."

"Gone where?"

"Off with Bento. She told her sister she was going out with him last night, and now she has not come back."

He paused, not sure what to do. Then he said he would go get help. "Maybe I can ask the other workers if they know anything."

"What would they know about this?"

"Well, I don't know, but maybe they would have heard something or know what this means."

"I know what this means. The man has kidnapped my daughter. I don't have to ask anybody about anything."

"So what do you want me to do?"

"I want you to go to the police right away. They were a big help when Jesse's experienced the trouble with their daughter."

"But," he insisted, "this is different. Her sister says she went out willingly."

"How dare you say this is different?" she said to his face. "My daughter is no different from anyone else. So what if she did go out to see the man? He kidnapped her from there."

He knew better, as did she, but maybe it made her feel better to think like this, so he left the matter alone. "I will go out and see what I can do."

Once out of her sight he slipped into the barn where his other two workers were gathered, waiting for his instructions for the day. In his halting Spanish, he asked them.

"Would any of you know where Bento is? My daughter went out with him last night and has not come back."

"No, we have not seen him this morning."

"Did Bento like my daughter?" he asked them.

They grinned from ear to ear. "Oh, yes, very much. And she liked him, too."

"What would it mean if she went out with him last night and has not come home?"

"Oh, that is how we do it down here. When a man likes a girl, they do not marry. We cannot afford to marry, plus too much trouble. What we do is ask her to meet us some place, usually after dark so no one sees us, and then go away together. That is how we do it."

"Why do you not ask to marry the girl?"

They really thought that was funny. "That we cannot do. The father would not let us marry the girl. Sometimes he does, but usually not. Most of the time they have to run away together, just like in this case. Would you have let them marry or given them the money they needed?"

"No."

"There you see, that is why they have run off. It is nothing to worry about. Bento will love your daughter. He is a good man."

"Is there any chance he could have taken her, like, by force?"

"No, no," they chuckled. "We do not do it like that down here."

Returning to the house he told his wife in no uncertain terms what he had learned, and she accepted it calmly. "You must find out where Bento lives, then, and go get her back. I cannot have her living with a man outside of marriage. That is just simply not acceptable. Just look how that is going to make all of us appear to the other people."

He nodded his head and made plans accordingly. By nine o'clock, he knew where Bento stayed in Guateteca, but there was no Bento or daughter there. Further inquiries got him information on where Bento's parents lived. One went to the next town closer to the capital and then an hour's drive to the north. No one knew for sure where in town, but he obtained the name and that would have to be enough.

≫

By noon Jesse Stolsfus heard the first details of the affair. It was quite by accident, as he happened to be in town when he heard and then confirmed what was happening. After getting back and letting his wife know where he was going, he walked up to the home place. His father was in the orchard, giving directions to the workers on some transplanting he was having done.

"I think I need to talk to you, Dad."

Peter could tell there was something wrong and left his workers with some instructions before walking towards the house with Jesse.

"One of the young girls ran away with a worker last night."

Peter was not sure he heard right. "One of our girls? An Amish girl? Ran away with a boy?"

"Well, Dad, it really was not a boy, more like a man. He is thirty-some years old. But yes, she did run away. As of right now, her father is out trying to find her and bring her back."

"Who was it?"

"One of the girls from the liberal families. She is sixteen years old."

Jesse told Peter some more of the information he knew, and then he left. Alone, the full impact of the situation began to hit Peter. He felt like a man hit in the stomach with a full frontal blow. A thousand specters arose and formed in his spinning mind. Not as in the haunting of the ghosts of Christmas past — those were much too friendly, dreadful as they were. These were ghosts from the hell of Amish depravity. He thought he saw before him the face of Bishop Wengerd, lean and windblown, riding on his buggy. It turned and looked at him with those eyes, hard from years of living with church responsibilities and people like himself.

"So you think you are better than the rest of us. Do you, Peter? You always thought you were so spiritual. How do you feel now? All your complaining about the wild young people from some of our communities, as if any of us could be perfect in this life. You didn't like, you said, the impure dating practices. You said you thought it was not right that anyone should fornicate. What do you think now, Peter? At least our young people are sleeping with others from within the faith. Yours are now sleeping with the heathens. I told you, Peter, that you should be careful with those spiritual ideas of yours. Even though you thought it was so wrong what some of our people were doing, most of them will turn out okay. Can you say the same for yourself? What have you got, Peter? Your young people are running off with the unconverted, off with the world. Is this how you were planning on making things better? Is this where your spirituality was taking you?"

Besides the face of Bishop Wengerd, he saw the faces of others. Men who stood up in the Amish church for what they believed was right. Men like Bishop Bontrager who took so much upon themselves in an effort to bring more of the truths of scripture to the Amish church. He saw his face looking at him with anger in his eyes. Peter knew the alarm bells would flutter out and out, and on out, deeper into the recesses of the Amish minds. Things would never be the same. Peter felt like throwing up. He tried to walk towards the house, but he staggered like a man under the influence. His chest hurt and it was hard drawing air into his lungs. Leaning against a tree he rested and tried to catch his breath.

"We have fallen," he said to himself. "We have failed to bring the world up to our level. Instead, the world has brought us down to its level. We have now become one with them."

The little car they were riding in went bouncing down the old gravel road towards the capital. In the back seat she turned around once and caught a glimpse of the late moon in its last quarter rising over the horizon. It looked friendly and familiar, like an old friend.

"Where are we going, Bento?" she asked.

"To my parents' place. We will be safe there."

"Safe? Who do we have to be safe from?"

"Your father, of course. Your brothers are too young to be dangerous."

"You, you sound like you are quite familiar with all this. Have you ever run off with a girl before?"

"No." He said it with a sigh in his voice. "No, I never have, but now I have you. I have you forever. I will always love you."

"But you are over thirty years old. Have you never loved a girl before?"

"Of course, once when I was younger. I liked a girl that lived next to our house when I was growing up, but we never got to live together. Her father took her off to stay with some relatives when he saw that we liked each other. I never could find out where the relatives lived." Bento tried to kiss her, but the road made it nearly impossible. "You are the first girl that I will actually live with."

The driver chuckled to himself. "Your girlfriend, huh?" he asked out loud.

Bento said yes.

"How long have you been with her? She looks kind of fresh. You just run off with her tonight?"

Bento said yes again. "You know, just the usual. This is my first time though. Her father will be real mad, I think. They come from a strange faith, called the Mennonites. They don't believe in shooting anyone. I should be safe."

"Oh, she is white." He noticed for the first time. The driver craned his neck around towards the back seat and tried to get a good look. It was too dark. "Well, that is a good catch, I should say.

I don't think you have much to worry about, do you? Even if her father were not from a different faith, when is the last time you heard of anyone getting hurt running off with a girl? You know our people do it all the time."

Bento nodded in the darkness. "That is true. I guess it is all just talk when it really comes down to it. It will be good to have a woman, though."

There was another loud chuckle from the front seat. In the back seat, she pushed him away from herself, although there was not very far to push. "I am not your woman, you hear that? We are not married."

"Makes no difference down here. Don't you know that? We hardly ever marry. It is much too expensive, and why go to the bother? This is how we do it. We will live like most of the others do, at our parents' house. You will not have to cook too much anyway, just wash our clothes and be there for me." He tried to kiss her and this time succeeded. "Later on maybe we can get our own cottage there in town."

"Bento, I am not sure about all this. I just came out with you for the night, and maybe a day or so. I am only sixteen, and all this is not what I planned on."

"But Darling, I love you, and you said that you loved me too."

"Well, I did, and I like you, but I do not like all this. You know, the living with you for a long time and never seeing my parents again."

He was silent for a long time. "I cannot believe you are saying this. You are breaking my heart. I went to all this trouble, because you are the only one that I love."

She felt bad about it, he could tell. Moving closer to him, she tried to make it right to him. "I do love you, Bento."

❧

After getting off at the next town, they caught a ride on the early bus north. It involved waiting alongside the road in the middle of the night, but the bus was the first thing to come along. Morning was just dawning when they pulled into his parents' hometown.

He took her by the hand as they walked halfway across town. She never knew anything like this before. The mother of the house was up already preparing the day's food. His parents did not seem to be too surprised at her as they welcomed their son home.

He knew his way around the place and took her to the spare bedroom. "We have to get some sleep after being up all night," he said, but there were other things on his mind too.

She noticed then how thin and close-in the bedroom walls were and how small the house was. It bothered her a lot right then, but from what she could tell no one else seemed to mind it. Maybe you grew used to this kind of thing if this was always the way it was. After he was done, she remembered how dusty she was from the travel and that there would be no running water in the house. Any bathing or washing would require a trip to the creek or someplace like that. Who knew where? This was the first time she felt so dirty, inside and out, and unable to do anything about it. What was there to do but follow his example and go to sleep? That proved to be a simpler thing than she thought it would be.

She awoke sometime later from a deep sleep not able to tell what time it was, but the sun in its full glory shone through the open window. On the other side of the wall, voices were talking in low tones. That was not what awakened her, though. What was it? She lay there thinking what it could be. There was no one with her in bed, and then it happened again. Her hand that was hanging slightly over the bed was nudged with an abrupt upward motion, followed by a high-pitched "oink." One of the little pigs that ran freely around the place had come calling. She jerked her hand up in disgust and wondered what in the world she was doing in this place.

Getting dressed with all the unfamiliar buttons and zippers, she pushed out of the way the slight door of the bedroom that was standing ajar and walked out into the kitchen. Bento was sitting in the kitchen/living room with his parents. Combined, the area consisted of maybe ten feet by twelve feet. A molded mud stove made out of clay with its 55-gallon drum lid for a stovetop stood at one end. On the other side was the small round table with some chairs around it. Bento was sitting on one of them while both of his parents were standing.

They greeted her with smiles.

"You are welcome here," his mother said. "We are glad to see that our son has found himself a girl to live with. You are very beautiful."

She blushed a little and said thank you. Bento's father nodded at her. "There is word that your father is in town looking for you."

"My father?"

"Yes, your father with some other men, maybe your brothers? We hoped that Bento here would not have so much trouble when he brings a girl home. Some boys have no trouble; others have much trouble. It looks like you have much trouble."

"Bento, I have to see my father right away."

"But Dear, if you see him, he will take you home."

"I want to see him."

Before they could continue, a knock came at the door that did not wait to be answered. Someone pulled the door open from the outside. A white man's body with a full-face beard, blue shirt, and Amish suspenders filled the doorway. He did not come inside; neither did he acknowledge Bento or his parents. Looking only at her, he said, "You will come with me, now."

She said nothing to him, nor good-by to Bento. Keeping her eyes straightforward she walked out the door. The Amish father swung the door shut behind her and made sure it was tightly shut as he left — like he wanted to be sure no one would follow him, but those inside the house held no plans to do so.

When they got home, they kept her inside the house for several days so that she wouldn't be seen and things could settle down a bit. On Sunday, Bishop Manny did a beautiful sermon on forgiveness and the granting of mercy to those who go astray. Not that anyone in the community would have done otherwise, but it helped to have the sacred words spoken for everyone to hear when they were really needed. The next week she told her mother that her cycle was coming at its regular time. They knew then that they would live through this with a little less grief both to her and to themselves than what they feared.

"God in his wisdom must have known what was best," the mother said.

Some in the community thought, in their private moments, that more reaping for the sin might have been the best route to go. The mother, though, was glad that they were spared and mistook the present lack of a bitter harvest as a sign that the storm passed — not knowing that some crops are slow in their growing so as to leave a yet more poignant harvest of evil when they come to their full growth.

❧

A little more than a month later, Bento met the father in town quite by accident. He used the occasion to express his great love for the daughter. Bento asked for permission to marry her. He said that he was willing to make any sacrifices necessary that were required of him. He would join the Mennonite faith. He would be converted in whatever form they wanted. He would be baptized and try to learn the German language. Whatever the requirements were, he was willing. The father told him emphatically no.

They never told her about that conversation, but they felt she needed to be told about what happened later that night. Bento, who was not given to drinking, entered a bar and intoxicated himself. Towards midnight he attacked the bartender with his machete. The bartender felt threatened to the extent that he pulled his gun out from under the counter. When Bento attacked him again he shot him three times. Bento died with two bullets through his lungs, but it was the one through his heart that killed him.

The story of Bento's sorrow over his lost love was so well known in town and by the family that no revenge was sought against the bartender by Bento's brothers, as would have been customary even in a killing of self-defense. The family tenderly buried him in his hometown, where none of the Amish attended the funeral services.

Bento was the brother of Homer's worker, Fostor. Bento was

also the brother of Peto who helped dig out Homer's basement by hand. Jason talked to Peto after the accident and funeral. Peto said there were no hard feelings. "Bento was so much in love. In his sorrow," Peto said, "he went looking for death."

CHAPTER THIRTY-ONE

I T WAS ALSO during 1973 that Peter Stolsfus had been troubled all day. It was now Saturday afternoon. Normally it would have been time for him to lift his spirits and get spiritually ready for the Lord's Day tomorrow. Somehow it seemed he just could not. Trouble was hanging over him and around him, with more coming on the horizon, if he was any judge of it.

Remembering that some of the fruit trees up behind the house were dropping their fruit before the workers got to them between pickings, he decided he would gather them up yet that afternoon. Summoning Jason, who was at the house, to help, he got ready to leave with the buckets.

Rachel often came to visit on Saturday afternoons, as well as other times too, for that matter. A simple walk across the fields helped in making her trips more frequent to see her parents. Maybe it was because Spanish did not come easy for her that she felt like visiting with people who talked English. These social needs were most easily satisfied at the home place with her unmarried sister and mother. Peter did not mind the state of affairs, and whatever the reasons were, she was there. He decided to use the extra free help to gather up and carry in the fruit.

Jason possessed plenty of energy and was quite capable of lugging the fruit buckets around. Peter gave Jason two empty buckets to carry and took the other three himself. Out under the trees there was plenty of fruit lying around, and Peter got right to it. Giving Jason a bucket of his own to fill, he started filling a bucket under the next tree.

Instead of filling the bucket, Jason found other things to do. "Ah, a bird. My slingshot — okay pull it out carefully. Birdie, birdie, look the other way."

What a handy little tool for a boy to use. These Honduras slingshots were not at all like the biblical slingshots that David used on Goliath. David's slingshot consisted of a leather pouch that held the stone. Attached to his pouch were two long strings that one swung around and around either over the head or sideways, releasing one of the strings at the appropriate moment.

Jason once handled such a slingshot. "Wow," he thought. "These biblical slingshots can really hurl a large stone, and to an amazing distance. I suppose Goliath ought to know if he were still around to say anything about it. How glad I am though that Honduras has not developed their slingshots like these big ones. I like theirs the way they are."

Theirs were simple wooden slingshots carved into a y-shape. The locals did this by hand with a machete, and later the Amish boys used a band saw or other such modern tools. Modern machinery was never up to the effort, though, and none of the Amish boys ever got good enough with a machete to produce anything close to the craftsmanship of those who held such things in their blood. Some tried the machete, but after just straight out failures and many cut fingers gave up on it. A nice long machete scar on one's hand can be a right beautiful thing for a boy, but it does not produce any quality slingshots. That left one with only the art of bargaining with the local boys to obtain a really good slingshot.

Jason now possessed a Honduras slingshot. It was a beautiful work of local art. He had purchased it for two limperas from a boy in town. The handle was round and fat and fit properly into the palm. If the handle was too narrow, the fingers went around too far and into each other on the other side. If the handle was too big, the fingers could not reach around it properly, resulting in a loose hold for shooting. Of course all that depended on the size of the hand. This one was just right.

Attached to each side of the y were the rubber bands used for the shooting propulsion. They were purchased by the yard without the ends fastened together. It was something like buying string, and tricky like string also. A tangle was almost impossible to get out. Strung carefully in one repetitious circle around and around between each end of the y and the small piece of leather that held the stone, your slingshot was ready to go.

The rubber bands went through a hole in the y, usually burnt in with a magnifying glass using sunlight. This burnt hole — as opposed to a hole drilled with a metal bit — added something very special to the slingshot.

At least Jason was sure it did. "When the hole is burnt in," he thought one day while holding the magnifying glass, "I think something special is happening. Not only is the wood already rounded down around the hole making for easy, non-snagging movement of the rubber bands, but also the native energy left over from the sun burning the hole gives one that extra accuracy and power to shoot the slingshot with great skill. I am just sure of it. The wood even feels lighter in one's hand when a slingshot has a burnt hole. I am so glad I have a burnt-hole slingshot."

Of course there is really nothing to all of that. There is no energy left over by the sun, but looking at those black burnt holes made one understand why Jason thought there might be.

"What other explanation can there be for how well the local slingshots handle?" Jason thought.

Jason stood beside his bucket that was supposed to have fallen fruit in it. Putting a small stone in the small leather piece and drawing his slingshot taut, he took aim at a blackbird hiding in the neighboring tree. Blackbirds as well as parrots usually traveled in large groups, but this one was alone. He was approaching a nearly ripe orange, no doubt thinking of the meal in store for him. Jason's stone whacked him hard on the lower anatomy but did little other damage. A hit on the head or neck area would have been his demise. Delighted even with a hit, if not a kill, Jason was grinning broadly as the blackbird flew off with loud protests. Honduras blackbirds are raucous, noisy critters, and this one's departure got Peter's attention.

"Why are you not picking up fruit, Jason?"

"I was supposed to shoot at the blackbird."

"You did not have to shoot at anything. Now leave your sling-shot in your pocket, and pick up the fruit."

"But he was going to eat the orange. Aren't we supposed to scare away the birds?"

"I don't care what you were supposed to do. Keep your sling-shot in your pocket, and pick up the fruit on the ground."

Jason was a little puzzled, as it was a general policy on the orchard grounds that thieving birds be dealt with in whatever way possible. Matthew even paid a small bounty fee for parrots, woodpeckers, blackbirds, and any other sort of bird that ate fruit. Whatever, he grabbed his bucket and went to picking up fruit with vigor.

"Now, don't throw the fruit in so hard. It squashes and injures things when they are dropped in that hard."

Jason said nothing but slowed down a little with the dropping speed. Two minutes later he forgot.

"Now, Jason, I said to stop throwing the fruit in the bucket so hard. And look how much of the fruit you are missing. Over there is one, and here is another one you missed. Here is one you stepped on. Look what you are doing, and be careful. These fruits are valuable."

Jason still said nothing, which did not seem to help matters much. He was not sure what was going on. His grandfather usu-ally was a mild-mannered, kind type of person. They went on in this way for an hour or so until the fruit was gathered up. Together they walked to the house and left the buckets in the basement. Rachel left for home soon after that, and Jason forgot about the afternoon's experience before they got home.

That night, though, Peter did not forgot. As he meditated on the scripture selection for the evening and prayed, he could not get the afternoon out of his mind. Outside it was already dark, and the full moon rose. A gentle breeze blew through the trees sur-rounding the house. Peter could hear it moving from where he sat by the open window. He could also hear in his mind the voice of someone else. Before him rose the face of a man. It was a kind face, dusty from walking the road, tired looking and lined already with pain at thirty years of age. Around him were gathered older men, men dressed in important clothing and signs of rank. The face of the man was looking somewhere else though. He was looking past the important people gathered around him, out into the crowd that Peter could see was gathered even further out. Motioning to come, he moved his hand towards what he was looking at. Peter saw what it was. It was a child.

"Let him come to me," the man said.

Soon there were many of them. The man gathered them around him, and across his face came the smile of pure delight. The sorrow vanished. He looked young, standing there like he was remembering what being a child was like.

Peter stayed by the window for a long time, thinking about the day and about the sorrow that he himself was facing. His chest pains were bothering him again, and then there were the church problems to think of. What was to be done about them? Yet Jesus always found time for the children. Was there really anything so important in life that a child should be hurt because of it? Peter thought of the afternoon and how short-tempered he had been. He wished it were not so.

〜

Sunday morning Homer and Rachel were walking to church, as was usual for them. They were using the main lane instead of the shortcut the school children used, a sort of beeline between the house and the building on top of the hill. The regular lane made a slight circular approach, veering off to the right towards the dam before swinging back to cross between the church house hill and the Children's Home. As they approached the hill and began to climb up, Peter could be seen standing off to the side by the walk waiting. He stood there by himself, not in conversation with anyone or pretending to be. The way he was standing imparted a sense of purpose, like he was facing something important that he was glad to do but must make sure that it got done. The rising sun from the east silhouetted and accented the form of his body. Jason thought it must really be important whatever the purpose was that required such a focus of time and energy.

As Homer and Rachel approached, he greeted the family with a good morning and a handshake with Homer. Homer paused, waiting to see if there was any problem Peter wished to address with him.

"I would like to speak with Jason."

"Sure." Motioning with his head towards Jason, Homer and Rachel went on inside with the rest of the children. Bewildered, Jason followed his grandfather a short distance from the sidewalk where Peter stopped.

Looking down at Jason he said, "I am very sorry for the way I acted yesterday afternoon when we were picking up fruit out there beside the house."

Jason shrugged his shoulders. "That's okay."

"I will try to do better from now on. Shall we go inside?"

Together they walked into the church house, the old man and the young one. Their hearts were at peace — one because he tried to become a little more like the Saviour he loved, the other not because his broken heart had been mended but because some-one who was important in his eyes took the time to fix what he thought was broken. Years later when the real hurts came and were left un-mended by people who should have known better, he remembered the man who took the time in the midst of so much that troubled him to reach down for what he thought was a hurt child. Jason remembered, and in remembering he believed that the Father in Heaven must be like that too, and his heart was made strong within him. Strong to go on in a world often so heartless and cruel, because he believed that somewhere on this earth there was still life that refused to pass by even the least of these.

Chapter Thirty-Two

Jason fell into a misguided adventure during 1973. One that not all boys get into, but he did.

The dog was a little critter of a dog. Not all that unusual from the others dogs, just mangy, tick-loaded, and with a nasty temperament. The side road to Peter Stolsfus' place went right past the house, and any dog of decent respect and deportment knew that people were allowed to walk on it. Jason knew that the dog knew it. This dog was not that stupid, he just possessed malice in his heart. Maybe his mother raised him wrong, a couple snaps in the wrong place, or his share of the milk perhaps never quite arrived. Such a thing was easily possible with Honduras dogs. Rare was the nursing mother who was not skin and bones. Honduras natives treated dogs a little like gods. Not that it ever occurred to them in those terms, but they professed a great reverence for dogs. Heaven, to the natives, forbade any harm being done to any dog. Starving them, though, for some strange reason did not qualify as harm. In this matter, the Honduras natives conducted their lives a little lower than, say, even the natives of India, who at least put platters of food out to eat for their idols. Here, a dog, being protected by heaven, was also expected to eat by the hand of heaven.

What it may really have amounted to was just another excuse for doing nothing in the face of need. It was hard to tell, though, and that conclusion would then hardly explain the need for the dog's godlike status. Maybe this status was once upon a time latched upon as a convenient way to keep your neighbor from killing the poor starved beast. In Honduras thinking, bestowing this status would no doubt have been easier and cheaper than feeding the thing and would have provided the additional benefit of some religious activity on top of it all — religious activity that was right there at home, free of charge, without having to go into town and paying the priest for something. That way you saved both on food for the dog and limperas for the priest.

Any of these things could have been imagined as the culprit for this dog's nasty disposition, but Jason declined all the moderating excuses and settled for simple wickedness as the explanation. How else could you explain a dog who came barreling out from underneath the house, without warning, when one walked by and attempted to do things with one's legs that were against the design of nature to have done with them?

This dog lived at one of the houses that were like most of the houses built by the Amish early on. The house was built on boards turned on edge. These were placed first on blocks and served as the foundation on which the floorboards were then nailed. Turned on edge like that, they left spaces between the boards running the full length of the house and open on each end — excellent spots for chickens and the like to nestle in from the heat of the day and for dogs to launch attacks on passing children. This little mutt hid behind the boards, of which he could make many choices, so it was hard to tell exactly where. Lying there beside the board, he would flatten out until his body became almost level with the dust. This no doubt provided amusement all of its own sort without the thrill of chasing little boys. What it provided Jason was not sure, unless it was that the dust and its mind were of similar substance and enjoyed each other's company.

Jason took to carrying a stick with him and then later a small bb gun that he acquired for the lack of real guns. These items stopped the exploding dog attacks, but the dog still lay there just waiting for any signs of weakness or a slack moment when opportunity might present itself. This unwillingness to attack when he carried a stick or bb gun present only convinced Jason further that the dog was not lacking in cunningness. How could it not be? A good-hearted dog, full of love for his home and property and knowing that he was doing his duty, would not fail to attack regardless of the peril. Many a dog of sterling character has risked himself to protect his master's property against much more than a stick or a bb gun. That this dog chose not to present its mangy hide for even the tiniest whack with a stick just showed the caliber of his character. Plus, it left Jason with no relief from the abuse that he already suffered, like at least one good whack on the dog's hind quarters would have caused.

The dog belonged to a lady who lived with her children on the ranch. Theirs was not all that sheltered an existence, right out there in the open where the road forked on the other side of the dam. They lived better lives, though, than what would have been the case if they lived off of Amish land. Here her needs were seen by everyone and were not easily forgotten.

So, Jason made the best of things for some time. Finally he got tired of it, and set his mind to thinking about this state of affairs. What could be done? He thought and he thought, and as he walked up to his grandfather's place he thought some more. Finally it came to him — a simple plan that could not fail. He would take some hamburger, which all dogs love, fill it with some poison, and leave it for the dog to eat. Pronto! There would be no dog hiding under the floorboards of the house.

But where would the poison come from? He thought and thought some more. He possessed insufficient money to buy such an expensive item; besides he did not know what to buy. Then it came to him. He saw his uncles mixing the chemicals used to spray the fruit trees at the orchard. They handled the mix very carefully, and he heard Matthew say once when he was mixing up spray during spraying season, "This stuff is very poisonous — don't ever eat any of it."

Would this not do the job? He thought some more about it and ran calculations in his mind. The conclusion was that it would do the job. From there it was a simple matter to take a handful out from where his father kept some in the storage shed at home. He was not sure that it was the same stuff his uncle used, but it did say pesticides on the bag. Borrowing a small patty of raw hamburger from his mother's supply, he hollowed out the center so that there was still hamburger on the bottom. Pouring the pesticides into the center he covered it with the hamburger left over from the hollowing out. Patting it all together made quite an innocent-looking hamburger patty. Would not a perpetually hungry Honduras dog just jump at the chance to eat it? He thought it would.

That very day he got a chance to walk up to Peter's place for some errand his mother sent him on. When he came down the side road after forking off at the dam, he nonchalantly slipped up to the house and left the patty of hamburger sitting just inside one of the sideboards. No one was around to see him, and even the little dog was not there. The hamburger lay there out of sight to the causal observer who might walk by, but dogs can smell, can't they? Jason figured they could.

Two days later he thought it should be about time to hear of news of the dear little dog's departure. Sufficient time passed, he figured, for the pesticides to do their work. He kept his ears open when he was around people who made contact with the mother for any reports they might have. No one said anything, and the little dog was still there the next time he passed by. Thankfully he brought along his gun, just in case. Why the plan failed he could not fathom. Surely the little critter was not smart enough to smell pesticides in hamburger. Then his aunt mentioned something that cleared up the whole matter. Rather it made the whole matter a lot worse, but at least he knew what happened. His aunt mentioned that all of the mother's chickens took to dying the other week. Mightily strange thing it was, she said. None of them looked ill, but they all died the same day.

Jason found himself smitten to his heart. Now here he was doing wrong again. His conscience tormented him mightily. After suffering its ravages for a length of time, he could handle it no more and told his mother about the situation. She did not say much, but the long and short of it was that Jason found himself visiting the mother one sunny afternoon. The world kept on going around while he walked to his heavy task. He took with him an apology and enough cash from his own stash of hard-earned money to pay for the chickens.

The mother could not understand why anyone would want to poison her chickens, and Jason could not get her to understand that it was intended for the dog. She expressed her gratitude for the money, though, and told Jason's aunt the next week that it was a satisfactory conclusion to the matter. Jason decided to leave the poisons alone from then on. It proved a little more expensive to take matters into one's own hands than he planned on.

Chapter Thirty-Three

LATE SUMMER OF 1974, although they do not count the seasons so in the tropics, something was brewing in the ocean as the hurricanes formed in the Atlantic. In August, Carmen, moving west, took aim at the Central American landline with its 150 mile-per-hour winds. The trajectory was a little high and it crossed the Mexican Yucatan without doing much damage to human life. Out in the Gulf again it made landfall in Louisiana after veering to the left of the city of New Orleans. Honduras barely knew that danger passed so close by. There was no coast guard, no early warning system, and no money to spend even if there was anyone in government who cared a whole lot what the hurricanes were up to.

Four days after Carmen turned into a tropical storm, Fifi became a hurricane. Keeping itself on the same path as Carmen only lower down, it raked almost the entire Honduras coast along the northern Atlantic shore with its 110 mile-per-hour winds. The eye never ventured too far inland, blasting the land with its west-side wind currents. No one knew it was coming in those days, other than the locals who obtained a little warning from watching the weather for themselves. What if it looked bad — where was there to go? Honduras has no storm shelters to speak of, no concrete stadiums or local firehouses to go to. It is just you and your little hut as you weathered the storm.

Bouncing hard off the Central American landline at the port city of San Pedro Sula in Honduras, Fifi veered north a bit before coming ashore at Belize. From there it crossed completely over into

Mexico and out on the Pacific side. Fifi left an estimated eight to ten thousand dead, and those were the ones they could count.

It had been raining hard all that night at the Amish community. It lay around a hundred fifty miles from the coast as the crow flies. When David Bunker went out to check his rain gauge it read over six inches from the evening before. He wondered right away what could be going on but thought little more about it. Most of the others did not keep rain gauges. They awoke to water running everywhere on the roadways in big torrents. That much rain in such a short time needed to go somewhere — and come from somewhere.

Matthew Stolsfus came back from town that morning reporting that a storm disaster happened on the coast. No one from town knew too much. The news on their radios provided only sketchy information of a hurricane sweeping the northern shore. It seemed important enough, though, that Matthew made another trip into town that evening just before dark. The grocery store people said the President made a speech. A hurricane inflicted great damage along much of the northern coast. San Pedro Sula was the hardest hit. The President said that US and other International aid was already on the way. Matthew thought it strange that the President did not ask for volunteers from throughout Honduras to assist the storm victims, although no one at the grocery store seemed to think ill of the omission or have any plans to go help.

This all sounded like serious business to the Amish, so the next morning they dispatched Matthew and Elmer Hurst to investigate. David Bunker, his weekly report to *The Budget* ready to go and almost sealed in the envelope, waited to mail it when he heard the news. Each week a writer from each Amish community or district would write in the news of the community. *The Budget* was the Amish newspaper of choice, published in Holmes County, Ohio, for Amish people. The writer at the time was David Bunker, although others might substitute for him. He quickly added a section on the reports they knew so far of the hurricane, mentioning the amount of rainfall he measured at his place a hundred fifty miles from the coast and what the rainfall must have been like there. It got in the mail that morning on fast delivery, as Matthew and Elmer dropped it off at a mailbox in the capital instead of in Guateteca as was usually the case. Once in the capital, they caught the mid-morning bus for the coast, another four-hour drive. Late that afternoon, as they neared the area hardest hit, the devastation soon became apparent. It started an hour from the coast and got worse the closer they got. Honduras is a hilly country, consisting at times of up one hill and down the other. Matthew and Elmer could see all along the road what the rains did to the hills. Hillsides everywhere had long brown streaks in them. On the bottom lay the piles of mud with trees and debris mixed in. Any hut caught in their paths did not survive. Splattered in the pastures and the occasional garden plots the oozing mud was still settling. It was on the coast itself, though, where the real toll was taken on human life. The storm surge took away whole chunks of houses that lay within its reach. At points the water moved in a half mile from the shoreline. The rest of the homes the wind chewed up to some degree or another.

Matthew and Elmer were forced to leave the bus where it stopped at a temporary station. The driver said this was as far as he was going. "It is not safe to go any further."

"Why isn't it safe?" Elmer asked him.

"I have not been told too much, but the roads are not passable ahead of here. There are many people looking for help and aid. In those conditions it can be dangerous, as the law officers cannot handle everything. I will be staying here for the night. If you want to return to the capital, my bus will leave at five o'clock in the morning."

With that they left the bus and set out on foot. It was as the bus driver told them. They did not get far before they found there was little they could do to help. Other than the obvious act of expressing sympathy to the people they met, what was needed were supplies, and they had brought none with them. Here and there were dazed people walking about. The Amish men could see little rescue work going on. When they asked about this they were told that everyone was waiting for a US military ship that was coming. The authorities spread the word that it would soon pull in and dock offshore with aid.

They were told by one man, "You see that we have no strength left, and no way of getting any strength. We do not even have tools to dig for the buried ones. Our homes are gone. Our families are gone. We cannot even find the will to bury our dead. Maybe tomorrow we can, but there are so many of them."

They left him weeping by the roadside. Before dark, they walked back to the temporary bus station. For a small fee the bus driver let them sleep on the seats for the night. A small store nearby was selling food at an exorbitant price. They decided to forgo supper and bought some bottled water, which did not go up much in price. The next morning they left with the bus and headed for home, shaken by the scope of what they saw. That evening in a meeting held at Elmer's place, they gave their firsthand report to the large gathering of people who came to hear what happened on the coast.

David Bunker wasted no time the next morning, firing off a letter again to *The Budget*. In it he detailed the report Matthew and Elmer brought and mentioned that a crew of Amish were getting together to leave in two days for the coast. They planned to go with what supplies they already owned or could purchase in Guateteca and were planning to stay for a week. For the present that was all the plans they possessed. Money of course was a big issue, but David did not mention it in his letter. It would take a lot of money to do any extensive aid at the coast. Few of them owned an abundance of material possessions. Not that they were starving, but something like this would take much more than their resources could provide.

The little group that was leaving for the coast met at Elmer's place for prayer the night before they left. They asked the Almighty for help and strength, both for themselves and for those who were staying behind, so that they might have strength to give to others when they arrived on the coast.

Matthew led the group once they arrived at the disaster site. That first week they spent in cleaning up and distributing the food they brought along. In Honduras you do not pass out bottled water — the local creek suffices, after a storm or otherwise.

The Americans purchased bottled water or boiled the local water for themselves until a safe water supply could be found. All those in the group were in Honduras long enough by then to know the basics of survival when off the community grounds — don't drink the water and don't eat the greens.

American ships arrived and unloaded supplies and medical people by the time Matthew returned with his group. Also, coming from the capital, the Mennonite Central Committee already established an aid station on site by the time the second Amish team arrived. In addition to distributing their own supplies, the Amish were asked to help at the Mennonite Central Committee's site. They were glad to do this, but they declined to get involved with the US or the local government's work. When they found themselves working in the same area or alongside a government project, it was always under their own authority structures. Government and the church must be kept separate in all ways and by whatever means necessary. To the casual observer watching them help with the work at the disaster sites it may have looked like a paper difference, but to the Amish it was important.

When the week was up they returned home with a report on the great needs still to be met. By that time the checks began to come in. David Bunker's letter to *The Budget* pulled on many heartstrings, and thousands of dollars were coming in though no formal appeal for funds was ever made. With this informal system of weekly letters to the Amish newspaper, the Amish of Guateteca mounted a serious relief effort of their own. In time, the aid station at San Pedro Sula was staffed full-time by someone from either the Sanson or the Lagrange communities. For over a year and a half they provided first cleanup services, held formal church services on Sunday, and then built extensive housing in the coastal area. Jason got to visit the site when the Amish school took a tour of the relief effort. The chaperoned group spent two days at San Pedro Sula. It was memorable primarily for having to sleep on concrete floors. Most of the damage that would have interested Jason was already cleaned up.

All of this was done with the money from David Bunker's

reports in *The Budget*. Amish are hesitant to send money to foreign aid work. First of all, because they do not trust overseas mission workers. Secondly, because they do not think that religion and money go together. The second reason is likely the reason for the first, since missionaries obviously are religious, and they are usually the ones asking for money. David Bunker never mentioned or asked for money in any of his letters — not that he would have wanted to, but if he had that would have been the end of it. Since he did not ask for money and was known of course as Amish, there was no inhibition to the flow of money.

When it comes to money, the Amish do not like to have the obvious stated. Everyone knows that it takes money to mount an aid operation. Therefore, they do not want their intelligence insulted by being told how much money must be raised to do so and so. Just say what is being done. That is all that is needed. They know that someone must be giving money to have it done.

Also the Amish expect those giving aid to use their own resources first before asking others to help. It was apparent that this first rule was being followed when David Bunker reported that a group went to the coast for a week. Everyone who read that knew things were being done with local funds. That was the only logical conclusion. That was a good sign and a great confidence builder. When David reported that the work continued, it indicated that money was being sent in from outside. Knowing that others were supporting the cause, yet more Amish people concluded that the cause was worthy of support.

With this method of simple reporting, the flow of funds was plenteous for the entire time the Amish kept their aid station open. When it came time to close down, it was done again by common understanding. David simply reported that the work was now completed, and that the local leaders thought it was time to close the aid station. Naturally, some had already mailed checks when they read the report, but they were confident that things would be handled correctly. Indeed they were. The bond of trust was held secure when David reported that any funds received above what was needed for the costal aid project would be used in the

"Poor Ladies Fund." This was the first and last time that money was mentioned. In this way the whole affair was handled in the highest traditions of honesty and integrity on the part of all parties concerned.

This aid project to unwed mothers was known as the "Poor Ladies Project," familiar by this time to many of the readers of *The Budget*, as David wrote about and mentioned it many times. What he did not mention yet were the problems associated with the project. The Amish were finding that aid to single ladies tended to produce single ladies. Recently forsaken wives showed up in large numbers, looking to be added to the dole.

In suspicion that this increase was not entirely natural, it was decided to appoint a three-man board responsible for overseeing the project. These men were to research each claim. Especially, they were to see whether it was true that the men were leaving their wives only so that they could be added to the "Poor Ladies Project" and then coming home some nights for rest and solace. Soon, though, the research itself became an embarrassment for all concerned. First of all little information was forthcoming, as the locals were not known for telling the truth. Secondly, it really started looking strange to have three married men visiting certain single women in town once a month on Saturday afternoon.

Even with these problems, the "Poor Ladies Project" survived for many years. The program was run above board, and reported properly. In David's style of reporting he waited awhile before mentioning that there were some problems associated with the aid program but that this was to be expected. In this way, northern enthusiasm for helping those who were in need stayed intact, and the "Poor Ladies Project" experienced a long life of many years.

One hard case was playing out right on the ranch itself. A lady and her children were given housing on Amish land. Some were now suspicious that she was entertaining a male friend during the night, although no one could actually catch him around. If this were true it would pretty much undo one of their best test cases. The lady was moved onto the ranch in the first place partly to prevent this very thing. Whatever was happening there was definitely a man involved. It produced a child every year or so. By the strange fluke that nature is at times, it was always a girl regardless of the particular father involved. These continued pregnancies, while the woman was living right there on their land, was the final consternation of the Amish charitable minds. They brought her onto the place out of the goodness of their hearts and now were forced to keep her for the same reason. They could not turn out the woman to starve on the streets. Plus, she made a point of becoming friends with some of the Amish ladies. Not that this was hard to do, as some minds were as yet unaware of the evils that lurk about, even in sunny faces. Yet those who knew wondered how they could keep the male friends away at night, or her away from the male friends — failing that, maybe at least the results of the visits. The several plans they came up with, though, all proved to be unsuitable in their implementations. It was finally left alone, to be one of those mysteries of mankind that only God can solve.

In the meantime, the hurricane that passed by on the coast mirrored the hurricanes that were passing through the church at Guateteca. Some scored direct hits, and some did not. If the damage were as easy to repair as some of the damage on the coast, many a soul would have been happy. It did not prove to be so. Issue after issue came up regarding the church rules and standards. Allowing the use of bicycles again became a prominent issue.

There still lingered the dispute over the women's dress code. It somehow never quite went away. Some hoped, with the night fiasco of the liberal family's daughter, that connections would be drawn and conclusions made. Obviously this was not happening, and being decent people, they considered it impolite to bring up the subject to the face of those involved. Those who agreed on the subject mentioned the matter to those who agreed with them, but never mentioned it in the presence of those who disagreed. The issues alone were mentioned and discussed, which did not make much sense without the larger picture in focus. So one side thought the other was courting the world and inviting the devil in, and the other side thought their minds were just being unreasonably stupid and uneducated.

Jason hardly noticed any of the church problems. He was busy with his own life and Christian growth. He was approaching fifteen years of age, and the one big issue, baptism, now lay behind him. The attention baptismal time had brought from people around him had been embarrassing. Not that he blamed anyone, as such occasions always arouse people's interest. He learned from past experience, though, that traveling under the radar produced less conflict with people. Jason much preferred an unnoticed and uncommented status.

He devoured the book *A Christian's Secret of a Happy Life* from cover to cover. He had observed other young people who were preparing for baptism before him going around the last minute confessing their wrongs. Three of them showed up to speak with his father on a Saturday night. This had all made an impression on him, and he decided then that since this was the way it was done, why not start right away? Better yet, why do things that would need confessing later? He found this a helpful and stimulating guide for Christian living.

Those were happy years. Schooling was now over, as they are for all Amish youth. Eighth grade is it. It seemed to him like life would go on forever, just like it was, unchanged until he was grown. Growing up to him was so far in the future as to border on the impossible. The adventures on the mountain came less often, now that he must work full-time in the shop. Homer taught him the elementaries of welding and drill presses.

It also brought him in full contact with grown men who were not shy about sexual matters. No longer was it just young boys, but now day after day the truckers pestered him with stories of their delight and obsession with sex. Jason found it a distasteful subject and felt not the least desire to enter their world. To him the world he lived in held foundations that could not be shaken. None of the men he was around — his father, his uncles, and Bishop Manny — were anything like this. He figured they slept with their wives, and yet he hardly ever thought of it when around them. It just seemed normal, not out of place or unusual at all. These men at the shop came across to him as worse than animals. For even animals are not always hungry and never satisfied.

Those years were the dreamy years. Times to build tree houses and hang on to the last vestiges of childhood. If he knew then how quickly it would all end, he would have hung on even tighter, but those things were hidden from the vision. No one knew how quickly the end would come. This attitude of joy carried over to the adults; the most notable was Matthew Stolsfus. Matthew just must go adventuring or bust. Yet even he did not know that these were the last days of summer. Nor did he know how long the winter would be that was coming.

CHAPTER THIRTY-FOUR

IT WAS ALSO in 1974 that Matthew Stolsfus's wedding date was coming up fast. He was getting married. His bride to be was Deborah Mast, Jacob Mast's daughter. Matthew and Deborah were a sweet couple — a tall, lanky boy standing beside his girl, who matched him well in size and wholesome good looks. On their dates they made a lovely sight, walking down the church house hill on Sunday afternoons. It lifted everyone's spirits to see them go, shyly glancing at each other and talking in low tones. Made one feel downright hopeful about the world just to see love on the prowl and looking to multiply and replenish the earth.

Now that Deborah was facing marriage, someone slipped her a book on the subject — Christian, of course, but full of explicit details and such. Deborah checked with her mother before reading the book and was told to leave the book alone.

"Nature," her mother said, "is well able to teach its own what needs to be taught. Better leave the book learning and all that to others. To the pure," her mother said, quoting from the good book itself, "all things are pure. Some things," she said, "are best left to themselves."

The advice must have been working, because Matthew went around floating in the clouds. Maybe that gave him the ideas for some of the things he decided to do. Before he got married and settled down in a year or so, he badly needed to take in some adventures. The first one he wished to go on was a rafting trip down the river Patuca.

Guateteca lies in the middle of Honduras surrounded by

mountains on the north, south, and west. To the east, on another four-hour drive in those days, was the town of Catamoras. Further east were the marsh plains and the real jungles of Honduras. The river Patuca passed in its meandering just east and south of Catamoras. On a bridge just outside of town, one could drive over the river and enter quite easily by boat from either bank. You could not drive through the river with a vehicle, as Honduras people believed should be done with any river, especially in the dry season and perhaps even in the rainy season. At that point the river had already become too large on its way to the coast for fording either on foot or otherwise.

In the view from the bridge the river looked muddy, brown, slow moving and ponderous. Its waters were deep but without any indication of danger or threat. Its flow was south-southwest for fifty miles or so after leaving the town of Catamoras. From there it looped back gently in a graceful turn to the north-northeast and headed for the ocean. The track of the river led straight through the least-populated jungle areas of Honduras.

Sitting at home with his map in front of him, tracing the route, Matthew heard the river calling his name. He could feel it. He just must raft down the thing. Checking the next day with the locals for information, he found out they could not give him much. It was hard for him to tell what was hearsay and what was actual fact. He obtained enough information that corresponded with the map, though, to give him confidence. The river did enter the real jungle, which was one thing he wanted to see, somewhere past the loop northward. There were also rapids involved — big ones, some said, though others thought they were not too bad. One of the locals knew of someone who could serve as a guide if he really wanted to raft down the Patuca. A guide was most important, apparently. This guide would even build the raft for them right on the river site itself.

Armed with these facts and supposed facts and with his enthusiasm, Matthew persuaded Elmer Hurst and David Bunker to join him on this expedition down the river. He did not ask Deborah what she thought of it, not that she would have dared say anything anyway. They were not married yet. She, being just informed of the facts as they progressed, kept her thoughts sweetly to herself.

"What is there to fear?" Matthew asked. "I will have Elmer and David along. Both of them are good strong men. We will have a guide, and when we come to the coast there is a missionary who worked there who has a plane. I believe that plane can be hired for transportation back home." Deborah still thought it sounded like a hair-brained idea.

Two weeks later they were all dropped off with their supplies at the bridge out of Catamoras. The guide was paid his advance a week earlier to get there in time and build the raft. There he sat all right, but as to the kind of raft they were expecting, that was the problem. They were not too sure what kind it was until they saw the one he built. Then they knew for sure that the guide's time had been spent in vain. The raft looked like something from Tom Sawyer and Huck Finn, only half as big. A couple logs strapped together with rope. But being stouthearted souls and full of adventure, they were not about to turn back now. They cheerfully told the guide that it was much too small, headed back to town with a ride they caught, bought some more rope, cut down some trees with the guide's tools, and strapped on the new logs to what was already there. It still looked small when compared to themselves and their luggage, so they made some raised racks with poles for the luggage.

Pushing the contraption into the water, they watched it sink nearly to the top of its logs. There it was, bobbing up and down, even without any people on it, as if daring them to crawl on board. What were they going to do? Pass up the challenge? Of course not. Life to them needed challenge, so they climbed aboard with the guide and the luggage. Nightfall found them drifting down the lazy river, bored and pushing with poles trying to go faster. They broke reluctantly for camp when the guide reminded them that the danger of snakes was bad after dark — it was hard then seeing the things. They agreed, as they already passed several sunning themselves on the rocks.

The second day was much a repeat of the first day, and they

really wondered about this trip. A little excitement would not hurt their feelings at all. On the third day they entered the first signs of the jungle. Monkeys swung from the trees, and bright-colored birds began to fly off at their approach. They were expecting the snake problem to get worse, but it did not yet.

The fourth day the rapids started. Nothing very rough at first, but then it got worse and even worse. The guide, who professed himself an expert of the river, now seemed confused. Late in the afternoon of the fifth day, after fighting rapids all afternoon, he raised the point that his friend lived in the village just ahead.

"A good place to stop," he said. "Maybe my friend, who is also an expert guide, would consent to help with this trip."

The American crew was skeptical of any expert guide, but what could they say. The time was here to stop for the night, and obviously this guy was in over his head. If the rapids got any worse, they held genuine fears as to their own safety. Not something they wanted to speak of right then and there, but they agreed readily to the plan.

"In the morning I will find my friend. He will agree to join us, for a price of course."

This caused grumbling among the Americans who would have to pay for it. They quit complaining when their guide offered to pay a small portion of the new guy's fee out of his own fee. Not that this helped much monetary wise, but it cast the situation in a true serious light. If a local expressed willingness to part with money, it surely was for a reason. In this case, what reason could it be but trouble ahead?

By nine o'clock they were on their way and soon found the first rapids in front of them. They waited and watched to see if the purchase of the services from their new guide was worth the expense. Soon enough they found out. The new guide took charge. This way, he said, when the river forked. That side leads to big rocks. Sure enough, five minutes later the opposite side of the river they were on showed the rocks. On their side were only small ones. Later on that morning the first roar arose from the river ahead. Guide number one lost the last of the opinions he was offering and gave himself to only following instructions. It was plain that every bit of money they spent on guide number two was going to be worth it. The rapids were awful. The currents pulled the raft this way and that. Thankfully, when there was a choice of ways or approaches, the new guide always called the right one. Being Amish, they worshiped God silently while riding down the river.

"He still has mercy on the sons of men," Matthew thought.

That night deep in the jungles of Honduras they made camp. Not one of them knew where their location was or were half sure how they got there. Over the treetops the moon shone down on them. Slowly, acting like the moon they were used to seeing, it sunk down out of sight behind the trees. All of them sat there watching the moon set, enjoying the feeling of familiarity and of home it stirred within them.

When it was out of sight, Matthew turned to Elmer and said, "That was nice, wasn't it?"

"Yes, it was. Only I wish I knew why it is coming back up over there."

"What do you mean?" Matthew was puzzled.

"I mean, look over there — the moon is rising again."

They all turned to look at what was coming. It cast light first and then stuck its round side slowly up past the treetops. There was no doubt. It was the moon.

"So tell me," Elmer said. "If that is the moon. What did we just see set?"

No one could think of any logical ideas, nor have they since then. Maybe they were just tired from too many rapids, but they all insist it looked like the moon setting. It sure was the moon rising, because it stayed there all night and was still there in the morning just getting ready to drop below the horizon when they got up.

They hit the river early, anxious to get back home. The rapids got no worse, although that is not saying they were easy either. Two days later things leveled out and stayed that way until they reached the coast. It took a day of walking to reach their ride out with the missionary. He was glad to give them a lift and happened to be flying that day.

They pulled into Guateteca late in the evening, having hitched a ride from Catamoras on the big bus. Matthew said his goodbyes to Elmer and David at the corner. Elmer left them out by the Taft road. Matthew walked along in the darkness. A couple hundred yards away across the fields was David's house. Suddenly roars of laughter split the night. David's children caught their first sight of their father. He just opened the front door and walked straight in on them. It is amazing what over two weeks of life without much bathing, shaving, washing, or hair cutting will do to a man. Matthew, glad someone thought the whole thing funny, snuck into the house when he got home, cleaned up, and changed clothing before anyone saw him.

Jason heard all about it at the family gathering on Friday night. Everyone was there — Homer and Rachel, Peter and Annie, Susie, Jesse and his family, Albert and Barbara, Abe and cousin Enos. Matthew told them all about the trip down the river as Jason sat in the back drinking it in. The Patuca River was now a place of wonder for him.

Chapter Thirty-Five

THE YEAR 1974 concluded with the entire Amish community stirring itself in concern, deeply so in some quarters. A certain girl living in the northeast corner of Lagrange held up well in public, but how she did in private no one who knew anything about it was saying. Matthew Stolsfus now was missing for over three weeks. That is, his letters were missing.

Three months from his wedding date, Matthew took into hand another idea that had been in his head for some time. He would like to tour all of Central America and South America before he got married. It should not take more than two months, he said. These plans were arrived at after studying the map and reading what other information he could obtain. It looked like the Pan American highway would be the best route to follow. It ran all the way from Mexico for 16,000 or so miles, right through the capital of Honduras and clear down close to the tip of Chile and Argentina. The highway had been supported and financed by the United States in the 1940s and 1950s. Sure there were still some gaps not completed, but nothing that could not be gotten around. The scenery varied, the information said, from lush jungle to cold mountain passes of up to 15,000 feet in elevation. Some places were not passable during the rainy season.

Matthew took all the information into consideration, deciding that since it was presently dry season, and the wedding date came in three months, if he really wanted to make the trip then it was time to go. He tried but found no success persuading anyone else to go along. Maybe the recent Patuca river trip memory exerted some influence. If it did, no one was stating so; they all just found something else to do more important at the moment. Besides, it cost a lot of money they thought. Matthew figured that angle too but thought he could keep the cost down by traveling with public transportation and sleeping outside when possible.

So that is how it came to pass. He put the final trip plans together and left by himself. Letters were to be expected from him, he told his immediate family. These would come at regular intervals when possible. This was especially true for Deborah. Matthew said he would keep her informed and up to date on where he was. According to his calculations he should be back in two months. That would be one month before the wedding and still in plenty of time to get ready for the big day.

Now it was five weeks into the trip and the letters stopped coming. The last letter had been from the tip of Argentina, posted from a town called Puerto Santa Cruz, close by the Laguna del Carbon. In it Matthew stated his intentions to head for Buenos Aires and from there on to the Mennonite community in Paraguay. No one knew if he ever arrived.

The community at Paraguay had been founded some years before the community in Honduras. Peter made special mention to Matthew that he ought to stop in if possible. "They are an interesting group," Peter said." Different from us Amish. A little more liberal, the Beachys are, but they too have a burden for missions."

Peter knew the Beachys drove automobiles and owned other such modern conveniences, but it did not bother him too much. He also met the Bishop after whose name the Beachys were called. He told Matthew, "Seems like every twenty years or so we go through this as Amish and Mennonite people. Someone starts preaching revival and then the new movement gets its own name from the founder."

Revival movements were never greeted with any great joy. The established leaders did not like them at all and at times would take disciplinary measures against people who attended any of the meetings. Then the cycle repeated itself as the new movements matured over time, settled down and took on the form of a new conference or denomination. They became like your cousin who, though related to you, might not be the sort you would want to have over to your house every day.

The Beachys were still in the first stages of their movement and not quite accepted in the family yet. Their zeal burned hot — hot enough to generate the energy it took for the founding of a mission outreach in Paraguay.

Peter told Matthew, "The Beachys have quite a spectacular beginning. I guess it always goes that way when believers are called into a personal relationship with God and their emotions are stirred. They seem not to mind the cost, things like the poverty of losing one's reputation, the persecution from the established church leadership. Such people are willing to pay the price it takes for advancing the Kingdom of God."

So it was not surprising that Peter wanted him to stop in. Both communities did hold a similar faith, and Matthew also wanted to see for himself how a more liberal church approached its mission work. So that was where he was heading. At least that is what his last letter said.

There was no way to contact the Paraguay folks by telephone. Mail was much too slow a method of communication to even be considered for this purpose. A telegraph was considered but not yet tried. Sending a telegram carried quite a serious connotation with it. Deborah was not sure yet that she wanted to go that route. If it came to it, she would have her dad send a telegraph of inquiry to the folks in Paraguay. As to what good it would do, no one was sure. South America seemed to them a vast and mostly untracked piece of country.

Matthew solved the whole problem by walking in late one evening a week after his scheduled homecoming. He was surprised at both the concern and gladness expressed by the first people who saw him. They wondered where he had been. He said he was held up a little longer coming home than planned but wrote all about it. Those letters were mailed, he said, for the whole length of the trip home. Matthew was informed that those letters were not received by anyone in the community.

"We were all really worried about you."

"That is understandable if you were not receiving my letters, but I did send them."

"There are going to be some people really glad to see you," they said, smiling in that knowing way.

Matthew knew what they meant but did not take the bait in responding. Instead, he changed his plans and instead of going home first went straight over to Jacob Mast's place. It was dark by then, and no one saw him walking up the Lagrange lane. He was glad for that, for if anyone came out to talk it would impede his travel speed. Walking around the back of the Mast's house, he found Deborah alone in the back yard. What they said no one ever knew, because no one else was there. They never told anyone either. When Matthew left an hour later the wedding plans were still on for the planned date.

The following week a family meeting was held in the evening for Matthew to give a talk on the trip. It was the usual informal affair, just supper and the tales afterwards. They held it in the basement where Enos Stolsfus was living. That was the old place Homer bought from Steve Stolsfus when they left for Canada. After supper, and a good time of laughter and talking, Matthew got up to begin his story. He started from the beginning and gave a running account of each day and location he visited.

On the way down he stayed on the west side of the Andes, taking in the Inca ruins at Ingapuca just a little off of the Pan American Highway near the town of Cuenca. These ruins in southern Ecuador take up nearly 240 square kilometers of populated area. For a long time the ruins were uncared for and its stones used for the construction of present-day homes. Placed under proper care after 1919, many of the sites have been reconstructed and presented for public observation.

He loved Peru where the lower part of the country is irrigated by the far western tributaries of the Amazon. Here also the Andes mountains exceed 20,000 feet. Going high into the mountains he visited the ruins of Machu Picchu and the world's highest navigable lake, Lake Titicaca.

After reaching Santiago he figured he saw enough of Chile. Swinging over the mountains and down to the tip of Argentina, he went back up the other side of the mountains and through Paraguay visiting the Beachy community there. The country of Paraguay failed to impress him. He said it was not like Honduras — something about being hot, dry, and dusty. Neither did he have much good to say about the community of Beachys. It was a great disappointment to him after having such high expectations of seeing another missions project run by Amish-related people.

The community itself he found in a discouraged state of mind, mentally and physically. From the talk he heard, thieving seemed even a worse problem than in the community at Guateteca. One of the founders of the community was openly speaking of returning to the States.

"They lacked a driving force," Matthew said. "A lot of them seemed not to know what they wanted to believe. We here at least know that we want to stay Amish. I think they are floundering around as their initial missionary zeal wears off."

Matthew also said that a big issue was the long distance from the States. Honduras was a mere two–three hour flight to Miami or Houston. There, south of the equator, it took big money and time just to make a trip home to see relatives. Communal feelings run deep in all Amish blood, and these were making themselves evident. Another thing that Matthew said he noticed — here he turned away a little bit from the audience — "They all impressed me as poor financially. I got treated well, and got plenty to eat, but you could just tell."

Even Jason knew what that meant. Most Amish people would not be content with an imposed poverty condition. He wondered if in their focus on missions they forgot how to work hard?

Matthew chuckled, "I didn't drink their tea. It was stuff you sipped out of straws. Uck!" Matthew shook his head then continued, "Part of their problem with money is that the country is too poor to support much industry. We have thought at times it is bad here, but they have it even worse."

From Paraguay he went through Santa Cruz in Bolivia on his

way to La Paz, the highest city in the Andes mountain range. At 11,910 feet in elevation it was something he just needed to see.

The most significant story of the evening was about his coming off the mountain from La Paz. The bus took him up, but he missed it coming back down. Not wanting to stay up there for the night, since he experienced a little trouble breathing, he managed to hitch a ride for the trip down. The fellow was middle-aged and was driving a BMW by himself. Maybe he picked up Matthew because he wanted company. Whatever the reason, just outside of town when they started down the mountain, the man took the steering wheel and violently shook the car back and forth. Matthew experienced his first serious doubts about the guy and wished he could get out of the car. Keeping quiet, though, he soon learned the reason. Apparently the fellow was testing the vehicle for one last check of roadworthiness, because after finding that the car stayed together from the vigorous shaking, the man took off down the mountain. That is, he took off at seventy to eighty miles an hour. Matthew said he was unable to see the speedometer but he knew it was that fast. Down the mountain they went. The curves were taken by driving on the left side of the road, and even then the tires squealed. Obviously they made it down safely, but it was apparently quite some ride.

The rest of the trip was largely uneventful, other than the nice scenery. He left Bolivia, traveling through San Borja on the way to Brazil. The language of Brazil proved to be very different than Spanish. He had been expecting Portuguese to sound something like Spanish, but it did not. Other than his letters getting lost, which he still did not understand, that was about it. No one volunteered that night to repeat the trip or to go with him if he were going again. Jason, though, was thoroughly fascinated with the story.

The day of the wedding dawned bright and clear. The only clouds in the sky were white and fluffy, holding no threat of rain. Everyone who could be there was there. The crowd spread out on top of the church house hill after the service, where tables had been set up for the noon meal. Food was everywhere in abundance — dishes of casseroles, meats, pies, cakes, and desserts you needed to taste to determine what variant of delight it was. By that time the Amish had made many acquaintances among the locals, and many of them came invited or not. You did not have to be a personal friend of Matthew. Most considered their friendship with Peter, of whom there were many, to be sufficient grounds for attending his son's wedding. If you held no connection with the family, being an acquaintance of Bishop Manny, since he was conducting the ceremony, could be taken as grounds for attending as well.

The food of course was the biggest attraction for those who lived their lives on tortillas and beans. One of the young men claimed he fasted the whole day before in preparation for the food Americana. Jason watched in amusement at his glee, as patting his well-filled belly he demonstrated how he let out two belt holes to get all the food in. That may have been true, but several older and wiser men said they learned from experience that a prior-stretched stomach holds more than a prior-shrunk one. They showed fat hanging over their belts to prove it, having long ago decided to leave the belt buckled where it was in the hopes of somehow stemming the tide of internal fat swelling up from their middles when they looked at the ground. These were all without fail gringos, that is white people. It is hard to get fat on the local diet. The young fellow who commented on his belt stood un-convinced. He left shaking his head. "They must have fasted a long time to fit that much food in."

The wedding ceremony lacked any of the Amish norms of the north, as the couple wanted a simple wedding. No elaborate dresses or any special fuss made. Matthew and Deborah sat on the front bench of the church, having walked in together five minutes before the beginning of the service with two pairs of witnesses following them, who then sat on each side. That was it. No walking down the aisle, no special music. The church service started and ended at the usual time. Bishop Manny called them up at the end of the sermon and asked them the vow questions. There was nothing in them containing the words love, honor, and obey. Those are modern vow questions, not considered suitable for the lifelong commitment required of the truly committed.

First of all Manny wanted to know whether they both believed that God led them together. Then he wanted to know whether they both knew that marriage was sacred and highly esteemed in the eyes of God. Then he wanted to know whether they were both willing to take up the work required of such a commitment as marriage. Would they stay by the other's side in sickness, in health, in good times, and in bad times? Were they willing to let nothing separate them from each other until the God of Heaven Himself deemed fit to separate them by death? Their answers could not be heard clearly throughout the crowded church house, but no one doubted what they were.

Manny took their hands, prayed for them in his own words, and said that they were now man and wife.

Chapter Thirty-Six

THE YEAR 1975 opened with the shocker which would prove to be the beginning of the end. It all began one fateful Wednesday evening, early. At Peter's place, Abe Stolsfus, with his local crew of helpers and Matthew, was loading the final things on to the truck for the next day's trip into the capital. Every Thursday Abe ran a produce route. With a hired driver and a flatbed truck with tall sideboards, they would drive into town loaded to the hilt with whatever was being grown and produced in the community at the time. They set up to sell the items on a one-day basis. The operation was run out of a little store Abe rented in the Tegucigalpa market area. It proved to be quite a thriving business venture and gave a steady and safe outlet for the Amish people who grew vegetable products.

Darkness came quickly, as it does in Honduras, around six-thirty at the latest. It was now seven. They were just finishing the last of the loading work by the headlights of the vehicle and by two gas lanterns hung off the latticework of the stairs going to the upper floor. The headlights of the truck stabbed deep into the surrounding darkness, reflecting back some of the light from where they hit the surrounding trees and brush. The lanterns tried to help out by casting their cheery flickering glow for fifty feet or so. It made a difference, but the light seemed swallowed up by the vast outdoor darkness. Above the hiss of gasoline being turned into light, Abe was giving the final instructions on how he wanted the items packed. Things needed to be just right or they would be bruised too much on the long bouncy trip into the capital in the morning.

Just before the tall sideboard that was the tailgate could be dropped in, there was still an empty area of space that needed to be filled. If this space were not filled with something, all the motion tomorrow would knock the rest of the produce right down the hole. One of the help suggested moving the higher things down lower, but Abe vetoed that. The higher things were higher for a reason — so they would not get squashed. If you moved them lower, the heavier things would end up sitting on top of them.

Something else would have to be done. Abe remembered seeing a couple empty crate boxes out at the orchard's edge, not far from the house. This might just be the answer. He told the others he would go get some crates and left to look for them. Following the headlight beams of the truck out as far as he could, there were still no crates to be seen. A small hedgerow of bushes ran along the irrigation canal between the house and where the land began to drop off towards the creek. Maybe the workers moved the crates behind the hedgerow to keep them from being an eyesore from the house. It sounded like good reasoning to Abe, as his father would think like that, and the workers probably picked up the training by now. More likely, though, his father moved them himself.

Walking over the little flat board bridge laid across the irrigation canal, Abe was now out of range of the truck headlights. His flashlight beam penetrated the darkness on the other side of the hedgerow. There were the crates. Going through the bushes he headed in the direction of the pile stacked not ten steps on the other side. He never got to where he was going. A pair of hands seized him from both sides, closing down on his arms and pulling them backwards. The third set came across his mouth from behind with the force of muscles hardened by labor and toil in the fields of many a landowner of Honduras.

"Do not make a sound," a voice said with urgency and whispered delivery.

Abe could not have made a sound if he wanted to. He felt faint and dizzy. This was way too much to absorb quickly.

"No noise," came the next instructions, followed by a loosening of the hands on his mouth. In its place, he could make out from the shadows of the night, were guns barrels held up close to his head.

"You will do what we tell you." There was no way anyone could see whether he was agreeing or not, so they asked him. "You understand?"

Abe said that he did in a one-word answer, "Yes."

There followed a whispered conversation between two of them, while the third kept his gun barrel up close to Abe's head. All was silent then for a while. Abe could not tell how long from the pounding of the blood in his head. Time seemed to be going by at an altered state. Yet it could not have been too long before the two were back in front of him.

"This is what we want you to do. You are to walk in front of us up to the truck." They pointed towards the lights shining on the other side of the bushes. "We will follow you. When we get up to where the people are, you are to tell them in your own language that we are friends. You are also to tell them that they are to do whatever we tell them to. Do you understand?"

Abe slowly understood. "What do you men want?"

"That is none of your business. You just do what you are told. Now get going up the path."

Abe got going, finding his way cautiously across the little foot-bridge, remembering even under these conditions not to miss the boards and step into the irrigation canal. The guy on his right did not know what was coming, let alone remember. There was a splash as water heaved up onto the canal banks. Abe felt a gun barrel being brought up sharply against his back, just to remind him, he supposed. Muffled curses filled the night air as the man floundered up to his knees in creek water. He must have twisted something, because when they came into the line of the truck lights Abe could see him limp. The limp was gone, though, by the time they got to the truck. What was not gone were the ever-present guns.

Matthew was the first person to meet the little party coming towards the truck. He walked around the edge of the house and caught sight of Abe first. Instinctively he started to ask, "What took...," and then he saw the others.

Before Matthew could react, Abe told him in a low voice, in German. "Do not do anything. They have guns."

A voice behind Abe told him in Spanish, "Tell him to go get his father. One of us will go with him."

Abe responded, "I do not have to tell him. He understands Spanish."

"Good, take him to find his father." The guy in the middle motioned to the fellow on the left with the dry pant legs. "Do not let him get away, and bring the father out here."

The dry pant leg guy put his gun on Matthew. "Let us go. You will tell your father there is nothing to fear, and that he is to come out of the house."

Up the stairs they went. In the night air, the steps seemed to creak extra loud, Matthew thought, or maybe it was just the blood pounding in his ears. On the top of the stairs the landing turned to the door on the right. At this time of the evening it would normally be locked, but with the truck sitting outside being loaded, it was not. There was nothing unusual about it, as lifting the latch Matthew went in without knocking. The fellow with the gun was right behind him.

Looking up from his chair in the living room, Peter looked at Matthew. Puzzled, he wrinkled his forehead at the guy behind him. "Does he want something?"

Matthew shook his head yes. "They want something. I do not know what. There are two more outside, and they said you are to come out."

Peter shrugged his shoulders. "Okay." He looked at the gun. "If they want money, I do not have much. They can have what we have in the house. Of our other things, they can have what they want. A man cannot take it with him anyway. Mother," he called out to Annie. "I am going outside with Matthew."

This was highly unusual, causing Annie to stick her head around the corner of the kitchen and freeze. Susie opened the front bedroom door of her room slightly, just enough to see out. She did not continue to open it.

The dry pant leg guy asked Matthew, "Can he speak Spanish?"

"Yes."

"Be quiet then, old man. Come out of the house with us."

Together the two of them walked down the hall leading to the stair landing and then down the stairs. The gunman followed close behind. At the bottom of the stairs they stopped and waited.

Again there was a long pause. This time Abe saw what was causing it. The leader of the gang of three went out into the darkness, was gone for a little while, and then returned. "He says there are two more people in the house. They are both women, and they are no danger to us. We are to go and search the house for guns and money."

"I wonder who 'he' is," Abe thought looking at Matthew. He shrugged his shoulders.

Wet pant leg broke in, "If there are women in the house, are any of them young?"

"Yes, he says one is young and the other is old, but you are to let the women alone. Both of you! He says we do not have time for women. Besides, he knows these gringos better than we do. Bothering the women will bring no good to us. You are to look for guns and money only. You will do what you are told. Now go look for the guns and money."

The two left for their search, returning ten minutes later with no guns, because Peter owned none, and a little money. They gave it to the third guy, who counted it, then left for the edge of the darkness. By now Abe figured it out. There was another robber out there in the night who was the real leader. Apparently he did not want to be seen or heard by them. What reason could there be for that other than he was somebody they knew, and knew well?

Number three came back with the instructions that things were as they should be. Peter Stolsfus was not known to have much money at the house, and the produce truck could not be expected to have any. It would need a trip to town first. It was time to move on to other prey down the road. They were heading for Homer Esh. Both Matthew and Abe would come along for hostage purposes and to open doors quickly and quietly.

Peter was sent back up the stairs and told to stay inside for the rest of the night. He agreed, as there was not much else to do anyway. There was simply no way to go for help, even if he wanted to. The party then set out down the lane in the dark. A proposal by wet pant leg to use the produce truck was rejected by the number three man. It would make too much noise and attract attention.

Up the lane they went with Matthew and Abe out front, followed closely by the three men with guns. The fourth guy must have followed behind them. He made no noise that Matthew or Abe could hear. Rounding the curve that turned to the right they went up the little incline that gave a clear view of David Bunker's place on the left. Occasional stones bounced around and the gravel crunched beneath their shoes. Abe was assigned to carry about a dozen gunny bags the robbers took from the produce truck. Loot bags, he assumed.

At the top of the incline, David Bunker's lights came clearly into view. The family was not known for early retiring and was still stirring about. Wet and dry pant leg both wanted to head across the fields toward the lights. In whispered voices they told number three that this looked like a rich target. It did look like it, enough so that number three halted the walk and went back to consult with the man in the darkness. He came back with instructions to continue. David Bunker was still up, and this could cause a dangerous situation. One of the children or David himself might be able to make a break for it and alert the community to what was going on. The real money was at Homer's place anyway, he said. They were to continue as quickly as possible.

From there they made the turn to the left, crossing over the dam. Matthew thought of making a run for it down the steep right side, but decided against it. There were simply too many unknowns, the fourth guy being one of the main ones. Having bullets hitting the ground around him was also a consideration. After the incident in the potato patch with Enos, there was no doubt left in his mind that the locals would shoot.

The three got a little noisy and louder with their conversations while they were not passing close to any residence, but went back to whispering as they approached the Children's Home. At the

Children's Home corner, they turned right and five minutes later were crossing the cattle guard on to Homer's property. Number three called them to a stop just on the other side of the cattle guard while he went to consult with the fourth man following in the darkness. It must have been a strategy session on how to best approach Homer's lights and siren. The plan arrived at worked. Number three told them to walk hard and fast towards the house, and not to stop or pause for anything. Halfway there Homer's faithful dog took off, making a big fuss.

"Go, go, go," number three said. "Do not stop. Get there quickly."

The dog recognized Matthew and Abe and calmed down a little, backing off to the side of the porch. "Up to the door quickly. Knock, knock, tell him who you are, and that he is not to turn on the lights."

Inside, Homer dimly heard the dog's barking and half woke up. Looking at the alarm clock on the nightstand with its glow in the dark hands, he could see that it was still early. "Too early for much to be wrong," he thought.

Matthew and Abe knocked vigorously on the door. "It's us. Open up. Don't turn on the lights."

Homer heard them well enough and was annoyed. "Just like them Stolsfus boys to come around this time of the night. Probably want something out of the shop to fix their produce truck. Yes, it was Wednesday evening. Why can people not go to bed at decent times?"

Fumbling with the bar across the door after finding his way in the dark, he lifted it and set it off to one side. Turning the lock open he swung the door in towards himself, stepping out into the opening. Three gun barrels hit him in the lower torso area. One caught him soundly in the ribs and the other two in the stomach. He gasped for air and reeled backwards, his left side burning like fire. Catching himself on the now swinging door, he kept from falling over. He was too dumbfounded and shocked to say anything.

"Don't move. You will not be hurt."

The voices were in Spanish, which he could understand just

fine. Where had the German voices of the Stolsfus brothers gone? That was what he could not figure out. Then he saw them, standing just outside on the porch. It was Abe and Matthew. He asked them in German, "What is wrong?"

"Silence!" came the order in Spanish. "You are not to talk with them."

The gravity of the situation and what they were doing seemed to be sinking into the robbers. It could also have been the lust for potential loot, now that they were at Homer's place, or the now multiple hostages that heightened the situation. Whatever it was, they pulled out rope from somewhere and tied everyone up, each man's hands behind his back and then all together in one long line.

This all took some time, and Rachel got curious about what was going on. She lit her kerosene lamp, heading out towards the front door in her housecoat. Getting to the front required going through the kitchen, which then led down three steps and out to a large foyer, where the front door opened on the left. The robbers saw the light coming through the kitchen opening. With the light in her eyes from the kerosene lamp, she could not see that far. She lifted the lamp away from her so that it would cast its light farther out. The maneuver worked just in time to reveal the gun barrels on the other side of the kitchen opening. They were pointed straight at her. Why she did not scream she never knew, but a great calm came over her.

In a voice that did not even tremble she asked in Spanish, "What do you want?" That was as far as it went. She did not understand the reply, as her Spanish was quite elementary even after all these years. For reasons even she did not fully understand, Rachel never learned to master the native tongue.

A voice that spoke German from beyond the kitchen opening said, "Just do what they tell you. They are robbers." She was sure it was her brother Abe's voice, but why was he on the side of the robbers? Was not he the one Homer went to open the door for? It really made no sense at all. But the immediate did make sense. There were three guns pointed at her. The men were talking rapidly to her in Spanish, and she could make no sense out of it. Words here and there came through. "Dinero" — she understood that. "Casa" — she understood that. So they probably wanted to search the house for money.

Still the calm stayed with her. Taking her kerosene lamp as the guiding point, she motioned the men to follow her. They did not like this and grabbed her by the arms, taking the lamp from her. With a man on each side of her and the third staying to watch the hostages, they began the tour of the house. First they went to the bedroom where she came from. Ransacking the closet and every drawer in the room, they threw clothes every which way right in front of her eyes. They found two guns in the closet, which produced smiles that could be seen even in the flickering light of the kerosene lamp.

Where was the money, though? So far they found a few limperas in the one drawer where she kept her spending money. She could tell that anger was rising up in them. They jabbered in her face with some more Spanish that she could not understand, gesturing with their guns. It then occurred to them to search the other rooms of the house. The kitchen was handily right there, but gave up nothing when searched, because there was nothing there. Next came the children's bedrooms down the hall, with the girls' first and then the boys'. When one of them looked in at the first bedroom it was obvious that it belonged to a child. Toys and clothing were scattered around and other such childlike signs.

He turned to her and asked something. The words she did not understand, yet she knew what it was. He was asking whether they were boys or girls. She just knew it, plus she understood "muchachos" or "muchachas." That was boys or girls, she was sure. She felt certain they would not go looking for money or guns in the children's rooms, but would they go looking for something else? For the first time that night fear gripped her. Her heart pounded and her head felt light. What was she to do? The man was still looking at her, waiting for an answer, as the kerosene lamp sent its bouncy light flickering off the paneled bedroom walls. She said, "Muchachos." Later she wondered at how easy it was to lie and the fact that the words had even come out at all. The man grunted to himself, moving on to the next bedroom. Looking in and seeing it was obviously another children's bedroom, they moved on.

Now the guns were up again and "Dinero" was back in the sentences. What was she going to do? She needed to get these men out of the house. Should she tell them about the safe? Homer designed a nifty sliding panel in the bedroom closet that opened up into a false ceiling in the basement. She was sure there was plenty of money in there. Too much, she thought, to be able to lose it easily. Homer would not want her to show it to them. What was the other option?

Then she remembered. Wasn't Homer planning to go to the capital this very morning? Wouldn't he have money on him for that trip? Supplies needed to be purchased for the shop with cash, as checks were not trusted in those days in Honduras. Where was that money? In his pants pocket, no doubt. Did he have those pants on? No, they would be lying beside the bed in preparation for the trip in the morning. What he wore now was an old pair he used for work. She would give them that money.

Having decided it, she motioned with her hand and said the one word, "Dinero." They were more than willing to follow. Taking them into the bedroom, she pointed at the pants lying on the floor. One of them picked it up and shook it. Nothing happened. She motioned for them to look in the pockets. They did, and found the billfold. It contained over 3000 limperas, about 1500 dollars in those days. It was enough, she could tell by the smiles. Quickly they left through the kitchen door opening and out the foyer. She waited a little bit and then stuck her lamp out into the foyer, expecting to see Homer sitting there, or something. There was nobody there. The foyer was empty.

Out by the lane the little party huddled while the routine was repeated. Abe filled Homer in on the details as the number three man went to consult in the darkness. He came back with the report that there should have been more money found. Since there was not, they would have to continue on to some of the other places. They were to go for Jesse's place next. The three hostages were ordered to get moving — Abe first, then Matthew, followed by Homer. Strung together like animals going to market, they headed down the hill towards the south and Jesse's place. There were two slight rises and falls in the land between Homer and Jesse. In the bottom of the first one, the number three man called for a halt. He untied Abe's hands at the front of the line and took him aside. Placing him under the guard of wet pant leg, he forced Matthew and Homer to kneel one in front of the other. Backing off a few steps to the side, he instructed dry pant leg to stand in front of them with his gun ready. There was no doubt as to what the plan was. The hostage number was too high for necessity's sake and was about to be reduced by the basest method available. Homer only felt numb as the certainty filled him that he would never see the dawn of another day. Matthew felt a great sorrow at having spent so little time yet with his young wife. Both of them prayed to God that He might have mercy on their souls.

Before number three could proceed, though, he needed to consult with the man in the darkness. Coming back from that, he showed disgust in his voice. "He will not let us do it. Let's go." Grabbing Abe roughly, he tied him back up to the front of the line after pulling the other two to their feet. The party of people started moving again, going up the incline towards Jesse's. Arriving there the same method of entry was used, yielding very little money or weapons. They left Jesse's without any more hostages, only warnings to stay quiet until daylight. From there they swung back up north by the Taft Road to Elmer Hurst, where they added him to the hostage line. The frustration level of the robbers was rising with their inability to get the quantity of money and guns they desired. A few hundred feet from Elmer's another hostage elimination attempt took place. Again it was stopped after consulting with the fourth man in the darkness.

By now it was two o'clock in the morning as they headed up the Lagrange lane towards Lee Stuzman's and Minister Robert Troyer's places. The robbers decided to stop in at both of them, but bypassed Jacob Mast's place. Their attention span was getting short as they quickly went through the houses after rousing the occupants from their sleep with German words and knocks on the door. The yield was getting yet lower, and they took no more hostages. From there the entire party went across the fields of Lee Stuzman, which led straight to the mountains to the north of the settlements. A little ways into the open field number three called a halt again, untying everyone from the ropes. He said nothing more as the three robbers picked up the gunny bags the hostages were carrying and simply walked off into the darkness.

The four Amish men waited until they were sure the robbers were not coming back, and then numbly started walking back towards their homes. Elmer split off just over the bridge on the Lagrange road, Abe and Matthew at the Children's Home complex, and Homer walked home by himself across the cattle guard. The first streaks of dawn were just breaking in the sky as he opened the sliding iron latch on the yard gate of his home. Rachel met him at the door in a total wreck of tears and weeping.

Two hours later the sun was fully up, but Homer did not open his shop or go to the capital. He just sat around all that day nursing his ribs and his shattered psyche, as the news of the night's event flew back and forth across the Amish community. Jason, who slept through the whole thing, sat on the board fence with his brothers and sisters watching as people came and went. Long discussions were held by the adults on what should be done. It was decided that the police must be notified, which they were. The local officer said it was too big a matter for him to handle. An assault of this magnitude would have to be referred to the higher authorities. Two days later the Honduras version of the FBI arrived and began their questioning. They soon came to a conclusion about who must have done this. A notorious criminal, "Carlos the Mano," was just released from a lengthy jail term for other armed robberies. They were sure that was the guy who masterminded this. He must have been the fourth man in the darkness. Some fellow was then captured the next week, whom none of the Amish ever heard of before. He was brought through the community on a flatbed truck. Homer as well as the others was asked to come out and identify the guy. He stood their scowling on the back of the truck, tied to the front iron bar beside a supposed accomplice. No one could identify anything — besides, no one saw the fourth man in the darkness. Jason came out of the shop to look at the two men standing on the back of the truck. They did not look dangerous at all, not nearly dangerous enough to cause all the uproar that was going on. Wise in Honduras ways by then, he assumed the police did not have a clue as to what was going on. These were just some men they had dragged in to make the gringos happy. Nobody really knew who performed the robbery.

Several of the Honduras Secret Service spent a few nights north of the communities near the mountains waiting for any repeat attack. Nothing happened other than some noise in the bushes and the same bushes being racked by the agents' gunfire. By the time all was said and done, the pall of that night would cast its shadow for many years, both in the memories and in the souls of those who were touched by it. How could things ever be the same again? Was it not true that once the glass was shattered it could not be put back together again? At least not quite like it was before. Jason knew now there was trouble ahead.

Chapter Thirty-Seven

Following the armed robbery and during the rest of 1975, talk of leaving increased. The motivation for doing so was already around before the incident. Now, though, it grew four-fold. Liberals and Conservatives formed their increasingly clear lines. Bishop Manny tried his best to bridge the gap between the two, but so far had not succeeded.

No one wanted to leave, if the truth were known. Too much was at stake — the mission vision on which the community had been founded, the personal delight of living in the country. To a man, they enjoyed Honduras in spite of its obvious drawbacks of thievery. Yet religious passions stirred beneath the surface and demanded attention.

The Liberal side wanted votes on the issues troubling them, perhaps feeling confident that their choice would carry. The Conservatives did not want voting on any issue, at least not under the new system of doing things. Bishop Manny pondered it all often and decided for now not to have any votes, but continue working on the problems. Perhaps there was some common ground between the two factions.

Jason listened, until he was told to go on into the house, to one of the conversations that were becoming ever more frequent. Homer and Rachel were talking with Jesse and Lois out by the sidewalk gate after church.

Rachel was saying, "I will simply not have it, the way the women are dressing. They want a vote to change the "ordnung," but they are already changing it by the way they are acting. How can we control anything if people can just do what they want without regard to the rules?"

Jesse said, "I know that, Rachel, but you know how close the ministers are. They must talk with each other all the time. Their wives have ideas too, and most of those are not what ours are. Bishop Manny must be exposed to all of that. It is just a great disappointment to me that Vern and Robert have turned out to be so liberal."

"There is nothing we can do about that now," Rachel continued. "Remember our conversations in Fraserwood, before we all moved? Dad wanted Amish ministers involved. He could never have done all of this on his own. You know that. It cannot be helped. How did we know who was going to be liberal and who was not?"

Homer joined in, "Do you really think things are serious enough that we should be talking of moving? I know the robbery shook us all up. It sure did me, but we can live with that. Things have kind of settled down."

"It is not the robbery, Homer," Jesse said. "All of us are saying that. We can stand to lose our worldly goods. What is really the real concern is the state of the church."

"But why do we need to go back?" Homer wanted to know. "I know that things like the bicycles, the suspenders, and women's dress issues are important, but remember how it used to be in Fraserwood? I can't even work in town anymore if I go back there."

Jesse shifted uncomfortably. "That was a little over-bearing what they did, but I understand it better all the time. Their concern was real, and they were trying to stop the very things we are dealing with here. Can't you see that, Homer? It was uncomfortable, and it cost you money. It would still cost you money if you moved back and had to work under those conditions. Yet look what's important. Do you want your children growing up in a liberal church? Look how some of the young people are acting. Look how they are running around without suspenders, parting their hair like English boys. Sure the medicine used by Bishop Wengerd seemed a little strong to us at the time. Yet I would be grateful for some of that strong medicine right now. Like in the church down here, for example."

Rachel jumped in to Bishop Manny's defense. "I do appreciate though how he stresses the spiritual end of things. Like being born again. Jason has been really doing well under his preaching and guidance. I would miss some of that in Fraserwood."

"There is no reason we cannot have that same thing in Fraserwood," Jesse insisted. "Amish people believe in being born again, they just say it differently than English people do. Why do we have to use all these English terms for things? It makes me uncomfortable at times. What good is it anyways to talk about the inside and getting it right, when the outside is so messed up. I don't give much for that kind of talk. It's all just talk to me, excuses taken by people who want to do what they want to do. I want to see the righteousness of God on the outside. To be around people who do what is right, not just talk about their good experiences they have in private. What good is that to anyone? What good does that do to the church? How does that benefit the community of believers? All this talk, talk, promises, promises about how spiritual they are becoming, when no one can see it."

Rachel nodded her head. "That's all true, but I would still miss it. You know, Jesse, that it is not the same. Bishop Manny has something in his life I would really miss."

"I suppose you would," Jesse said. "He is a real nice fellow. He just doesn't know how to keep any discipline in the church. I get tired of niceness when things need to be straightened up."

"But Jesse," Rachel continued, "it is more than niceness. He really has that spiritual life he preaches about. I know he can't keep church discipline, and that is the bad side of it. Does it always have to be that way? I wonder sometimes. Are spiritual people always liberal leaning, and conservative people always a little mean?"

Jesse chuckled. "I hope not. I'm not mean, am I?"

Rachel joined in the humor, "No you're not. You're a nice person. Yet it's hard to figure out. People that look right on the outside, which you can see, say they are right on the inside, but they often don't act like it. Then the people who look wrong on the outside say it doesn't matter anyways because the inside is all that matters. Although I can't see that most of them act any better. Why is it like that? What does it take then to really make the inside right? It's all very confusing."

"That's just my point," Jesse said. "It's not safe to say we are right on the inside if the outside does not match up. That kind of confession does not hold water. No one is impressed. The most important thing that we can control is the outside. That is our responsibility to get right. The inside, only God can make right. We have to trust him for that. If some people fail to allow God to do that, I would still take my chances with that bunch. At least they are trying to do what is right. That seems better to me than not trying at all."

"It is just hard for me to think of going back, though," Homer jumped into the conversation. "It was not a nice place to live. My brother and how he acted. Think of how different it is down here."

Jesse was pensive as he thought. "I know it would be hard, Homer, but I am afraid it will have to be done. Hopefully I am wrong, and things will work out. Maybe Bishop Manny will come to his senses and choose to rein things in, but for some reason I do not have much hope. His sympathies are just drawn so deeply into all this spiritual stuff. He has a hard time seeing the dangers that lie along the way. I think his heart is in the right place, but he has to use his head too. God does not intend for us just to feel and not to think."

Standing by the front window looking out, Jason saw them wrapping up the conversation and part ways. Jesse and Lois went on down the lane towards their house. Homer and Rachel were still talking coming up the walk.

The following Sunday, after church, Bishop Manny called a members meeting for Wednesday night. There, he proposed a surprise move. His fellow ministers obviously were in on the news, but no one else knew anything about it. The proposal was this: ordain a new minister.

It was obvious by their faces that this was an unexpected turn of events. So the Bishop continued with an explanation. "I know this comes as a surprise to many of you, but I feel like this might be an answer to our problems. We are, first of all, short on a minister since Robert is working at St. Marks. Then, perhaps God could show us the way this church is to go by giving us direction on a minister."

Those explanations were all the reasons they needed to hear. Everyone knew what was being proposed. The dice was to be rolled. Not that they would have used such English terms, but the lot was to be cast. Not just cast in the choice of a minister, but cast for the direction the church was to go. That was what the Bishop was proposing. He never said it, but they understood. Things were out of his hands, and he was appealing to the Almighty for help. The bishop felt that he was helpless to solve this problem, and like the scriptures said, "The lot causeth contentions to cease, and parteth between the mighty" (Proverbs 18:18). This was what the Bishop was proposing.

They thought about it. Threw the options around in their heads. If the lot ordained a liberal minister, then the church would go liberal. If the lot ordained a conservative minister, then the church would throw its weight onto the conservative side. They thought some more and went for the idea, each side comfortable in the decision. The liberals were convinced their cause was right and that things must go their way. The conservatives were willing to cast it into the hands of God. If they died, they died. So it was decided. Another minister would be ordained. The vote was unanimous with no abstentions.

Since communion was in two months, Bishop Manny set that as the date. It felt like it came rather quickly, considering what was at stake. The tension in the church house was palpable that morning as the service continued through the day of preaching. By three o'clock communion was served and the feet washing done. It was time for the ordination.

Four men were in the lot that morning. Two were clearly liberal. One young man had ideas not yet fully baked. One was a strong conservative. After the books were set up and taken, the men lined up on the front bench. Bishop Manny came to the first man in line and took his book, opening it. The inserted paper almost fell to the floor as the Bishop's hands shook. The first man was the conservative.

Jason could see the shocked looks on some of the faces as Bishop Manny officially announced who was chosen. They were still there as the ordination continued and church closed.

Outside the church-house steps the talk started. "I thought God would give us someone who could speak Spanish," someone said.

The speaker's neighbor concurred. "We so desperately need that. What with the great need for evangelization and outreach."

"How could we have been so wrong in our expectations?" the first speaker continued. "I was sure God wanted us to increase our outreach. We can't do that if our preachers can't even speak Spanish."

"I can't understand it either," the neighbor said.

So they did not understand it. A month later they still did not understand it. The new preacher was somewhat new to Honduras. He had moved there two years prior, but Spanish speaking still came hard to him. Nowhere was the fluency with which Bishop Manny could speak Spanish evident, or any signs of that fluency flourishing anytime soon. To really make matters worse, from the liberal point of view, was that he cared more for church purity than for evangelistic outreach.

The liberals would have none of it, lot or otherwise. There must have been a mistake made. The conservatives said little, because they had after all won, had they not, and one must be charitable. Whether this was a wise course of action throws one into one of the great questions of the ages. Why do decent people have such a hard time closing the deal? They rely heavily on the virtue of their stand, shunning the gritty politics of consolidating power.

In this case it did not work. Six months later Bishop Manny was clearly being swayed by the invigorated liberal movement and was on the edge of openly joining the cause. A month later he did, announcing his intentions on Sunday morning.

Jason was in the living room when he heard his parents talking in the kitchen.

"Looks like this might be it," Rachel said.

"I'm afraid so," Homer agreed. "I still hope we don't have to move back to the States."

"I will do it before I go liberal," Rachel said. "We have to think of our children."

Chapter Thirty-Eight

It was also during mid 1975 that Jason was baptized. In Amish culture baptism is an important but lengthy affair. Not the actual baptism — that is accomplished by three little splashes of water. Jason had watched the rite many times. In drama it ranked only after communion time and an ordination. Tied in with the six-month cycle of Amish church affairs, the opportunity for entering the next baptismal class was announced within a few weeks of communion time. Jason was now old enough and had joined the instruction schedule some five months earlier.

Each Sunday morning, on what was called "Church Sunday" versus "Sunday School Sunday," the class met. In Honduras there was no division between "Church Sunday" and "Sunday School Sunday," so instructions were taken every second Sunday. After church starts, Amish ministers always file out for consultations between themselves. "Out" is an upstairs room if church is being held at a home, or into the house if church is in a barn. In Honduras it was on top of the church-house hill.

If there is a baptismal class the applicants follow the ministers out, after an appropriate pause for respect. Once out, the applicants are instructed in church doctrine for thirty minutes or so. The applicants then file back in by themselves, and the ministers come back later led by the bishop. This drama and rhythm of church life lends to and encourages the feeling of permanence and importance of Amish life in general.

Baptism was in two weeks, and Jason was tense and worried about it. Bishop Manny had dispensed with the normal Amish tradition of drilling the applicants on the importance of Amish traditions. Instead he had stressed over and over again that one must be born again.

"I want you to understand," he said on many a Sunday morning while the ring of ministers and applicants sat on top of the church hill under the wide-open skies, "that we are not saved by anything else but the Lord Jesus Christ. If we are not born again the Amish lifestyle will not save us. Are each of you sure that you have been born again?"

The insistent questioning could have undermined his confidence if Jason had not been so sure of his own conversion. Perhaps because of this, Bishop Manny let the parents know individually, in case there was any misunderstanding, that he was not trying to question anyone's experience.

"I just want to be sure someone is not being baptized unconverted. That is a real problem among us Amish," he told them. "I don't want it to happen under my care."

Homer told him, when the bishop spoke with them, that the concern was appreciated and respected. It was hard not to like Bishop Manny.

With baptism on his mind, Jason was surprised when one of the older youth of the community approached him with a plan. "We are getting a group together to walk back to St. Marks next Sunday. We would like you to join us."

Jason wanted details. St. Marks was a mission outreach farther back into the mountains to the south of Guateteca. Two Amish families, led by Minister Robert, manned the post under an experimental agreement with the main Amish church. If things worked out, perhaps more Amish families would join the two; if not, then no hard feelings would be held. So far, all was going well and the locals were attending the Sunday services in moderate numbers. Contact was kept up with the front community on a regular basis, with visitors encouraged to visit often. The trip by vehicle took around an hour and a half across mountains and roads much worse than those into the Capital. St. Marks was where the youth planned to go.

"Five of us youth want to visit, and we would like for you to come along," the youth leader told Jason.

"But my baptism is the Sunday after next," Jason brought up right away.

"I know that, but there is no problem with getting back in time. This is what our plans are. We will walk back on Sunday morning, attend the services, and then catch a ride back with someone on Monday morning."

"Walk back. How in the world can you do that? It takes an hour and a half by vehicle. That's a long way." Jason was emphatic.

"I know, but it's not as bad as it sounds. The road actually goes by a long round-about way," which Jason already knew from personal knowledge. "There is a trail that goes almost straight as an arrow from Guateteca to St. Marks," a fact Jason did not know.

"How do you know this?" Jason asked. He was not unfamiliar with the surrounding countryside and had never heard of such a trail.

"One of the men who lives back there told me. He has himself walked the trail a few times when there was no ride out. Granted, he is a fast walker, but he does it in three hours."

"In three hours. You have to be talking of Al Yost." Jason guessed correctly. Al was an outdoorsy type of person, ruggedly built with a full face of hair. He did not shave his beard into the normal right-angled Amish style. Instead he left it to grow wherever it could, just clipping it into manageable length. Jason could well believe the tale of him walking back to St. Marks in three hours. But for the normal person to repeat the deed was another matter.

He probed further. "So how are you going to walk it in three hours, and with girls along? We are not anything like Al Yost."

The young fellow said, "I know that, but I figure if we allow ourselves a few extra hours, we can do it."

"So what are the times?" Jason wanted to know.

"We start out from here in the community at three o'clock a.m. Sunday morning. That should give us an hour extra to reach Guateteca. With an extra hour added on to Al's three from Guateteca to

St. Marks, that should give us five hours total. That would be seven o'clock for our arrival time at St. Marks. Plenty of time for them to serve us breakfast and be at the service by nine o'clock."

Jason was skeptical but so what. Adventure was adventure, and he was not the one responsible if something went wrong. Why worry? He knew Honduras and its hills, and something did not add up.

"Why can't we just hire a vehicle?" he tried one last time.

"You know it's too expensive, plus no one goes back on Sunday morning. Are you going with us or not?"

Jason said he would. That was on Wednesday evening. Sunday morning he got up at 2:30, met the group at the rendezvous at 3:00, and they were off. If off it could be called. There were three boys and three girls, all in their Sunday dress with Sunday shoes on ready for Sunday church, with five hours of walking in front of them.

They shuffled through Guateteca an hour and a half later. Jason sincerely wished for his horse, but the horse was at home. There was not a vehicle anywhere to be seen on the roads. The whole town seemed to be asleep. South of town where the road dipped to cross the river they had to take off their shoes and socks to get through the water. One of the boys tried to use some stones that appeared to be set up for crossing purposes. Whether it was his slippery Sunday shoes or the dark moonless night he lost his footing and fell in. Thrashing around in the shallow water only made matters worse and convinced the rest to do it the other way — take off the foot-wear, cross over, and put the foot-wear back on.

No one had brought a flashlight along or any other basic element for hiking. Even Jason had brought nothing. He wondered about this later. Never did he leave for the mountains without a knife, his canteen, and if at night for sure a flashlight. What had gotten into him to leave without any of this? He knew then, as he became assured of it even more later, that it was the dressing in Sunday clothes that had done it. Sunday clothes meant going to a safe place where one was protected from the weekday dangers and necessities. It also spoke of a power exercised by religion that makes men and women change their normal behavior patterns. In this case it was not so good, because they rather needed those weekday patterns.

"In the future I will wear my normal clothes and change when I get there," he thought. But then on second thought he knew that would take a lot of daring, as the instructions had been specifically to dress in Sunday clothes so that no time would be lost once they arrived at St. Marks.

If the others were thinking the same thoughts they said nothing, but got up after putting their socks and shoes back on and started off again. The moist Honduras night hung heavy in the sky. Dawn was still an hour away. A slight river mist rose up to fill the valley in front of them. To the right they found the walking trail that broke off from the main road. That was what they thought it was anyway. No one was very sure about anything anymore.

The group of young people walked off into the darkness, their feet moving slowly as they approached the first hills. Up they went and down again, winding this way and that. Trails soon began to break off from what was clearly the main one. Then soon no one knew which was the main one. Here it forked again with both trails looking equally well traveled and going to the south. They took the best choice according to their own judgment.

Dawn found them in the hills somewhere, thirsty and hungry. The first concern with the coming of light was to find the St. Mark's mountains. They were the distinctive mountain range behind the town. No doubt they had an official name, but the Amish called them the St. Mark's mountains. In finding the mountains they would know if they were going south or not. On the top of the next hill they found them, to their right instead of dead center. That meant they were off course by a few degrees. This was corrected at the next trail choice and served as the compass from then on.

The next problem was water. All of them were well informed as to the dangers of drinking surface water of any kind. High in the mountains was the one exception. There a person could be fairly sure of the quality of the water. This was not high in the mountains though, but it would have to suffice.

Another of the numerous little trickles of water soon crossed the trail. They paused, contemplated the steepness of the hill, and then decided to climb closer to the top before drinking. Boys and girls together scrambled up the greenery to where the water pooled in a shallow little corner by some rocks. There were no huts in sight either higher up the hill or below it.

"This looks okay," one of them said. They took turns cupping up the water with their hands and drinking deeply. Such little mountain-fed streams have their own taste, deep and mineral like, and satisfying.

As the morning wore on the St. Marks Mountains seemed to come no closer. They continued up and down the little foothills.

"We are never getting out of this by next Sunday," Jason finally ventured.

They others assured him that they would. An hour later they found their first hut and asked for directions. The result was a general waving of the arms towards the St. Mark's Mountains and assurances that riders often came through here going to St. Marks. That sounded reassuring.

"How far is it to St. Marks?" they asked her.

"Oh, an hour or so. I don't know. I have never been there. Often I go back to Guateteca, but St. Marks I go not to," she told them.

"How far is it to Guateteca," they asked her.

"Two hours on foot, I think, but I go with horse. It is faster," she said.

So they continued on, not much comforted in their journey. It was now nine o'clock in the morning. Church would be starting by now.

"Maybe if we hurry we can be there for a part of it," one of them said. They all knew he was dreaming. They had yet to find any familiar landmarks at all. Thirty minutes later they did find one — a larger river they knew from driving in by road. Crossing again was a hassle and took time. Beyond would lie the main road, and they quickened their pace at the thought of its familiarity.

Finding it rather quickly after leaving the river they now knew they were no longer lost. It would only be an issue of arriving.

They did that at a quarter after twelve, walking up to the house of the first Amish dwelling feeling dismayed and disheveled. Services were already over and dinner was on the table.

"So where have you been?" Minister Robert asked them in a questioning tone. "We were expecting you hours ago."

Jason was glad he was not answering the questions. It was not lightly looked upon for youth to be unaccounted for, especially if they were by themselves without adult supervision for an extended period of time. After explaining that they had been lost, the matter was settled satisfactorily. Jason could see the reason why, though, and it was not for the reasons given. Without the youth leader's reputation with Minister Robert, which was impeccable, their tale would hardly have been believed.

On Monday morning the group caught a ride back to Guateca, where they ended up walking out the rest of the way. Their ride continued on westward away from the community.

The rest of the week was uneventful for Jason. Sunday morning found the class seated outside on the hill for their last instructions.

"After today," Bishop Manny said, "you will now be full members of the church. As that, you are expected to take your responsibilities seriously. When matters come up for voting, consider the matter well. You boys will be asked, from time to time, to give testimony on the sermons."

Jason's heart froze in fear, but what was there to say? "I am just sixteen years old. How in the world am I supposed to give testimony to a minister's sermon?"

The Bishop continued, "I do this because I have confidence in our younger members and want to hear what you have to say on church matters. Another thing we have not spoken on yet is the 'Holy Kiss.' You will now, after today, be expected to participate in it. Sisters with sisters," he nodded towards the girls in the class. "And brothers with brothers."

Jason's stomach turned again, but not with fear this time. He had often, when he was younger, kissed his mother goodnight on the cheek, but kissing a man on the lips? That was another matter.

Yet he knew that it was decreed, and such a law could not be broken.

When class was done they all filed back to their prepared places on special benches. It was on the front row, boys on the men's side and girls on the women's side. The service seemed extra long in such an exposed situation, but it finally came to an end.

Bishop Manny asked them all to kneel. He then read the vows, pausing after each question for their response. The sound of yeses proceeded down the front row modulated by the degree of voice change in each boy and expression in the girls' voices.

When he was done, the bishop took the pitcher of water standing behind the pulpit, gave the pitcher to Minister Vern, and then cupped his hands over each applicant's head. Minister Vern poured the water at the sound of each mention of the Trinity.

Bishop Manny recited from memory, "On the confession of your faith and before these many witnesses, I baptize you in the name of the Father, the Son, and the Holy Spirit."

Going back to the start of the line he took the hand of each boy, helped him up, and greeted him with a kiss. For the girls he took their hands and then made room for his wife, who had joined him by then. She completed the introduction for each girl into Amish church life.

Jason was glad he was baptized, but he was also glad the day was over.

Chapter Thirty-Nine

Now late into 1976 and a year after the ordination, Jesse Stolsfus decided that he and his family were at their end. They were moving back to Ontario, the home territory near the town of Fraserwood. The Amish community there was still going strong and would welcome them back with open arms. It was not just the armed robberies. The church problems coming to a head were the real problem.

Bishop Manny finally gave in to the pressures from the reformers and put some of the issues to a vote. The first one to come up was the bicycle. Changing the rules passed by more than a sixty percent vote. So now the community was full of young Amish boys, Jason among them, riding their bicycles, native plastic streamers still attached from their former owners. Up and down the lanes they rode, honking their air horns in high glee at their newfound freedom. It was enough to make the soul cringe. Several of the men quickly banded together and removed the horns from the young boys' bicycles. At least then the riding would be done in silence. There was no reason, they thought, that insult should be added to injury, like the proverbial salt rubbed in the wound.

The issue that had been voted on, the bicycles, was bad enough, but the dynamics behind it were what really hurt. Jesse told his father, "This is just not the Amish way of doing things. Nowhere can you find in any stable Amish community where the rules are changed with anything less than a one hundred percent vote. Maybe in extreme cases a vote could be passed with one or two dissenting votes, but then only with the presence and consent of an older and experienced Bishop. This is the bedrock on which the whole system rested securely. If we remove that, then really we already have a liberal church before any votes are even cast.

"You know how majority rule is spoken of at Fraserwood. They would be horrified at what is happening. It would be anathema to them. This change of the rules by Bishop Manny can be easily seen for what it is. Now that we have crossed the line, the whole community here in Honduras will be little better than a tree caught in the currents of whatever winds blow up the valley. If the people feel like it, they can change anything. All it takes is a solid majority vote, stirred up by whatever passions are around at the time. Today it could be this, and tomorrow it could be whatever they please it to be." Jesse looked with horror on the situation. He was leaving while his family could still be saved from the coming destruction.

Bishop Manny heard about all of this, many times, in his conversations with the conservative members of his congregation. But it was a concept Bishop Manny was not sure about. Things looked a lot simpler to him than this. Was it not just a vote? A vote was not such a big thing. If it did not work out, could they not change back? How was he to know that Jesse and the others knew better? One thing the Bishop did know was that rules could be overdone. Was this maybe what was happening?

Peter told Jesse, "I never dreamed things would come to this point. From the beginning I planned to operate this missions outreach fully within the Amish culture. Sure, the others say this culture is not necessary. They say it is simply the general culture of the world frozen in time from a hundred and fifty years ago. That is true. I agree with them. It is just that I do not see the culture as a negative thing.

"The Amish have believed for a long time that living in the culture of a hundred and fifty years ago produces a measure of the mindset associated with that culture. We like what the old culture possessed. Not just the fact that they used horses and buggies and lived simply — that is incidental. It is really because, by and large, that culture was amenable to the practical applications of scriptural Christian living. Women generally wore some form of headdress like we wear today. They also dressed modestly with well-covered bodies. Nowhere was there seen the partial nudity of either men or women, as is seen today. Most mainline Christians now think nothing of this state of affairs. Back then divorce was almost unknown. No young people needed to take a chastity pledge to stay a virgin until marriage — their culture required it of them. Children, back then, were raised by parents, not by their grandparents, as many are today. Older people were respected and taken care of by their relatives. Community was a priority, and people belonged to each other. All this is really what the Amish are after, Jesse. This attitude and willingness of prior generations to live Scriptural teachings, which, even when known, are mostly ignored today. I see the Amish culture, then, in its best moments only as a tool to accomplish something greater."

"I know that," Jesse said. "This is, of course, the ideal. It seems precious — all the more so as I see it slipping away. We held this ideal with such optimism after starting this new community here in Honduras. It hurts even more since so little time has passed, and the hopes are still fresh within us."

"Yes," Peter continued. "The corruption that crept into the older communities has been swept away down here by our new beginning. We could see clearly the possibilities of where we wanted to go. Where we wanted to go was to leave the problems that arose in the old communities when the culture became its own focus and the meaning behind it all forgotten. This happens to us Amish people, frequently. Then the extent to which the culture becomes an end unto itself is the extent to which the greater goal is lost. Don't you think, Jesse, that the practice of most beliefs and ideals brings about a gradual decline in the integrity of that practice or ideal?"

Jesse thought about it. "It could be. I just never thought of it in that way before."

"It is like this," Peter said. "A man has a barrel of apples in the fall of the year and enjoys the taste of the first one, the second one, and then the third one. After winter grows long, the apples in the barrel grow old too. They become corrupted and no longer taste as good. So it is with everyone unless they have renewal or revival. We here as Amish people in Honduras have left whatever corrupted version of the Amish ideal we lived with and have started to eat from a new barrel of apples. There has not yet been enough time to corrupt our version of it before it is being snatched away from before our very eyes. I planned on being different, and on having a constant renewal at the church here. Now it is not to be. It just makes the pain yet more acute."

Nodding his head, Jesse agreed. "I can see that. There is just no way that we can sacrifice the Amish culture at this point. It puts us into uncharted waters where neither of us knows where we are going.

"The Amish firmly believe, and I agree with them, that it is not possible to practice and maintain a truly biblical Christianity in the present day culture. While others dialogue the subject, I am not interested but firm in my conviction that this is so. I have no plans to discuss the subject if it entails any hint of compromise. It is a non-negotiable point. I am not about to buck the mainline Amish position and decide that maybe things could be done without the Amish culture. And look, Dad, my conviction to hold fast is buttressed by much of the practical experience we have with our own people. Few Amish who truly leave the culture retain much of the biblical teachings meshed in with the culture."

Peter agreed. "Look at the Mennonites. They are really just a liberalized version of us Amish. You can see how little success they have with holding the line, either with their watered-down culture or with biblical teachings."

Jesse was emphatic. "I have no desire to go out into that world where we start questioning things. We need to stick with what we have. Look how many variations and divisions there are in the Mennonite and Amish faiths."

All this debate left the great question for Jesse and the others. How far were they willing to go to protect their beliefs? Was moving really an option? As far as Jesse was concerned, the answer was still "yes," every time he thought of it. He made known his position and his plans to move in a family meeting at Peter's place.

Jason could hardly believe what he was hearing. "Leaving Honduras? His Honduras? Just leaving it?" Jesse's decision, though, set things in motion that six months later emptied nearly half of the members of the Amish community at Guateteca.

Then, as things would be, the very next week after the family meeting two government officials from high in the Honduras administration showed up at Jesse's place. They came looking for help from the Amish. Their report said that the government was proposing a program to help poor farmers in the San Lucas area, located south, down by the coast. The plan was to teach the natives farming techniques using the horse-operated and hand skills practiced by the Amish. All the two officials wanted were two young Amish men skilled in farming who could supply teaching for the program. Funds, tools, and the rest would come from the government. The young men would be paid for their time. The officials said the activities of the Amish in the Hurricane Fifi restoration work, as well as other reports of their industry, impressed the Secretary of Agriculture himself. It was for him that they came to ask for help. He would personally authorize and fund the program in San Lucas.

Jesse and his boys could not believe what they were hearing. Was this not exactly what they came to Honduras for? Yet, knowing what the answer would have to be, Jesse still told the officials he would pass the word on to the others. After talking with Peter and Matthew, it was as he thought. First, there was the big problem of working with the government. That would be tough to overcome, but maybe something could be worked out. Maybe the Amish boys could refuse to get paid or to handle any government money. That might work. Second was the problem of the bad influences upon the two boys, whoever they were, while away from home those six months. Maybe having them come home frequently could solve that? There remained, then, the third problem — the ones interested in doing this sort of work were moving back to the north. That problem could not be overcome. The moving was a sure thing. Jesse mentioned something to one of the reformers who was staying about the government's offer and request for help. No interest was expressed in pursuing the idea. That evening the weather fit Jesse's mood, and as night fell it began raining softly and continued for two straight days. It was strange weather even for Honduras, as if Heaven itself were weeping.

Moving was not as simple as it sounded when the plans were made. By this time the roots were down deep in Honduras. Jesse, plus several of the others, had acquired a large herd of registered milk cows. These cows had been their pride and joy to acquire and in large part to raise until they reached a standard that rivaled what they experienced up north. Milk production was at an unheard of high for cows in Honduras. No one of the local natives believed them when they told them how much the milk average was per cow. They were content to buy the milk, but God did not, in their minds, make it possible for one cow to give that much milk. These were just gringo tales to tickle the fancy with.

So deep went the unbelief that no milk cows in the history of the community were ever stolen. If the locals really believed the cows possessed that much value, they would have stolen them. What they did steal for was meat. That was a concept they could understand, taste, and handle. Young heifers, in contrast to bony cows, held value as objects for meat consumption. A quality heifer that could produce many times over its own value in milk and calves during a lifetime was gladly eaten in its youth. The Amish learned this lesson early. Lee Stuzman came out one morning, after having lived in Honduras only a year, to find his registered bull lying in the pasture reduced to bones and entrails. The bull was shipped in only the week before from the States using the "Heifer Project," a group that supplies help to startup farmers in third world countries in the form of registered stock to get their herds going. There it lay, the hope of a thousand quality calves, slaughtered in one night to feed man's hunger for a day — when a vision and faith in the future could have produced enough to meet the needs of a hundred lives for decades to come.

These herds of cows would have to be sold. They could not be left here or taken with them, so the decision was made to have one mass cattle auction on the appointed day. Neither Jesse nor Matthew was entirely sure how it would go, or if the cows would even sell. But it needed to be done, so they did it. They printed up flyers listing each cow separately with its record in detail. They decided not to worry about the locals' opinions, but to give the information in terms they were used to, using American formulas and milk production per cow. Matthew even went to the capital and paid for the advertisement's publication in the national paper, *El Tiempo*. Making inquiries about an auctioneer, he found that only two existed in Honduras. Contact was made and a date contracted with the one best recommended. He made some suggestions of his own, which they followed.

The results were beyond anything anyone imagined. On the day of the auction they came from every corner of Honduras it seemed, and from the neighboring country of San Salvador. Cubans, Americans, more foreigners and successful businessmen than they knew existed. Out under the mango trees in Peter's place they set up a temporary corral to bring the animals through. Mini-stadium seats were built for the occasion. Food was made and served by the Amish women. The auctioneer did a tremendous performance. Jesse's boys and other young men from the community led the animals through as they were sold. Prices went to a level the Amish did not know was possible for Honduras. It was as if, after all these years of work, the civilized world came to say good-by for a job well done.

That evening the trucks rumbled out the lane past Homer's place — cattle trucks with high sideboards, through which you could see the cows with their heads raised to get more comfortable from their packed existence; and flatbed lumber trucks especially designed for the occasion to carry animals. Jason stood there, beside his father's little barn by the lane, and watched as the head of his white horse, looking out over the sideboard, disappeared out the driveway. When the dust settled by six o'clock, it all became strangely quiet. There were no cows walking up from the west pasture to Jesse's place for milking, mooing as they went. No Amish horseback riders came riding through the whole afternoon. All the horses on the Sanson side, except for David Bunker's, had been sold. Jesse and his boys, along with Matthew and Peter, were counting up the money. A neighboring rancher, whom they all trusted, offered to keep the money until they could run it into the capital tomorrow. It was simply not safe to leave it in the Amish community overnight. When the final total was rung up, they would have been smiling under normal circumstances. What they found was what all men find. Money is a small compensation when a portion of the life that you love is sold.

Two months later Homer Esh would hire a Fruehauf semi-trailer to transport his shop equipment up north. He did the calculations and decided not to sell his things by auction locally. The likelihood of another good auction was slim indeed. Anyone can milk a cow, but running a lathe was another matter. There was not enough skilled labor in the country to supply a market for his tools. It made no sense to Homer to give the stuff away for half price or so. Jason helped as best he could. Everything was packed into the trailer over three-days time, including the heavy pieces. When it was over, Homer was glad the job was done. He never was glad to leave, though, but that was just the way things were. All this moving was planned and would be controlled as the need arose. What was not planned happened the next week. The One who does all well came calling a soul to move up higher.

Chapter Forty

THE YEAR OF 1977 opened with the end in sight. It was also the end not just for the whole, but for one very important part. His chest pains started early that morning. Peter Stolsfus was no more than out of bed and starting to move about that Wednesday when he knew he was in trouble. For the last two years his heart had been giving him strong signals that all was not well. The doctor in the capital told him that a mild heart attack had occurred some years before. There was really nothing, the doctor said, that he could do about it. Peter needed to rest and take things a little more slowly. That advice is all well and good, but Peter liked to work. Even when he was short on breath, the working continued. Some more help from the doctor would have been appreciated, but in those days there was not much they could do about heart trouble, especially in Honduras.

As the day wore on, the trees around the house swayed gently in the breeze. The five tall ones on the east side of the house stood watch as they always did. Peter's chest pains were getting worse. By ten o'clock he told Annie she should call the children. Word was sent out by foot. Rachel was the first to arrive. Albert came soon after that, along with Jesse. There was not really much they could do, but they stayed there as the hours and the pains got worse.

By one o'clock it was obvious even to the untrained eye of the others that this would be the end. Jesse knew for some time already. They sent Albert out earlier in search for wine. It was possible, they thought, that it might slow the chest pains down. Albert remembered that the little store down by the river might carry some. It was the closest place they could think of.

By two-thirty it was over, and Peter Stolsfus left for the other side. His last words repeatedly were, "Come quickly, Lord Jesus," as the pains got ever worse. He said them in German, the last words he ever spoke on this earth. Ten minutes later Albert got back from the store. Jason arrived on foot about that time also. He knew since that morning when his mother left that Peter was sick. How serious he never imagined, but came over drawn by a desire to know what was going on. Rachel showed him into the house and his grandfather lying there in death.

The funeral was the next day. There was no time to do more than notify the children who lived up north. They could not be expected to come, since it was physically impossible in the time available. A telegram was sent to Beth, who was told to let the others know. Bishop Manny preached the sermon to a church house filled to the max, with the overflow filling most of the one schoolhouse wing. Peter Stolsfus was a beloved man, both in the community and by the locals.

They buried him on the east side of the church house hill, just a little below the building. Jason stood there that afternoon and watched them throw the dirt onto the coffin. The ground slopes away only gradually at that point, and they faced him to the east towards Jerusalem, from which will come the morning. A plain marker placed the following week on the gravesite read simply, "Peter Stolsfus 1915–1977." To this day it still is there.

So ended the era of adventure and courage of a great people who rarely venture far from home. A time that some of those who lived through it saw clearly for what it was. In that land of poverty and desperation, the light of heaven broke through to the dwellings of men — casting shadows, through no fault of its own, for in this world of sin and sorrow it will always be so. Here men reached for the stars only to find them slip from their grasp. Yet the light shone, ere briefly, to bear witness of that day still to be. There, in a better country, the light will shine where no darkness can enter. Is that not the day when it will truly be a time to live?

Before his family moved, Jason went out to his tree house for one last time. He did not cry — it hurt too much for that. Climbing up, he sat there and looked around. The mountain rose in its grandeur to the north, wispy clouds clipping its highest peak. Fruit trees hung heavy with tangerines, oranges, and mangoes on the ridge behind him. The smell of the tropics was all around. Before him lay the land he played and hunted and loved for so many years. When he climbed down, he knew he was leaving it all. What he did not know would be left was the child that life now called to be a man.

As a young boy, Jerry Eicher was part of the Amish venture to Honduras. He now lives with his wife and four children in central Virginia. His other books include *Living Christianity* and *Transforming the Believer*.